HOOD ACADEMY

SHELLEY WILSON

HOOD ACADEMY

bhc
press™

Livonia, Michigan

Edited by Susan Cunningham

HOOD ACADEMY

Published by BHC Press

Library of Congress Control Number:
2019938916

Hardcover: 978-1-64397-009-7
Softcover: 978-1-64397-035-6
Ebook: 978-1-64397-046-2

For information, write:
BHC Press
885 Penniman #5505
Plymouth, MI 48170

Visit the publisher at:
www.bhcpress.com

ALSO BY
SHELLEY WILSON

FICTION TITLES

Guardians of the Dead
Book 1 of The Guardians

Guardians of the Sky
Book 2 of The Guardians

Guardians of the Lost Lands
Book 3 of The Guardians

ANTHOLOGIES

In Creeps The Night: An Anthology
Featuring "The House On The Hill"
by S.L. Wilson

For Lee, Jamie, and Ella

PART ONE

OATH
BREAKER

ONE

The blue flashing lights pulsed through the fractured front window, illuminating the blood splatter on the walls. The click-click of the forensic team's camera ate into the sterile silence as the officers combed through the living room.

Like something out of a macabre horror show the blood covered everything, coating the threadbare rug in front of the fireplace with its crimson wash. The splintered remains of the coffee table littered the overturned chair, and the smell of death clung to the walls.

I lifted my eyes to look at the police officer who knelt in front of me, his face a mask of professionalism even though he must be wishing he was anywhere but here.

'Did you see who killed your dad?' I slowly shook my head as the officer tried to determine what had happened.

'Someone tried to kill you, miss. I want to help. Did you see who broke in and attacked you?'

I couldn't answer. The words were stuck in my throat. How could I tell him that my dad was the one who tried to kill me and that a wolf had jumped through the window and ripped out his throat? Who would believe me?

The paramedic dropped a medical kit at my feet and began wiping the blood from my face, the sudden cold of the antiseptic wipe causing an involuntary shudder to run through my bones. The police officer and paramedic exchanged a look. The same kind of look that my teacher and headmaster used to give each other when I tried to cover up the bruises down my arms.

I slumped a little further into the kitchen chair, letting my long dark hair fall around my face.

'Anything you can give us by way of a description will help.' The police officer clicked the end of his pen and poised it over the clean sheet of notepaper.

'Big,' I managed to say. My lips cracked as I spoke, and I could feel a trickle of blood slide down the side of my mouth. The paramedic wiped it up before moving to the gash on my forehead.

'It...he was big. Dark hair. Brown eyes.'

The officer noted it down and let out a deep sigh. Not the best description for them to go on, but it was all I could give him. If I'd told him the attacker was hairy, with sharp claws and fangs, the paramedic would have had me committed. I didn't need to escape from one prison to then find myself in another.

'It's late. Who can we call?' the medic asked as he secured a small bandage to my head. 'Any family?'

The police officer grabbed the radio from his shirt pocket. 'I've already called social services. As she's a minor we need to find her a bed for the night. I'll chase them up.'

'No!' I could hear the flicker of panic in my voice as the threat of being sent away loomed. 'I can call my brother. He'll let me stay with him. He's much older than me and has his own place. It'll be fine.'

They exchanged another look.

'What's his number and we'll call him for you?'

Shit.

I hadn't seen Zak since he walked out nine years ago. He'd promised to come back for me but he never did. He left me alone with that bastard who called himself our father.

'I'll find it,' I mumbled, standing up and moving towards the living room. The police officer barred the door.

'It's probably best that you don't enter the crime scene, miss. You've been through enough tonight already, so why don't you take a seat and tell me where to look?'

Double shit.

I needed to stall for time. If only someone were willing to lie to the police about being my brother then I wouldn't have to go with the social worker. Unfortunately, friends were a luxury I never got to enjoy.

My heart beat faster as I wrestled with the possibility of leaving this house. If I went with them, Zak would never be able to find me. I stumbled against the dresser, knocking a vase to the floor with a loud crash.

The paramedic led me back to the plastic kitchen chair and I lowered myself into it, resting my head on the wooden table and letting my long hair fan out around me. The softly murmured voices of the police officer and the medic washed over me as I closed my eyes.

Throat torn open—blood gushing from the wound as it sprayed across the furniture—his eyes wide in shock and panic as he fell to the floor.

Keeping my head on the table, I tuned into the conversations around me. The officers were speculating on the attacker, trying to understand how someone could cause that much carnage.

Strong assailant—nothing missing—bloody mess—no chance of survival.

They went on, talking through all the possibilities. Of course, none of them came close to the truth—how could they?

I squeezed my eyes more tightly shut as I tried to block out the images that danced across the inside of my eyelids. His eyes. The blood.

A man's deep voice cut through the air and a shudder skittered down my spine. The sharp tone and arrogance reminded me of my father, and I had to lift my head to check he hadn't risen from the dead.

I opened my eyes and blinked against the stark brightness of the kitchen light.

'This is Sebastian Roberts, miss.' The police officer led him into the room.

The well-dressed man filled the kitchen doorway; his dark suit and long overcoat looked as if they cost more than my dad earned in a year. His shoes shone in the bright light of the kitchen, and I instinctively tucked my tatty trainers under the chair.

I figured him to be middle-aged and he had thick black hair that was neatly clipped around a square face. The hard lines of his nose and jaw worked to highlight the cold grey eyes that stared down at me.

'He says he's your uncle.' The police officer gestured for Mr Roberts to take a seat, but he remained where he was, watching me with predatory eyes.

I'd only met this man a couple of times when I was a kid, but the striking resemblance to my father would have convinced anyone that he was who he said he was. They could have been twins apart from the difference in hair colour and the small fact that this man was clean-shaven and professional, and my father had been a drunken mess with a violent temper.

'We were about to call her brother to come and get her.'

My uncle huffed. '*If* Mia's brother gets in touch, then do feel free to pass on my details so he can come and visit her at my home.' Sebastian Roberts looked pointedly at me as he said it, and I understood immediately that I was busted. He knew I didn't have a clue where Zak was.

Shit.

THE POLICE OFFICER took Sebastian to one side as his female colleague escorted me towards the stairs to pack a bag and collect anything I needed. I took my time ascending the steps as I strained to overhear their conversation.

'Is there a number where you can be reached, sir?'

'Of course. Here's a business card with my direct number and the address where Mia will be staying for the time being.'

Where I would be staying remained a mystery to me. The only flicker of hope I could hold onto was that it couldn't be any worse than here.

As I gazed around my dismal bedroom, it struck me what a pathetic life I had led so far. A handful of books, some of my mum's handwritten poetry that I'd managed to salvage after she died, underwear, four tops and two pairs of jeans. My worldly belongings fit into one backpack. I avoided looking directly at the female officer as she glanced around the dank bedroom. The pity on her face was almost too much to bear. Staying in this house was supposed to have been temporary. Zak had promised that he would come back for me. I didn't need a new bed or lots of pretty things, not if I needed to get away quickly when he came. Of course, he never had come back to get me.

I gave a sharp nod to indicate that I was done, and we made our way back down to the kitchen.

Sebastian was waiting by a large black car when I arrived. The medic pressed a spare bandage into my hand as I stepped out of the front door, and the police officer gave a grim nod of his head as I walked towards him.

'We'll be in touch, miss,' he told me. I didn't care if he did get in touch. I just wished this whole brutal night would disappear from my memory, but I forced a smile and whispered my thanks.

The fresh night air settled around me like a cloak, the sky dotted with grey clouds that swept across the full moon, its creamy light bathing the front garden in an eerie glow.

Sebastian watched me as I trudged down the path and joined him on the passenger side.

'We have a long drive ahead of us, Mia.' He opened the door. 'We better get started.'

I didn't look back. I didn't want to see the broken window or the blood splattered across the walls. The neighbours had congregated on the pavement and were watching the events unfold. I avoided their staring faces as I slid into the leather seat and closed the door.

The tinted windows offered me some comfort as the black car slid past the gawping faces. I shut my eyes and let the exhaustion creep over me.

THE SOUND OF the car engine cutting out stirred me from a frenzied dream of blood, teeth and carnage, and I was grateful for the reprieve as the whirlwind of images steamrolled through my brain. Sebastian sat motionless at the wheel and stared ahead through the windscreen.

'Are we here?' I wasn't quite sure where *here* was, as my mysterious uncle had been a bit vague on our destination. I'd been too distracted to bother asking and now my uneasiness troubled me.

He grunted and shifted his gaze to look over at me, his eyes sweeping over my face and hovering on the split lip and bandaged forehead.

'Not yet. We've been driving most of the night, and I thought you might need a bathroom break.'

He had stopped at the motorway services. I noticed the glass-fronted building in the distance and saw the steady stream of people rushing in and out. The car park was busy with motorists in need of a caffeine fix before resuming their journey. The flickering sign for beverages beckoned to me, and I sat up straight in my seat.

'I could do with a coffee.'

We entered the building side by side but in silence. I didn't know this man and he didn't know me. If I was going to spend the next God knew how long with him, I needed to open my mouth and at least attempt to hold a conversation with him.

'Two white coffees.' He handed over the cash, ignoring the pleasant smile from the barista as he motioned for us to sit in a free booth.

'I'm not sure that sixteen-year-olds should drink coffee.'

I almost laughed.

'You don't have kids?'

'No, my brother was the sibling graced with offspring.'

I did laugh at that.

'I don't think my dad thought he had been *graced* with anything.' I stirred my coffee a little too violently and watched as it slopped over the rim and left a muddy puddle on the table.

'Your father had a lot to deal with. The death of his wife, the loss of his son. It all took its toll on his mental health and...'

'How dare you.' I dropped the teaspoon with a clatter as I raised my voice. A couple of patrons glanced in our direction.

'What do *you* know about our life? Dad was a bastard, plain and simple. These bruises were from him and they weren't the first. They wouldn't have been the last either if that...if he hadn't been killed.'

I dropped my gaze and lifted the coffee cup to my lips. My hands shook slightly as I let my little outburst settle. I'd never done that in the past. I'd never verbalised what my dad had done, even when my teachers tried so hard to get me to admit it. It all went back to Zak. If I had spoken out about the violence, social services would have taken me away. Zak wouldn't have been able to find me when the time came. I couldn't risk that happening, so I kept my mouth shut.

'I'm sorry.'

Sebastian's words surprised me.

'What have you got to be sorry about? He was the bad one, not you.' I realised that there was every possibility that Sebastian was also a bad one. Could this be a family gene?

As if reading my mind, he began to shake his head.

'I'm nothing like my brother, Mia. You are perfectly safe with me. The death of your mother changed him in ways none of us could understand. He was such a kind man once. A long time ago.'

'Well, I must have been out that day because I never saw any kindness, not a single moment of it.'

I wanted to say more, but as I opened my mouth to speak his phone began vibrating in his pocket.

'I need to take this. I'll be back soon.'

With that he stood up and walked away, his mobile pressed up to his ear.

THE SMELL OF diesel and strong coffee assaulted my senses. I took another sip of the hot liquid and screwed my eyes shut. I'd never really liked coffee, but I opted for it in a bid to convince Sebastian that I was a sophisticated teenager. Why I believed that drinking a cup of coffee would make me look less of a child was a mystery to me. I remember seeing it on a TV show once. Road to nowhere and a cup of coffee, please. Stupid. As he was paying, I should have gone for the hot chocolate with extra cream.

The tiny screen above the entrance showed the network of motorways, giving out up-to-date advice on scheduled roadworks and estimated travel times. The southbound route was busy, even at this time of night, with a flow of vehicles heading to the capital. The traffic heading north was much lighter. North; I had a faint memory of Zak telling me that he wanted to go to Scotland. He had shown me a map once, trailing his index finger up to the centre of the United Kingdom and tapping the spot over the county of Nottinghamshire.

'This is the belly button of the UK,' he had said. 'I'm going to start here and work my way up north until I make it to the Scottish mountains.'

Zak's need for adventure was palpable. Being outdoorsy kids, we thrived on that glimpse of freedom. I only wish that I'd been allowed to venture further than the garden gate more often.

We both loved the smell of the trees after a rainstorm, and lying on the grass to watch the clouds or the stars in the sky.

We had been brought up in a colossal concrete jungle. Grey boxes stacked on top of each other with a token patch of green grass at the centre of each estate. The trees were dead and the animals were either feral cats or angry dogs.

I shifted in my seat as I tried to shake the memory of home, or rather, the house I had lived in. My thoughts were interrupted when a young man placed a steaming mug of hot chocolate in front of me.

'Can I join you?' He didn't wait for an answer but slid into the space opposite and took a long drink from his own mug.

'Please.' He gestured for me to drink. 'It looks like you need an injection of chocolate.'

The skin around his mouth crinkled when he smiled and his front teeth were slightly crooked. I guessed him to be in his early twenties.

'It's a gift,' he continued as he nodded at the cup. 'A simple act of kindness.'

I fidgeted in my seat and looked around for Sebastian.

'People aren't kind and gifts don't exist,' I said, pushing the mug away and waiting for the explosion of anger that normally accompanied my backchat.

'Hmm, I see.' He put his own mug down and laced his fingers together, studying me with mysterious brown eyes that seemed much older than the face they occupied. His gaze rested only briefly on my split lip.

'You don't believe in acts of kindness?'

I shook my head, my hair swishing around my shoulders.

'No, I don't. Nobody does anything without wanting something in return.'

'So if I offer you a hot chocolate what do you suppose I want in return?'

I sat back in my chair and squared my shoulders. The gravity of a sixteen-year-old girl sitting in a service station all alone in the middle of the night suddenly hit me.

'My uncle will be here any minute and he won't be pleased to find you in his seat.'

'I've scared you,' he said, holding his hands up. 'I'm sorry, that wasn't my intention. I was looking for a bit of light conversation to pass the time, that's all.'

He picked up his mug and took another gulp, his eyes still fixed on me.

'I'm sorry,' I whispered. 'I didn't mean to be rude. I'm...' I stopped myself from opening up to this mysterious stranger.

Reaching for the mug, I smiled weakly at the young man. 'Thank you for the hot chocolate.'

He watched me as I sipped my drink.

'I'm Terry.' He extended his hand across the table and I took it, shaking it firmly just as Zak had taught me.

'I'm Mia.'

19

'So Mia, where are you heading on this chilly morning?'

I hesitated; regardless of the sweet, hot chocolatey gesture I needed to lie to this guy. I wasn't ready to spill all the gruesome details of my screwed-up life, especially to a stranger.

'I'm going to Scotland.'

He raised his eyebrows and let out a long, low whistle. 'That's a hell of a long journey.'

I laughed at his expression and managed to relax my posture, realising for the first time how tense I was.

'I'm visiting my brother, and he lives in the Scottish mountains.'

Terry cocked his head to one side as if weighing up my answer.

'How do you know he lives in the mountains?'

I blinked. 'Excuse me?'

'How do you know your brother lives in the Scottish mountains? Did he tell you?'

I shook myself out of the shocked silence and stammered a reply, 'Yes...he told me.'

The fact that Zak had only mentioned Scotland to me nine years ago didn't matter. It was the first thing that had popped into my head. This conversation was making me feel uncomfortable, and I looked around again for any sign of Sebastian.

Terry slipped out of his chair, and I curled my fists ready to fend off an attack, but he smiled and moved towards the exit.

As he reached the door, he glanced back at me.

'You might be interested to know that your brother is closer than you think, Mia. I wouldn't bother going all the way to Scotland. Perhaps stay close to the belly button, and be careful who you trust.' He winked and then he was gone.

The gasp froze on my lips. The 'belly button' was Zak's phrase.

I flew out of my seat and rushed to the door, stumbling over my own feet as I went. The cold air hit my face as soon as I stepped outside. I scanned the car park for Terry, but he was nowhere to be seen.

'Mia?'

I whirled around to find Sebastian standing behind me, his posture rigid, deep grooves trailing along his forehead.

'I...I was worried about you,' I lied. 'Thought you'd dumped me and run.'

My eyes continued to roam the car park.

'I'm sorry. It was a business call that couldn't wait.'

I trailed after him as we made our way back to the car. Sliding into the seat, I scoured the dark corners, the parked cars and the surrounding area for any sign of Terry.

Hope filled my chest like a helium balloon.

There was only one way that he could know about Zak's quirky phrase. Whoever this guy was, he knew my brother, and if that was the case, then my brother knew where I was.

OATH BREAKER

TWO

When Sebastian told the police that I would be staying with him, I'd pictured a semi-detached house with a front lawn and overgrown flower borders. As he pulled through the tall, wrought-iron gates and into the winding driveway of a stately home, I began to feel slightly cheated. How could he live in such a grand place while my dad barely scraped enough together to afford the dirty hovel that I'd called home?

'It's a school,' he mumbled, as if sensing my animosity.

Panic gripped me and my fingers tightened around the car seat. I was briefly reminded of Terry's warning about who I should trust.

'You're dumping me into a boarding school?'

'No, Mia, this is my home. I run this school for gifted girls.'

I snorted. 'I'm sorry to disappoint you but I'm not gifted. In fact, my grades are about as good as my conversational skills.'

Sebastian huffed, the stony exterior wavering momentarily but snapping back into place as he stopped the car in front of two huge wooden doors.

'I apologise. I should have forewarned you about the nature of my job and home, but Hood Academy is not for the academically gifted, Mia, it's for the physically gifted.'

'What, like a prep school for Miss United Kingdom? Ohmigod, do you run an underage brothel?'

'Mia!' For the first time since he walked through the door of my ruined house and into my mess of a life, Sebastian looked flustered.

As we sat in the car, and I waited patiently for a worthy explanation, the front doors opened and a stream of girls burst through. They were dressed head to foot in tight-fitting grey jumpsuits with long poles strapped across their backs. Like water breaking around a boulder in a stream, they swarmed past the car and sprinted off across the open lawn to the right of where we were parked.

A tall, lithe student with long red hair split from the group and began shouting commands. The others quickly manoeuvred into pairs and began sweeping their arms in slow, deliberate movements.

'Are they dancing?'

Sebastian shook his head and reached for the door handle.

'They are training, using Tai Chi movements to prepare their bodies ahead of the hand-to-hand combat.'

'Hand-to-hand combat! What the hell is hand-to...?'

I didn't get a chance to finish my sentence as the girls swung the poles off their backs and began fighting each other, using them as weapons. The clash of wood on wood filled the early morning air as I stepped out of the car.

They moved with grace and determination, and I was transfixed at how fast they could wield the long staffs. There were a few grunts and yelps as fingers got caught in the onslaught, but none of them gave up.

'This way, Mia. I want to get you settled into your room before breakfast.'

Reluctantly I followed Sebastian up the front steps, losing my footing as I kept an eye on the girls.

I HAD TO admit, the interior entrance hall of Hood Academy was impressive. The high ceilings bore lavishly painted frescoes from Greek mythology. The walls were decorated in rich, golden, wood panelling that gleamed in the warm light cast from the chandeliers. Chunky pieces of furniture hugged the walls. Intricately carved sideboards, full of dusty old books and red sofas occupied every available space. The room was clearly designed to be multi-purpose. An inviting entrance for visitors and a communal gathering space for the students. To the left, through an open door, I could see a large dining area. Several tables and long benches filled the floor space, and I heard the gentle clatter of cutlery being laid out.

Directly to my right a half-glazed door stood slightly ajar with a name plaque in the centre. Dr Sebastian Roberts.

So my uncle was a doctor; interesting.

Two staircases leading off from the hallway dominated the space; one veered to the left and the other to the right. Sebastian walked up the left-hand stairs and I followed, swinging my rucksack over one shoulder.

'Breakfast will be served at eight in the dining room. Follow the smell and you should be fine. If you need me, come to my office, anytime.'

'What is this place?'

Sebastian stopped suddenly on the stairs, and I walked straight into the back of him. Jumping back, I grabbed onto the handrail to steady myself.

'Mia, there is so much you don't know, so much that your dad probably should have told you but didn't. I need you to be open-minded about this place.'

When he looked at me, I noticed the dark circles under his eyes, and I allowed myself a brief moment of guilt. Was he grieving over the loss of his brother? In the horror of the aftermath, I hadn't considered it, or maybe I just didn't care enough.

He turned his back and kept on walking up the stairs. It seemed that neither of us could communicate our true feelings.

We stopped on the first-floor landing and Sebastian gestured to the higher levels.

'The second and third floors are for the older students and teachers. This floor is for our newest students. We do maintain a basic curriculum of maths, English and science, but predominantly your studies will be centred around learning to fight, defend yourself and hunt.'

My mouth went dry, and all I could hear was the sound of a clock ticking somewhere off in the distance.

'What exactly is it that I'm learning to hunt?' I said, deliberately grinding out each word.

'Werewolves, Mia. You will be hunting werewolves.'

I SAT ON the end of the bed and stared at the wall. He had been so matter-of-fact when he'd told me. So cold and clinical. Not once did he stop to think that I might not believe him or that I'd laugh in his face and tell him there was no such thing.

Memories of a huge brown wolf crashing through our living room window stomped through my thoughts. I'd seen it with my own eyes. Fear had crippled me as I watched the creature pace the floor, broken glass crunching beneath its immense paws. The only other sound had been the whimpering sobs from my dad. He didn't move to protect me, he just mumbled words I couldn't understand. And then, the creature launched itself forward to rip my dad's throat out. As it turned to face me, all I could focus on were the hazel eyes and blood, lots and lots of blood, smeared over a long snout, and sharp fangs.

I stood up and paced the floor.

Sebastian had dropped his bombshell, dumped me in my new room and left. He had nothing more to say to me. Did he know what I'd seen? Was he fully aware that a werewolf had killed his brother?

My head was spinning as I tried to comprehend everything that had happened. In twelve short hours, I'd watched a mythical creature murder my dad, been whisked away by an estranged uncle werewolf hunter and had an odd conversation about my brother with a complete stranger.

I'd just hung my coat on the hook behind the door when it burst open and a pretty, young blonde girl dashed inside and collided with me. We both fell and hit the floor with a bang.

'Oh no, I'm so sorry. Are you okay?' She jumped to her feet, extending her hand to help me up. 'I didn't know you'd arrived.'

'I didn't know you were expecting me.' I fumbled to my feet with her help and dusted off my jeans.

'You're Mia, Dr Roberts's niece. He told us you were joining the school and I, for one, am so excited to be your roomie.'

I glanced around the bedroom, seeing it properly for the first time. There were single beds on either side of the room with a large mahogany dressing table separating them. Single wardrobes and a huge chest of drawers sat on the opposite wall. A doorway led to a private bathroom. Fresh cream linen and soft blankets covered the bed I'd been sitting on, whereas the other bed was covered in multicoloured cushions and an assortment of stuffed animals. Rich purple curtains framed the window and a plush grey rug stretched across the centre of the room.

'I'm Elizabeth, but my friends call me Lizzie.'

I shrugged and sat back on the bed, crossing my legs underneath me.

'I guess you know all about me, then.'

Unfazed by my abrupt manner, Elizabeth sat on the end of her bed and scrutinised me.

'You look so similar to your mum.'

I recoiled.

'How the hell do you know what my mum looks like?'

'Oh, there are tons of photographs in Dr R's office. When I first arrived here, I thought the pictures were of his wife. I actually told him I thought his wife was pretty.' She laughed and her blue eyes twinkled.

'What did he say?'

'He got all embarrassed and told me she was his sister-in-law but that they were close. I felt like such an idiot.'

Her smile was infectious, and I could feel the corners of my mouth twitching in an attempt to return her warmth. She was nice. I didn't know how to handle nice. So I did what I do best and clamped down on any attempt at being friendly.

'Have you eaten? Breakfast is great and there's plenty of it. Come on.'

My stomach growled, confirming that I hadn't eaten for far too long. Elizabeth giggled, and grabbing my hand she pulled me off the bed and towards the door.

She ignored my veiled attempts at being moody and didn't stop talking all the way to the dining hall, filling me in on which student stayed in which room, who held the best parties and where to get my equipment. As we got to the ground floor, I noticed another door close to Sebastian's office. I hadn't seen it when I first arrived.

'Where does that lead?'

Elizabeth pondered the existence of the door for a moment then shrugged her delicate shoulders.

'I think it's Dr R's storeroom. It's always locked and I don't remember ever seeing anyone use it.'

I followed Elizabeth into the dining hall. The smell of bacon and eggs filled the air and I realised just how hungry I was.

With a full plate and a large mug of hot chocolate, I trailed behind Elizabeth to sit at one end of the dining table. The hall was full of students, in their grey jumpsuits, chatting and eating and laughing. It was strange to think this was a school. The lunch hall back at my old school hadn't been as upbeat. In fact, nobody dared to eat the slop they dished up or to take on the *popular* kids who taunted anyone with a pulse.

I was halfway through my sausages when a hush fell over the room. I glanced up to see the tall red-haired girl from the garden saunter into the hall with what looked like two bodyguards bringing up the rear. I rolled my eyes. Apparently even Hood Academy had its own *popular* crew.

Elizabeth stiffened beside me as I became aware of the redhead hovering over me.

'You must be Mia.'

I chewed the remains of my breakfast and swallowed before staring up at her stern face.

'Stay out of my way.'

With that, our introduction was over, and she left as quickly as she'd arrived. The hush lifted and the laughter resumed.

'Who the hell is she?'

Elizabeth glanced nervously around her.

'That's Felicity. She's a true breed.'

'A what?'

'True breed! Her father, grandmother and great-grandmother were all hunters. She's the latest in a long line of dedicated hunters. They've written books about her family.'

'Well, I don't give a crap about her ancestors or her inbreeding, she's a freak.'

Elizabeth sniggered. 'True breed not inbreed.'

'Whatever. I don't like her.'

'No one does. Because of her family's connections, she gets to run some of our training sessions and pushes us to the limits, and it's hard for the younger kids.'

'How long have you been here?'

'I'm still in my first year. A werewolf attacked my sister and me when we were camping last summer, so my parents enrolled me here.'

'I don't get it. Why did your family ship you off and not your sister?'

'She doesn't have the sight. Only I could see the werewolf.'

'So you only get to be a hunter if you can see werewolves?'

'Yes, you can't fight something you can't see. When did you see your first werewolf?'

I closed my eyes and then thought better of it as the scene unfolded in my mind for the millionth time.

'Yesterday, when it jumped through our living room window and murdered my dad.'

THREE

Elizabeth was right. Sebastian's office was full of old photographs, not just of my mum, but my dad too. I picked up a brass frame with a faded picture inside; three happy faces beamed up at me. I'd never seen my dad smile. Being so young when my mum died meant that I missed out on the pleasant side of family life.

Sebastian opened the door and stopped midway between his office and the hallway, his jaw slack and eyes wide.

'You did say I could come and see you anytime, remember?'

With a deep sigh, he walked into the office and closed the door behind him.

'Sorry, Mia, I'm still getting used to seeing your face.'

'Oh, thanks. I see we both need to work on our family bonding skills.'

I flopped into one of the armchairs that sat in front of his desk, tracing the intricate carvings with my fingertips.

'You've got a lot of old stuff in this house.'

He huffed and I realised that was as close as he came to a laugh.

'The original owner of the property left the house and its contents to me in their will. I've just added the odd piece over the years.'

I stood up and walked across to the large picture window. The view looked out over the front lawns, the same piece of land where I'd watched a bunch of schoolgirls thrash the living hell out of one another.

'I can't do this.' I watched as it started to rain, big fat blobs of water chasing each other along the imperfections of the glass. 'Actually, scrap that. I don't *want* to do this.'

I spun around to catch him studying me from his leather desk chair, his fingers laced together behind his perfectly coiffed head of hair.

'I understand now why you brought me here, but I don't know why I could see that werewolf. I do know that I don't want to get that close and personal with another one anytime soon.'

He lowered his arms and placed his large hands flat on the desk. He addressed his knuckles when he finally spoke.

'Why didn't it kill you, Mia?'

'What?'

'How is it that you survived a werewolf attack that claimed the life of your father?'

I opened my mouth to speak, but the words dried up in my throat. I'd asked myself that same question over and over. The sight of all that blood, the broken glass and the piercing scream as the creature's fangs ripped out my dad's throat. Those huge brown eyes that looked...sad. It had played out in my mind a million times. I was paralysed with fear, unable to move a muscle, and I thought I was going to be next to die. The wolf watched me for a long time as if it was studying my reaction. When it approached, terror had vibrated through my entire body, but it licked my hand and then left.

'Werewolves know when they are facing a hunter, Mia. That monster could see that you were dangerous and it fled.'

I shook my head. That wasn't right.

'No, it could have killed me, but it didn't. It just walked away.'

Sebastian rose from his chair and walked over to the nearest bookshelf. He pulled out an old book, bound in soft green leather, and handed it to me.

HOOD ACADEMY

'The history of the hunter line is in this book. I suggest you read it before making any rash decision to dismiss your calling.'

'My calling! I don't have a calling, I'm a sixteen-year-old orphan with no friends, and I have severe trust issues.'

He huffed again.

'What about your roommate, Elizabeth? She's a pleasant young girl.'

'Oh, now I get it.' I threw my hands in the air. 'How much did you pay her to befriend me?'

'I didn't pay anyone, Mia. Have a little faith in people.'

'It's very hard to have faith when your own flesh and blood made your life a living hell.'

'What your father did to you was unforgivable. He can't change what he did, and he can't make it right, but I can. I can take his place and look after you.'

I had a highly inappropriate urge to giggle. It was clearly well out of Sebastian's comfort zone to act the all-conquering uncle, but here he was, pleading for me to stay put.

'Give it a try,' he said softly. 'If you're still unhappy here in a few months, I'll enrol you in the secondary school in town. You can go off and be a normal teenager and leave all this behind.' He swept his arm out in an arc.

'I'll do my best, but I'm not making any guarantees. I'll try to fit in with your weird hunters, but if this doesn't work I'll hold you to that promise of a normal life.'

The corner of his mouth twitched as he nodded.

'I promise, Mia. Now, let's go find your tutor. She's a lethal hunter and an excellent teacher, and I *do* have to pay her to be your friend.'

I laughed and followed him out of the office. Mysterious uncle had a sense of humour; maybe there was hope for this place yet.

MISS ROSS SWEPT an analytical eye over me before piling two jumpsuits, a tracksuit and various other outfits into my arms. Topping the pile with a pair of dark grey pumps, she steered me out of the stock room and back to the staircase.

'Drop it all off in your room and then meet me back here. I want to give you the grand tour.' She beamed at me and nudged me gently towards the stairs.

None of my teachers back home had been so nice. They'd tried to help me, but I'd turned away from all of them. With nobody to talk to, and no friends to speak of, I was easy to forget, and so, after a while, they stopped checking up on me. I became a ghost.

Here, in such a short time, I'd potentially made a friend and engaged positively with a member of the teaching staff. There was a lightness about me that felt alien, but not at all unpleasant.

When I got back to the entrance hall, Miss Ross was waiting patiently for me. She led us out of the front door, and we deviated towards the side of the building, walking along the flower beds until we came to a low stone wall.

We stopped briefly, which allowed me a glance at the extensive grounds that spread out across the back of the property. Huge circular lawns divided by gravel paths and neatly trimmed shrubs stretched for miles around us.

'The building dates back to 1866,' said Miss Ross, sweeping a hand wide to encompass the Victorian architecture. 'The gardens were designed at the same time to complement the buildings.'

I glanced to the right of us where a large willow tree with a stone bench beneath its branches stood proudly. A young man tended to the borders nearby with a long-handled spade.

'That's Adam. He's the groundsman.'

Adam looked up at the mention of his name and gave us a wave.

We moved off and cut across the open lawns until we reached an old wall. The aged stones were discoloured and covered in overgrown ivy revealing the level of neglect on this part of the estate.

Beyond the wall lay a dirt track, leading down to what looked like outbuildings or a stable block.

There was a row of four cages with iron bars and heavy doors, all of them empty. The ceilings were far too low to accommodate a horse but were just high enough for a person to stand up if they curved their shoulders.

'What is this place?'

'Years ago, we used to catch the werewolves and hold them in the animal cages, but these days Sebastian prefers to keep any captives in alternative accommodation.'

'Captives? What do you mean?'

'Well, the creatures are only wolves at the full moon or if they are provoked by attack. The rest of the time they are as human as you and me. Sebastian thought it more humane to let the prisoners rest inside rather than on the ground outside.'

Shock reverberated through my bones, the image of those sad brown eyes flashing across my mind. Yes, the animal was terrifying, but imagining it in its human form was too much to take in.

'Come on, I want to show you the gymnasium next.' She bounded off up the track heading back to the academy, leaving me reeling at her revelation.

The wind picked up ever so slightly and ruffled my hair as I watched the lethal hunter bounce lightly up the path. I glanced back at the cages and swallowed down the nausea. A snap behind me made me jump, and I whirled around. There was nobody there, only the endless woods that bordered the property. I shook my head to dislodge the unease, certain that my mind must be playing tricks on me. The trees swayed gently as the wind lifted the leaves and shook them, the scent of damp earth and moss filling the air.

I backed away from the forest with a heavy heart. Would my hunter training keep me from enjoying the woods and nature? Was I destined to shed blood and cage these creatures? I'd told Sebastian I'd give him a couple of months and I would do my best to stand by that promise. But as I rushed past the animal cages I felt closer to despair than anything else.

'I WAS SORRY to hear about your father.' Miss Ross stepped in front of me and I forced myself to look up into her face. She was probably in her late fifties and still strikingly beautiful, her dark skin complemented by the bright blue jumper she wore.

Her voice echoed around the huge room with wooden floors and ropes suspended from the ceiling. She'd referred to it as the gym, but it looked more like an army assault course.

'Thank you. The police said they'd contact my uncle if they find anything out.'

She smiled at me, her gaze flickering to the fading bruise on my cheek. 'Mia, I want you to prepare yourself for the possibility that your father's death will be classed as a cold case. The investigators won't find anything because it was a supernatural death.'

She paused to fiddle with a stack of boxing mitts. 'What happened to your father is happening all over the world. It's our job, as hunters, to put a stop to these attacks. The murders remain unsolved as the police fail to find answers.'

Was it wrong to tell her that my father may have deserved what happened to him? He had been an evil monster too, no fangs or sharp claws, but what made him any different?

I didn't think my confession would help the situation, so I shut my mouth and nodded along as she explained the need for hunters and how the work they did was for the greater good.

When she started to talk about my mum, I snapped to attention. 'You knew her?'

'Yes, I knew her. She was a lovely lady, a very talented photographer and a welcome visitor to the academy. Your uncle was very close to her.'

'Yeah, I've seen the photos in his office. It was a bit creepy. Dad didn't even have any pictures of her at home.'

'Well, I'm sure her death was a huge blow to your father. Grief can cause ordinary people to do extraordinary things.'

'Was my mum a hunter too?'

The silence stretched out. A tiny muscle in Miss Ross's jaw worked hard as she formulated a response. I began to think I'd rather not know until finally she spoke.

'She was passionate about the work Sebastian was doing here, and she understood the importance of the hunters' oath, but no, she wasn't a hunter.'

'What's the hunters' oath?'

'Once you begin your full training you will be sworn in to the academy. It's a great honour to serve as a hunter, and we uphold that tradition by requesting that our students swear allegiance in front of their fellow students to be loyal and fierce.'

'If my mum wasn't a hunter, how did she know about the oath?'

'I believe your uncle explained the ceremony.'

By the tone of her voice, I knew that more questions weren't going to be welcome, and as she made her way to the exit, I realised that my tour was also at an end.

'We'll catch up tomorrow in class, Mia.'

Then she was gone, leaving me with a head full of questions and an ache in my heart.

I ATE LUNCH alone, as the other students were in class. The silence was a welcome distraction. It was hard to take in some of the information I'd received since Sebastian had turned up at my house.

After devouring a burger and fries, I found my way back to the front entrance and ran up the stairs two at a time, eager to get back to my room.

Three figures blocked the way as I reached the corridor to the bedrooms. Felicity and her squad watched me as I made my way towards them.

'You don't belong here.' Felicity crossed her arms over her chest and swung her fiery hair over her shoulder.

'Why not?' I didn't really want to get involved in a war of words with the resident school bitch, but the look on Felicity's face told me I wasn't getting away from her anytime soon.

'Sebastian has worked incredibly hard to build this academy into a respected school for hunters, and the likes of you will lower the tone.'

'I wouldn't be here if I hadn't seen a werewolf, so I guess that makes me a hunter, and that means I am eligible to attend the academy.' I crossed my arms to mirror her standoffish body language.

She laughed loudly, a cruel sound that dripped with malice.

'You may have seen a werewolf, but you will never be a hunter. Sebastian knows it, I know it, and soon enough you'll realise it. When Sebastian rushed off to collect you, my father called your uncle and told him exactly what he thought about you coming here. You're not welcome. You are weak like your mother and a waste of space just like your father.'

Her smile was callous as she spun on her grey pumps and stalked off down the corridor. I felt winded. The lightness that I'd felt earlier left in a whoosh and a heavy rock settled on my chest, squeezing out any emotion I had managed to claw back.

Through a haze of tears, I ran back down the stairs and out through the front door. I didn't falter, sprinting across the open lawn, down the gravel driveway and into the woods beyond. I kept running and I didn't look back.

THE AIR WAS crisp as I ventured deeper into the woods. I don't know how far I ran or how long I had been running but the further I went the more relaxed I became. Eventually, I stopped running and strolled through the trees at a more leisurely pace, noticing the fauna around me. When the sky began to darken and my stomach growled, I realised I must have missed dinner.

I kicked myself for not taking more notice of my surroundings; I was in a strange town and didn't know anyone, and yet being in the woods felt familiar and safe.

I remembered the times Zak had taken me to the park close to our house, which had a small pond. The neighbourhood boys had set up a tyre swing across the water and dared each other to swing across. I used to climb one of the trees and sit in its branches, watching the boys fall in the pond or cut their knees. They were happier times full of laughter and innocence.

I pushed through the drooping branches of a willow tree and stopped. Beyond the trees was an outcropping of rocks; big boulders bleached a sandy colour by the sun were now illuminated by the light of the moon. I climbed the nearest rock, its surface smooth and cool to the touch. Swinging my legs over the edge, I marvelled at the view.

Far below, the countryside stretched out like a blanket. On the horizon, I could make out the twinkling lights of Ravenshood, the town Sebastian had driven through on our way to the academy.

I watched the world ready itself for the evening, and a sense of peace settled over me. A cool breeze ruffled my hair, and I wished I'd grabbed a jumper as I ran away. I was pondering how I would find my way back to the academy when a sharp noise in the bushes behind me made me jump.

Shit.

Standing up, I backed away from the edge, keeping an eye on the surrounding bushes and trees. The moon was large and bright in the sky, bathing the woods in a creamy iridescent glow.

Double shit.

Looking up through the overhanging branches, I watched the wisps of grey cloud float across the moon, momentarily hiding it from view. Last night the moon had been at its fullest, and as Miss Ross told me only hours earlier, werewolves changed on the full moon. Did she mean for just one night, or did they stay in their wolf form for a few nights?

Shit, shit, shit.

The bushes ahead of me stirred. My heart hammered inside my chest. I strained to see what was in the bushes. My palms were sticky and a bead of sweat trickled down my spine. Whatever it was, it was getting closer. I backed up to the nearest tree and felt the bark dig into my shoulders. The bush parted and a wild rabbit hopped forward, sniffing the ground as it searched for food.

I let out a deep breath and leant my head back against the tree trunk, my shoulders sagging against the rough bark.

All the talk of werewolves and hunters had me spooked, and I was turning into a quivering mess. The rabbit was oblivious to my distress and continued foraging for its dinner as I pushed away from the tree and turned in the direction of the academy.

My heart froze and my legs trembled as I came face-to-face with four sets of eyes. The huge wolves were standing in a semi-circle just ahead of me. Their eyes gleamed in the moonlight, and the fur on their hides shimmered under the bulbous moon. They were immense, much larger than any of the wolves I'd seen on *Animal Planet*.

A brown wolf, this one even bigger than the rest, separated from the pack and took a tentative step forward, sniffing the air.

My dad's screams echoed in my head as the other wolves followed and circled me. The terror I felt held me in its rigid grip; the only part of me I could move were my eyes. I wanted to close them, squeeze them shut so I didn't see the blow when it came, but whether it was morbid curiosity or something else, I couldn't stop watching them.

They walked around me, never looking away. Sebastian had said the wolf that killed my dad knew I was a hunter. If these wolves had any suspicion that I could be dangerous, they weren't showing it. In fact, they probably knew I was a hunter-in-training and would snuff me out before my first lesson.

My legs were shaking as I struggled to stay upright. Every inch of my being wanted to lie down and curl up into a tight ball.

The brown wolf growled, and I braced myself for the attack, but instead of launching itself in a flash of fangs it turned its back and walked away. Two others followed, and I watched them disappear into the darkness of the trees. The last wolf was much paler than the others, the light of the moon reflecting off its golden fur. I was drawn in by its blue eyes, which sparkled like the ocean. It hung its head to one side, and I got the distinct impression that it was giving me a lopsided smirk. I blinked and it spun away, bounding off into the woods.

It was a good twenty minutes until I could move any of my limbs. For a short moment, I thought it had started raining but then I realised I was crying. Whether that was from fear, relief or a mixture of the two, I wasn't sure. This was the second time in as many days that I had escaped death or at the very least serious injury. I was too numb to process what that might mean, but I knew I couldn't chance the wolves returning to finish me off. Eventually, the feeling in my legs returned and I stumbled through the trees, slowly at first and then picking up speed until I was sprinting through the woods and hoping it was in the direction of the academy.

FOUR

I hadn't realised I was still holding my breath until I spotted the glaring lights of the school in the distance and I released a loud sob. As the woods petered out and the lawn came into view, I raced the rest of the way.

Sebastian was waiting for me on the front steps when I approached the old building. His face was a mixture of anger and relief.

'Where did you go?'

'I needed some fresh air so I went for a walk in the woods.' I leapt up the stairs until I stood in front of him and then stopped, folding my arms protectively across my chest. If he had even a sliver of my dad's temper, I was in for a barrage of abuse.

It was clear to anyone that I had been crying, but he either didn't notice or he chose to ignore it. The dark cloud that crossed his face lifted temporarily as he let out a long, slow breath as if he'd been holding it in for hours.

'I have dealt with Felicity. She was bragging about her treatment of you to some of the girls in the common room and Miss Ross overheard.'

I cringed. If she had received a roasting because I'd skipped out, I was certain there would be repercussions. If not from Felicity, then from her girlie goons.

'There was no need for that,' I said. 'She's a bitch and doesn't know how to behave in any other way. I can handle her.'

'I don't want you to have to handle her. She can be passionate about the academy, and it doesn't always come across in the right way.'

'Passionate! Oh, she's definitely passionate, especially when it comes to her hatred towards my parents. What the hell's that about?'

Sebastian sucked a breath in sharply.

'I want you to ignore her and keep out of her way. Her family are wealthy benefactors for the academy, and she believes this gives her a right to interfere in how I manage the school. Clearly she is a young girl out of her depth.'

'She's an idiot, and I'm more than happy to stay out of her way. Is that all?'

Sebastian studied me for a while longer before nodding. If he had any inclination that I'd had a run-in with wolves, he wasn't letting on.

'Yes, get some sleep, I know Elizabeth was worried about you, so she'll be glad to see you're back safe.'

I smiled to myself as I walked through the front door. It felt nice to know that someone cared.

'Mia.'

I looked back over my shoulder. Sebastian was standing with his back to me, looking out over the grounds and into the woods.

'I don't want you to take a walk in the forest at night again. Do you understand?'

He couldn't see me nodding as he was still staring at the trees, but I knew that walking in the woods at night wouldn't be on my to-do list any more.

'Sure, whatever. Goodnight, Sebastian.'

'Goodnight, Mia.'

THE LAMP WAS on in the bedroom when I crept through the door. I had thought that Elizabeth would be sitting up waiting for me after what Sebastian said, but the long wait had clearly exhausted her. She was fully clothed and propped up on her pillows, fast asleep and surrounded by masses of stuffed animals. She looked incredibly young as I checked her sleeping form, but she was the same age as me. Maybe the dark circles under my eyes were a side effect of a lousy life.

I slipped into my sleep shorts and T-shirt and climbed between the clean sheets. The bed was soft and comfortable, and I was suddenly aware of my aching limbs. Running wasn't an everyday occurrence for me, especially at the breakneck speed I'd fled the woods. My mind wandered back to the wolves. Despite Sebastian's warnings, the animals hadn't attacked. Did they believe I was a hunter and could destroy them? Somehow I didn't think so. There had to be another reason I had been spared—twice—and I intended to find out why. Sebastian's office was the best place to start. Tomorrow. First, I needed to get a good night's sleep.

There was a light tap at the window and then another. Something struck the glass. Elizabeth stirred and I was just about to open my mouth to warn her to be quiet when a male voice called her name. Elizabeth's eyes flew open and she grinned at me in the pale moonlight streaming through the curtains.

'It's Adam,' she whispered, bouncing off the bed.

'The groundsman?' I recalled the handsome, dark-skinned gardener I'd seen during my tour of the grounds earlier.

She nodded enthusiastically and climbed on the desk. I raised an eyebrow as she unlocked the window latch.

'We're two floors up,' I hissed. I knew I was stating the obvious but I worried that in her euphoria Elizabeth had forgotten this simple fact and would launch herself into midair.

She giggled. 'I know, silly.'

There was a light tap and the top of a ladder appeared against the frame as Adam's face appeared at the window.

'Come inside, quickly.' Elizabeth grabbed his arms to help steady him.

With his dark skin and black clothing, Adam was perfectly camouflaged against the night sky. He swung his long legs over the sill and jumped down to the floor.

Elizabeth laced her fingers through his and glanced in my direction. Her expression was one of delight and also apprehension. Was she worried that I'd disapprove?

'Mia, I'd like you to officially meet Adam.'

I climbed out of bed and extended my hand to the handsome young man who fidgeted on the spot.

'It's lovely to meet you.'

Adam's posture relaxed as he took my hand and shook it. His palms were rough to the touch, no doubt from working in the academy garden, but his smile was genuine and I found myself warming to him.

'It's great to meet you in person, Mia.'

Elizabeth grinned at me and bounced up and down on the balls of her feet.

'I'm so sorry I didn't tell you about him sooner, but with everything that's been going on I didn't get a chance, and then you weren't at dinner and...'

I put my hand up to stop her chattering.

'It's fine, really. You don't need to tell me your business.'

'Oh, but I do; we're friends and roomies. We must share our deepest secrets.' She turned to smile up at Adam, then added, 'And he's mine.'

I suddenly felt the urge to flee. Soppy looks and romantic gestures were for romance novels and chick flicks and I didn't have the first clue how to *be* around that.

'I'm going for a walk,' I said, rather too loudly. 'I'll give you guys some privacy.'

I slipped my feet into my grey pumps, grabbed a hoodie and the small book Sebastian had given me and headed for the door.

'You don't have to leave, Mia.' Elizabeth's brow creased as she watched my fumbled attempt at escape.

'I know,' I said, smiling at my roommate, 'but I fancy exploring and hopefully I'll be able to avoid a certain redhead at this time of night.'

'Be careful,' she said.

I DIDN'T WANT to think about the teenage romance that was unfolding back in my room. No matter what Elizabeth said, it was her business and nothing to do with me. I was, however, pleased that Adam seemed to be a decent lad. The boys back home had been cruel and relentless in their bullying. Zak had taught me at a young age who to avoid and how. A tip I should remember when trying to stay out of Felicity's way.

The redhead pushed her way into my thoughts as I crept along the first-floor corridor towards the staircase. Why did Felicity hate me so much? Why did I care? It wasn't that I wanted us to bond and braid each other's hair but she possessed a deep-set vindictiveness that involved my entire family and that bothered me.

There was no one around at this time of night. Sebastian's office door was closed and no light shone through the glass to indicate he was up and still working. I realised I didn't even know where his bedroom was. He had failed to share that with me. Clearly I only had access to him during office hours. The cafeteria was in darkness and the heavy wooden doors that I'd sprinted out of earlier today were now shut and bolted. I curled up on one of the many sofas hugging the wall in the entrance hall, flicked on a small table lamp and pulled out the green leather book Sebastian had given me.

The pages were well worn and yellowed, their edges marked in gold. A handwritten inscription on the first page read: '*Never stop searching, love C x.*' I recognised the handwriting instantly from the rescued pages of my mum's poetry, and my pulse quickened as I thought about my mum, Cassie Roberts. This message was from her. I raised an eyebrow as I turned the book over in my hand, searching for some other message sent from beyond the grave. The book had come from Sebastian's bookshelf, and judging by the number of photographs of my mum in his office, they obviously had a deeper connection than anyone realised.

The book covered every topic from the history of hunters to weaponry through the ages. It was the strapline on the title page that caught my eye.

To every pack, a cub is born.
Unleash the hunter to protect and serve.

The author, a man named Dr P.S. Neale, had written a long-winded introduction, dated 1862. He waffled on about the importance of hunters and how they were necessary to correct the balance of nature, of creatures so vile and brutal that Queen Victoria herself had assigned him as a master hunter to the realm.

Impressive. Not only was I now a member of an elite werewolf hunting academy, but apparently we were to report directly to the royal family.

According to Dr Neale, it was the birth of a child to a werewolf mother that triggered the hunter gene in a human child. Mother Nature's way of balancing good and evil. For every werewolf that gave birth to a cub, a hunter was born to kill it.

Closing the book, I rested my head back against the wall. Did I believe that all this supernatural crap was true? Sebastian believed in it. He ran a school dedicated to that principle. I certainly couldn't deny that werewolves existed, but hunters being born for the sole purpose of killing them? I wasn't so sure about that. Besides, there were hundreds of girls in Hood Academy. Surely there weren't hundreds of werewolves hiding in the surrounding woods.

From somewhere upstairs I heard hushed voices and the sound of people approaching. I switched off the light and slid off the sofa to crouch on the floor, hiding myself away behind a large mahogany dresser.

Felicity's voice was clear and harsh. 'It's a privilege to see what I'm about to show you. Nobody else in this god-awful school even knows about the lab.'

The two girls walked across the foyer oblivious to my presence and headed for the door beside Sebastian's office. It was the one I'd seen yesterday, the one Elizabeth had thought was a storeroom. From the pocket of her jeans, Felicity produced a key and quietly unlocked the door, swinging it open. She glanced around the dark foyer and I crouched lower, curling myself up so as not to be seen.

Satisfied that they were alone, Felicity ushered her companion inside.

I raced across the carpet, catching the handle so the door couldn't click shut behind them. A torch light bounced off the walls, and I waited until their muffled voices had faded away before following.

The small space looked like a typical storeroom until I moved further in. Shelves covered the walls from floor to ceiling with stacks of paper, printer inks and dusty exercise books, but beyond the shelves was a long corridor hidden from view behind the shelving unit. A faint light glowed in the distance, and I could see shadows moving about. Felicity and her companion disappeared through an opening to the right.

My heartbeat was rapid as I tiptoed after the two girls. Maybe this was an unknown route to the science classrooms. Somehow I didn't think that was true. The same feeling of dread I felt earlier, coming face-to-face with the wolves, trickled back into my veins.

A low moan filled the darkness and I dropped to my knees. It didn't sound like Felicity or her companion. The sound was masculine. The moaning ceased and I was about to creep forward when a scream filled the air. The hairs on the back of my neck rose at the desperate sound. I was close to the entrance where the girls had disappeared. Hugging the wall, I skulked closer until I was alongside the opening. I risked a quick look around the corner and saw that it opened up onto a staircase that went to a lower floor. The screams were coming from below.

Felicity's wild laughter floated up the staircase.

Although they were faint, I could hear her words clearly.

'Do it again. That's right, hold the knife in your right hand and press down. Don't worry, nobody in the school can hear us. The lab is soundproofed.' A dreadful howl followed, and I felt bile rise up in my throat. Whatever they were doing down there, it wasn't good.

'You deserve to die.' Felicity's voice filled the darkness and her friend laughed.

I spun on my heel and ran. The entrance hall was still empty when I emerged from the storeroom. Nobody heard those terrible screams because the rooms were secure. Did that mean Sebastian knew about the lab, or the prisoner? I knew that I should run and tell my uncle what I'd heard, but my gut instinct told me not to trust him. Not yet. I pushed the door closed behind me and rushed to the stairs, taking them two at a time. I needed to get back to my room. I wanted to feel safe, but I doubted that I'd ever feel that way again.

FIVE

The morning sky was overcast as the student body filed through the huge wooden doors and assembled on the front lawn. Miss Ross stood on the top steps surveying the bleary-eyed girls like a kestrel watching its prey. I spotted Felicity and her squad congregating by a tall flagpole stuck in the grass and steered Elizabeth to a stop at the furthest possible point from them.

'Avoidance tactics,' I mumbled when Elizabeth gave me a quizzical look.

When I returned to our bedroom last night Adam had left and my roommate was fast asleep. Something I was grateful for. I wasn't sure if I could, or should, confide in Elizabeth about what I'd seen and heard in the secret storeroom. I didn't want to get her mixed up in any trouble.

Miss Ross punctured my thoughts as she called for silence.

'Today's assignment is our boot-camp training run,' she said.

A rumble of discord filled the air.

'Yes, yes, I know how much you love these runs, but our stamina, strength and agility are what make us deadly. The only way to maintain the high level of fitness that Hood Academy is famous for is to push ourselves to the limit.'

'What's a boot-camp training run?' I asked Elizabeth who was stretching her calf muscles out.

'We've got to run through the woods, loop around the town and return before dark.'

'Doesn't sound so bad. Why does everyone look like she just cancelled Christmas?'

'It's about fifty miles.'

'Whoa, fifty! That's really far. How often do you do this?'

'We run regular circuits once a week but Miss Ross likes to spring the ultra-marathon on us at least twice a year.'

'Terrific,' I mumbled, grabbing my ankle and bending my leg back in a vague attempt to warm up my quads. 'There's no way I'll be back before dark. Do they send out search parties?'

Elizabeth laughed. 'The route is marked with green flags. Just follow them and you'll be fine. If you're not back at the academy by nine, Miss Ross collects the stragglers in the minibus.'

'Well, that's a relief. Maybe I could just take a book with me and lounge around at the final marker until it gets dark.'

'I'll run with you and we'll take it slow.' Elizabeth beamed at me and my mouth tugged in something resembling a smile of gratitude. She was really sweet and so far hadn't given up on me. Maybe I wasn't so unlovable after all.

MISS ROSS WAS now standing next to the tall flagpole with a whistle in her hand. The students spread out across the lawn in varying degrees of panic. There were the ultra-sporty girls bouncing on their heels as they eagerly awaited the shrill screech of the start whistle, and then there were the rest of us. The *I can't believe we have to do this* brigade, loitering near the back.

'Remember to follow the markers, girls. The green flags are there to keep you safe and protected. We can't venture into unmapped territory, and I wouldn't want anyone to risk their lives for a training exercise.'

I spun to look at Elizabeth who quickly held her hand up as if expecting me to have something to say about this latest revelation.

'It's just a precaution,' she said. 'There are huge parts of the forest that even the tutors don't know about. Just stick to the path that's marked. No need to panic.'

'Panic! Who's panicking? It's my second day at this place and so far I've risked my life three times...' Elizabeth's eyebrow rose. 'Well, you've tasted the food here!'

She chuckled and I released the breath I'd been holding. It wasn't the right time to reveal my extracurricular activities or my run-in with the local werewolf pack.

The whistle sounded and everyone swarmed forward, jostling for elbow room. Miss Ross nodded at me as I passed her, giving me a pity thumbs up. She knew I wouldn't be able to breathe after the first mile. Maybe that thumbs up was her way of telling me she'd meet me soon with the minibus.

ELIZABETH WAS CLEARLY using all her energy to stop herself from running at a half-decent pace and I felt a pang of guilt.

'You should go ahead,' I rasped, already struggling to talk let alone suck air into my lungs. 'I'm fine, honestly. I'll meet you for dinner.'

'It's okay,' she said. 'I promised to look after you on this run.'

'Lizzie, I insist. You can look after my blisters when I get home later.'

She giggled. 'If you're sure.'

'Hundred percent, now go.'

She gave me a sympathetic wave then shot off up the path, overtaking the other girls who were also striving to survive this physical assault Miss Ross had forced on us.

As I rasped my way further along the path the hairs on the back of my neck prickled, and I turned to look behind me, half expecting to see a few stragglers, but I could no longer see any of my fellow students. Even the most unfit girl in the school had overtaken me and disappeared into the trees. I was alone once more, and yet I had the strangest sensation that I was being watched.

I slowed down to a fast walking pace and wiped the sweat off my face with the bottom of my T-shirt. The sound of the birds high up in the branches filled the air, and I could hear the distant trickle of a stream. My breathing steadied, and I felt a deep sense of belonging. Zak would love it here. The small dell back home had been our sanctuary but these woods, with their endless paths and beautiful clearings, would have kept us amused for days at a time.

The path ahead split in two directions; the western route seemed to be the more obvious track as I knew the town was that way, but the green flag stood further along the eastern path.

I veered right and picked up the pace again heading away from town. The further I ran, the more uneven the path became. The compacted earth of the running track had given way to moss and weeds. Tree branches dangled across the trail making it difficult to run without bending to avoid a twig in the eye. There hadn't been a green flag for about half an hour, and I worried that I'd somehow missed a turning.

Sweeping aside a beautiful willow tree, I stepped into a clearing and froze. I knew this place. The same sandy-coloured rocks hugged the edge of the overhang where I'd marvelled at the view under a full moon.

Shit.

My heart began to race as I looked around the clearing. Not twenty-four hours ago, I'd stood here, face-to-face with four huge wolves. How could Miss Ross lead her students through woods that the enemy had claimed? My mind wandered to the uneven path and the lack of green flags.

'Felicity.' I said her name aloud as if looking for confirmation from the trees that she had something to do with this. It had to be her. She was the kind of person who would change the flags and send me into danger. But I didn't feel like my life was in danger. In fact, I felt calm and comfortable. Finding this place again was like discovering silence in a storm.

There was no full moon to unnerve me this time, so I climbed onto the smooth rocks and took in the view. Fields, wooded glens and paddocks of grazing horses stretched out below me.

'Beautiful, isn't it?'

I jumped at the sound of a voice behind me. Scurrying to my feet, I half expected to find Elizabeth or Miss Ross. Instead, I was looking into the bluest eyes I'd ever seen.

A boy stood in the clearing, his hands shoved deep into his jeans pockets. His hair shone like brass despite the cloudy sky. He couldn't have been much older than me, perhaps seventeen.

'Sorry, I didn't mean to startle you. I'm Cody.' He gave me a lopsided smile.

'Mia.' I lifted my hand in a lame half wave.

'Can I sit with you?' He motioned to the overhang and I jumped back, giving him room to manoeuvre.

He walked to the edge of the rocks and lowered himself down, his long legs disappearing over the ledge, the lightly tanned flush to his skin deepening as he glanced back at me.

I hesitated for a moment before joining him, making sure I was a safe distance away.

'I love it here,' he whispered. 'It's always so quiet.'

'Why would you need to find a quiet spot?' I asked, wondering if he attended a boys' version of the academy.

'My family can get a bit loud so I like to escape.' His smile lit up his entire face, and I couldn't help but smile along with him.

'Do you have a large family?'

'My parents are foster carers and over the years we've grown as a family.' He laughed out loud. 'At the moment, I've got four brothers and two sisters.'

'Wow, that is...loud!'

He laughed again and I felt my shoulders relax with every second that passed.

'Your parents must be amazing,' I said.

'They were,' he replied softly. 'Unfortunately they were killed a few years ago.'

I mentally kicked myself.

'I'm so sorry. How did it happen?' I scolded myself a second time for asking such a personal question. It was none of my damn business, but I felt a strange bond with this boy. We were both orphans who had been touched by tragedy and looking for an escape.

Cody didn't seem to notice my discomfort.

'It was a car accident. They were here one minute and gone the next. My brothers have looked after me ever since it happened.'

'I'm sorry to hear that. My mum was killed in a hit-and-run, so I understand that pain, but it sounds like your parents did a wonderful job of raising all those kids, if they're still here for you when you need them.'

I didn't mean to sound so envious, but it slipped out in my tone. Cody must have noticed as his eyebrows lifted slightly as he looked over at me.

I didn't want him asking about my tragic past, so I jumped in with another question.

'Do you live in the woods?'

He nodded, his fair hair flopping into his eyes.

'We live in a farmhouse deep in the woods. Luckily there's a lane that leads us to the outskirts of town so we're not totally cut off. My parents ran a vegetable store and sold all the produce they grew in the fields. We've kept it running ever since they died.'

'You don't look like a farmer.'

He laughed again and the sound melted something inside my chest.

'What do I look like?'

I could feel my face burning as I thought about an appropriate answer.

'You know, don't answer that. I don't think I want to know.' He smiled and tilted his head to the side. 'Want to see something cool?'

I grinned and he took that as a yes.

We left the outcrop and ventured further into the woods. Somewhere deep inside my subconscious I knew I shouldn't be wandering through the forest with a strange boy, but my gut told me a different story. I had the oddest sensation that I knew him— on an emotional level. We'd suffered the same tragedy and our grief united us.

The smell of the earth and woods filled my senses and calmed my nerves the further we walked. The trees began to thin out as we reached a clearing with a huge oak tree in the middle. It was like no tree I'd ever come across. The trunk was immense and someone had chiselled a seat into the wood.

'My dad carved this for me when I was little. I used to come here after they died so I could feel close to them again. This tree and the overhang are special places.'

I could understand that. After my mum died, I would sit in the bottom of her wardrobe soaking up the scent of her clothes and the lingering smell of her perfume. Loss is hard, but when you are so young it is life-altering.

'It's also a great climbing tree.'

He winked at me, extending an unspoken challenge, and strode off across the clearing until he stood beneath its branches. He reached up and grasped the lower bough, then swung one of his long legs up and over until he was perched in the tree.

'Come on up.' His voice was teasing as he began to swing higher and higher.

I hadn't climbed a tree in years, not since the days when Zak had taken me to the park as a kid. It came back to me in a rush of adrenaline and I scrambled up the branches, catching up to Cody in no time.

'Ah, an expert in tree climbing, I see. What other talents does the mysterious Mia hide beneath her grace and beauty?'

I couldn't stop myself from laughing. He had a way of making it feel easy.

My T-shirt clung to my back as I moved from branch to branch. I knew I looked like someone had thrown me in an oven and finished me off in the swimming pool, my mediocre run through the forest adding to my not-so-glamorous appearance. Cody, however, didn't seem bothered by my frizzy hair and blotchy cheeks. By the time we reached the top I was wheezing, but I felt fearless. Cody nestled into the crook of two branches and I did the same, our feet planted side by side.

'I can understand why you like coming here,' I said, trying to catch my breath.

Through the top layer of leaves we could see for miles. The houses and shops down in the valley glinted in the sunshine and the faint outline of the peaks framed the horizon. It was a breath-taking view.

We talked, mostly about our likes and dislikes, favourite music and authors. It was nice. Apart from with Elizabeth, I'd never really experienced the joy of a normal conversation without there being an ulterior motive. My dad always managed to twist my words, leaving me with an incessant fear of saying the wrong thing. His way of picking a fight. However, Cody was easy to talk to, and I was about to tell him this when he spoke up.

'So then, Mia, are you going to tell me what you were running from?'

I flinched slightly as suspicion flooded my senses. Had I misjudged my bad boy radar? I didn't think so. Cody didn't give off that homicidal maniac vibe, but how did he know I'd been running? Had he followed me to the outcrop? Realising that I'd done nothing wrong and was merely on a training exercise, I relaxed my shoulders.

We stared at each other across the branches of the tree. My mind whirled with possible scenarios that I could share without divulging too much. I opted for part truth in the hope that it would pacify his curiosity and spare me from the fear I felt at opening up.

'My dad recently passed away and my uncle brought me to live with him. He has this strange opinion that family should stick together.' I laughed, nervously.

Cody's head automatically dropped to the side in the universal language of sorrow and I glanced away. I didn't want to see the pity shining in his beautiful blue eyes. I omitted to tell him the part about the werewolves and the gore. It seemed safer sticking mainly to school-related topics, so instead I told him about my new life amongst the spawn of Satan, who happened to have red hair and her own set of bodyguards.

'Felicity and her crew are determined to make my life a living hell, but all I want to do is melt into the background and get on with my studies.'

'Are you talking about Hood Academy?'

'Yeah, I arrived yesterday, and I've already run away twice; doesn't bode well, does it?'

He smiled but his features were tight, not the open, warm expression from earlier.

'Is something wrong?' I asked.

'I've heard things about that school—bad things.'

'What kind of things?' I was starting to feel uneasy. Cody didn't seem to be talking about schoolgirl bullies. Did he know about the werewolf hunters? Could I ask him? I only realised at that moment that the academy might be a secret society, and here I was telling the first guy I stumbled across.

'I think I better go,' he muttered.

He began climbing down the tree, slowly at first and then much faster. I struggled to keep up and worried that he would run off and leave me. I didn't play the damsel-in-distress card very often, but I was lost in the woods and I kind of needed him to guide me back in the direction of the school.

I sat on the lowest branch and steadied myself to jump, but Cody raised his arms to help me down, and as I leapt he caught me.

His hands felt solid at my waist, and our bodies were so close I could smell the tang of his shower gel. I looked up into his bright eyes and saw a flickering of pain there.

'Follow the trail to the right and it will lead you back to the academy. Stick to the path and you shouldn't get lost again.'

'I feel like Dorothy in *The Wizard of Oz*,' I said quietly, trying to lighten the tension that was evident on his face and in the tightness of his hold.

He smiled, a fraction of that warmth returning to his eyes. If I had given some serious thought to the situation I would have said that Cody looked scared.

'Stay safe, Mia, and be careful who you trust.'

With that, he turned away and jogged off into the woods, leaving me reeling from his words and his touch.

BEING THE FIRST to return back from the ultra-marathon should have been a memorable occasion. However, as I strolled across the lawn I could just make out Miss Ross's outline through Sebastian's office window. She threw her hands in the air and disappeared from view, only to reappear with Sebastian by her side at the main door, rushing down the front steps of the academy and heading my way.

'What's wrong?' It was Sebastian who spoke first, worry etched in the frown lines across his forehead.

'Nothing. I got totally lost when I missed a green flag, but I managed to find my way back.'

I'd been proud of myself for following Cody's vague directions but the look of horror on Sebastian's face made me wish I'd stayed lost for a few more hours.

Miss Ross waved him away and herded me towards the school, wrapping her arm around my shoulder like a protective mother hen.

'You appear to have an aptitude for getting lost in these woods, Mia.'

'It was an easy mistake,' I told her. 'I was far too busy enjoying the scenery, and I must have missed a couple of flags.'

'Hmm, I doubt that very much.'

'Miss Ross, we don't *know* that Mia didn't get lost of her own accord.' Sebastian strode alongside us, his jaw taut.

'Sebastian, you know as well as I do that young Felicity had a hand in this. In all the years we've been doing these exercises, *nobody* has missed a flag. Felicity is behind this because she is unruly and petulant and...'

'Bitchy.' I waded in with my opinion and Miss Ross cackled.

'Indeed.'

Sebastian paused on the top step and rubbed his hands over his face. He looked tired.

'She is still a student and I have an obligation to protect her as much as anyone else in this academy.'

'With all due respect, Sebastian, you do everything you can for these students, but your talents lie in the management and structure of their education rather than their emotional welfare.'

Well, that explained his lack of paternal instincts. I'd wondered if his coolness towards me had been down to the distant relationship with my dad but now I understood. He didn't know anything about teenagers, especially teenage girls.

'Mia, could you wait in my office, please.'

I nodded at him and thanked Miss Ross for her kindness. Pushing open the front door, I wandered through the foyer to Sebastian's office. The storeroom door was closed and I couldn't resist trying the handle as I went by. Locked. How did Felicity have a key? I made a mental note to ask Elizabeth if her friend Adam had a set of keys to the academy's many rooms.

The lights were blazing in Sebastian's office and there was a fire roaring in the grate. I warmed my hands before ambling over to his desk. Documents and open books littered the surface. He had obviously been in the middle of something when I strayed out of the treeline. I glanced at the papers filled with data that made no sense to me.

I was about to flop into the chair opposite the desk when a Manila file caught my eye. The label in the top-right corner read 'Private & Confidential—Fatalities'. Taking a quick peek through the window, I saw Sebastian and Miss Ross were still deep in conversation, so I risked a look at the file.

There were lists of names inside the folder, dating back to the 1970s. Three column headings stood out on the crumpled page. Name, Drug Trial Administered, Date of Death. I ran my finger along the long list of names until I reached the bottom of the page. My heart froze. The last name was Cassandra Roberts. My hands began to tremble as I read the information alongside her name. Trial notes: Prototype 0118 failed. Subject fell into a coma. Bite site infection. Unable to resuscitate. Date of Death: October 11th.

My chest was tight as I fought against the tidal wave of tears that threatened to fall, and I found it difficult to breathe. The back of my throat burned, but I refused to allow myself to cry. Sebastian would be here any minute and I was reading his private files. *His* files. Files that contained information about my mother's death.

Memories of my brother's arms wrapped tightly around me barrelled to the front of my mind. He held me as I wept, both of us listening to the police officer who told our father about the hit-and-run driver who had left our mother by the roadside. Zak's strength had kept me glued together over the weeks that followed.

He was fifteen and I had just turned six. Our dad had lost it, drinking more than usual in a miserable attempt to blot out his pain. The shouting was too much for me, and I would sit on my bed with my hands clasped over my ears, blocking out the sounds of Zak and Dad screaming at one another. Zak left me a year later. Mum's death hit our family hard. A tragic accident that tore us apart. And it was all a lie.

SIX

By some miracle, Sebastian was called away to deal with a parent and Miss Ross excused me for the rest of the day.

'The other girls should be at the halfway marker by now and won't start returning until dinner,' she said. 'Go get a shower and enjoy your free time.'

I avoided eye contact as she happily chatted about having the school to myself. If I raised my head, she'd know I was upset. It was torture keeping my emotions in check as she prattled on. A loud crash in the cafeteria attracted her attention and I used the distraction to shoot off up the staircase.

The corridors were deserted as I'd expected, and the silence hit me with such force that when I finally reached the bathroom, I slid to the floor and sobbed. I was still crying when I stepped under the hot stream of water and washed away the dirt and sweat from my unsuccessful run.

Why had the police lied to us about Mum's death? The strange file on Sebastian's desk referred to an infected bite. A sense of clarity settled over me as I realised what that meant. A werewolf killed my dad, his throat ripped out in front of me, and now it seemed that my mum had also died because of a werewolf bite. Becoming a hunter suddenly made absolute sense.

Sebastian was somehow involved, but I couldn't figure out if he was covering for someone or being protective. The photographs of my family in his office could be a sign of guilt or love. Whatever it was, I intended to find out. I made a vow to myself that as soon as Elizabeth returned from the marathon, I would confide in her. My stomach churned as I thought about opening up to someone new, but I wanted to tell her everything. For nine years I'd dealt with life alone, and now I knew it didn't have to be that way. Zak was the only person I'd ever spoken to about things that mattered. He was my best friend and brother rolled into one. Until he left. Then I didn't have anyone to share my pathetic dreams and stories with.

'Be careful who you trust.' Twice in as many days those words had been spoken to me, first by Terry, at the motorway services and earlier this morning by Cody. Although I couldn't trust my uncle or Miss Ross, I could turn to my friend. I needed her help. Someone had to know about the academy. Cody said he had heard bad things about this place. Maybe his brothers knew more.

Determination powered my actions as I threw on my jeans and jumper, pulled on my tattered old Converse and dragged my wet hair back into a ponytail. Cody had mentioned that even though he lived deep in the woods, he often visited the town, and Miss Ross did tell me to enjoy my free time. She didn't specify I had to stay on school property.

MY DARING ESCAPE plan was going smoothly until I bumped into Adam as I skulked around the side of the building heading for the animal cages and the tracks beyond. Feeling flustered, I made up some lame story about exploration.

'You want to explore the forest?' he asked with some trepidation in his voice when I voiced my hastily hatched lie.

'Well, it's such a beautiful day and I love being in nature.' We both looked up at the overcast sky and the grey storm clouds rolling in as the words passed my lips.

'Uh huh.' He wasn't convinced.

Shit.

'Okay, truth is I need to escape this place for a few hours. I'm going stir crazy and Elizabeth won't be back for ages.'

His eyes twinkled at the mention of Elizabeth's name and I couldn't help but smile.

'You want me to keep you company?' he asked.

'Thanks, but I think I need some time alone.' I was genuinely touched that Adam was willing to give up his time for me, but I was on a mission, and nothing would deter me.

'Fair enough,' he said. 'If you stick to the left-hand track it leads down into town where you'll find a few stores and Taylor's Coffee Shop. Don't be long because Lizzie will kill me if anything happens to you.'

The track did indeed lead into town, or at least to a farmer's gate at the top of the high street, which I climbed over, then I headed down the hill.

I'm not sure I would call Ravenshood a town. With only a smattering of local shops, one pub, a church and a bandstand, it looked more like those photographs of rural villages from the geography textbooks we'd had at my last school.

I spotted Taylor's Coffee Shop in the distance with its brightly painted green window frames and potted bay trees on either side of the main entrance. The chalkboard outside boasted the best Bakewell pudding in Nottinghamshire. I dug into my jeans pocket and pulled out the ten pound note Sebastian had given me for emergencies. A cake sounded like the perfect fuel to inspire my search for Cody.

A plump lady in a Robin Hood apron smiled at me as I approached the counter.

'Hello, my love, what can I get for you?'

'Hot chocolate and a slice of Bakewell pudding, please.'

She busied herself with my order as I thought about my next tactic. If Ravenshood was indeed a small community, the smiling woman adding a mountain of whipped cream to my mug might know where I could find a certain farm boy.

'Do you know if Cody lives nearby?' I tried to act nonchalant, but the burning sensation rising up my neck and spreading to my cheeks was a bit of a giveaway.

The lady lifted her eyes to meet mine and studied me for a long moment.

'Friend of the Mills family, are you?'

'Er, yes, Cody and I are friends but I've mislaid his address. I'm from out of town and promised I'd pop in for a visit the next time I was here.' I was babbling but couldn't seem to stop. If she believed anything that poured out of my mouth, it would be a miracle.

She finished with the cream and shook a small silver canister over the mug, showering everything in chocolate flakes.

'Cody will be in soon for his lunch. He delivers produce to Mr Thompson over the road and always stops for a cheese roll before heading home.'

I handed over my money and tried to resist the urge to do a little jig on the spot. My face felt warm again and I had an odd sensation in the pit of my stomach.

I positioned myself strategically at a table for two on the left of the entrance.

The café owner was right and just as the hands on the clock above the counter turned to one o'clock I saw a truck pull up opposite the café. The signage down the side panel confirmed that it belonged to the Mills Family Farm. Cody climbed out of the passenger side and lifted a box of vegetables from the back of the truck. He wore the same jeans from earlier but a new T-shirt beneath a navy apron. The muscles on his arms flexed as he hoisted the box up onto his shoulder and disappeared into Mr Thompson's store.

I wiped my hands down my jeans and cursed the butterflies that were swirling around my stomach. I remembered thinking how good-looking he was when we first met in the forest, but as I sat staring through the window, I realised I'd underestimated how much. Cody was gorgeous. Drop-dead, blond hair, blue eyes gorgeous. The stuff of movies or rock bands. I dragged the band out of my hair and shook out my ponytail, letting my long hair fall around my shoulders. I heard a chuckle from behind the counter but refused to turn around. I knew I was having a girlie moment, but I didn't need to see the café owner's amused expression.

The door to the coffee shop swung open and a large man with a square jaw and shaggy brown hair stepped inside.

'Afternoon, Jane.' His voice boomed across the café and made me jump.

'Hello, Byron, usual is it?'

'That'll be great, thanks love. I'm starving. Do me a cheese roll for Cody while you're at it.'

I wanted to turn around and look at the man now standing at the counter. This had to be one of Cody's brothers, someone who could give me answers, but I kept my eyes fixed on Mr Thompson's shop. Cody hadn't come out yet and I didn't want to miss his entrance.

There was a hushed conversation behind me, and I realised too late that Jane was making Byron aware of my existence. I stayed as still as possible, straining to hear what she was whispering.

I nearly flew out of my chair when a large hand landed on my right shoulder.

'Hello miss, I understand you're a friend of my little brother.'

Byron slid into the seat opposite me and smiled. His eyes were warm and filled with good humour. He was clearly enjoying seeing me squirm.

'How does a pretty young lass like you know our Cody?'

'We, I...'

Shit.

He smiled again, wider this time until I could see nearly all of his perfectly white teeth.

'No need to be shy. We could be family if the two of you are, you know, a couple.' He winked and his shoulders began to shake as he laughed.

'Oh, no, we're not a couple,' I said, finally finding my voice. 'We haven't known each other very long. I'm new in town and he's the only person I know. Sort of.'

Byron rested his elbows on the table and scrutinised me.

'That's a shame. I think you'd make a lovely girlfriend for my baby brother.'

I felt my cheeks grow hotter as I lowered my gaze and nibbled on my lower lip. How had I got myself into this?

Byron roared with laughter and slapped a big hand on the tabletop.

'I'm sorry. I'm only teasing. It's not often we get pretty strangers in Ravenshood. I don't mean anything by it.'

I looked up at him and found it easy to return his warm smile. His eyes twinkled with mischief, and I remembered when Zak used to look at me in the same way when he was teasing me about something or other. I suddenly missed my brother more than ever.

The café door opened and Cody breezed in with a big smile and a cheery hello for Jane. His eyes slid towards Byron and me and he stopped dead, still clutching the door handle.

'What are you doing here?'

He looked shocked and confused, but he also looked scared. His eyes flicked between Byron and me as if he'd caught us doing something wrong.

Byron didn't seem to notice his brother's discomfort and stood up, swinging his arm across the newly vacated chair.

'I was just keeping your seat warm, baby brother.'

Cody finally released the door and took a tentative step towards me. I tried to keep my face as neutral as possible. I was just a girl in a coffee shop enjoying a hot chocolate and hoping to make a friend.

I smiled up at him in the hope that he would take that as a peace offering. It appeared to work as he slowly lowered himself into the seat. His long fingers rapped at the tabletop and his left leg bounced up and down on the spot. He had either become really shy since our time spent in the woods or he was a nanosecond away from making an escape.

'I'm sorry. I didn't mean to surprise you,' I said finally, keeping my voice low so Byron and Jane couldn't hear.

He looked at me then, his intense blue eyes boring a hole into my soul.

'What you said to me earlier about the academy, I need to ask you about that. I didn't know how else to find you.'

He nodded and wiped his hands down his apron, constantly glancing behind me at where his brother was talking to Jane.

'We can't talk here. It's not safe. Meet me in the woods after dark.'

It seemed odd to assume the woods were safe after dark, and if I arranged to meet him, I was agreeing to something I knew was against Sebastian's rules. However, if Cody had answers, then it was worth the risk.

'Where shall I meet you?'

'There are some cages on the edge of the academy's land. If you follow the track on the right, you'll eventually come to the overhang where we first met. I'll meet you there at midnight.'

He took a pen from his apron pocket and scribbled something on a napkin, then slid it across the table towards me.

'Here's my number just in case you have any problems.'

Without waiting for an answer, he got up and walked over to his brother. Muttering his thanks to Jane, he took a foil-wrapped sandwich from her.

Cody stormed out of the coffee shop but Byron stopped by my table.

'It was lovely to meet you...' He spread out his hands and widened his eyes as he waited for me to fill in the blank.

'Mia,' I said. 'Nice to meet you too.'

Byron took a step backwards as if I'd slapped him. He looked through the window to where Cody was climbing into the truck and then back at me.

'Right, of course, Mia.' His smile was growing thinner by the second, and with a tight nod of his head he rushed for the exit. I watched him fumble with the door handle, all the earlier bravado and jokes a distant memory.

I'd never seen anyone screech the tyres on a truck before, but the Mills Family Farm vehicle left a cough-inducing cloud of dust as Byron tore off down the high street.

Perhaps Cody had told his brother about our earlier meeting and that I was a student at the notorious Hood Academy. There was so much I wanted to know. So much I needed to know.

I looked up at the clock above the counter. Only another ten hours until I saw Cody again. Maybe then I'd get some answers.

WHEN ELIZABETH BURST through our bedroom door looking like a cross between the swamp monster and a yeti, I couldn't resist laughing at my roommate's misfortune.

'It's not funny!' Elizabeth squelched across the floor towards the bathroom, shedding clothing as she went.

'I know, I'm sorry. How was the marathon?'

'Oh, you know. Long, tiring, wet and bloody awful.'

'I'll see if I can rustle us up a couple of hot chocolates from the canteen.'

I left her to shower in peace and made my way downstairs. Clusters of students huddled in the corridors and sat on the stairs wrapped in blankets and dressing gowns, sipping from steaming mugs of chocolatey goodness.

I spotted Felicity and her squad languishing on the sofas in the entrance hall. She glanced at me as I walked towards the canteen, a look of surprise and then malice registering on her features. She was evidently hoping I was still lost in the woods.

Now wasn't the time to confront her. I was happy to wait until the right moment to take my revenge on that bitch. In the meantime, I was going to follow Sebastian's orders and keep out of her way.

ARMED WITH TWO mugs and a large packet of popcorn, I hurried back to our room. Elizabeth should be out of the shower by now. She was easy to talk to, and although I didn't want her to get mixed up in my crazy life, I knew the time had come to ask for help. It was new territory for me and my palms were slick just thinking about it.

Surrounded by an army of stuffed animals, Elizabeth flicked through a schoolbook as I walked in.

'I'm sure they'll let you off doing your homework for one day,' I said, handing her one of the mugs.

Sitting opposite her, I watched as she sipped her hot chocolate and let out a contented sigh. Her long blonde hair was wet and hung loosely around her shoulders, and her bright eyes sparkled in the lamplight. I could see why Adam was so enamoured with her. Elizabeth was one of those rare people who were beautiful on the inside as well as the outside.

'Miss Ross told me you got back first. She mentioned something about you getting lost again.'

I nodded and fished a marshmallow out of my drink before answering. 'Yeah, I missed a couple of flags and ended up in the middle of nowhere.'

'Hmm, I agree with Miss Ross about your missing flags. It had to be Felicity.'

I waved my hand dismissively. 'I don't care about Felicity's stupid prank. As it happens I met a boy who helped me find my way back.'

That got her attention. She put the mug down on the dressing table and shuffled forward until she was teetering on the edge of her bed.

'A boy? Who is he? Is he cute? Ooh, tell me all about him.'

I laughed at her wide-eyed expression. 'Are you obsessed with boys and romance or something?'

'No, but I believe there is a soul mate for each of us, and if we find someone who makes us happy, we should cherish every moment.'

'Is that how you feel about Adam?'

Elizabeth's face lit up at the mention of Hood Academy's groundsman. 'Adam is sweet, kind and warm-hearted, and I love spending time with him.'

'Is he a good kisser?'

I watched her cheeks grow pink as she squirmed on the bed. 'We've only kissed a couple of times and only recently.'

'What took you so long?'

Elizabeth frowned. 'We had to overcome certain...problems.'

Now I was intrigued.

'Adam only arrived at the academy a month ago,' she continued. 'I'm sure you can imagine the impression he made on the girls—one girl in particular.'

'Felicity!'

Elizabeth nodded and dunked a marshmallow with the tip of her finger.

'Felicity flirted with him outrageously. It was embarrassing.'

I stifled a laugh at Elizabeth's horrified expression.

'So what happened? Did he only have eyes for you?'

She blushed. 'I used to share a room with Felicity and just before you arrived here she found me and Adam...together.'

I was aware that my mouth was open but no sound came out. The revelation that sweet, gentle Lizzie had been paired up with that red-headed monster startled me more than the love triangle.

'Felicity went mad. She was screaming and shouting, and in the end Adam dragged me out of the room for my own safety. Miss Ross assigned me a new room, this one, and I tried to keep out of Felicity's way.'

'Something we have in common,' I mumbled.

'Felicity tried to get Adam fired while Sebastian was out of town collecting you, but Miss Ross was brilliant and stood up to the governors. I don't think Felicity will ever forgive me.'

'Well, all I can say is Adam has great taste. He's smitten with you, that's obvious.'

'Do you really think so?'

'Hell yeah. When I mentioned your name earlier, his eyes twinkled. Of course, that was when he helped me escape the academy.'

Elizabeth's head jerked up at the mention of my extracurricular activities, and she scrunched her brow.

'Why did you want to escape?'

I took a deep breath and launched into my day's activities, then told her about Cody appearing in the woods and the strange conversation about Hood Academy.

'If I hadn't got lost and met Cody, I may never have ended up in Sebastian's office and seen the file on his desk.'

I paused to check she was taking it all in. She studied me for a moment then urged me to continue with a wave of her hand.

'The file was a list of fatalities and at the bottom was my mum's name. There's more to Hood Academy than just training and taking an oath. I think Cody can help me find out what that is, so I'm meeting him again. Tonight. At midnight.'

'Are you crazy?' She jumped off the bed and began pacing the floor. 'You can't meet a strange boy in the woods and especially not in the middle of the night. It's too dangerous.'

'I know it sounds dangerous, but I'll be careful. It's odd but I feel like I can trust Cody.'

'You don't know anything about him!' Elizabeth placed her hands on her hips and towered over me as I sat on my bed.

'I know you're worried about me, but I can take care of myself, and besides, I need to know what he was talking about. There's something going on at this school that potentially involves my family. Something is not as it should be and I need to find out what it is.'

Her shoulders sagged as all the fight drained out of her.

'I'll come with you,' she said.

I wasn't expecting that. Elizabeth was full of surprises, and it felt nice to be able to confide in someone and have them back me up.

'I can't ask you to do that, but I do need your help. Do you think you could ask Adam for a spare key to the front door?'

She flopped down on her bed and wrapped her arms around herself.

'The front door is bolted from the inside after lights out, but he does have a key to the kitchen door. I'll ask him.'

We smiled at one another and I had the strangest sensation of being at peace. I'd shared a part of my life with someone and they hadn't pushed me away or laughed at me.

'Thanks, Lizzie,' I whispered.

She came and sat next to me, threading her arm in mine and resting her head on my shoulder.

'That's what friends are for.'

Friends. I had a friend. Zak would be so proud.

ADAM AND ELIZABETH turned out to be the best wingmen anyone could wish for. Adam gave me a spare key to the back door off the main kitchen that led to a dark courtyard which housed the wheelie bins. A short jog across the side lawn took me to the animal cages and the track that Cody told me to follow. Adam even loaned me a torch and a black waterproof jacket.

Elizabeth pushed a small penknife into my hand with strict instructions to use it if my life was threatened. I sincerely hoped it wouldn't come to that.

They waved me off and told me they would wait up until I returned. I prayed that I would come back in one piece. Glancing up at the night sky, I noticed the moon had started to wane, and once again I kicked myself for not asking Miss Ross how many nights the wolves would be roaming the forest.

I FOUND THE overhang easily this time as if I'd memorised the route after using it so many times. Ravenshood lay below me, the town in darkness apart from the odd lamp in a window. The air was so still that all I could hear was the beating of my heart.

'You made it. Did you have any trouble finding this place?'

I spun around at the sound of the voice behind me. Cody stood a short distance away dressed in dark jeans and a black jacket. He looked like a secret agent. I tried not to think about his role as the next James Bond and dropped my gaze to his feet.

'No, your instructions were spot on, thank you.'

He gave a short nod of his head.

'So, what do you need to know?' he asked.

His question surprised me. He had been so elusive and cold before that I assumed it would be difficult to get any information out of him tonight. Either I'd misread the signs of his earlier inner struggle at the coffee shop, or he didn't have the answers I wanted.

'You told me that Hood Academy was a bad place. What did you mean?'

He gestured for us to sit on the boulders that looked out over the valley. I dropped down and swung my legs over the ledge as Cody did the same. His thigh brushed up against me, but he didn't flinch away this time. Instead, he remained that way with his leg touching mine. My mouth went dry. I tried to concentrate on anything other than the sensation of how close he was to me. If I could have slapped myself without looking like a total fool, I would have.

I cleared my throat and tried again. 'I know I've only been at the school for a couple of days, but I don't see any evidence that it's a bad place.'

I hoped he wouldn't notice the quiver in my voice as I lied. The screams from the storeroom certainly pointed towards something very bad happening within the walls, and then there was the list with my mum's name on it, but did he know any more than I did? I didn't want to blurt out everything I'd discovered until I was sure I could trust him to be honest with me.

'It's mostly myth and legend that surrounds Hood Academy, but something bad seems to happen to people who come into contact with the students,' he said. 'According to my brothers, the superstitions surrounding the school have been passed down over many generations. Did you know Queen Victoria is supposed to have opened it?'

I smiled, remembering the small book Sebastian had given me with the reference to Dr Neale, the master werewolf hunter for the realm.

'Yeah, I heard that the original owner worked for royalty.'

'Well, Byron told me the old queen believed in the supernatural, and so she founded the school to protect the town.'

'Supernatural? You mean like vampires and stuff?'

Cody nodded, his blond hair falling across his face. He swept it back in one fluid motion and continued with his story.

'Yes, but I don't think it was vampires that she was worried about.'

He was clearly gearing up to break the news that werewolves were real, and I felt a bubble of panic rise up my spine. Was I supposed to act shocked when he announced it? Should I scream like a girl and run or should I express disbelief? He saved me from doing anything.

'Of course, it's all a load of rubbish. Theory has it that a big dog bit someone and the townsfolk got all hysterical. The reports were twisted and by the time they reached the queen she believed that huge beasts were roaming the forests. Everyone knows that it's not true.'

He looked out over the valley, and I took the opportunity to study his profile. Any girl would kill for his cheekbones. He had the most handsome face, with a strong jaw, but I couldn't help settling my gaze on the fullness of his lips. I had a brief desire to see if they tasted as good as they looked. He sensed me staring and swung round to look at me. I was thankful for the darkness so he couldn't see me blushing.

'So, according to the town's history, my school was created to scare away big dogs?'

Cody chuckled. 'Told you it was rubbish. The stories have escalated over the years and now the entire town believes the academy, and its students, are cursed.'

I wasn't buying it. When he had helped me out of the tree, he was visibly shaken when I'd mentioned Hood Academy, and earlier at the coffee shop he hadn't been pleased to see me. He didn't seem the sort of guy who believed in curses. So why was he feeding me a useless story? Unless he did know the truth but couldn't tell me and was fobbing me off. It was time to call his bluff.

'Well, that's a shame,' I said. 'I was hoping you would be able to tell me more about the werewolf pack and why my fellow students are training to kill them.'

SEVEN

The silence stretched out between us as I watched every kind of emotion flash across his pale face. Eventually, he settled on a deep sigh and a defeated slump of his shoulders.

'I think you need to start from the beginning,' I said, folding my arms like a disgruntled teacher. 'There's no curse. The school is a training centre for wannabe werewolf hunters, and we both know it.'

In the fading light of the moon, I noticed the anguish in Cody's expression. The breath caught in my throat and I grabbed his hand, squeezing his fingers.

'I'm sorry, Cody. I never meant to be so blunt about it.'

Damn! Maybe he *did* believe in the curse story, after all.

He rubbed at his face with his free hand but kept the fingers of his other hand wrapped tightly around mine. I felt a warmth spread down my limbs.

'It's okay,' he whispered. 'I guess I'm actually relieved that you know.'

My quizzical expression urged him on.

'All my life my dad told me to keep the town's wolf secrets to myself. Byron said it's all hush-hush for a reason and if we start talking about the werewolves, then it'll attract bad luck. When you told me you'd just arrived at the academy, I was worried that you either didn't know about the place, or you were going to go all ninja on me.'

'You think the hunters are a danger to the town?'

'Yes, I've seen some of the students in action, and when they get started it doesn't end well.'

'You've seen them kill a werewolf?'

'No, I've seen them attack a boy because they *suspected* he was a werewolf. I wasn't sure if you were the same as them.'

I squeezed his fingers. 'I'm not.'

He smiled down at me and held my gaze. It was like he could read my thoughts, see into my soul. I suddenly felt exposed—naked. I averted my eyes and looked out over the sleeping town.

'Do you and your family know where the wolves are?' I asked, filling the silence.

'They keep to themselves and if people don't bother them, they don't stray near to town. The folk here keep the peace with the wolves but that's at risk if your school keeps churning out Barbie-sized hunters.'

I burst out laughing at his comment and made him jump.

'I'm sorry, but now you mention it, it's kind of true. There's a particular student who fits the plastic doll stereotype perfectly.'

Looking down at my hand, I examined our entwined fingers. Cody wasn't in any rush to let go, so I relished the feel of his rough hand in mine and the warmth that continued to vibrate through our connection.

'So, that's why you said Hood Academy is a bad place, because it threatens the truce between Ravenshood and the wolves.'

He dropped his gaze to study our interwoven hands, rotating them so that his was on top of mine. It felt strangely comforting.

'There's a rumour in town that the students at Hood Academy capture the wolves and do experiments on them in class.'

I flinched involuntarily. Sebastian hadn't mentioned any kind of warped biology lesson to me, but that didn't mean that Cody wasn't right. I'd only been at the school a few days and didn't know enough about the curriculum to confirm or deny Cody's rumour.

A memory of the late-night screams rumbled through my mind. Was it true? Did the student body catch the wolves and keep them locked up until it was time for a macabre show-and-tell?

I quickly steered the conversation around to basic werewolf legend, eager to find out more about this mythological species. 'Is it true that the werewolves only stay in their wolf form on the night of a full moon?'

Cody lifted his head and looked over at me, his bright blue eyes filling my vision.

'They always turn on a full moon but can also change at will in case they need to defend themselves...according to Byron.'

'So if your rumour was true, the school would be full of extra people and not animals.'

'I guess so, unless they stayed in their animal form as a method of defence.'

The very human-sounding scream that had come from the underground lab told me the captive wasn't in wolf form.

'What if they couldn't remain in their wolf mode?' I whispered.

Cody's eyes shone in the soft moonlight as his gaze trailed over my face. He lingered a moment on my lips.

'If they couldn't stay in wolf form, I dread to think what your classmates might do to them.'

'You sound like it's a bad thing that the school experiments on them. Not that I'm condoning animal testing or anything, but surely if the students kill the werewolves, your town is safe.'

'It's not that simple, Mia. Ninety-nine percent of the time they are as human as you or me, and they don't deserve to be harmed. Not for any reason. Whether there are good intentions at the bottom of it or not.'

I looked out over the valley as I digested Cody's words. He was right of course. No creature deserved to be in pain, and the screams I'd heard the other night proved that someone was indeed getting hurt. Could I trust Cody with what I knew? I'd trusted Elizabeth and Adam and they hadn't let me down so far. Perhaps my luck would continue.

'I can find out if the rumours are true,' I said softly, studying his face for any spark of mistrust.

'You'd put yourself in danger for the werewolves? Aren't you going to be training to hunt them down?'

'Yes, on both counts. At the moment, I've had light lessons but my full training starts tomorrow. I'm going to learn what they have to teach me, Cody, but I have no intention of using those skills to harm anyone...or anything.'

He smiled at me and this time it reached his eyes. The tight smile from yesterday had vanished and he appeared calmer and more relaxed. I was still very conscious of our hands tightly clasped and our legs touching. My stomach did a strange lurch as my neck and cheeks flamed. I was grateful for the cool early morning air.

We sat in comfortable silence for a long time, watching the slumbering town and listening to the nocturnal activity surrounding us. I felt peaceful and dare I say it, safe. I never wanted to leave the calming influence of the forest. Being in Cody's company was enjoyable as he felt like a kindred spirit, but I knew Elizabeth and Adam would worry if I didn't return soon.

'I better get back before anyone misses me.'

Cody got to his feet and pulled me up so I was standing beside him. His scent was intoxicating, and I vowed to remember that smell so I could recall it whenever I wanted to reminisce about this night—this moment.

'Promise me you'll be careful, Mia.' He ran his thumb down my cheek, and I swear I felt an explosion go off in my head. 'Your uncle won't want you snooping around, so be on your guard.'

I couldn't answer as he leant in and pressed his lips to mine, softly at first but then applying light pressure.

His hands cupped my face as he pulled away and smiled down at me.

'I don't want anything bad to happen to you, Mia. For the first time since my parents' death, I feel like I've found someone I can talk to properly. Someone who understands me.'

A glow spread through me at his touch and his words. I knew exactly what he meant. I'm not sure that Zak would have approved of me snogging in the middle of the woods at midnight, but I believed that he would have liked Cody and that filled my heart with hope. An emotion I thought I'd never experience again.

'You've got my number. Message me when you know more and we'll meet back here,' he said, brushing my hair behind my ear.

I nodded and leant into his hand, kissing his palm as it swept down my face.

'Okay,' I said. 'I'll find out as much as I can.'

He kissed me again, full on the lips, taking my breath away, before turning and disappearing into the treeline. I stood for a while in silence, willing my heart to stop thumping so loud. It wasn't my first kiss, that prize had gone to Tom Nook in the last year of junior school, but this was like nothing I'd ever experienced. I touched my fingertips to my lips and smiled. Life had taken a turn for the better.

Adam was still awake when I tiptoed into the bedroom. He was leaning against the wall with Elizabeth's head resting on his chest. She was out cold and oblivious to my stealthy return. Adam smiled as I closed the door behind me.

'You're alive,' he whispered with a wide grin.

I snorted as I untied my shoes and kicked them into the corner.

'So how did it go?'

'It went better than I thought. Cody was...very helpful.'

Adam bent his head to the side and watched me carefully. I felt every inch the naughty schoolgirl.

'That good, eh?' He winked and I felt my face grow hot.

I ignored his knowing smirk.

'Cody told me about the werewolves and a pact between them and the town. From the sound of it, Hood Academy is the threat, not the wolves. The townsfolk believe that we're experimenting on the werewolves as part of our science classes.'

Adam's eyes widened and I had a moment of panic when I thought he was going to say that Werewolf Dissection 101 was at nine o'clock the next morning.

'That explains the noises,' he mumbled.

'What noises? Do you know something?'

'When I started working here, I was given a bunch of master keys. I can access every classroom, office and door in this place. The other day, I unlocked the storeroom in the foyer.'

'You went inside?'

He nodded. 'Yes, but just for a second. I heard this faint grumbling and moaning sound coming from behind the shelves. Your uncle arrived and ushered me out, so I couldn't investigate.'

'What did he say?'

'He told me I was imagining the sounds and said it was only a stationery store. Then he took my key off me.'

'I saw Felicity go inside the other night,' I confessed. 'She took one of her heavies in with her and I managed to follow for a bit. The storeroom opens up to a long corridor with stairs leading down to a basement room.'

I paused as I let Adam digest everything I was saying. He knew this school better than I did, and I was pretty sure he trusted his employer. Was I about to shatter all his misconceptions? Would this knowledge put his career at risk?

'I didn't see what they were doing down there,' I continued, 'but I heard someone screaming. It sounded like a man or a boy; definitely human.'

We sat in silence for a moment listening to the soft snores from Elizabeth, neither one of us wanting to admit that whatever we thought we knew was not as bad as the reality could be.

'I can try and get my hands on that key again,' he said, stroking his hand down Elizabeth's golden hair. 'The three of us will work out what's going on.'

'The three of us?'

'Yes. Elizabeth and I were talking about it while you were gone and we want to help. You can't do this on your own, Mia. You need extra eyes and ears and we can provide that. Your uncle will be checking on you and that puts you in full view of the one person we're trying to avoid.'

'So, if he's watching me, he won't be watching you.'

'Exactly!'

I flopped back on my bed and stared at the ceiling. In such a short time I'd gone from a beaten and broken girl to werewolf hunter and spy. I wondered what Zak would think if he knew.

Adam slid out from under Elizabeth and lowered her head to the pillow. He bent over and kissed her tenderly on the cheek. I smiled to myself, recalling my first kiss with Cody earlier this evening. I was still reeling from it and if I hadn't been so exhausted, I might have sat up all night reliving it.

'Take care of yourself, Mia,' Adam said, climbing up on the desk and throwing his leg out of the window to descend the waiting ladder.

'I will. Promise me you'll be careful too.' I didn't want him risking anything for me.

He nodded and then disappeared from view, his dark skin blending in with the darkness.

Elizabeth stirred and opened her eyes.

'You're alive,' she said, her voice croaky from sleep.

I chuckled as she mimicked Adam's exact reaction on seeing me again.

'I'm alive. It went well. Cody was helpful but I think I can find out more here at the school. Do you remember the file I mentioned, the one with my mum's name on it?'

Elizabeth nodded.

'Well, it also had a number; prototype 0118. I need to find out what experiments they did on her and why.'

Elizabeth yawned and I noticed how late it was.

'Go back to sleep and we'll talk more in the morning.'

Her lips twitched in a half-asleep smile and she was steadily snoring again before I could turn off the light.

Starting tomorrow I was going to embrace everything Hood Academy could teach me. I was going to take that hunter oath, and then I was going to use it all to discover the truth about my mum's death, the werewolves and the part my mysterious uncle had to play in it all.

OATH BREAKER

EIGHT

reakfast at Hood Academy was a messy affair. I sat next to Elizabeth at the far side of the room, keeping a wary eye out for Felicity. I still owed her for getting me lost in the woods, but, without her assistance, however ill-intentioned, I might never have met Cody. Maybe I should be thanking her instead of thumping her.

Miss Ross appeared in the doorway and waved me over.

'I guess my training is about to begin,' I murmured to Elizabeth as I cleared my plate and dropped it in the used crock bucket.

'Good luck!' Elizabeth's sing-song voice followed me as I weaved in and out of the breakfast tables.

Sebastian had decided to pull me from certain classes so I could have one-on-one sessions with Miss Ross. He wanted me to catch up so I could integrate fully into class activities as soon as possible. I should have been glad that I was getting out of double maths, but looking at the glint in Miss Ross's eye I doubted I was getting off lightly.

We walked across the grounds and back to the gym that she had shown me on my original tour. I spotted Adam cutting the grass as we marched down the gravel path. His head lifted as we trotted past and he raised a hand in greeting.

'Such a nice lad,' Miss Ross said as she waved back.

'Yes, he is.'

THE GYM WAS just as I remembered it, and I couldn't shake the feeling of being at an army training camp. Two large blue mats filled the centre of the room and there was a long staff at each corner. They were the same weapons I'd seen the girls using on the front lawn the day I arrived. About five foot long and smooth to the touch. There were two black rubber strips equally spaced along the staff for ease of handling. The way my palms were sweating, I could imagine causing additional damage to the surrounding area if that thing slipped from my grasp.

'Grip the staff like so.' Miss Ross flicked the weapon off the floor. She stood in the centre of one blue mat with her feet together.

I lifted the other staff from the floor and mirrored her stance on the opposite mat.

'When you start to fight, bring your less dominant leg and arm to the front. This allows you to swing your dominant arm forward with more strength, like so.'

She lurched forward, bouncing on the balls of her feet and flipping the wooden staff forward at a tremendous pace. If I had been standing a foot closer, my nose would have been a bloody mess right now.

'In a few weeks Hood Academy holds its annual sparring assessment. If we get your training up to an agreeable standard, there's no reason why you can't take part.'

'Do I have to?'

'You'll be fine. Besides, the assessment is the perfect stage for taking your hunter oath.'

'You mean the bit where I swear my loyalty to crown and country?'

Miss Ross smiled. 'It's a huge honour, Mia. You get to stand in front of your peers and promise to be a part of something special. A new family if you like.'

I'd had about as much 'family' time as I could stomach, so I shut my mouth and followed Miss Ross's lead.

For the next hour, she taught me how to roundhouse kick, thrust, block and sweep. My arms ached and I was convinced that every inch of my body would be covered in bruises. I needed to work on my defence if I was going to stand any chance against my fellow students.

'You learn fast, Mia. Your uncle will be proud of you.'

It felt strange to hear that. Only Zak had ever used the word proud around me and that was on the day he left. 'You're the best little sister anyone could wish for,' he had said, 'and I'm so proud to be your brother. Never forget that.'

'I promised Sebastian that I'd try to fit in here, and if that means I need to throw myself into my training, that's what I'll do.'

'It's not all about school, Mia. Sebastian wants you to be able to defend yourself. I'm sure you wish you'd had this kind of training from an earlier age.'

She glanced over at me with a knowing look on her face and wide, expressive eyes.

'Did Sebastian tell you about my dad?'

'If you mean about the beatings then yes, he did. I'm sorry, Mia. No child should have to put up with that behaviour, especially not from a loving parent.'

I gave a sharp laugh and whirled the staff around in my hands.

'Just for the record, my dad was *not* a loving parent. He was cold, calculating and a violent drunk. If Sebastian knew about that, why didn't he come and get me earlier? Why wait until I had to watch my dad get his throat ripped out by a bloody werewolf?'

Miss Ross watched me carefully as if deciding on the appropriate words.

'Your uncle couldn't interfere even though he wanted to. When your mother died it created a rift between him and your father, and I don't think Sebastian knew how to repair the damage.'

'He didn't have to repair anything, he just had to take me away.' I could feel my shoulders slump as I caved in on myself. It was an automatic reaction whenever I thought about my dad. Like an inbuilt safety mechanism that helped me to shrink away and become invisible.

'Sebastian didn't realise it was that bad, Mia. Give him a chance to make it up to you at least. He cares about you and he can keep you safe.'

'Like he kept my mum safe?'

The dark shadow that flashed across Miss Ross's face told me she knew more than she was telling me. Should I divulge the information I'd found on the file in Sebastian's office? Maybe she could tell me why my mother's death was covered up.

As if sensing my imminent questions, Miss Ross dropped her staff in the storage bucket and headed towards the door. She pulled at the handle and exposed the lush gardens beyond the gym, calling over her shoulder as she went. 'That's all for today, Mia. I'm happy for you to join the rest of the class for group training.'

As she marched off, leaving me alone in the gymnasium, I felt that familiar prickling sensation down my neck. Turning to the bank of windows, I surveyed the forest beyond. Nothing.

I huffed at my reaction. Clearly, Miss Ross's input had unnerved me more than I realised.

ELIZABETH FOUND ME sulking in the common room a couple of hours later. I'd taken it upon myself to start reading through the textbooks Sebastian had dropped off early this morning. History and science hardbacks together with a volume on myth and legend. Not the kind of schoolbooks I would have had in my old life.

'I'm impressed,' she said. 'I never had you down as the studious type.'

Her eyes twinkled as she teased me and I smiled. It was easy being around Elizabeth. She made me forget that I was ever alone.

'For the record, I've spent my day catching up on schoolwork and learning to fling that bloody staff around. I'm exhausted.'

'Well don't nod off just yet. I've come to collect you for class. You need to survive one more staff-whirling session then you can finish for the day.'

I groaned and Elizabeth laughed. 'You'll be fine, just hide at the back.'

We made our way to the gymnasium with the rest of the student body and took up our positions on the wooden floor. No mats this time. Miss Ross had obviously been extra kind to me earlier.

My stomach lurched as I spotted Felicity stride to the front of the room. If she was running this group, I was in trouble. Elizabeth glanced over at me and gave a little thumbs up sign. She had obviously had the same thought.

'We're going to break off into pairs.' Felicity's voice cut through the air like nails on a chalkboard. 'Try to pick a partner that you've never sparred with.'

There was a rush of movement as the girls scuttled back and forth finding partners. I stepped up to Elizabeth's side and claimed her before anyone else could.

'This will be fun,' she whispered.

I doubted that my mediocre skills with a staff would be any competition for Elizabeth's training.

'You mean fun for you when you whip my ass.'

She giggled. 'Exactly.'

With everyone in position, Felicity blew her whistle and the sound of wood on wood exploded throughout the room. Elizabeth thrust forward with her dominant arm, and I lifted my staff in time to block her advance. I spotted what looked like a mixture of surprise and pride flutter across her face.

We tested one another's skills, breaking through the defensive barriers every now and then, but I was satisfied at being able to hold my own against a more experienced fighter.

As we were so caught up in our training, neither of us saw Felicity approach until she'd lunged forward with her staff, knocking both of us off balance.

'There's no need to go easy on this one,' she said, tossing an icy glare in my direction. 'If anything, we need to push her more than anyone else so she doesn't hold the class back.'

Elizabeth tried to intervene, but I stopped her with a raised hand.

'It's fine, Lizzie. If Felicity thinks I need additional help, who are we to argue? Maybe she could teach me.'

A hush fell over the gymnasium as I took my position across from my nemesis. I knew I didn't stand a chance against her, but if I could get at least one or two brutal swings in I'd be happy.

We circled each other like vultures around a fresh kill. I could feel everyone's eyes on us and prayed that I could land one half-decent strike.

Felicity lurched forward, flipping her staff skyward with her toe. Distracted momentarily by the flying weapon, I didn't see her fist coming. She punched me hard in the stomach and I folded, dropping to my knees.

Over my shoulder, I could hear Elizabeth urging the rest of the group to keep working and hustling them back into pairs. At least if they were occupied, I wouldn't have an audience for my downfall.

Still slightly winded, I slowly dragged myself up to my full height. Felicity was bouncing on her toes, balancing her staff in one hand and grinning at me like a feral cat. If she thought she was leaving this gymnasium without at least one bruise, then she was mistaken.

I whipped my staff up so fast she failed to see it until it connected with her chin. The loud yelp she made when my weapon found its target filled me with hope.

She snarled at me. 'You're going to pay for that.'

I didn't doubt it, but I allowed myself a small moment of pride.

She pushed forward and I blocked her advance. She tried again but I was there to prevent the strike. This carried on for a while, and her frustration was evident in her angry cries. Relentlessly she attacked and I continued to defend myself. Her eyes blazed with pure hatred.

An eerie hush fell over the room as the other students watched our exchange. One of the girls called time, telling us that the class had finished and it was time to leave but nobody dared move.

During the short distraction, Felicity advanced once more and the staff flew out of my grasp as she flipped her own weapon with ease. She swept her leg out, cutting me down at the knee until I was sprawled on the floor, my staff clattering beside me.

I lifted my chin and steadied myself to stand but the butt of Felicity's staff struck me on the side of the head. Stumbling backwards, I landed on my backside.

'Hey, that's not allowed.' Elizabeth's voice splintered the silence.

I waited for the spinning sensation to pass. The last thing I wanted was to throw up in the middle of the gymnasium with everyone watching.

Elizabeth barrelled her way to my side, pushing the girls out of the way until she reached me.

'Leave her alone, Felicity!'

'I'm fine, Lizzie, honestly. It was just a tap.' The spots that swirled across my vision told another story.

Felicity laughed and whirled her staff around her arms like a baton twirler in the middle of a parade.

Grabbing onto Elizabeth's arm for support, I let her pull me up and tug me towards the exit. I didn't want to make a scene. Sebastian had warned me to stay away from Felicity, but I hadn't been able to resist the opportunity to get my own back on her. Maybe it was time I started listening to him. Even if it meant ignoring the smug bitch. As I brushed past her, she hissed in my ear. 'You should be used to getting a smack around the head. Think of it as a cure for homesickness.'

Somewhere on the other side of the hall, I heard someone suck in their breath. The air whooshed out of me as Felicity's words punctured my heart. I felt like I'd floated out of my body and was watching the scene pan out in slow motion below me. The hunter and the hunted.

The clock above the door ticked painfully on to the next second as if the effort to move was too much. Elizabeth's eyes widened and her mouth began to open in readiness to shout something, but I never got to hear what she wanted to say.

From deep within my gut, the rage built up and bubbled over. My fingers tensed and curled into fists as a red fog descended over me, blocking out all sound. The image of my dad's face steamrolled through my mind, and I let out a choked sob. All I could think about was squeezing the life out of the redhead who stood in front of me.

It all happened so fast. My fist connected with Felicity's jaw with such force that we both fell. She crashed to the gymnasium floor with a loud yelp and I landed on top of her, crushing her to the wooden floor.

She squirmed and bucked in an attempt to throw me off, but the anger that roared through my veins held me firmly in place. I straddled her body so that I was sitting on her stomach, my knees pressing into her ribcage, pinning her to the ground as I pounded her face with my fists, repeatedly, left then right.

Her arms flailed as she tried to block my advances, but something had taken over me, a darkness that I'd never felt before.

Then it was no longer Felicity's face that I saw, it was mine, bloody and broken and begging for my father to stop.

With a rush of noise, the world came crashing back down. I could hear the screams and shouts around me and felt Elizabeth's hand pulling at my arm and shouting my name. I looked up into her face and saw the panic in her eyes, then I felt the warmth coating my hands. I flinched as I realised I was still sitting across Felicity, who was screaming hysterically and using her arms to protect herself. The warmth I'd felt was blood, her blood. I'd punched her until her nose bled and her eye began to swell.

'I'm...I'm so sorry.' I jumped up and fled from the gym, Elizabeth right behind me.

NINE

My hands shook as I sat in the armchair facing Sebastian's desk. I hadn't had time to clean myself up before he whisked me into his office. Felicity's blood had dried over my knuckles and I frantically rubbed at it as if this simple act would erase the memory of what I'd just done.

'I warned you to stay away from her.' Sebastian had been shouting at me for the last ten minutes. He hadn't stopped pacing his office and waving his arms in the air.

'She provoked me,' I said again.

Sebastian held his hand out to shut me up, the skin at the corner of his eye twitching as he glared at me in anger. I recoiled involuntarily and his expression softened slightly.

'Felicity's family will demand your expulsion, and I don't know if I can prevent it,' he said, folding his arms across his chest and slumping against the wall.

'I thought *you* ran this school. So much for family loyalty, eh?'

'You really think they care that we are related? That just makes things worse, Mia.'

I shrugged my shoulders. 'Maybe it's not such a bad thing. I could go to school in Ravenshood but still live here, with you.'

He stared at a spot over my right shoulder for what seemed like an eternity then resumed his pacing.

'No, I need you to remain here and continue your training. It's important.'

My ears pricked up at his words and I felt a rumbling of unease.

'Why is it so important to you that I stay here and train to be a hunter? Is it because a werewolf killed my mum?'

He stopped suddenly and spun around to face me, a startled expression on his face.

'What did you say?'

I squared my shoulders and sat up a little straighter in the chair. It was time to test my uncle and his loyalties.

'I saw a list on your desk with my mum's name on it. The cause of death was an infected bite not a hit-and-run. Why didn't you tell me?'

Sebastian sank down into the chair behind his desk and rubbed a hand over his face. He looked exhausted.

'It's true, your mother was killed by a werewolf. You were far too young to understand, and so it was much easier if you thought it was an accident.'

'But you let *all* of us believe it was a car accident. My dad. Zak. We were together when the police came to the door and told us. How could you do that to us?'

I analysed my uncle as he hung his head. Any fear I may have had about standing up for myself vanished and I felt angry. What gave him the right to decide what we knew?

'Were you having an affair with my mum before she died?'

My direct question obviously shocked him as he spluttered an incoherent jumble of words before resting his elbows on the desk and holding his head in his hands.

'I loved your mother very much, but no, we weren't having an affair.'

'Why did you love her? It wasn't your job to love her, it was ours. Me, Zak and Dad. I don't understand how she could be involved with werewolves unless *you* put her in harm's way.'

'Mia, there is so much you don't understand, and that's why it's important that you stay here and train. Werewolves murdered both your parents. Surely that's enough motivation to behave and trust in my judgement.'

I stood up, curling my blood-encrusted fists into tight balls. I'd had enough of people telling me how to behave, and I was fed up of the bullying and all the lies.

'You don't get to decide what's right for me. As you say, werewolves killed my parents and that should be enough motivation to stay the hell away from them.'

Sebastian burst from his chair and was around the desk in a heartbeat. He stood over me and hissed menacingly into my ear. 'I have every right to decide what's right for you, Mia. I'm the only family you have left. Stay here until I work out what to do with you.' With that, he stormed out of his office, slamming the door behind him.

I lowered myself into the chair, afraid that my wobbly legs wouldn't be able to hold me up for much longer. It appeared that my dear uncle Sebastian was more like my dad than I'd first realised. It wasn't long until the tears began to fall. I curled up in a ball and sobbed for a long time.

CONFINED TO SEBASTIAN'S office, I pulled a couple of books from the shelves and busied myself by reading. The rain hammered at the picture window and the fire popped in the grate. For such a big school, full of hundreds of girls, it was extremely quiet.

At three o'clock I heard the rumble of footsteps as the students made their way to the last lesson of the day. Only one hour to wait and then I'd be in for another slanging match with Sebastian. I briefly wondered if he'd starve me to death as part of my punishment. My stomach rumbled as if to confirm my suspicions.

I wandered over to the back wall of Sebastian's office which was made up of floor-to-ceiling bookshelves. There was an impressive library here, intermingled with photo frames of my family. I picked up a picture of my mother taken a few months prior to her death. I remembered her long brown curls and the way her cheek dimpled when she smiled. Sebastian had said he loved her very much but that they weren't having an affair. Did she know he loved her? Is that why she came to the academy so often? Miss Ross had told me she was a frequent visitor.

The door burst open causing me to lose my grip on the frame, which fell to the floor with a crash. Elizabeth stood in the doorway, her brow creased with worry.

I glanced down at the smashed glass of the frame and sighed.

'Jeez, Lizzie, you frightened me to death.'

'Sorry. Dr Roberts let me off my last class so I could come and get you. He's asked me to take you out for something to eat. Even gave me some money.'

I looked across at her, my mouth hanging open.

'Why the hell would he do that? He spent most of the day screaming at me. I'm supposed to be getting expelled, not taken out for a meal.'

'He did mumble something about keeping you well away from the student body until lights out.'

'Ah, so it's a hide her away and deal with it later ploy. How unoriginal.'

I crouched to clear up the glass, dropping it into the bin by the side of Sebastian's desk. The frame wasn't damaged so hopefully he wouldn't notice. As I set it back on the shelf, my mum's photograph slipped out of the bindings and drifted to the floor.

'What's that?' Elizabeth pointed at a yellowing piece of paper hidden behind the photograph with a sealed envelope clipped to the page.

'I don't know.'

As I unfolded the paper, I spotted my mother's handwriting, her expressive curly letters covering the page.

'It's from my mum.' Excitement fluttered in my chest as I started to read.

Elizabeth placed her hand over my arm and tugged me towards the door.

'Maybe you should read it in private. We've been given a free pass and by the look of your puffy eyes, I'd say you need it.'

I smiled at my friend and nodded. Some time away from Hood Academy was just what I needed. Grabbing the broken frame, photograph and letter, I stuffed them inside my training jacket and followed Elizabeth out of the office.

ADAM WAS WAITING in a beat-up old Ford when we rushed down the front stairs of the school. With the engine running and him glancing backwards and forwards, it made me think of a getaway after a bank robbery. I sniggered to myself as I climbed into the back seat.

'You okay?' Adam glanced at the red welts on my hands.

'Yeah, my fist connected with someone's face.'

'Fair enough.'

Elizabeth jumped into the passenger seat and leant over to give Adam a kiss.

'Thanks for doing this,' she said.

'It's my pleasure. Miss Ross came and found me before you did. She said I might be needed for a speedy escape.'

Elizabeth laughed and slammed the car door behind her.

'Well then, you better do as she asked and get us away from this place.'

'I'm on it.'

The car jolted forward and we made our way down the winding drive. It seemed like an eternity since I had first seen the wrought-iron gates of Hood Academy after my father's death.

ELIZABETH SUGGESTED GOING to Taylor's Coffee Shop for homemade burgers and chips, and I briefly wondered if Jane, the proprietor, would remember me.

The café was bustling with conversation and laughter when we crowded through the door and settled ourselves into a booth. I sat facing the window, secretly hoping to see the Mills Family Farm truck.

'The burgers are amazing, Mia. Do you want one?'

I nodded absentmindedly. I didn't care what I ate as long as it was hot and there was plenty of it. I was impatient to read the strange letter in my pocket and explore the contents of the envelope. I needed to see what my mum had written.

Adam went to order our food and drinks as I slipped the letter from my jacket. The tattered page had been read multiple times, one of its corners torn and the paper flimsy to the touch.

I glanced up at Elizabeth who watched me with wide, eager eyes. She nodded her head as if I was waiting for her to tell me it was okay to carry on. I peeled open the page and began reading.

My dear Sebastian,

I wish I had good news for you but I don't. I met with Joel and spoke about our situation. He was so cross when I explained that I'd made a mistake marrying Frank and that I wished to leave him and join you at the academy. His rage got out of hand and he hurt me. I'm scared, Sebastian. Joel wouldn't let me leave. I tried everything to convince him that this is where my heart belongs, but he refused to listen. He believes that the work you are doing is dangerous and instead of loving you I should forget you exist.

I'm defying his orders by writing this letter and I fear retribution should he discover we're still in touch. Zak is growing suspicious although he hasn't asked me outright. I'm so glad Mia is too young to understand. I only hope that I can persuade Zak to come to you instead of Joel when the time comes. He is nearly sixteen so it's getting close.

I believe in what you're doing, Sebastian, and if it will save Zak and Mia from this fate and allow them to have a normal future, I hope you carry on without me.

I'll try and write again soon but in the meantime know that I love you with all my heart and I wish we could all be together.

Yours forever, C x

I stared at the paper for a long time, unable to think, move or comprehend what it meant. Elizabeth's mouth hung open as she struggled to find an appropriate response too.

Adam snapped us out of our stunned silence when he returned with three Diet Cokes.

'What have I missed?'

I handed him the letter and waited until he'd finished reading. He let out a long, low whistle and passed it back.

'So your mum and Sebastian *were* a couple?'

'It certainly looks that way, but earlier, when I asked Sebastian if he had been having an affair with my mum, he said no. He admitted to loving her but nothing else.'

'Who's Joel?' Adam cut in.

'Never heard that name before. He sounds like her boss or something, but that doesn't explain why Zak would go to him. Whoever this Joel is, he doesn't sound very nice.'

'How did he hurt your mother?' Elizabeth asked.

I skimmed over the letter once more. 'It doesn't say, but she was definitely scared. I wonder if he had something to do with her death.'

'I thought you said a werewolf killed your mum?'

'Yes, that's what it said on the file, and Sebastian confirmed it earlier. Maybe this Joel knew where they were and he took her to their lair. Do werewolves have lairs?'

Adam chuckled. 'I think they have three-bedroomed houses and attend church every Sunday.'

I groaned. I was more confused than ever.

A young waitress arrived with our food and gave us a cheery smile. The burger smelt good and my mouth started salivating before I could unwrap the cutlery from the napkin.

'What's in the envelope?' Elizabeth asked between mouthfuls.

I tugged the prize from my coat and tore it open. There was a single photograph inside, but this wasn't a pretty shot of my mum smiling or even a family portrait. My appetite disappeared as I studied the bare-chested boy chained to a laboratory table. He wore a shabby pair of trousers and dirty socks. With his arms and legs shackled, he strained against his restraints. A man in a long white lab coat was injecting something into the boy's upper thigh.

I covered my mouth with my free hand as a wave of nausea washed over me. The photograph was old, its colouring faded, but the anguish, fear and pain that distorted the boy's features were as raw as the day it was taken.

I flipped the photograph over and gasped. Printed in capitals on the reverse was *Prototype No. 0102.*

OATH BREAKER

TEN

The next morning passed in a blur of one-on-one fitness training with Miss Ross and private tuition on a hastily erected table under the picture window in Sebastian's office. I believed it was partly Sebastian's way of keeping a close eye on me and partly his need to keep the student body safe from his homicidal niece. I alternated between reading and watching the distant woods with longing.

The sound of raised voices pulled my attention from my books and I jumped out of my seat to investigate. Outside Sebastian's office window, partially obscured by shrubbery, stood a large, bald man in an expensive-looking grey suit. He towered over Sebastian by a good foot and a half and jabbed my uncle in the chest as he enunciated every word.

'I. Want. Her. Gone.'

'Mr Parker, please. I assure you I have punished Miss Roberts severely and...'

'I don't care if you threw her in the goddamn animal cages, she *attacked* my daughter and half killed her!'

I rolled my eyes at the exaggeration. Yes, Felicity looked like a ton of falling rocks had landed on her but 'half killed' was not even close.

'Mia is devastated over her actions. She was hoping to fit in at this academy after witnessing the brutal murder of her father—at the hands of a werewolf.'

The big man squared his shoulders and studied my uncle like he was a bug he'd just found in his dinner.

'I understand that your niece is damaged but that does NOT give her the right to...'

'I know, I know.' Sebastian raised his hands in submission. 'I beg you to let her complete her training, even if it's just to give her the basic skills she'll need to protect herself in later life.'

Mr Parker looked as if he was considering Sebastian's proposal, and I pressed myself closer to the window in anticipation of his response.

'Very well. She can fulfill her training, take the oath, and *then* I want her gone. If you fail to get rid of her, Dr Roberts, I shall have no other choice but to withdraw my funding.'

'There's no need for such a rash action, Mr Parker.'

'It took me a long time to find that tribe in Africa, Dr Roberts, and it took me even longer to find you. I needed a doctor qualified to use the tribe's knowledge to develop the serum. Do not make me begin my search again.'

Sebastian squirmed under the bald man's deadly glare.

'I assure you, sir, I am doing everything in my power to develop the correct transfusion. You will have your serum and the wolves will never need to turn or hunt again.'

I pressed my hand to my mouth. Was it possible that Sebastian was the person responsible for the screams I'd heard?

Felicity's father moved closer to Sebastian and spoke through clenched teeth.

'I don't care about them turning, or hunting, because when this serum is ready, you, and your little band of hunters, will use it to destroy them all. For good.'

The door to Sebastian's office opened, making me jump and leap away from the window with a yelp. Miss Ross stuck her head in.

'You can take your lunch break now, Mia. Elizabeth is still sitting in her science exam, but I think I saw Adam in the canteen.'

I didn't need telling twice and shot for the door, knocking the books and papers flying as I did. Miss Ross chuckled as I hurtled past her and headed towards the sounds of clattering plates.

'Hey!' Adam waved a hand in the air to attract my attention, and I headed towards him with my plate piled high.

'I'm starving,' I said.

'I can see that!' Adam's eyes twinkled as he laughed at my haste to eat. He had become as much of a friend to me as Elizabeth had. They were like a package deal. He clearly idolised her and therefore he got her friends as well.

'I'm going to sneak out later and see Cody.'

Adam showed no signs of surprise at hearing about my escape plans; he just shrugged his muscular shoulders.

'You need any help getting out?'

'Not if you leave your ladder at the window. I'll use that and keep to the shadows. I'll message Cody and tell him to meet me at the overhang at midnight.'

Adam nodded.

'What do you know about Felicity's dad?' I asked, recalling the conversation between him and Sebastian.

'Mr Parker? Not much. I know he's wealthy and travels all over the world visiting tribes and trading their knowledge of herbal medicine for western goods. I also know he despises werewolves. Why?'

'I've just overheard him and Sebastian talking and I don't think I've got a lot of time left. Mr Parker wants me out.'

'Well, if Mr Parker is anything like his daughter, I can't say I'm surprised. That family despises anyone who isn't like them.'

I nodded and stuffed a chip in my mouth.

'I was thinking, you might want to put your meeting with Cody off until tomorrow, Mia.' Adam wiggled his eyebrows at me.

'Huh?'

'I've got a present for you and you might need to use it as soon as possible so I can put it back before anyone realises it's gone.'

My eyes widened as he produced a small silver key from his pocket.

'You got it!'

'I got it,' he said, puffing his chest out with pride. 'But I need to return it fast. If the so-called storeroom *is* the entrance to a secret lab, someone will notice that this key is missing.'

I nodded and turned the object over and over in my hand.

'Okay, change of plan. We'll sneak into the lab tonight and I'll meet Cody tomorrow. I might just have something to tell him by then.'

I slipped the key into my jeans pocket. An odd feeling circled in the pit of my stomach and it wasn't indigestion. I'd heard a scream when I followed Felicity and her minion that night, and I didn't relish the thought of what we might find down there.

'I have a staff meeting tonight so I won't be able to come with you, but that also means Sebastian will be there too and not wandering around the school.'

'Perfect. That should give us time to do some snooping without worrying about the staff finding us.'

'I'll meet you back in your room when I'm done to make sure you're both back safely.'

I smiled up into Adam's handsome face, his mocha eyes twinkling under the fluorescent light. He'd wait to make sure *Elizabeth* was safe, but I appreciated the gesture of including me in his thoughts.

I pushed my empty plate away and pressed my fingers against the pocket of my jeans, checking that the key was safe. Tonight we might have some answers. Tonight we might discover the truth.

THE SCHOOL WAS in darkness as we crept down the main staircase and into the lobby. There were no lights on in Sebastian's office, the bolts were secured on the front doors and the canteen was silent for once.

Adam had told us the staff meeting was taking place in the library and to ensure that they weren't interrupted, a curfew had been set for the entire student body.

As we approached the storeroom door, I tried not to think about breaking school rules. Calming my nerves was top priority, but my hand shook slightly as I fished the key out of my pocket and pushed it into the lock. My scalp tingled with the anticipation of what we might discover.

The long corridor opened up beyond the stacks of paper and ink, and I gestured for Elizabeth to follow me. She secured the door behind us and rushed to my side.

Her clammy hand clutched at my elbow was strangely comforting. Adam had given us each a torch and we shone them across the grey walls until we found the stairwell leading down into the lab.

Elizabeth's eyes flashed with fear but she nodded at me to carry on, giving me the strength to place one foot on the top step and move down.

The staircase was made of stone and led to a large open room with a low ceiling. The floor was stained with dark splodges that looked to be years old. I tried not to think about where the stains had come from. At the back of the room, carved into the rock, was a large glass window and a steel door. We hugged the edge of the room as we made our way to the door, neither one of us wanting to walk over the dark marks that littered the concrete floor.

I grabbed the handle and pushed, relieved to find the door was unlocked and opened easily. The room was bright, white and clean, a contrast to the stone cavern we had left behind.

Locating the switch on the wall, I flicked it up, instantly flooding the area in a stark light from the fluorescent strips overhead. In the centre of the room was a silver trolley. I trailed a shaky hand across the shiny surface with a growing feeling of panic. The smell of antiseptic filled my senses, making me gag. Two leather straps connected to heavy chains hung from the metal gurney. Even though the straps had been recently sterilised, I could still see the muted red stains ingrained into the leather.

'What is this place?' whispered Elizabeth, her complexion ashen.

'Well, it's not the nurse's office.' My voice shook slightly as I offered my friend a weak smile.

Above the long metal bench that stretched across the length of the room was another large window. Through the glass, I could make out the dull shape of filing cabinets lining one wall.

'We need to get in there.' I stabbed my finger towards the window for Elizabeth's benefit as I made for the connecting door.

Turning the handle as I put my shoulder against the steel, I prayed that it wouldn't be locked. It gave with a loud squeak and we both froze to the spot and listened for any sound that someone had heard us. Silence. We walked inside.

In the far corner was yet another connecting door. It appeared that the underground lab consisted of single rooms leading off one another. Just how many rooms and what they all contained was a mystery. One that I might not be willing to discover tonight.

The filing cabinets were in alphabetical order and I went straight for R. Flicking through the tightly packed Manila files I found what I was looking for. Cassandra Roberts—my mother's file. I tucked it into the back of my jeans and pulled my hoodie down over the top to conceal my stolen goods. Elizabeth hissed and beckoned me over.

'Look at this one.'

She shone the torch over the worn label and I gasped. Written in bold pen was a single name—Joel Mills.

'Joel was the name in your mum's letter. Maybe it's the same guy.'

I nodded and took the file from her. Flipping open the front page, I found a brief summary sheet. Name, date of birth, family. My heart froze. There was a single name written under the title 'children': Cody Mills.

I couldn't stop my hands from shaking as I read the words. How could Cody be connected to a man who knew my mother? Knew her and hurt her. It had to be some mistake. Maybe a complete coincidence and not my Cody.

A noise just beyond the next door made me jump. Elizabeth grabbed at my arm and brandished the torch as a weapon. I was starting to wish we'd brought our staffs with us, even if purely for show.

We inched towards the steel door, keeping our backs to the row of filing cabinets. The bright light from the first room splashed long shadows across the floor.

'Are you going to open it?' Elizabeth's voice quivered in terror as I took hold of the handle. 'We don't know what's behind there. It could be a werewolf.'

Part of me wished it was. I'd come face-to-face with quite a few over the past couple of weeks and so far none of them had hurt me.

A rattle of chains and a low moan arose from beyond the door, which quickly reminded me of the screaming. Maybe whoever Felicity had been torturing was still here.

Drawing on all my resolve, I turned the handle and pushed the door wide.

ELEVEN

lizabeth froze next to me and I felt my own limbs lock into place preventing me from fleeing. I couldn't move or look away. The dark room smelt of blood, wet dog and something else, something I knew and loved. It was the scent of the woods. Earth, leaves, moss and the clean air. But it was tainted. Spoiled by the horror that we faced.

A man lay strapped to a long metal bed secured by two silver chains anchored into the concrete floor. Dried blood caked his upper torso and thin scars littered his skin. He wore tattered jeans but nothing else: no socks, shoes or T-shirt. His brown hair was long and scraggly, matted with blood.

'Oh my God!' Elizabeth let out a wracking sob as she pressed her hands to her face.

I took a tentative step forward and then another. Elizabeth whimpered behind me.

The man moaned again, a low keening sound. His head lolled to the right, and he opened his eyes to look straight at me. I gasped and stumbled backwards, bumping into a small silver stand covered with scalpels, needles and vials. They crashed to the floor as I sorted through my jumbled memories. A motorway service station. A mug of hot chocolate. Twinkling eyes full of mischief.

'Terry?' I stepped forward, my initial shock dissipating.

'You know him?' Elizabeth moved to my side and leant over the now motionless body.

'I met him on my way to Hood Academy, the night my dad was killed. I think he knows my brother.'

'What shall we do?' Elizabeth's voice had regained some composure, and it helped me calm the thumping sensation that flooded my ears and sucked all the moisture from my mouth.

'We have to get him out of here.'

'But how?'

I looked around the dank room. Apart from the metal bed and the tray of grotesque instruments, there was only a small stool. I hooked it up with my toe and flipped it upside down. Using one of the long, thin legs, I slid it inside the loop of Terry's chains near to where they attached to the floor. I twisted and twisted until the chain and the stool leg were tight, and then I twisted some more. Eventually, the chain link gave and snapped free. I moved to the other side and repeated my action.

With Terry now loose it was going to be up to Elizabeth and me to balance his weight and try to get him back through the rooms and up the stairs. It seemed an impossible task.

'Where are we going to take him? We can't exactly hide him in our room?' I dabbed at a cut on Terry's lip with my sleeve and he groaned. Elizabeth flinched.

'We can take him to Adam's room,' she suggested. 'It's on the ground floor next to the library, and he's got access to the lawns. Maybe we can hide him until he's strong enough to make a run for the woods.'

I mulled this plan over, nodding in agreement.

'We'll get him upstairs and then you can try and get a message to Adam. We need his help to carry Terry the rest of the way,' I said. 'We must get him out of that meeting somehow.'

'Okay, I'll try.'

Terry coughed and rolled onto his side. His eyes found mine again and I tried to give him a reassuring smile.

'Terry, it's me, Mia. This is my friend, Elizabeth. We're going to help you.'

He nodded and tried to sit up. Whatever drug was pumping around his system clearly affected his coordination as he would have fallen to the ground if I hadn't stopped him. I hooked my arm around his shoulders and winced at the heat of his body. He was burning up.

We helped him swing his legs off the trolley and stood on either side of him as he tentatively tested the power in his limbs. Although very shaky, he was able to hold his own weight with a little help from us. We threaded our way through the maze of rooms. Elizabeth stopped to scoop up the information on Joel Mills before exiting the files room and closing the door behind us.

The concrete stairs were much harder to navigate. Terry had little strength left by the time we reached them.

He slid down the cold stone wall and sat on the bottom step with a defeated slump to his shoulders.

'Go get Adam,' I said to Elizabeth. 'Be careful and stay hidden.'

Elizabeth gave me a tight smile, shot a glance at Terry and then bolted off up the stairs, her torch light bouncing off the walls.

I knelt on the ground in front of the crumpled boy and stroked his hair away from his face. When I last saw him, he had been so full of life and energy, with a cheeky smile and a confidence that I could only dream of. I felt a heavy weight pressing down on my chest as I looked at him now.

'What happened to you?'

He lifted his gaze and gave me a weak smile.

'Captured. Tortured,' he whispered.

Tears threatened to fall and I blinked them away and carried on stroking his face. He reminded me so much of Zak. I knew now wasn't the right time to ask, but I couldn't help myself.

'Do you know where my brother is?'

Terry dropped his gaze and licked his parched lips. I wished I had a bottle of water I could give him.

'Yes,' he said eventually, his voice hoarse. 'He's here, in Ravenshood.'

I thought my heart might explode with joy at hearing his words. My breath caught in my throat and a million questions bubbled to the surface, but before I could ask any of them, I heard foot-steps above us.

The blood in my veins ran cold as I recognised Felicity's voice.

'The beast has been moved to the interrogation lab,' she said, 'but it just means we've got more knives to play with.'

Her sadistic laugh ricocheted off the stone walls and circled my throat like a noose. I had to move Terry. It would be catastroph-ic if she made it down the stairs and found us.

'Can you stand?' I whispered, urging Terry to his feet.

He grasped my arm for support and leant heavily against the wall. I noticed the smear of blood he left on the stone from his wounds.

My mouth felt like a sandpit, and yet the moisture that trickled down my spine did nothing to offer any refreshment.

I spun around looking for somewhere to hide, then I spotted a darkened alcove beyond the stairwell. It housed a mop and bucket and a janitor's uniform.

I shoved Terry without any preamble into the shadows and wrapped the grey uniform around his bare shoulders.

Felicity and her three friends reached the storeroom just as I melted into the alcove, my back to Terry, pushing him into the tiny space.

'You gonna let me have a go at torturing the monster tonight, Flic?' said Elena Fields, one of Felicity's longest-serving squad mem-bers, pushing herself to the front of the group.

'I suppose you deserve to have a go,' Felicity said, standing by the connecting door to the bright room. 'Just remember, we can't kill him. He might be disgusting vermin, but he's vital to Dr Rob-erts's work.'

I flinched at the mention of Sebastian's involvement. I hadn't wanted to believe it when I overheard him talking to Felicity's father. I knew he was doing something, creating some kind of serum, but I hadn't believed he was capable of torture.

The girls moved off into the other room, the door clicking shut behind them. I let the breath I'd been holding in rush out in one go.

'Come on, we've got to move.'

I supported Terry the best I could as we made slow progress up the stairs. It wouldn't take Felicity long to discover that Terry was missing.

We reached the stockroom just as I heard raised voices coming from the bottom of the stairs. I pushed Terry out of the door, and we crashed straight into a large man blocking the exit.

I recoiled before noticing the kind eyes peering down at me.

'Oh, thank goodness. Adam, we've got to move. Felicity is right behind us.'

Adam wrapped his arm around Terry's back and manoeuvred him across the foyer and out of sight. I followed, hearing the stockroom door burst open just as I escaped from view.

We hurried down the dark corridor until we arrived at a brown door with a number seven painted on it. Adam knocked once, then twice in sharp succession. The door opened and Elizabeth peeked out. She moved out of the way to allow Adam room to carry Terry through.

'Are you okay?' Elizabeth grabbed my hand and squeezed it as I entered Adam's bedroom.

'That was too close. Felicity turned up with her rent-a-torturer crew. I didn't think we'd make it.'

I flopped into a chair by the patio doors and stared out at the inky blackness. My heart was still pumping like crazy and I shoved my hands under my legs to stop them shaking.

'Is he going to be okay?' I asked Adam, who was settling Terry into the bed.

'Most of the surface wounds are already healing, but the drugs he's been given may take a while longer to come out of his system.'

Terry mumbled something and I moved over to the bed, sitting next to him and taking his hand.

'You're safe now, Terry.'

'The pack,' he said. 'He wants the pack, your uncle. It's my pack he wants.'

With that he slipped into a deep sleep. Gentle snores filled the room as Adam, Elizabeth and I looked on in shock.

'What if Felicity raises the alarm?' Elizabeth asked, her voice nothing more than a faint quiver.

I shook my head. 'She won't want to risk exposing herself and what she's been doing. She might be working on my uncle's behalf, but I'm not sure he knows about her cruel extracurricular activity. Terry should be safe here until the morning, and hopefully he'll have regained his strength by then.'

'I'll replace the key first thing tomorrow,' Adam said, moving to Elizabeth's side and wrapping a protective arm around her shoulder. 'You two need to act as casual as possible.'

'Casual? You mean not own up to breaking into a secret lab, stealing confidential files and rescuing a werewolf?'

That's right—a werewolf. Terry was a werewolf.

Adam grinned. 'Precisely.'

'I've never seen a werewolf in its human form.' Elizabeth's soft voice floated across the room.

'Cody told me they are as human as you or me, but I guess I wasn't expecting them to be people we know.'

'What are you going to do now?' Adam asked.

It was a simple enough question, but if I was being honest with myself, I had no clue what to do next.

'All we can do is wait for Terry to recover and see if he can give us any answers. He's a werewolf, with a pack that's clearly in danger, but he also knows where my brother is.'

'And what about the fact that Cody's dad might have had something to do with your mum's death?' Elizabeth whispered.

I rested my elbows on my knees and allowed my head to drop. Where the hell should I start?

'I promised Cody that I'd meet him and keep him up to date on any news.'

'Well, you've certainly got news to share with him. Do you think he knows Terry too?'

I couldn't think about that because if Cody *did* know Terry, that meant he probably knew Zak. I didn't think I could face it if anyone else was lying to me.

'What do you think Dr Roberts is going to do when he finds out Terry is gone?'

I stared at the silhouettes of leaves dancing across the floor. Sebastian was going to flip out when he discovered the werewolf was gone, but I wouldn't like to guess at what he would do if he knew it was me who helped it escape.

'I don't know,' I said quietly. 'I'm sure we'll find out soon enough.'

I TAPPED LIGHTLY on the office door as I pushed it open. My books were pressed into my chest as I hugged them close, using them as a shield against any impending danger. Sebastian sat behind his desk staring into a coffee cup. He didn't acknowledge my entrance.

I dropped into the chair at my table by the window and began unloading my pens and paper. The rustling of pages roused Sebastian from his stupor and he glanced around the room, noticing me for the first time. There were dark circles under his bloodshot eyes and stubble dusted his square jaw.

'Sorry, Mia, I didn't hear you come in.'

I smiled and flipped open one of my textbooks. 'That's okay, you looked...busy.'

His attention slid back to the coffee cup and he resumed his staring. My stomach churned as I wondered about the reason for his apparent lack of energy. By now, he must know that the werewolf was gone, but instead of the explosion of anger that I had expected, he looked defeated, broken and lost. I felt a sudden pang of sorrow for my uncle.

'Are you okay?' I couldn't help myself. I needed to know.

He lifted his head and looked across at me, his gaze drifting over my head and settling beyond the window and on the distant woods.

'All my work, those long years of hard study, all for nothing.'

'What do you mean?'

He stood up and scratched at his unshaven chin, carrying on as if I hadn't spoken.

'Take the day off, Mia. Go do teenage girl stuff with your friends.'

He pushed a small button on a control panel built into his desk and a speaker system crackled to life.

'Due to unforeseen circumstances, all classes will be cancelled today. All students have the day off.'

Through the heavy wooden door, I could hear the cheers and cries from the rest of the students and a thunderous clatter of feet as everyone dashed for their rooms or escaped out of the front doors hoping that the head of the academy wouldn't change his mind.

I collected my things, keeping a wary eye on Sebastian as he braced his hands against the edge of his desk, his head hung low.

'Can I get you anything?'

Sebastian shook his head and turned to face the bookshelves and the many photo frames that held images of my mother. I scooped up my books as quickly as I could and edged towards the door.

'I'll see you tomorrow.'

He didn't answer.

I RAN UPSTAIRS, dodging the masses of excited students who didn't know what to make of their impromptu day off. Elizabeth arrived back at our room just after me and we both dumped our books, changed into jeans and jumpers and darted back down the stairs.

'What have you decided to do with your day, girls?' Miss Ross blocked the head of the corridor leading to Adam's room. She wore a light turquoise running top and stretchy black joggers. 'Fancy joining me for a run?'

I screwed my face up as I thought about the last run I'd gone on. The only pleasant part of it was meeting Cody.

Elizabeth was faster with a reply. 'Sorry, miss, we're heading to the library. I want to show Mia the mythology section.'

'Excellent idea, Elizabeth. There's plenty to keep you busy in there.' With that, she jogged off across the foyer and out into the bright sunshine.

'That was quick thinking, Lizzie.'

She grinned at me and nodded at the sign hanging from the ceiling. The painted wood was starting to peel but the word 'Library' was still very clear.

We rushed along the corridor until we reached the nonde-script brown door with the number seven painted on it in wobbly lettering.

The door opened a crack when we knocked but was swung wide when Adam saw it was us. Elizabeth darted forward to fling her arms around his neck and I nodded my hello as I squeezed past my friends.

Terry was sitting up in Adam's bed looking much better than he had last night. He had showered and was wearing one of Adam's navy T-shirts, which highlighted the twinkle in his eyes. He grinned as I approached.

'Mia!'

'Hello, Terry. How are you feeling?'

I perched on the edge of the bed and folded my hands in my lap. He watched my every movement.

'I'm doing okay, thanks. Your friend will make a fine doctor if he ever gets bored of gardening.' He laughed and it rumbled from deep inside his chest.

I couldn't help but smile up at him. When I'd met him on the night my dad was brutally murdered, I never thought our paths would cross again, even though he had left me with cryptic clues and warnings. Yet here he was, a werewolf in human form, lounging in my friend's bedroom.

'You want to know about Zak, don't you?' He lowered his voice and lay a big calloused hand over mine. 'It's okay to ask me about him.'

I couldn't hold back the tears as they tumbled down my cheeks, hot and sticky. Terry pulled me closer and I nestled in the crook of his arm like *he* was my big brother and could protect me from the world.

'Zak never left you, not really. He had to move out so he could discover who he was, but he understood that you needed protecting, so he assigned some *friends* to check in on you every now and then. I was one of those friends.'

'What do you mean by he *had* to move out? Was it because of our dad? He should have taken me with him when he went.'

'You were far too young, Mia. Where he was going, it was too dangerous for you.'

'I don't understand. What could be so dangerous that he couldn't take his kid sister along? Where did he go?'

Terry tightened his hold around me and leant his head back against the wall. I spotted Elizabeth and Adam move closer to the bed as they listened to Terry's story.

'He needed to find Joel, the pack leader. He was sixteen and the time had come to commit to his family.'

'Pack leader? I don't understand. Did he go after Joel for hurting our mother? If Zak's a hunter too then surely he could have told me.'

Terry shook his head slowly. 'Your brother isn't a hunter, Mia. He's a werewolf. Just like your mum.'

TWELVE

My world spun away from me. I was aware that strong, warm arms were holding me, and I could hear the soothing tones of Elizabeth's voice in the background, but the noise in my head was terrifying.

'Are you absolutely sure?' Elizabeth asked Terry, her hand placed protectively on my shoulder.

'Of course I'm sure. We've been friends for ten years. I should know if my best friend is a werewolf.'

I pushed myself upright and felt instantly chilled as I untangled myself from Terry's arms. Elizabeth's hand remained on my shoulder, her way of telling Terry that I was *her* best friend and no one was going to mess with either of us.

'How?' It was all I could ask.

My brain couldn't comprehend the magnitude of Terry's revelation and the number of questions that bubbled up inside me.

Terry gazed down into my eyes and I noticed a kindness there. He didn't want to hurt me or frighten me. Apart from Elizabeth and Adam, he was the only one who had been honest with me from the start.

'How is my brother a werewolf?'

'It's hereditary,' he said, studying my reaction. 'Your mother was a werewolf, as was her father and his mother, and so on.'

I stored this genealogical insight for later and turned to Elizabeth.

'You told me that a person has to have the sight to become a hunter. I *saw* a werewolf kill my father and that's why Sebastian brought me here. I'm a hunter.'

Elizabeth nodded. 'It's true...or so I was told.'

We both looked at Terry for confirmation.

'In every pack, a cub is born, which unleashes the hunter to protect and serve...'

I jumped off the bed, holding my hand out to silence Terry, and began pacing the floor. 'Don't start quoting Dr Neale to me. I've read his dreary little book and nowhere in there does it say anything about siblings hunting each other.'

'Whoa! Who said anything about hunting each other?'

I stared at Terry with my mouth hanging wide open and the best 'duh' expression I could muster spread across my face.

'I'm a hunter. Zak's a werewolf. You do the math!'

'Mia, there's a reason you can see werewolves and it's not because you sparked the hunter gene. You come from a family of werewolves.'

Elizabeth gasped and took an involuntary step away from me.

'What is it?' I asked her.

She dropped onto the bed, her face as pale as the moon. Although she was looking at me, she was talking to Terry. 'When will she turn?'

'Turn? What are you talking about? Lizzie, who will turn?'

All eyes settled on me and I froze.

'I'm not a werewolf,' I said, but the tremor in my voice betrayed my doubt.

'It's okay, we'll work it out between us.' Elizabeth was at my side before I slid down the wall of Adam's room and curled up into a foetal position.

I MANAGED TO escape the overly protective embrace of my best friend and disappear into Adam's small bathroom. I could hear the voices of my friends waft under the door as they analysed my family history, future options and moon cycles.

Staring at my face in the mirror, I tried to picture how I would look as a wolf. My hair was dark brown like Zak's and curled over my shoulders. Did that mean I'd look like one of those Scottish long-haired cows? I groaned and pulled at my top lip—was that a fang?

There was a soft tap at the bathroom door and Elizabeth's gentle voice pulled me back from studying my fingernails—had they grown in the last hour?

'I'm fine, Lizzie,' I whispered, although if I was brutally honest, I didn't think I'd ever be fine again.

I opened the door and swept my gaze across the room. Terry was sitting up on the bed, the shape of his strong muscles visible beneath his borrowed shirt. He gave a short nod of his head as I caught his eye. Adam stood close by watching me with a crooked smile, and Elizabeth was eager to grasp my hand and squeeze my fingers. They looked just the same as they always did. No horror, fear or judgement in their eyes, just love and friendship.

'How are you not freaking out about this?' I asked Elizabeth and Adam.

Adam wrapped his arms around his torso. 'I have a confession,' he said. 'I've been around werewolves all my life, Mia. I knew Miss Ross when she worked at the academy down in Cornwall, and it was on her recommendation that I got the job here.'

'How didn't I know about that?'

Elizabeth shrugged her delicate shoulders. 'Sorry, Mia. I only just found out myself, but I should have told you.'

'It sounds like your teacher was getting all the players in place before you arrived,' Terry said.

'What do you mean?'

Elizabeth pulled me across the room and sat us both down on the bed next to Terry.

'Don't you find it all a bit odd?' she asked. 'Miss Ross brought Adam here just before you arrived.'

'Yes, and it was Miss Ross who suggested Elizabeth as a room-mate for you,' Adam added.

'But Miss Ross couldn't know I was coming here. Nobody knew until the last minute. My dad was killed and within hours Sebastian turned up. It all happened so fast.'

'Mia, I wasn't the first of my pack to be captured and tortured. I'm just one in a long line.'

'You're the first to escape,' added Adam with a soft laugh.

Terry grinned. 'I am indeed. Despite the drugs, knives and questions, I never gave in. I never told them what they wanted to know.'

A chill crept along my spine as I listened to his words and imagined the horrors he had endured.

'What did they want to know?'

'Your uncle was only interested in our pack. He wanted Zak above everything else.'

'Is that why they captured you? To get to Zak?'

'I was careless. After our meeting at the service station I followed you here. I watched from the treeline to see if you'd been taken to the laboratory too, but when I saw you training with all your hunter friends, I knew I had to tell your brother.'

'What did he say?'

'I never made it. I got too close to the school and didn't see the attack coming. I was taken to the lab and stayed there until you found me.'

'So, if you didn't report back to Zak, does he even know that I'm here? Does he think I'm the enemy?'

Terry shook his head. 'I'm not the only one keeping an eye out for you, Mia. Don't worry.'

I thought about all the times I'd imagined someone was watching me and shivered. It was creepy rather than comforting.

'What if Miss Ross knew what was going to happen?' Elizabeth asked.

I swallowed the bile that rose up like a tsunami threatening to roar from deep within my throat.

'You think she was behind the attack on my dad?'

Adam knelt in front of me. 'No, she couldn't have been. I've known her my entire life and she would never cause *you* any harm.'

'Me? Wouldn't cause me any harm? Why just me?'

'Adam?' Elizabeth's brow creased as she watched her boyfriend splutter for the right words. 'What aren't you telling us?'

'Miss Ross...and your mother, they were best friends from a young age.'

Both Elizabeth and I sucked in a deep breath.

Adam continued. 'Just before your mum died, she asked Miss Ross to keep an eye on you. To bring you here if you were ever in any danger. Miss Ross recruited me to look out for you too.'

I noticed the hurt flicker across Elizabeth's face at Adam's revelation and felt relieved that I wasn't the only one he'd kept in the dark.

'That doesn't explain how she knew about my dad's murder before it even happened.'

'Maybe she has contacts with the werewolves.'

We all turned to Terry looking for confirmation.

He threw his hands in the air. 'Maybe. I don't know who Zak is in touch with outside the pack. We're brothers, not a married couple.'

I stood up and began pacing the small floor space.

'It's like she *wants* you to know the truth,' Terry said. 'Bringing in her own team.' He nodded towards Adam who was trying to placate Elizabeth. 'And ensuring you had a friend here to support you.'

I thought about it for a moment, and it started to make sense. Of all the hundreds of students in the school, why put me with Elizabeth? She was light and full of energy and passion. I was dark, moody and broken. We were at the furthest ends of the friendship spectrum, and yet I couldn't imagine my life without Elizabeth in it. She'd helped me to see the spark of a life that flickered deep inside my gut. Miss Ross had made that happen.

'But why does Miss Ross want me to know the truth?'

Elizabeth shrugged her shoulders. 'Maybe it's a way of repaying a debt or some strange bond between hunter and werewolf—her and your mum.'

I chuckled at Elizabeth's observation. 'A bit like us, you mean?'

She smiled and her bright blue eyes sparkled.

'No matter how hairy you get, I'll always be your roomie.'

'Hey!' I thumped her on the arm as she darted away from me laughing. She hid behind Adam, who circled his arms behind him in a mock attempt to protect her. He was clearly forgiven.

Terry stood up from the bed, towering above all of us. I didn't remember him being so tall last night.

'As much fun as it is to debate the inner workings of the minds of Hood Academy's teaching staff, I need to get back to my pack and let them know I'm alive.'

He made for the patio doors and the rest of us rushed to block his path.

'The entire student body is roaming the campus at the moment. If you step outside, you'll be seen and reported. Or worse, recaught.'

Adam nodded in agreement. 'Mate, you *look* like an escaped werewolf and some of these girls are itching for a fight.'

My thoughts turned to Felicity and what she would do if she discovered that Terry was hiding in the gardener's bedroom.

'Adam's right,' I said. 'Let me go meet my friend, Cody. He might be able to help me locate your pack and get word to them. Once that's done, we'll break you out when it gets dark.' I pulled out my phone and sent Cody a quick message.

Terry cocked his head to the side and considered me for a moment.

'What?'

'How do you know Cody?'

'Never mind how *I* know Cody, how do *you* know him?'

'He's my brother!'

The silence was so overwhelming, even the insects in the garden behind us held their breath.

'How is that possible?'

'Well, he's a foster brother. His folks took me in years ago along with a few other kids and we've stuck together ever since.'

'So you're one of the loud brothers he told me about.'

Terry nodded his head and gave me a goofy grin.

'Does he know you're a werewolf?'

'He found out a long time ago and he's...cool about it.'

I nodded, stunned by this admission. Cody knew his brother was a werewolf. Maybe that explained his initial reaction when I mentioned Hood Academy at our first meeting. He was concerned for his family, not the town. I turned towards the door but Terry stopped me, tugging at my sleeve until I was facing him, a sly smile twitching at the corner of his mouth.

'Why did you blush when I mentioned Cody's name?'

I knew he was teasing me, but I couldn't stop the additional burn as it shot up my neck and coloured my cheeks. I stuck my middle finger up at him and flung the patio door open.

'I'll see you all later.'

I could hear them all laughing as I stomped off across the grass.

THE SUN WAS high in the sky as I reached the overhang, and a cool breeze ruffled the luscious green patchwork of leaves overhead. Cody wasn't there when I arrived but I knew he wouldn't be long.

I pulled my mum's Manila file from my bag and flipped through the pages of notes inside. I was still shocked at the discovery she had been a werewolf. One of the sheets in her file detailed the infection she had contracted from a werewolf bite. Was that how Joel hurt her? Had the pack leader bitten her?

Someone had scrawled a page of notes detailing the injection dose and dates of administration. Beneath this, in Sebastian's neat handwriting, were some footnotes, added like a journal entry.

> *Unfortunately, I was unable to stabilise the serum for prototype 0102. It appears the dosage was lethal to the subject. Several modifications were made, and it is my belief that prototype 0118 may be working. The werewolf gene is diminished slightly.*

I digested the words as a growing sensation of dread pooled in my gut. On the surface, the idea was a good one. It meant that no human being would have to go through the pain of turning every full moon. But the idea that Sebastian tested his serum on my mum knotted my insides. The thought of Terry chained to the

119

steel trolley in the cold, dark basement steamrolled through my brain. Had Sebastian chained my mum to the same gurney?

I pulled the other file from my bag, and the tattered label with Joel Mills written on it gleamed in the sunlight. Near the back of the folder was a colour photograph of a young couple. They were smiling and had their arms circling each other. It was a happy image, full of joy and love.

'Why do you have that?'

I jumped at the sound of Cody's voice close behind me and dropped the picture back into the file.

'You scared me.' I held a palm up to my chest as if trying to stuff my heart back into my ribcage.

'That photo...it's of my parents.'

I blinked up at the wide-eyed boy who stood over me, his blond hair dulled by the halo of sunlight that burnt behind him.

So the file was right. Joel Mills was Cody's father. I wasn't sure how to break the news that his dad might have killed my mum, but as I looked up at his sorrowful eyes, I knew I couldn't hurt him like that.

He dropped down to sit beside me and held his hand out for the file. I gave it to him without a sound. From what I'd read on the opening page, Joel and Pauline Mills were not killed in a car accident as Cody believed. I could relate to the shock of discovering the lies, having found out that my own mum hadn't died in an accident. I needed Cody to know the truth, however hard it might be.

'If it helps, they lied to me about how my mum died too.'

His blue eyes found mine and my heart almost broke at the pain I saw there.

'I thought...' He shook his head, his chest heaving as he struggled with the emotions churning inside of him.

'I know.' It was all I could say. I understood his pain only too well.

I reached out and took his warm hand. I had so much to ask him, but I didn't know where to begin.

'You were right about the academy,' I said softly.

His head hung low as he hunched over the photo of his parents, his blond hair gleaming in the sunshine. At the sound of my voice, he lifted his gaze to meet mine.

'They are doing experiments on people...werewolves,' I added. 'We rescued someone last night and we're keeping him safe until nightfall.'

Cody just watched me, not making a sound or rushing me to fill in the blanks for him.

I took a deep breath and blurted out the rest. 'It's your brother, Terry.'

I don't know what I'd been expecting him to do on hearing the news but sitting in silence and watching the coming and goings in the valley below wasn't it.

'Did you hear me?' I asked, my voice rising slightly. 'Your brother was being tortured in the basement of my school and I saved him.'

Nothing.

I collected the files and thought about snatching the photo of Joel and Pauline from Cody's hand but decided against it. Stuffing everything into my bag, I got to my feet and dusted off my jeans. Cody still hadn't moved or reacted to my news.

Giving him one last look, I uttered an exasperated sigh before storming off into the trees.

I'd almost made it back to the academy when I heard his heavy footsteps running behind me.

'Mia, stop!'

I whirled around to face him, clenching my fists as I watched him approach. I had risked a lot to save his brother and he was being ungrateful and infuriating.

'I'm sorry,' he said as he stopped in front of me. 'It was such a shock seeing that photo and finding out that the academy had something to do with my parents' death. I wasn't thinking straight. What you've done, for Terry, and me... My family mean the world to me.'

'I know they do,' I said. 'So do mine.'

He moved a step closer and took hold of my hands.

'I haven't been totally honest with you, Mia.'

I held my breath; this was the moment he either told me that he knew his dad had hurt my mum or that he was fully aware of Terry's full-moon activities.

'My brothers and sisters, the ones that were saved by my parents, they are my family, no matter what blood flows in their veins. Terry, Byron, Sean, Jenna, Katy and...Zak.'

I stared at him for a long moment, aware that I'd heard his words but unable to process them and sort them into a suitable emotional category. Zak? My Zak? So he did know him.

'Your brother came to live with us when I was seven, long before my parents were killed. He became part of my family straight away and my dad helped him through...certain changes.'

My voice sounded tinny and distant when I finally spoke. 'I'm fully aware of the changes my brother had to go through. Terry filled me in on the whole werewolf DNA that runs in the family. What I want to know is did you know who I was when we met?'

Cody dropped my hands and they swung through the vast void that separated us even though we were only a few steps apart.

'Yes,' he whispered. 'After I saw you in the woods that night, I wanted to meet you in person but I didn't know how I could. Going anywhere near the academy is dangerous for us, so I...'

I held my hand up to silence him.

'When did you see me for the first time, Cody?'

'It was the night you ran away. You came crashing through the trees and we had to investigate the sound, so Zak led us to the overhang. You were leaning against a tree trunk looking really sad. Then you saw us.'

I gasped and pushed my fingers to my lips. The four wolves in the forest.

'You...you're a werewolf?'

I mentally kicked myself. Now I thought about it, he was part of a random family that included Terry and Zak—werewolves. How had I not put the pieces together? Even after Terry told me Cody was cool about his brother being a wolf, it still never dawned on me that he was one too. Or perhaps I hadn't wanted to believe it.

Cody nodded, his blond hair flopping into his eyes until he brushed it away. I watched his hair dance in the sunlight and thought back to that night. A large brown wolf had broken away and circled me. Was that Zak? There was another wolf too, its fur golden and its eyes as blue as the ocean.

'Oh my God.' My knees gave way and I dropped to the dirt track with a thud. Cody rushed to my side.

'I'm so sorry, Mia. Zak told me to stay away from you and the academy, but I couldn't. I had to meet you and speak with you.'

'All this time and you knew about the werewolves, my brother and me. Did Byron know who I was that day in the café?'

'Not until you told him your name. When we're in wolf form we don't really see you in the same way as when we're human. The scent is the same, but you were scared that night in the woods. You just smelt of cinnamon in the café.' His voice trailed off as he caught my mortified expression.

'So why hasn't Zak come for me?' That hurt more than the lies. My brother knew where I was, had always known where I was, but remained in the shadows—or in his wolf form. I felt abandoned all over again.

'When my parents died, Zak became the alpha wolf. He has to be careful. Coming anywhere near Hood Academy is more dangerous for him because of your uncle. It's like he has a personal vendetta against our pack. He suspected that Terry was being held here, but we couldn't do anything about it.'

'So you used me. You sent me to free him instead of getting your hands dirty.'

'I'm so sorry, Mia. I never wanted to put you in danger. Neither did Zak. He's spent his life trying to keep you safe and prepare for your future.'

Tears spilt down my cheeks as I sat in the dirt trying to digest Cody's words, but they stuck in my throat.

'But I wasn't safe,' I cried. 'I was never safe. Our father beat me until I couldn't see, he hurt me so I couldn't walk and he terrorised me every day of my life. Zak didn't keep me safe. He left me to rot.'

I jumped up, grabbing my bag as I did, and ran past the old animal cages and across the lawns, wiping frantically at the tears that flowed down my face with the back of my sleeve.

I stumbled through Adam's patio doors and collapsed in a heap on the floor, sobbing hysterically until Terry scooped me up and set me down on the bed. He stroked my hair until I felt the tears subside and the ache in my heart lessen.

'I'm guessing you spoke to Cody.'

I nodded and blew my nose on the tissue Adam handed me.

'Yes, he told me everything. How he's a werewolf too and that Zak's your pack leader.' I hiccupped as the sobs wracked through me. 'Zak chose his pack over me, Terry. I'm not sure I can ever forgive him for that. And now, I'm all alone. Again.'

THIRTEEN

We spread the contents of the files across both beds. I propped my mother's photograph on my pillow. It gave me a warm feeling in the pit of my stomach, like she was there with me, trying to sort out the lies from the evidence in front of us.

'Terry said he was sorry.' Elizabeth had only just returned from Adam's room. The night was dark and overcast and Terry had made his escape, running for the treeline wearing one of Adam's navy hoodies and joggers.

'I'm not interested. Zak, Cody and all his pack of werewolves can rot in hell for all I care.' Of course, I didn't really mean that. I was just so angry at all of them. Mad at Cody for not telling me the truth from the beginning, cross with Terry because he could have given me more than cryptic clues at our first meeting, and as for Zak—I was furious at my brother for everything. I'd believed in him and he'd let me down.

Elizabeth gave a little half laugh in response and carried on reading through the file on Joel Mills. She had been nothing but supportive since I returned to our shared room with puffy eyes and incoherent babble about renegade siblings.

I wondered if it was possible to adopt Elizabeth as my sister and trade off a hairy, slobbering man-wolf. A giggle escaped my lips and Elizabeth raised a single eyebrow.

'Something funny?'

I shook my head. 'Not at all. That's why I'm laughing. My entire life has fallen apart in a matter of weeks, and now I discover I'm descended from werewolves.'

We both giggled. Then we laughed out loud. It wasn't long until we were rolling around the floor, clutching our sides and wiping away the tears that fell. It felt so good to have fun.

After we had exhausted all inappropriate humour, we sat with our backs against the wall and stared at the mass of photographs and graphs that littered the room.

'Do we even know what we're looking for?'

I hiccupped a little and shook my head. 'Not a clue.'

'Okay, let's look at what we do know.' Elizabeth clambered up from the floor and stood over the mountain of paper with her hands on her slim hips.

'We know that your mum was a werewolf and that Joel was the pack leader. We assume from her letter to Sebastian that your mum was a member of Joel's pack and he didn't let her leave.'

I stood up and adopted the same stance as Elizabeth. Surveying the yellowed pages, I processed Elizabeth's findings and voiced some additional thoughts that had been brewing in my mind for a while.

'Terry says that once you're sworn in as a pack member you can't leave without good reason. Apparently, falling in love with a werewolf hunter was frowned upon in Joel's pack.'

Elizabeth laughed.

'We now know that my brother is a werewolf and abandoned me to join Joel's pack after Mum died.'

Elizabeth snatched up the crumpled letter we found behind my mum's photograph in Sebastian's office and opened it up.

'Your mum wanted Zak to come to Sebastian and not Joel. Why? What could your uncle offer Zak that a werewolf pack leader couldn't?'

'Freedom.'

Neither of us had noticed Miss Ross slip inside the room, nor did we hear her creep up on us.

We squealed in unison as she spoke.

'So it *was* you two who helped our guest to leave.' She wasn't asking. The glint in her eye told me she knew exactly what we'd been up to.

A sharp tug of fear pulled at my gut.

'Don't worry, I'm not going to tell Sebastian. Believe it or not, girls, I'm on your side.'

She stared down at the papers strewn across the bed, and I noticed the small muscle in her jaw twitching. If she had information but didn't know if she should tell us, it was down to us to coax it out of her. Miss Ross could have a vital clue from her friendship with my mum and her working relationship with Sebastian.

'We didn't mean any harm,' Elizabeth said, her voice barely a whisper.

'Oh, I know you didn't.' Miss Ross patted Elizabeth's hand and the warmth returned to her eyes as she turned to look at me.

'I wanted you to know the truth about your mother, Mia. No child should be left in the dark about their heritage. Your mother was a kind, caring and beautiful woman, and she was my dearest friend. I felt obliged to point you in the right direction. It was obvious that Sebastian was never going to tell you.'

'So you hired Adam to help you out.'

'Kind of,' she said. 'I've known Adam a long time and when I asked for his assistance he was only too happy to come to Hood Academy. I needed someone I could trust on the inside to watch out for you without arousing suspicion. Adam fit that role perfectly.' She moved around the bed, glancing at the collection of evidence. 'When young Elizabeth here had her altercation with Felicity, it presented me with another way of keeping a closer eye on you.'

I balked and instinctively took a step away from Elizabeth. Her eyes widened.

'No! I didn't know anything about that, I promise.'

'Relax, Mia. Elizabeth was as clueless to my plans as you were. I just felt it would be advantageous for the two of you to be friendly, so I persuaded Sebastian to put you together as roommates.'

My initial panic subsided as I moved to stand beside my friend once more.

'I'm sorry,' I said quietly.

She smiled and reached for my hand.

Miss Ross continued, 'It all worked out quite well when Adam was dazzled by Elizabeth before you arrived.'

Elizabeth blushed and lowered her head.

'Oh, don't worry, my dear. Young love is a wonderful thing and I wouldn't do anything to harm your relationship.'

'Did you help Adam to get the key to the underground lab?' I asked, trying to work out how Adam had helped Miss Ross when he had seemed as much in the dark as the rest of us.

Miss Ross chuckled and took a seat on the end of Elizabeth's bed, pushing the pages of Joel Mills's file to the side. Her eyes were bright and sparkled in the light cast from the table lamp.

'No, I only told Adam to befriend you. I didn't give him any more information than that. I thought it would be a slow task with everything you had been through at home. But it appears that you girls, and Adam, discovered far more than I had planned all by yourselves.' She fiddled with the hem of Elizabeth's blanket as if choosing her next words carefully. 'I merely wanted you to learn that your mother was a werewolf so you could prepare yourself for the change should you carry the gene. But you dug a little deeper and unearthed Hood Academy's secrets.'

'I think you're giving us too much credit, miss. We might have found my uncle's files and the hidden lab, but none of us have any clue what it all means.'

I grabbed a file from Elizabeth's bed and waved it in the air.

'Did Joel Mills kill my mother?'

A shadow passed over Miss Ross's face and she took a deep breath. 'Joel was Cassie's pack leader and when your mother told him she wanted to leave the pack he became angry. You have to understand; it *is* possible to leave a pack without issue but the reason your mother wanted to leave was what caused the tension.'

'Why did she want to leave?'

'Sebastian,' Miss Ross said softly. 'Your mother fell in love with Sebastian when they were young but he was a hunter and she came from a family of werewolves. They tried to hide their relationship from the world but Sebastian's brother found out the truth. He didn't have the hunter gene but he understood the laws.'

'So my dad threatened to expose them?' It was a guess, but understanding how cruel my father could be, I presumed that I wasn't far off the truth.

Miss Ross nodded. 'Your dad told them he would go to the pack and tell them everything unless she agreed to marry him.'

Elizabeth sucked in a deep breath. I'd moved beyond being shocked by my dad's actions long ago and urged Miss Ross to continue.

'Your mother had no choice but to agree. They got married and then went on to have Zak. She tried so hard to make a go of the marriage and forget about Sebastian, but the pull was too great. They were like magnets and every time they tried to separate, an unseen force would pull them back together.'

'That's why Dr Roberts has all the photographs of Mia's mum in his office.' Elizabeth squeezed my hand as she spoke and I was once again grateful that she was with me.

'Yes, he never stopped loving her,' Miss Ross said with true affection in her voice.

AFTER MISS ROSS left, I squared my shoulders and leant back against my bed. I couldn't feel sorry for Sebastian; what he was doing to the werewolves wasn't right. I thought about Terry. He was a human being ninety-nine percent of the time. Torturing him wasn't the right thing to do—it was beyond cruel.

'Do you think it's Felicity that hunts them?' Elizabeth asked as she collected the files from the bed.

'Yes, I do. She's the one with a secret key to the lab, and I heard Terry's screams when she was down there with him.'

'She isn't just catching them, is she?'

'No, she isn't, but I don't know if Sebastian is even aware that she's torturing them for pleasure.'

'Are you going to tell him?'

I flopped onto the bed and picked up the letter my mum had written to Sebastian.

'I can't tell him without owning up to our part in all of this.'

'So what now?'

I couldn't answer her. I didn't know who to trust to help us. I glanced over the letter again, my eyes settling on the final words.

'I believe in what you are doing...I hope you carry on without me.'

It was my mum's wish that Sebastian continue to work on the serum, but why? Realisation hit me and a chill spread over my skin. She did it for us. Me and Zak. I'd only just found out that it was even possible that I could turn into a werewolf, but beyond the shock and horror I hadn't given much thought to the practical side of things. Would I be prepared to undergo treatment to avoid turning?

'If my mum wanted Sebastian to finish the serum, I think she hoped it would work on Zak, and me.'

Elizabeth stopped what she was doing and sat beside me.

'But Zak's the alpha. The pack needs him.'

'I doubt he would be interested in a cure.' I felt despondent that I didn't know anything about my brother anymore.

'Your mum was a willing test subject, Mia. From what Miss Ross told us, Sebastian treated her with care.'

'So she wasn't shoved in the animal cages then,' I mumbled.

Elizabeth wrapped her arm around my shoulder.

'We'll figure it all out, don't worry.'

The smile I gave her didn't quite reach my eyes. I felt numb all over. When she moved away, I wrapped my arms around my legs, hugging them to my chest like a protective barrier. I couldn't shake the feeling that it was Sebastian's fault that my mum had died.

There was a faint tap at the door and a small square envelope appeared under the gap. We both stared at it for a while until Elizabeth scooped it up and handed it to me.

Inside was a photo of my mum and Sebastian; they looked so happy, with twinkling eyes and radiant smiles. On the reverse was a short note from Miss Ross.

Sebastian was protecting you by not telling you the truth about your mother's death. He arranged for the police to notify you about the car accident. He wanted to finish his work before Zak came of age and turned for the first time.

'I guess that explains why your mum wanted Zak to go to Sebastian instead of Joel,' Elizabeth said over my shoulder.

If Frank had ever realised that your mum was secretly seeing his brother, it would have been catastrophic for you and Zak. Sebastian thought he was doing the right thing by keeping the truth from you.

I gave a little huff as I read her words and thought about how catastrophic my life had been regardless of whether we had known the truth or not. I wished that my dad had chosen to cherish and care for me in the aftermath of Mum's death instead of beating me. It was as if he had taken all his hatred for Sebastian out on me.

Miss Ross's note continued, *Look closely at the photo, Mia. What similarities can you see?*

A wave of understanding washed over me as I thought about how my dad would look at me from beneath a furrowed brow. His face would twist into a mask of loathing for the little girl with dark eyes and long brown curls. As I reached my teenage years I had always been so grateful that I hadn't inherited his lacklustre mousebrown hair but had a deeper, richer hair colour—the identical colour to Sebastian's.

At the bottom of the note, Miss Ross had scrawled a single sentence.

Yes, Mia, Sebastian is your real father.

FOURTEEN

I couldn't sleep. The room felt claustrophobic and I longed to escape to the woods beyond the academy. If I was honest, I longed to see Cody and tell him everything I'd discovered. To share my world-changing news. Sebastian was my real dad. I didn't know how to even start to handle that.

Part of me was shocked that my mum had cheated, although the overwhelming evidence proved that she had loved Sebastian above anyone else. There was also a part of me relieved to discover Frank wasn't my flesh and blood.

I'd always wondered if that violent gene was hereditary and after going all ninja on Felicity, I'd questioned it even more.

Lizzie and I had talked long into the night about it, not necessarily looking for answers but just voicing our thoughts. It had helped. Eventually, she'd fallen asleep and now here I was staring at my mum's file and wishing I could drift into a dreamless slumber.

I flipped back to the notes and resumed reading the handwritten entries. It read like a personal diary with Sebastian mentioning their conversations as he administered the injections. Stories about life, me and Zak, and how they would be reunited one day.

It felt strange to be reading something so private, even if it was about my mum.

At the bottom of the page was a hastily written addition, the messy scrawl almost illegible. I could just make out a few of the sentences.

The serum is working—Joel has found out about us—Cassie is injured. I can't believe Joel bit her, but I'm so proud that she fought back—side effects—catastrophic results—immunity to the werewolf venom has been stripped away— I can't save her—bite infection worsening—she can't self heal—I can't save her—I can't...

The final words remained unwritten, instead the ink trailed down the page as if Sebastian had lost the will to write any more.

Everything was different now. Things were going to change. I didn't know how I was going to cope with what was coming, but as I listened to the soft snores of my roommate, I knew, without any doubt, I wouldn't have to cope alone this time.

AFTER THE STARTLING revelation that my uncle was, in fact, my father, I managed to successfully avoid all contact with him for the next few days. I needed time and space to get my head around it all. With the end-of-term assessments, it was easy to throw myself into schoolwork and training.

Miss Ross managed to get my ban lifted, telling Sebastian how isolation would only damage my mental health further and that if I was going to heal I needed to mix with the other students. This meant I could attend regular classes, much to Elizabeth's delight, but I made sure to stay far away from Felicity.

The redhead had made a few snarky comments on my first day back, but ultimately she kept her distance. The faint outline of her bruised eye stopped me from seeking her out and confronting her about Terry. That and the fact Sebastian was still unaware of my involvement in the werewolf's escape.

I hadn't managed to sort through all my emotions yet. Discovering the truth about who my family were had been like hitting a brick wall at full speed. Finding out I was descended from werewolves and the result of an illicit relationship had blown my entire existence apart.

'Ready for the sparring assessment?' Elizabeth bounced up and down, balancing on her toes and jabbed her fists forward in quick succession. 'Our annual Karate Kid-meets-Buffy tournament to the death.'

I remembered Miss Ross telling me about the assessments during my first one-on-one session, but I didn't remember her telling me it was to the death.

At the look of absolute horror on my face, Elizabeth laughed out loud before assuring me that 'death' meant a winner's medal.

'Nope,' I mumbled, struggling into my pumps. 'The last thing I want to do is punch anyone in the face again. Look what happened last time.'

'In my humble opinion, Felicity deserved what she got, and after what Miss Ross told us, the girl needed a good slap to shut her up.'

'I guess it did give Terry a few days' break while she was recovering in the nurse's office.'

We giggled as we made our way through the gardens towards the gymnasium. Adam rushed over to give Elizabeth a good-luck kiss, and I couldn't help but roll my eyes at just how damn cute the two of them were.

When the handsome groundsman had vanished back behind the rose bushes, I elbowed Elizabeth and wiggled my eyebrows.

'So, it's going well?'

She lowered her voice to a whisper and leant in close.

'It is, but we've had to take it slow the last few days because Terry was in Adam's room and it would have been, well...awkward.'

I laughed, imagining how Terry would react to playing gooseberry to two teenagers. He didn't strike me as a romantic type of werewolf.

My mind flitted to Cody. We hadn't spoken since my little outburst in the woods, and I was beginning to regret being so upset with him. He was the first person I'd wanted to tell when I found out about Sebastian. I knew he was only trying to protect his own family and, in his own weird way, he was also shielding me. I decided to send him a message to meet me at the overhang after the assessments were over and make it up to him.

My cheeks grew hot as I contemplated the various ways I could say sorry. Our first kiss still vivid in my memory, I prayed that the tournament wouldn't take long.

FOUR SECTIONS WERE cordoned off inside the gymnasium, each with a fighting arena in the centre and rope barriers. Along the far wall were several rows of chairs full of everyone's family members. Elizabeth waved at a couple sitting in the back row, and I deduced that the beautiful woman who shared Elizabeth's long blonde hair and blue eyes was her mum. I spotted the imposing figure of Felicity's father sitting in the front row between Sebastian and Miss Ross, his wide shoulders held taut as he surveyed the students with a predatory glare while we streamed into the gym.

Sebastian stood and walked into the centre of the hall, turning to face the visiting guests with a forced smile on his face. He had shaved and wore a clean suit, but the dark circles under his eyes were a giveaway that he was a troubled man. I felt a sharp pang of pity but shook it off. I couldn't afford to care for the man who had ultimately caused my mum's death, even if he was my biological father. If he hadn't given her the flawed serum, she would have healed and been alive today.

It was hard to believe Sebastian was unaware that I was his daughter. My mum had confided in my teacher but never dared to utter the truth for fear of what my dad would do if he found out. With the benefit of hindsight, I now realised that *Frank* wasn't stupid and had clearly worked it out for himself. Something Sebastian had failed to do.

'Ladies and gentlemen, welcome to Hood Academy.' Sebastian's voice was clear and crisp as he spoke to the assembled crowd. 'Before we begin the tournament, I have the great pleasure of swearing in our newest member of the academy, Mia Roberts.'

I flinched as all eyes in the gymnasium slid my way. My cheeks were burning as I made my way to where Sebastian was standing.

When Miss Ross told me about taking the oath, she failed to mention the pomp and ceremony involved. My hands felt slick and I surreptitiously wiped them down my T-shirt. The gymnasium fell silent and the only sound I could hear was the roar of blood pumping through my veins. My stomach churned as I drew closer to Sebastian.

He gave me a tight smile as I approached and lifted a tattered old brown leather book. Taking my hand, he placed it on top of the book and rested his hand over mine. I felt myself tense up at his touch, but he misread it for nerves.

'Don't worry, Mia. It'll be over very quickly,' he whispered.

Lifting his head, he spoke loudly so the gathered guests could hear.

'To every pack, a cub is born. The hunter shall be unleashed to protect and serve. Mia Roberts, do you swear to uphold the hunters' oath and serve this academy and cause?'

I really wanted to tell him to shove his oath and run screaming from the gymnasium, but instead I nodded my head and replied, 'I do.'

'Then I hereby declare you to be a hunter of the realm.'

There was thunderous applause from the parents and students and I wondered if I'd burn in hell if my werewolf gene were ever triggered.

Sebastian patted my shoulder to dismiss me and turned to address the audience.

'You are here today to support your children in this assessment. These tournaments have been held for many generations, and the student with the most points at the end will win the coveted prize.' He held aloft a gold medal on a red ribbon, and the crowd erupted into applause.

'So we get to beat the crap out of each other for a chunk of metal?' I whispered to Elizabeth as I returned to her side.

She snorted. 'Pretty much. It's one point for a strike to the arm, two for the legs and four for a body blow. Just let whoever you're paired with punch you in the gut a couple of times and then you'll be out and can sit back and watch.'

She had a valid argument, but deep in my stomach, I could feel the rumblings of my competitive streak. I'd never bothered to interact with anyone at my old school and I certainly wouldn't have taken part in tournaments, but joining Hood Academy, meeting Elizabeth, Cody and Miss Ross, had awoken something inside me. Something dangerous.

Sebastian had taken his seat and was talking to Felicity's father when I made my way to zone number one. We were allocated a partner and stood at the barrier until Mr Peterson, the boxing coach turned commentator, called our names.

One by one the pairs were ushered into the arena. The cries of the parents carried above the grunts and yelps of the students in the ring. A young girl called Helen stood next to me as our names were called. She was slightly smaller than me, but I'd seen her using the staff in training and knew she was fast and methodical. My inner wolf, if I even had one, was likely to slink off with its tail between its legs as soon as the whistle blew.

'Hey, Mia.' Helen grinned at me. 'I'll try not to hurt you too much.'

She said it in jest, I knew that, but I couldn't stop the roar of power that shot through my core and into my limbs on hearing her words. Helen's eyes grew wide as I growled, the sound escaping before I could stop it. I clenched my fists and waited for the whistle.

I COULD HEAR Elizabeth's shouts of encouragement above the overwhelming din in the gymnasium. We had been fighting for well over an hour, and I had moved through the tournament with surprising ease. Elizabeth was out of the contest and sporting a fat lip courtesy of a large girl called Nessie. Helen sat by her side clutching a cold compress to her bruised shoulder caused by my roundhouse kick.

It had surprised us both when I launched my full-scale attack. I wasn't sure how or when I had retained all my training skills but I was able to use them with deadly precision. I wondered if Sebastian was proud of me.

'Mia Roberts and Stacy Calver, please move to zone four.' Mr Peterson's voice boomed out over the hubbub. He was in charge of the scoreboard and directing the students to their respective pairings and appeared to be enjoying the brutality far too much.

Something that felt oddly like pride washed over me as I approached the next contest, and I felt my shoulders straighten and my chin lift. Never had I felt this powerful or so in control. I'd had any semblance of confidence thrashed out of me from an early age and I honestly thought that capability was gone for good.

I understood all too well the irony of it being Sebastian who I had to thank for bringing me to Hood Academy and for persuading me to give the school a chance. I risked a glance in his direction and caught him watching me. A warm smile lit up his face as I took my place on the mat opposite my next opponent.

Felicity's father was concentrating his attention on the other side of the hall where his daughter was pulverising her latest victim. I felt the side of my mouth twitch slightly as I gave Sebastian the smallest of smiles. The look of delight that flashed across his face touched a long dormant part of my heart. I tried to shake it off. I didn't want to let him in. I couldn't form any attachment to the man other than that of a distant relative. So why was I so happy to have his support on the sidelines? And why did it feel so right to have him there supporting me?

The whistle blew, bringing me back to the present with a jolt. Stacy secured her first point as she took advantage of my distracted mind. I rolled my shoulders back and bounced from one foot to the other then circled my prey. It was at that moment I realised that *prey* is exactly what she was. If I did become a werewolf, I would need to hunt and this tournament was becoming a useful experiment for honing my skills.

Stacy didn't see me coming as I leapt forward and punched her once in the stomach and then swung my leg out to swipe her feet from under her. She fell to the ground with a thud and the referee waved his flag in my direction.

'Six points to Mia Roberts,' he shouted.

Elizabeth cheered and I saw Sebastian rise to his feet, clapping his hands enthusiastically.

I bowed once more to Stacy, who glared at me from across the mat. Too bad. My competitive streak was strong, and I was going to take her down.

IT WAS LATE afternoon when I finally got a break. Although each fight didn't take very long, I was still exhausted when Elizabeth pulled me out into the fresh air of the gardens. Adam was waiting with a long, cold drink and I took it from him gratefully.

'You are rocking this tournament,' Elizabeth squealed. 'I'm so damn proud of you.'

I grinned at her as I handed the empty glass back to Adam.

'It's like all the training has suddenly clicked and I can anticipate everyone's moves. I don't think Stacy will ever speak to me again, though.'

'Pft, no great loss.' Elizabeth flicked her hand to the side as if to dismiss Stacy's entire existence. 'You're a way better fighter than her anyway.'

'How many fights do you have left?' Adam asked.

'Two. I'm through to the semi-finals.'

'That's amazing, Mia,' he said, lowering his voice and adding, 'must be that werewolf DNA.'

I thumped him on the arm and Elizabeth clipped him round the ear at the same time as he burst out laughing.

'We don't know that Mia will inherit that gene,' she scolded him. 'She could just be an extremely skilled hunter.'

'Yeah, so you better watch it, Adam, or I'll kick your butt too.'

We laughed together, chatting and discussing tactics for the next half an hour, enjoying the relative peace of the gardens. Once they cleared the space and erected one big fighting arena in the centre of the room then the remaining competitors could return to the gymnasium.

The air was much colder as the afternoon vanished and the sky darkened. I found my gaze wandering to the treeline, and I thought about Cody and the wolves.

'I wonder if Terry got home okay.'

'He did,' Adam said. 'I saw him earlier today in Ravenshood. He was in Taylor's Coffee Shop with his brothers.'

I snapped my head around and gawped at Adam.

'You saw them all?'

Adam nodded.

'Was Zak there?'

'I don't know what he looks like, Mia, but there were three others with Terry, so I can only assume one of them was Zak.'

I hadn't seen my brother in nearly ten years. I clung onto the faint memory of his dark hair and hazel-coloured eyes, the developing muscles, and the early signs of stubble on his face. He was sixteen back then, still so young and naïve. He would be twenty-five now and was a pack leader. I was sure the muscles would be well defined and he might even have a full beard.

My chest felt constricted and I struggled to breathe. I was crazy mad at him but also missed him so much. Once this tournament was over, I would ask Cody to set up a meeting. It was time to be reunited with my brother.

Mr Peterson's booming voice cut through my musings as he announced the first semi-final match.

Elizabeth jumped to her feet and held out her hand to help me up.

'Come on, champ. It's time to win that medal.'

IF I BELIEVED in fate, or planets aligning, today would have been the perfect day to confirm those theories. As I walked into the gym sandwiched between Elizabeth and Adam, I looked up to see my name scrawled across the whiteboard directly above Felicity Parker's name.

The air left my lungs instantly and I stopped dead in my tracks causing Elizabeth to stumble as she spun towards my now motionless body.

'What is it?'

'I'm paired with Felicity,' I said.

Elizabeth looked over at the board and then closed the distance between us, grasping my hands tightly in hers.

'You can do this, Mia. You have pretty much cleared the board of other competitors. She's just another student who stands in the way of you winning that medal.'

I nodded blankly at my friend. I wanted to tell her that I wasn't scared or worried. I was elated. The gods, goddesses or universal energy had delivered this to me and I wasn't about to mess it up.

I looked into the bright blue eyes of my best friend and squeezed her hands.

'Don't worry about me, Lizzie. I'm going to kick that bitch's ass.'

WE WERE THE second team to fight, having already watched one of Felicity's squad, Elena Fields, obliterate Nicole Berry to secure her place in the final. Elena stalked up and down the gym like a lioness on the hunt, eyeing us both with hungry eyes.

It annoyed me and I prayed once more that I was the one who made it through this fight and got to wipe the smug smile off her face. Although I had the strangely comforting thought that if Felicity did beat me, she wouldn't think twice about taking down her friend.

I took up my position opposite the redhead, who glared at me from across the mat. She was clearly unimpressed that I'd made it this far in the tournament.

Mr Peterson drew us close and repeated the rules of the fight. We nodded our understanding and stepped away far enough to bow, first to the referee and then to each other.

The whistle blew and we began the fluid dance of sizing each other up and looking for an opening. My heart was hammering in my chest as adrenaline surged through me, powering my confidence and keeping my mind sharp.

I watched her step to the right and then to the left, her long legs carrying her across the mat with grace. My fingers ached from clenching my hands into tight fists, but I remained in a defensive stance. We mirrored one another as we explored every inch of the mat, both of us weaving and ducking, neither ready to strike first.

Felicity jabbed forward. I sidestepped her, blocking her strike and managing to get in an uppercut to the gut.

'Four points to Mia Roberts!'

Half of the audience cheered, the other half gasped.

I stepped away and looked over at the front row. Felicity's father's face was a mask of stone. He stared at his daughter with a loathing that I understood all too well.

I darted forward and landed a punch on her left shoulder. She yelped and circled towards me, baring her teeth like a rabid dog. She jumped and spun in a full circle, knocking me off my feet with a roundhouse kick. I flew into the referee who managed to stay upright and keep me from hitting the gymnasium floor.

I steadied myself and nodded my appreciation to the referee, walking back into the arena with purposeful strides. I caught Elizabeth's eye as she gave me a double thumbs up sign. Sebastian had moved away from Felicity's father and was now sitting next to Elizabeth and Miss Ross. They looked like a rent-a-crowd and it made me smile.

'Something funny?' Felicity spat the words at me.

'Not at all, I just hope they've kept your bed warm in the nurse's office.'

Felicity roared and sprang at me, her anger wiping away all rational thought and training. I punched out in quick succession, left then right, two blows to the chest.

'Eight points to Mia Roberts!'

Felicity screamed and swung her fist forward, aiming for my head. I lifted my right arm to block her advance, pushing her away and slamming my own fist into her nose. I heard the crunch as I circled away from her.

The referee blew his whistle and called me over.

'No direct blows to the head, Miss Roberts. Two points will be deducted.'

I didn't care. This fight wasn't about the points anymore. I was doing this for Terry, for Cody and my brother. For all the wolves that Felicity and her family had tortured over the years. I was going to win for my mum, for Elizabeth and Miss Ross, for Adam and all the students that ever feared the bully who stood in front of me.

FIFTEEN

I nestled the gold medal into the folds of my jumper, feeling the heavy weight of it against my chest. I never wanted to take it off again. I'd beaten Felicity by two points and went on to annihilate Elena by eight points to claim the prize.

Felicity's father had stormed out of the gymnasium before the end of his daughter's fight, and I spotted Sebastian hurry out after him. I'm sure it hadn't helped his cause that his 'niece' had beaten the main benefactor's only daughter.

I didn't have time to think about that now. Darkness blanketed the sky, and I was eager to get to the overhang and speak to Cody. Winning the medal had pushed all my angst and disappointments to the side. I wanted to share my happy news and, somewhere inside me, I hoped that Zak would hear about my win and be proud of his sister. After seeing Felicity's father at the tournament today, I understood just how dangerous it was for Zak to come anywhere near the academy. I needed to look beyond my own needs and appreciate that being pack leader had its risks. He knew where I was, and I would be waiting when it was safe for us to meet.

I left the building and walked through the garden towards the patio doors of Adam's room. I wanted to tell Elizabeth that I was sneaking out again.

The gravel crunched underfoot as I manoeuvred my way along the path. When I reached the centre of the garden, I heard the low murmuring of voices.

Through the curtain of leaves, I could see two figures sitting on the old stone bench, beneath the willow tree. The pale light of the bulbous moon glistened off Elizabeth's long hair. She threw her head back and laughed. The sheer delight at making her happy was evident on Adam's face. It filled my heart with a warmth that I'd thought was alien to me. Over the past few weeks, Elizabeth had become an important part of my life, like the sister I never had.

Her happiness meant a lot and I knew that Adam would continue to make her laugh that loud for a long time. Her beautiful face lit up when she smiled at him, and I was genuinely happy for her.

I let the branches fall back to shield them from my view as Adam leant in and tenderly kissed Elizabeth. They didn't need an audience.

The warmth I felt at my friends' happiness spread through my limbs as I thought about my own private rendezvous. Quickening my pace, I wound through the thicket of trees, eager to see Cody and tell him about winning the tournament.

As I reached the edge of the academy wall, I surveyed the empty windows of the house. All clear.

I raced across the lawn at full speed, but before I could reach the shelter of the animal cages, a single figure stepped out from behind the wall and blocked my path.

I skidded to a halt in front of Felicity, conscious that I was in full view of the academy windows. If anyone spotted me out of the building, I was in deep trouble.

Shit.

'Going somewhere?'

Her squad stepped out to stand behind her. Elena grinned insanely, folding her arms across her chest. Goon number two followed suit. They looked like a couple of bizarre statues.

I couldn't afford for Sebastian to see me near the forest, not after he had forbidden me to venture into the woods at night, so I edged to my right in a bid to shelter behind the bushes. As if expecting my move, Felicity mirrored my steps, forcing me onto the open lawn.

'I don't have time for your pathetic games, Felicity.'

Like a penalty shooter, I had three options: go left, go right or straight down the middle. I chose the last option and was pleased to see the shock register fleetingly on Felicity's face as I barrelled into her.

I shoved her hard as I passed, using the full force of my body. She regained her composure quickly and snapped her fingers. The two goons sprang to life and grabbed my arms in a vice-like grip. I flinched and tried to pull myself free, but they were surprisingly strong.

'Not this time, Roberts.' Felicity's face twisted into a snarl as she skulked forward, bringing her nose close to mine. 'You humiliated me today and I'm going to show you what happens to people who get on my bad side. Your uncle can't save you this time.'

I launched my head forward in a short, sharp snap and felt the crunch as her nose burst open. Blood spurted over her face, dripping off her chin, as she staggered back with a scream.

She swung her fist and connected with my left cheek. I felt my lip split and licked the blood away quickly. She could keep punching me all night, but I refused to show her any weakness.

I braced myself for the next onslaught but it never came. Instead, the girls dragged me down the path behind the animal cages, wrestling my phone out of my jacket pocket as they pushed and shoved me down the path. My first thought was that we were heading to the overhang and I hoped that Cody would be there to help me, but they veered left and worked their way down the path leading straight to the cages.

One of the iron doors stood ajar. I didn't register their intent until they shoved me unceremoniously through the opening. I landed heavily on the concrete floor, my hands and knees taking the brunt of the fall. The cage smelt of wet dogs. As I sat back on my legs, the cage door slammed shut behind me.

I swung around in time to see Felicity click the padlock through the door, locking me in.

'What the hell, Felicity?' Fuming, I stood and grasped the bars of the cage, pushing my face up close to the metal. 'Let me out.'

She pressed her sleeve against her face, trying to stem the flow of blood from her busted nose.

'You're not going anywhere, wolf girl.'

'What did you call me?' I could feel the anger stirring deep in my gut.

'Wolf girl! Don't pretend you're clueless. You must have worked it all out by now. Your precious mother was a wolf and it drove Sebastian to near madness. Now the academy is at risk again, and it's all because of you.'

She stabbed a finger through the bars and I used all my strength to avoid biting it.

'My mum was a good person and she wanted to leave her pack to live a human life,' I said quietly. 'When I get out of here, I'm going to do the same.'

Felicity laughed hysterically. With her face covered in blood, she looked deranged, almost demonic.

'The pack protect their own, so if it's proof you need that you inherited your mother's genes then allow me to educate you.' She moved to the side and Elena stepped closer, holding a small crossbow in one hand.

I didn't have time to move or cry out as she fired it through the bars, the bolt hitting me hard in my left shoulder. The agony was immediate; a hot, searing scream of pain shot through me as the force of the bolt sent me crashing into the far wall.

I slid to the floor, tears coursing down my face as I grabbed the shaft and tried to tug it free. Blood poured down my arms and chest.

Felicity stood close to the locked door and sneered down at me.

'The pack protect their own; you'll see it soon enough, wolf girl.'

The three of them walked away as if they'd been on a calm stroll through the grounds.

I swore as I tugged again at the bolt; it was in deep and every movement caused more blood loss.

Shit.

The animal cage was empty aside from an old tin bucket with a hole in the bottom. Dragging myself across the filthy floor, I grasped the handle. Swinging it hard, I smashed it against the iron bars. The vibration shot through my limbs and made my teeth hurt, but the loud clang echoed out into the woods with a satisfying sound.

Someone would hear. Someone would come.

I lifted the bucket again and swung it repeatedly until my arm grew tired.

THERE WAS A definite chill in the air, or perhaps my limbs were numb from the loss of blood. Either way, I was freezing. Felicity hadn't returned and so far my lame attempts to call for help had remained unanswered. Part of me hoped that Elizabeth and Adam would take a romantic amble through the woods and find my crumpled form, but no such luck.

The bolt from the crossbow, still embedded in my shoulder, hurt like hell. I'd ripped a strip of fabric from the bottom of my T-shirt and tried to bind the wound as best I could to stem the flow of blood.

I felt light-headed. I was cold to my bones. I was alone.

As if in answer to my prayers, I heard a rustle in the distant forest: the unmistakable crunch of boots on the ground.

'Help!' My voice cracked slightly and I coughed to try to loosen up my vocal chords before trying again. 'Please, help me!'

Like a vision sent by the angels, Cody stepped out of the treeline and stopped short. His obvious shock at seeing me locked in a cage and covered in blood subsided fairly quickly, and he cleared the space between us in a couple of strides.

'What the hell happened?'

'Long story,' I said, threading my arm through the bars so I could hold his hand.

'You're like ice, Mia.'

He examined the bolt and wound in my shoulder with a grim set to his jaw.

'Who did this to you?'

'There's a girl with an inherent hatred of wolves, and as my mother was one, she's taken it upon herself to make my life a living hell.'

I shuffled towards the door, and it took all my strength to pull myself up to standing. I grabbed the padlock and wiggled it.

'Have you got a penknife or anything that will break the lock open?'

Cody felt in his pockets and then began searching the compressed soil outside the animal cages looking for any kind of tool that would suffice. There was nothing and I felt the wave of Cody's anger and fear hit me as he raised his eyes to mine.

'I need to go get help,' he said, taking a step backwards.

'No! Please, Cody, don't leave me.'

'I *have* to, Mia. You've lost so much blood and you need medical help. I'll go get my brothers. They'll know what to do.'

I flinched away from the cage door as he stepped forward and took hold of my hands through the bars. As situations went, this one sucked, but I didn't want to sit in the dark on my own for a moment longer.

'I'll fetch Zak.'

'No! It's dangerous for him to come here. If Sebastian sees Zak, he'll try to capture him and inject that horrible serum into him.'

'Sebastian won't find out. I'll run fast and be back before you know it. Zak's your brother, Mia. He'll want to help.'

I felt a rush of heat flood through my system and even though I knew it came from Cody and his wolf genes, I couldn't help but associate the warmth with the prospect of seeing my brother again.

'I'll be fast. Tomorrow is a full moon so my senses and reactions are already heightened.'

He leant close to the bars and pulled me gently forward, kissing me lightly on my split and bloody lips.

'I'll be back soon,' he whispered.

Cody shrugged out of his jacket and passed it through the cage bars, helping me slip it around my shoulders. His scent wrapped itself around me and calmed my frayed nerves.

'I'll see you soon.' I said it more to convince myself than as a goodbye.

He nodded and turned towards the treeline, releasing my hand only an inch at a time as if it hurt him as much as it pained me to lose that physical contact.

I watched him walk away across the dirt track heading to the bushes and waited for him to turn around one last time. I knew he would because it was the kind of thing I'd do. We were more alike than either of us would let on.

As his shoulders shifted in my direction, there was a blur of movement followed by a feral cry. I shouted out in warning but it was too late. Felicity pushed through the branches and swung her staff at Cody, beating him square on the back and knocking him off his feet.

Felicity and her two goons towered over Cody, hitting him repeatedly with their staffs. The sound of wood on flesh filled the air and a wave of nausea rushed over me.

'Cody!' I screamed his name and rattled at the cage door, desperate to get to him.

Felicity moved away from her friends and smirked at me. The silvery light cast from the moon high up in the sky highlighted the evil glint in her eyes.

'Wolf for a mother and wolf for a boyfriend. I shouldn't have expected anything less.'

'Leave him alone, Felicity. It's me you've got the issue with, not him.'

She laughed, a high-pitched hysterical laugh that stopped her goons in their tracks. The three of them circled towards me. I glanced over their shoulder to where Cody lay still on the ground. Elena prodded her stick through the bars, taunting me.

'My mother was murdered by a wolf,' Felicity said, her voice dripping with venom. 'I watched it happen right in front of me.'

'Yeah, well, both my parents were murdered by wolves and yet I've learned to forgive.'

'Forgive scum like that?' She pointed her staff in Cody's direction. His shoulders were hunched over, but he was trying to push himself up. I looked back at Felicity, eager to keep her eyes on me and not on Cody.

'They deserve to die,' she shouted through the iron bars at me.

I needed to stall and give Cody time to recover. He could still get away and fetch help.

'Where would you be if there were no werewolves, Felicity?' I stepped backwards and held my hands out palms facing upwards, the action causing pain to flare through my shoulder. I winced but continued, 'You'd be out of a job, attending a normal school where the popular kids would kick your ass. You'd be a nobody.'

Felicity's cheek twitched in the moonlight and I knew I'd struck a nerve. I pushed a little more, digging at her with my words, hoping for a reaction. It was a trick I'd picked up from my father.

'Of course, you already know what it's like to be a nobody, don't you? I bet *Daddy* thinks you're a waste of space after losing the tournament to a *wolf girl*.'

The taunting worked and Felicity launched herself at the cage, flinging her arms through the bars in an attempt to scratch my eyes out. I grabbed her wrists and bent them backwards so she couldn't back up and get away. She screamed and kicked out at the bars.

The pain in my shoulder was almost too much to bear, but I couldn't lose my advantage over the redhead.

'Open the gate and I'll let her go,' I shouted at Elena who stood open-mouthed watching events unfold.

She fumbled for the key to the padlock and rushed to the door. Her hands were shaking so much that she dropped the key twice until I finally heard the clunk of the lock.

'Throw the padlock into the woods, open the door and then step back, both of you.'

Elena and minion number two did as I asked, moving away from where I held Felicity, who was still spitting and swearing at me.

When they were far enough away, I released Felicity's hands and made a run for the open doorway. Stepping out into the clearing, I took in a lungful of the forest air, a welcome relief after the wet-dog smell mingled with my blood.

Felicity threw herself at me, grabbing the bolt in my shoulder and twisting. I screamed and fell to my knees, taking her down with me.

'I'm going to kill you,' she cried.

At that moment, when I looked into her eyes, I believed that she would indeed kill me. I'd seen loathing, hatred and wickedness in my father's eyes on numerous occasions, so I recognised it when I saw it. Felicity wasn't just a nasty school bully, she was evil incarnate, and if I was going to get out of this situation alive, I would have to fight dirty.

I grabbed a handful of her long red hair, and using my good arm I swung my fist up, connecting with the underside of Felicity's chin. Her head snapped backwards, giving me the space I needed to wriggle out from under her.

Leaping to my feet, I moved out of her reach. With the woods behind me, I faced the animal cages and could just make out the twinkling lights from the academy in the distance. I momentarily wished that Sebastian would come looking for me, but then I remembered Cody and thought better of it.

As if reading my mind, Felicity grabbed her staff from the floor and sprinted across the clearing to where Cody was crouched, rocking on his hands and knees.

She swung the stick and I heard the sickening crack as it collided with his head. He pitched onto his side and started twitching and shaking all over. Felicity held the staff above her head. She was ready to continue with her barrage of abuse but stopped in mid-swing to observe Cody's strange movements.

I wanted to run to his side but something inside me warned against it.

The convulsing grew in intensity, and he looked like he had lost all control of his body. A ripping sound filled the air at the same time as a low, deep growl rumbled from the back of Cody's throat.

I was transfixed as I watched Cody's clothing shred and fall to the ground. He cried out in pain but I willed my feet to stay put. There was nothing I could do to help him now. His hands stretched out in my direction as if he was reaching for me, but where his fingernails should have been, long claws broke through the skin. He arched his back and I watched the smooth, pallid skin disappear as his spine contorted and snapped into an alternative shape. His nakedness faded under a shiny coat of golden fur. His beautiful face distorted as a long snout and fangs tore through the flesh.

The wolf snarled and flicked a long pink tongue over its teeth, sniffing the air as it uncurled to its full height. It cast its gaze across the clearing, looking at each of us in turn. I gasped as it looked at me. Its eyes hadn't changed. They told me that Cody was still inside, and my heart played tug-of-war between fear and friendship. Felicity cowered beneath it as it grew to the size of a horse, but I saw the shift in her stance as her hunter instincts kicked in and she swung the staff at the werewolf. At Cody.

In one fluid movement, the wolf pounced, its jaw wide open and the sharp fangs sparkling in the moonlight. Felicity collided with Cody and then screamed as he bit down on her shoulder, causing the staff to fall harmlessly out of reach. He didn't let go and shook her like a rag doll. Blood sprayed across the clearing hitting my face. Elena yelled and grabbing her friend's arm, they tried to make a run for the woods, but as I watched them abandon their leader to her fate, a row of eyes in the treeline halted their progress.

I stood frozen to the spot as six huge wolves stalked out of the trees. The biggest was a dark brown wolf with massive paws and hazel eyes. It stopped and raised its head towards me, sniffing the air. I felt a trickle of fear along my spine as I remembered the last time I'd looked into those eyes. It was just after the creature tore my dad's throat out. This fearsome beast that stood in front of me was the wolf that had saved my life. Suddenly all the pieces fell into place.

'Zak?' I whispered.

SIXTEEN

Elena and her companion were hysterical and remained huddled together as they backed away from the advancing wolves. I wondered if Miss Ross would reprimand them for crumbling under pressure.

Zak padded forward and stood over Cody. The difference in their size shocked me. I had thought that human Cody was tall but seeing his wolf form beside the towering form of an alpha put the whole leader-of-the-pack vibe into perspective. His dark brown fur shimmered in the moonlight, and I could make out the lines of the muscles on his limbs. His paws were as big as dinner plates and thumped the ground with a resounding echo that vibrated through our bones.

He growled and his long snout crumpled up to reveal the deadliest fangs I'd ever seen. A low, deep rumble came from his throat, and Cody bobbed his golden head up and down, dumping a bleeding Felicity on the ground.

She scrambled away from the wolves, blood pouring from her shoulder. Elena helped the redhead regain her footing as she reached the stone wall. Felicity took a shuddering breath and vomited over her friend's shoes, tears shining in her wide eyes. Their faces turned towards the wolves in terror, but I found myself in a state of fascination rather than fear. Surrounded by wolves, I faced the three girls.

'You better leave, Felicity, before anyone else gets hurt.'

'Oh, someone is going to get hurt when my father hears about this.'

There was no doubt in my mind that her father would indeed hunt Zak and his pack for harming his daughter, but that was a worry to assess at a later time. Right now, my main aim was to get rid of the girls before they provoked the wolves into another attack.

A rustling to the left of the wall echoed through the clearing and a group of shadowy shapes emerged out of the darkness. I noticed Miss Ross immediately as she planted her feet in a defensive stance and appraised the sight in front of her. Elizabeth, Adam and a couple of students I recognised stepped into the clearing, armed with staffs and crossbows, and on seeing the blood and disarray around them they all assumed a defensive position ready for a fight.

I crept forward, not wanting to startle the wolves, and held out my good arm, suspending my hand in a lame attempt to stop Miss Ross and the pupils from advancing. Zak and Cody backed away until the wolves were on the edge of the treeline and I stood between them and my fellow students.

'Please, Felicity needs a doctor. Just get her out of here.' I hoped that by showing compassion for the redhead I would be able to give the wolves some time to retreat.

Miss Ross nodded at a couple of students on her left who broke away to escort Felicity and her friends away from the clearing. Felicity's high-pitched voice carried through the night sky as she swore and berated Miss Ross's methods, asking her chaperon why they hadn't run in and killed the wolves on sight.

'Step aside, Mia.' Miss Ross's voice was calm and steady but her eyes told a different story. 'They attacked a student and need to be dealt with.'

'No! They were defending themselves. It was Felicity who attacked them. She locked me in the cages and used me as bait. They were just trying to protect me.'

As my teacher digested this new information, Sebastian burst through the bushes brandishing a shotgun. The wolves growled as one and the sound caused the hairs on the back of my neck to stand on end. Zak took a step forward and snarled, lowering his head and immense shoulders as if in readiness to pounce.

'Stop it!' I shouted. Sebastian halted in his tracks as his gaze fell upon the circle of wolves.

I turned to look at Zak. He lifted his ginormous head and blocked out the moon in the sky.

'Please, they're my friends,' I whispered.

He nodded his huge head and let out a low rumble. One by one the wolves disappeared into the trees. Cody lingered until last and only left when Zak huffed at him to move.

I heard the intake of breath from Elizabeth, Adam and Sebastian as they sucked air into their lungs, relieved to have evaded a brutal battle.

With the wolves safely out of the area and Felicity on her way to the hospital wing, I was able to assess what had just happened. It hit me like a steam train and I dropped to my knees feeling drained.

Elizabeth rushed to my side and yelped when she spotted the crossbow bolt sticking out of my shoulder. Cody's jacket had hidden it from view, but now that I had time to think about it, I started to feel a little light-headed and nauseous. Yes, I was definitely going to vomit. I bent over and coughed my guts up onto the dirt floor.

'I don't feel so good,' I said to Elizabeth as the darkness began to push at the corners of my mind. In the blurriness, I saw figures approaching me and felt Adam's strong arms under my legs and shoulders. I felt weightless as I drifted off into a deep sleep.

THE STRONG SCENT of antiseptic roused me from a silent, dreamless sleep, and I rubbed at my nose to try to clear the smell. My eyes fluttered open but the lights were so bright it took me a while to focus.

I glanced around the sterile room of the hospital wing, remembering the events that had landed me here. Instinct made me reach for the bolt in my shoulder but it was gone. I was strapped up tightly and dressed in a highly unattractive blue jumpsuit.

'Good morning, Miss Roberts.' A wrinkly faced doctor walked through the open doorway and grabbed my wrist. He pressed ice-cold fingers to my pulse point and monitored the second hand on his wristwatch. 'You are very lucky to be alive, my dear. You lost a lot of blood.'

I huffed, not quite sure I wanted to commit to any conversation at this early stage in our acquaintance.

'If you're up to it, I have a couple of visitors for you.'

I looked over his shoulder and spotted Elizabeth and Adam waiting in the corridor. I couldn't stop a wide grin and Dr Wrinkly took that as an invitation. He waved my friends into the room and scribbled something on a chart attached to the end of my bed before leaving us alone.

We waited until he had gone before speaking and then we all rushed to say something at once.

'Are you okay?'

'Does it hurt?'

'Thanks for everything.'

We laughed and I let my shoulders relax against the starched hospital pillow.

'I'm so glad you guys are okay.'

Elizabeth sat on the end of my bed and started fiddling with the hem of a blanket.

'What's going on, Lizzie?'

I looked across the bed at Adam who also kept his head lowered. 'Adam?'

'Felicity has been running her mouth off about you and Cody,' he said. 'Although Sebastian has tried to cover up any link.' He stood up and began pacing around the room. 'He's told everyone that you were seduced by Cody so that the wolves could try and learn the academy's secrets.'

I gawped at him.

'Your uncle has told the governors and the students that the wolves weren't able to get the information from you because you were actually working with him to capture another wolf for experimentation.'

'Oh my God, and people believe him?' I was horrified.

'Yes, the governors have no reason to doubt him, and the students believe pretty much anything they're told.'

'Everyone's going to think I'm either a failed werewolf hunter or a traitor for breaking the school's oath.'

'Sebastian was only doing what he thought was right,' Adam said. 'He's really messed up about the whole thing and has hardly left your side since we brought you in here last night.'

A flicker of warmth stirred in the pit of my stomach at Adam's words. Sebastian cared and it felt strangely comforting.

'He'll be coming to see you soon but don't let on that we told you.'

'I'll try not to,' I said, wondering if I could honestly refrain from shouting at him when he did arrive.

I DIDN'T REALISE that I'd drifted off to sleep until I heard the faint sound of a chair leg scraping across the floor. I opened my eyes and saw Sebastian heading for the door.

'You don't have to go,' I whispered.

He whirled around at the sound of my voice. His face was unshaven and he wore jeans and a jumper instead of his usual smart suit, collar and tie.

'Oh, Mia, are you okay?'

I wriggled up to a sitting position and let him take hold of my hand.

'I'm fine, just a bit groggy and sore.'

'If anything happened to you I would never be able to forgive myself.'

I stopped myself from saying anything too harsh by biting my bottom lip. Instead, I offered a weak smile.

'You mean the world to me, Mia.'

I examined his face, noting the dark smudges beneath his eyes. It looked like he hadn't slept in days. Gone was the strong, confident man who had walked into my life only a few weeks ago.

'When did you last have a good meal and sleep through the night?' I asked him, surprising myself with the intensity of emotion that welled up inside me.

'It's been a testing time for the academy lately but it'll all work out for the best.'

'Best for who? You or the academy?'

He huffed and squeezed my fingers between his hands.

'You are so much like your mother, Mia. She was so full of compassion and hope for a better future, but not everyone thinks the same way.'

'If you're talking about Felicity's father, I understand that. His little princess made it quite clear why he has invested in the school. He wants to kill all the wolves—no exceptions.'

Sebastian lowered his head until it was resting on my fingers. I had the strangest urge to stroke the top of his head with my free hand.

'I can't...escape his hold,' he mumbled.

I wasn't sure what he was talking about and was about to suggest that he explain himself when he suddenly broke down. Tears soaked the bed linen as his shoulders shook with the release. I was stunned into silence. I'd never seen an adult cry. My dad hadn't even shed a tear at my mum's funeral.

'It was my fault, Mia. She'd still be alive if I'd waited until the serum was ready.'

He was babbling but I could make out every word and they chilled me to the bone.

'When your mother was injured, I sat by her bedside, just like I'm here with you now, and I willed her to get better, but she didn't. She got worse every day. The serum had taken away all her healing abilities and there was nothing I could do to help her.'

I knew that the reason my mother died was because she couldn't fight off the venom from Joel's bite. I'd read that much in her file. But why was he spilling this to me now?

He let out another wracking sob and carried on talking. 'When she passed away, I needed to cover it up, to save the academy and my work. Felicity's father said he could help. He had connections with the police commissioner. He helped me hide the truth.'

I clenched my free hand into a tight fist. That's how Felicity had known so much about me and my family when I first arrived at

Hood Academy. Her dad had been blackmailing Sebastian for nearly ten years.

'Do they know that you're my real dad?'

Sebastian gave a small hiccup and lifted his head. His eyes were
awash with unshed tears. His mouth dropped open as he struggled
to find the words which eluded him. It told me everything I needed
to know. He hadn't expected me to say that.

'No... It can't be true.'

'I'm afraid it is. Mum confided in Miss Ross and she was the
one who told me. She thought I had a right to know.'

'I...I half suspected at the time, but Cassie was trying to make
it work with Frank, so I told myself that you must be my brother's
child.'

'Well, I'm not. I'm your daughter.'

He released my fingers and ran his hands through his hair.

'What do we do now?' It only dawned on me in that moment
that Sebastian might not want a daughter. Running the school and
keeping his distance from the teenage element might be his only
ambitions. He might not want to be a father to me, and I didn't
think I could cope with anyone else rejecting me.

He stood up and walked around the room, rubbing a hand over
the stubble on his chin.

'We need to find out which DNA is the most prominent.'

I blinked. Not what I was expecting to hear from my new dad.

'With any luck you'll have inherited my hunter DNA, but I
don't want you to worry, Mia. If you do have your mum's genes, we
can fix that.'

I watched him pace back and forth as I chewed over his words.
A bubbling of dread began to inch its way up my spine as I understood his intentions.

'You're not going to do any experiments on me, Sebastian.' I
folded my arms across my chest and fixed him with my sternest
glare.

'I can help you,' he said, returning to sit beside me and take
my hand.

'You're not listening. I don't *want* your help, I'm perfectly happy as I am.'

'Your mother would have wanted this.' He continued talking as if I hadn't said anything. 'She hoped that I could cure Zak of his lycanthropy prior to him turning for the first time, but I was too late. Joel Mills got to him first and he was lost to us.'

'Zak isn't lost,' I said quietly. 'He's the pack leader.'

'I had hoped that the pack would scatter after Mills was killed. It would have been so easy to cure the entire group, but I hadn't expected them to rally round Zak and assign him as the alpha so quickly. He was so young.'

I was still reeling from his statement about the death of Cody's parents.

'Did you have something to do with Joel's death?'

Sebastian fell silent. The darkness in his eyes told me everything I needed to know, but I wanted to hear the words. I wanted my *dad* to admit what he was.

'He killed your mother,' Sebastian said in a brisk, matter-of-fact tone. 'Or at least his venom did.'

I flung the covers off my legs and swung them over the side of the bed. Jumping to the floor, I began to back away from Sebastian.

'Did you kill them?' I asked him again.

The silence stretched out between us until eventually he answered. 'Yes, I killed them.'

My hands began shaking as I balled them into fists at my sides. My head ached from the pressure of hearing all of Sebastian's revelations.

He knocked the chair to the floor with a swipe of his hand and made me jump.

'Joel Mills was a ruthless man who made your mother's life a living hell. He denied us the future we deserved, Mia. We could have been a proper family.'

I couldn't deny that the idea of a happy home with loving parents appealed, but killing people to get them out of the picture wasn't the way to achieve it.

'Cody thought his parents were killed in a car accident. You pulled the same trick with the Mills family as you did when Mum died. Did Felicity's father cover that one up as well?'

Sebastian remained quiet.

Anger roared through my veins, and I wanted more than anything to escape this hospital room and Sebastian's company, but he was standing between me and the door.

'I want you to leave,' I said.

He dropped his gaze to the floor and I watched his shoulders slump.

'I'm sorry, Mia. Please understand that everything I do is executed with the right intentions.'

'Everything you've *done*, you mean.' I had an uneasy feeling in my gut.

He looked up at me then, but there was no emotion in his eyes. Before I could question his words he had backed out of the door. He closed it behind him and I heard the definitive click of the key in the lock.

'No!' I ran to the door and tried the handle. Locked. He had actually locked me in the hospital room.

Shit.

I frantically looked around for a window but the room didn't have one. There was only one explanation for the lack of a window— the hospital wing was in the basement of the academy and probably very close to Sebastian's laboratory. I'd survived the cruelty and horrors of living with a physically abusive father, and now I was going to die by the hand of my biological and utterly psychotic father.

Panic set in and I slid to the floor with a strangled cry. I let the tears fall as I lowered my head to my knees and wept.

SEVENTEEN

'Where am I?'

'What does Sebastian plan to do with me?'

'I want to see Elizabeth.'

Each plea landed on deaf ears as Dr Wrinkly checked my pulse, changed my bandages and gave me painkillers. I examined every tube and tablet he put in front of me for mysterious serums but the doctor was merely there to ensure I was still recovering.

Sebastian clearly needed me in optimum health to administer his crazy DNA test. I tried not to think about the results, but I was a little bit curious. Was I destined to be a wolf? My mum had only hated it because she fell in love with a hunter. Although I wouldn't call it love, I had certainly developed feelings for a wolf. Was I so similar to my mother that we could both destroy our lives because of our emotions?

I pushed the mashed potato and peas that Dr Wrinkly had delivered on his last visit around the plate. My appetite had vanished the minute Sebastian locked me in. Judging by the contents of my plate, it was early evening. The moon had been full last night and I wondered if the wolves had stayed safe. For all I knew, Sebastian could have sent his mini army of hunters out in force. Keeping up appearances for the good of the academy seemed to be his top priority.

A scratching noise on the other side of the locked door tugged at my attention and I bristled. Ever since I'd had that conversation with Sebastian about him wanting to fix me, I'd been dreading his return. Every noise could mean the start of experimentation, injections or my ultimate demise.

However, it was Elizabeth who entered the room, dressed head to foot in black. She had pulled the hood of her jacket over her head to conceal her long blonde hair and had a staff strapped across her back. I couldn't help but grin up at her, relief flooding my chest. She looked like a cross between an avenging angel and a warrior.

'You are the best surprise I could ask for,' I said, jumping to my feet and pushing the uneaten dinner to one side.

'We thought you might want to get out of here,' she said, her voice shaking almost as much as her hands.

'We?'

Another figure entered the room, also dressed in black. Half expecting to see Adam's handsome face beneath the hood, I was shocked to spot Terry's mischievous grin.

'Terry? What the hell are you doing back here? Are you crazy?'

He chuckled and the sound came from deep in his throat.

'I volunteered to help Lizzie.'

I raised an eyebrow. 'Lizzie!'

'Oh yeah, we're BFFs now, aren't we, Liz?'

Elizabeth giggled as she pulled jeans and a jumper from a bag, dropping them on the bed with a pair of trainers and a torch.

'He has been incredibly helpful to our cause,' she said with a smile. 'Adam is on lookout upstairs and Miss Ross is in Dr Roberts's office keeping him busy, but I need you to get changed—and fast!'

Still reeling from the fact that Miss Ross was in on my daring rescue attempt, I stripped out of the hideous blue jumpsuit and wriggled into the clothes that Elizabeth had fetched. It felt good to be wearing my own clothes again.

I followed my friends out through the door. I was right; the room was in the basement and part of the maze of rooms that Elizabeth and I had explored the night we found Terry. The hospital wing was further in than we had ventured and consisted of a main office for Dr Wrinkly, a storeroom, and four patient rooms.

All the hospital areas fed off a large circular space with direct access to the school through the main office. To any unsuspecting visitor, it was a fairly mundane hospital wing, but the seventh door, set into a dark alcove, led to the secret laboratory and all the horrors it held.

As we hurried through each section, I grew more and more anxious. If Sebastian found us, it could be bad for all of us. It wasn't only me who would end up in trouble—or dead. Sebastian would no doubt torture Terry, and Lizzie and Adam would be thrown out or maybe kept prisoner so they couldn't tell anyone about what was going on beneath the school.

We pushed through another door and entered the sterile room where we had discovered Terry chained to the gurney on our last visit. The silver tray, prepped with utensils, stood alongside a clean trolley with fresh folded linen on the end.

'Looks like they were all ready to start another experiment,' Terry said, holding the door open for us to walk through.

'It's for me,' I mumbled.

Elizabeth sucked in a breath and grabbed onto my hand.

'Sebastian wants to find out if I have werewolf DNA, and if I do, he is going to use a modified serum similar to the one he gave my mother.'

'We won't let him do that to you.' Elizabeth squeezed my hand. 'We'll get you out of here, I promise.'

Terry urged us forward and we navigated the rest of the maze with ease. Adam was waiting by the stockroom door when we emerged into the academy foyer.

He held his finger up to his lips and motioned towards Sebastian's office door. The light shone through the glass, and I could hear muted voices coming from the room. Miss Ross's voice sounded louder than normal, and I realised she was either shouting at Sebastian or covering up our footsteps.

Elizabeth and Adam travelled the floor space across the foyer with ease, treading lightly to avoid any squeaky floorboards.

They beckoned me over and I looked to Terry for support.

'It's okay, I'm right behind you.'

I'd made it two steps when the office door flew open and Sebastian stormed through the opening. He hurtled towards me, his eyes blazing with rage.

'Do you think I'm that stupid to believe you wouldn't try and escape?' He grabbed my arm and I winced as his fingers tightened their grip.

Terry moved forward to intervene but Sebastian whirled me around, using me as a shield.

I saw Adam step out of the shadows, but I shook my head vehemently at him. I needed them to stay safe. He retreated back into the darkness.

With his free hand, Sebastian punched Terry hard in the face, causing him to stumble backwards and land heavily in the open doorway.

'Inside, both of you.' He shoved me through the door after Terry and then turned slowly on a stunned Miss Ross.

'You are dismissed, Miss Ross. I will deal with your indiscretions later, in accordance with the oath.' Sebastian's jaw was rigid as he spoke through gritted teeth. 'I think you've done quite enough for your goddaughter for one evening.'

I sucked in a sharp breath. It explained her need to help me discover the truth about my mum and her plans to protect me.

'Why didn't you tell me?' I whispered.

'I...I don't know,' she began.

Sebastian steered her to the exit, pushing her into the foyer, slamming the door and turning the key in the lock.

'No! Why did you do that?'

Sebastian turned his cold stare upon me and I stopped talking. Gone was the emotional man who had sobbed at my bedside. The man who stood in front of us was nothing but a monster.

He inclined his head at Terry but spoke to me. 'Am I to assume that you were the one who freed this creature from the lab?'

I stiffened and clenched my fists.

'He's *not* a creature, he's my friend.'

Sebastian laughed, the sound void of any humour.

'You don't honestly believe that, do you? Surely even you, Mia, can see how dangerous these beasts are. You've witnessed it firsthand.'

The images of Zak tearing Frank to pieces flashed through my mind.

'The pack protect their own,' I said, straightening my shoulders.

Sebastian was across the room before I could blink, his nose mere inches from mine.

'You are no wolf, Mia. Your genes follow the hunter line, *my* line, and you will do as I say because I. Am. Your. Father.'

Terry lunged forward, knocking Sebastian back a few steps.

'She's one of us and belongs with the pack. There's nothing you can do to stop me taking her.'

'Oh, really.' The glint in Sebastian's eye filled me with dread. Self-preservation kicked in and I took a step backwards, still reeling from the venom in his verbal attack.

He circled the desk and grabbed the phone from its cradle.

'It's me. Prepare the lab. I have two test subjects.'

I sat with my back to the wall, gripping my hands together so Terry couldn't see them trembling. Sebastian had stormed out after making his call, locking us inside his office. We tried to open the windows but they were sealed shut. It was hopeless.

'What are we going to do?' It was a stupid question because we were trapped. There was nothing we could do, but the silence freaked me out and I needed the comfort of conversation.

Terry slid down the wall to sit beside me.

'Don't worry, Mia. I'm sure Adam and Lizzie have found Zak by now and they're all on their way to rescue us.'

'Zak can't come here,' I gasped. 'It's too dangerous. If Sebastian gets hold of him, he'll end up with three test subjects.'

'Your brother will be careful. He's managed to keep an eye on you all these years without being discovered, hasn't he?'

I shrugged my shoulders. 'Why did he have to hide from me? My life was full of pain and anger and I could have done with a friend.'

'When Zak turned up at Joel's house, he was in bad shape. He didn't understand fully what was happening to him, why he was drawn to that town, that pack, and those people. Joel took him in, just like he did with the rest of us, and taught him the ways of the pack.'

Long shadows trailed across the office floor as I listened to Terry speak.

'He was a fast learner,' he said. 'Eventually he became Joel's second-in-command. He talked about you all the time and how he needed to keep you safe, but our pack was in constant threat from the hunters.'

'You mean, Hood Academy students?'

'Yes. It took all our efforts to keep ourselves safe. Zak sent me to check up on you from time to time. When I saw how you were being treated, I knew we had to do something.'

'How did you know?'

'I'd watch you on your way to school and you'd have a fresh bruise, or I'd hear the shouting from outside your house. Zak knew it was time to end it.'

'So he decided to kill Frank.'

Terry nodded.

'Why didn't he take me with him?'

'You're sixteen, Mia. You've come of age.'

The realisation dawned on me. 'I haven't turned.'

'No, you haven't. Zak thought you hadn't inherited the were-wolf gene from your mum so he asked someone he could trust to help you instead.'

'Who?'

'Miss Ross. I only found out about her after you set me free from the lab. I had no idea Zak even had a contact at this place.'

So she *was* on our side. She had instigated everything because of her close friendship with my mum, and because Zak trusted her.

I smiled up at Terry. 'As messed up as all of this is, it's nice to think I had people fighting for me, even if I didn't know it at the time.'

He wrapped his muscular arm around my shoulder and hugged me tightly.

'I won't leave you, Mia. We'll protect each other, okay?'

'Okay.'

The door handle rattled as we heard the key turn in the lock. My stomach lurched. Was this the end? Was I about to die?

EIGHTEEN

ebastian stood in the doorway, silhouetted against the dim light cast from the lamps in the foyer. We scrambled to our feet, Terry pushing me behind him protectively.

'You don't have to do this,' he said, his voice nothing more than a whisper. 'She hasn't turned yet. There's every chance you're right and Mia is a hunter.'

'I can't afford to take that chance any more. I've dedicated my life to this school, to this project. I lost the woman I love. I've only just discovered that Mia is my daughter and I'm not prepared to let wolves take her from me too when we've got a lifetime to catch up on.'

I stepped around Terry so I was facing Sebastian, his colourless face and sunken cheeks guiding me to believe that he wasn't psychotic but only exhausted.

'I can help you, Mia,' he said.

'Like you helped my mum?'

'She understood what I was doing.'

'But did either of you ask if you should be doing it?' I said. 'The wolves only turn on a full moon and it's a night they spend enjoying nature, not killing. I have to work out where I belong, Sebastian, without your help. I don't know if I'm a werewolf or if I'm a hunter, but surely it's my choice to discover what I am in my own time.'

Sebastian shook his head. 'No, I can't risk you turning. I can't risk them finding out I have a werewolf daughter.'

'Who?'

'They'll ruin me. Take everything. Mr Parker will…'

'Wait!' The pieces started to come together. 'You're not bothered about me at all, are you? You're more worried about Felicity's father taking his funding from you.'

'I need that money!' he screamed. 'For you. To save *you*. It's what your mother wanted.'

I backed away, bumping into Terry who placed his big hand on my shoulder. I'd escaped one hellhole only to discover that I'd ended up in a worse situation. Sebastian was mad. Stark raving mad. I was going to die by his hand and yet he believed he was doing what was right for me.

I looked around frantically. We needed to get out of here and fast. Terry sensed my panic and grabbed my hand, squeezing my fingers to show me he was there supporting me.

'It's time to go,' Sebastian said right before a loud crack filled the air. He pitched to his knees, crumpling in a heap at our feet.

Out of the shadow of the doorway, Adam stepped forward swinging a cricket bat in his hand.

'Adam!' I launched myself at my friend, wrapping my arms around his neck. 'I'm so happy to see you.'

He chuckled. 'You didn't think I'd leave you in here, did you?'

Terry stepped over Sebastian's unconscious body and pulled me after him. As one we disappeared into the shadows and rushed to Adam's room to meet Elizabeth and Miss Ross.

'What now?' I asked.

It was clear that I couldn't stay at Hood Academy, but suddenly I didn't want to leave. I looked around at the faces in front of me. Elizabeth's big blue eyes shone as they filled with tears. Adam's warm smile melted the fear that threatened to suffocate me, and Terry, the lone wolf who risked his life to save mine, waited patiently for me by the open patio doors leading to the gardens and the woods beyond.

I could smell the earth and the trees, and I longed to run across the lawn and disappear into the forest, but half my heart belonged here.

Elizabeth stepped forward and circled her arms around me. I squeezed her tightly and breathed in her scent, never wanting to forget the first friend I'd ever had.

'I'm going to miss you so much, Lizzie.'

'I know, but we'll stay in touch.'

She released her grip on me and wiped her eyes with the sleeve of her jacket. Adam put a supportive arm around her shoulders and I smiled up at him. I knew Elizabeth would be well taken care of.

Not wanting to leave without letting Adam know that he was as much a friend to me as Elizabeth, I flew at him and hugged him until he couldn't breathe.

'Look after her,' I whispered.

Miss Ross held her arms out wide and I allowed myself to be swallowed up in her embrace.

'If I am a werewolf, like my mum, then I'll accept that life and honour my pack because that's the right thing to do. It means we might never see each other again.'

I could feel my eyes filling up with tears, but I blinked them away.

'And if it turns out you're a hunter?'

I sighed deeply. 'If that's the case, I'll return, I promise. You can train me to be the best hunter you ever had, but I won't kill any wolves, or people, for you.'

'I doubt Sebastian will allow you to return, Mia. He's a broken man. I'm not sure what the future holds for Hood Academy.'

'Maybe you can train me in secret.'

She laughed and held my face in her hands.

'It would be my honour.'

Terry coughed and pulled my attention to the open patio doors and the wilderness beyond.

'Time to go,' he said. 'We've got a long walk.'

I turned once more to Elizabeth and smiled. Tears poured down her beautiful face as she nodded at me. Adam stood close behind her as solid as ever.

'Take care of yourselves.'

WE SHUFFLED OUT into the night air and I took a deep breath. The scents of the flowers flooded my senses and I relished the clear air after the oppressive academy.

With one last look at my friends, I joined Terry and began jogging across the lawn.

'It's a couple of hours' walk to the farmhouse,' Terry said. 'I'll race you if you like. Winner gets to have the first hot bath.'

I snickered and thumped his arm just as a loud crack filled the air. Terry stumbled next to me, falling to his knees and releasing an anguished cry. I had no time to comprehend what had happened before I heard Sebastian's voice calling my name.

I whirled around to see him rushing across the lawn with a gun in his hand. My head spun and I looked down at Terry who lay crumpled at my feet. Blood pooled on the lawn leaving a dark brown stain.

I grabbed at Terry's arm and helped him to his feet, his shoulder hanging forward as he tried to protect the wound. The bullet had travelled clean through his shoulder and blood coated his back and chest.

'I'm okay,' he said, his voice nothing more than a faint whimper. 'I'll heal, don't worry.'

I couldn't help but worry as I struggled to support his muscular frame. Another gunshot rang through the night air, and I felt the bullet brush past our heads as we limped towards the cover of the trees.

Sebastian shouted again. I looked behind me and saw Felicity and Elena sprinting across the lawn alongside him.

I unhooked myself from Terry and looked into his kind eyes.

'Go on without me. Get home so that your family can help you. I'll be right behind you, I promise.'

Terry faltered until I motioned towards the forest, urging him to escape before Sebastian could finish the job.

He gave a curt nod of his head then vanished into the trees.

I spun around to face the academy building and waited for Sebastian, Felicity and Elena to come to a halt a few feet away.

In the distance, I could see my friends moving out across the darkened grass, heading in my direction.

'I won't allow you to leave, Mia.' Sebastian's hand shook from the adrenaline of firing a gun. Sweat covered his face, and his hair was unkempt and matted with blood from the wound caused by the cricket bat.

'So you're going to shoot me?'

'It's what you deserve, wolf girl,' Felicity sneered at me, but I ignored her, keeping a wary eye on Sebastian and the gun in his hand.

'Just let me go,' I said. 'It's over, Sebastian.'

Under the pale light of the moon, he looked like a homicidal maniac. His eyes darted back and forth as he wrestled with his emotions.

Elena cried out as Elizabeth snuck up behind her, swiping her legs from under her and knocking her to the ground.

Felicity's head shot around at the sound and she leapt at Elizabeth, grabbing her arms and shaking my friend with such force I heard her teeth rattle. Adam didn't waste any time rushing to Elizabeth's aid, and in one fluid movement he elbowed the redhead hard in the face. With my friends safe and rallying to support me, I turned my attention to the man who stood in front of me.

'I'm sorry,' he said.

Fear curled in my gut as he raised his gun, but before he could bring it up high enough to shoot, Miss Ross stepped out of the darkness and pressed the barrel of a shotgun to his temple.

Sebastian didn't say anything but the exhaustion that swept across his face confirmed his surrender. Adam rushed to take the gun from Sebastian's hand, smiling across at me as he rounded up Felicity and Elena.

'I've got this,' said Miss Ross. 'You're safe to leave now.'

I backed up towards the trees, watching the lights flicker on in the academy as the students and staff came to investigate the sounds of the gunshots.

I grinned at Elizabeth and Adam and lifted my hand in a silent salute. I let my gaze drift to Miss Ross, who was still holding the gun to Sebastian's temple. She gave me a wide smile. She had been friends with my mum and understood my need to discover who I was. It was her guidance that had led me to this place and I would remember her forever.

I was following my instincts just like my mum had done ten years ago and there was love and pride in Miss Ross's smile that filled me with hope.

Finally, I looked into Sebastian's dark eyes, and for the first time I saw my father looking back. Neither Sebastian nor Frank deserved my love or respect. They had both failed me, but it meant that I'd learned how to be strong.

I spun around and vanished into the forest without a backwards glance. I could hear Miss Ross snapping instructions at the approaching staff members, and the quiet sobs of my best friend. Felicity's shrill tone cut through the night air, and for a moment I worried that the redhead would rush after me, but Miss Ross's authoritative manner punctured her complaint and silenced her in an instant.

My eyes had adjusted to the darkness of the woods as I faced forward and pushed my way through the brambles and overhanging tree limbs. Before we left the safety of Adam's room, Terry had given me a brief outline of the route we were to take, just in case we were separated. It turned out to be a good idea. I had a long walk ahead of me, but there was a lightness in my heart that I'd never experienced.

I was free.

STROLLING THROUGH THE woods after midnight had never been on my to-do list in my other life, but as I listened to the hoot of an owl and the rustling of nocturnal animals in the undergrowth, I began to feel more at peace. The further I walked, the more I was able to release the tension and anxiety that I'd felt at Hood Academy. Maybe I would end up returning one day, or maybe I would get to live out my days in the forest, surrounded by the beauty of nature and a new family.

After I'd been walking for over an hour I reached a winding lane. To my left rose a quaint farmhouse with walls of red brick and a roof of dark grey slate. A low white fence wrapped around the boundary, stretching towards a garage block. In the driveway I could see a truck with the Mills Family Farm sign emblazoned down the side.

Through the small cottage window, silhouetted against the lamplight, I could see Terry's outline. Byron was binding his shoulder with a strip of bandage as Cody looked on from over his shoulder. They were laughing and joking with one another and the sound travelled over to me, circling itself around my body and inviting me in.

A tall, muscular figure with longish brown hair that curled at the nape of his neck leant against the garden gate leading up to the house. His eyes twinkled in the moonlight as I approached, and a broad grin spread slowly across his face.

'Hey, Mia.'

I sprinted the rest of the way and flung myself at Zak. He wrapped his strong arms around me and spun me in a wide circle.

'Welcome home, little sister.'

OATH BREAKER

PART TWO

OATH KEEPER

ONE

A trickle of sweat trailed down the side of my temple, and I swiped at it with a trembling hand. I wished the tremors in my limbs could be blamed on the unusually balmy weather conditions, but they couldn't. I was being hunted, and every part of my body screamed at me to run.

The bulbous moon shone overhead disappearing from view momentarily as the clouds drifted across the sky. The night was warm and muggy, the heat of the summer sun still clinging to everything in its path.

A breeze ruffled the canopy of leaves above, and I held my stance until the rustling subsided. Cody had told me to move in the shadows and to *be* the silence, whatever the hell that meant. He wanted me to become one with nature, to be able to see the ebb and flow of wind currents and smell out the danger. Of course, my gorgeous boyfriend had the advantage of being a werewolf with super-strength and an inbuilt satnav for all things nocturnal. I, on the other hand, was still only a human.

With my seventeenth birthday one month away, it was looking less likely that I had inherited the werewolf genes carried by my mother and brother. Instead, I seemed to be destined to follow my father's hunter line.

My mind wandered briefly to Sebastian. The last time I'd seen him, he was pointing a gun at my head. Not the most fatherly thing to do. Only a few hours ago I'd tried, yet again, to communicate my feelings in a letter to him. The words flashed through my mind as I picked my way through the forest.

Dear ~~Dad~~ Sebastian,

I'm disappointed with the way we left things, and I hope you don't hate me for walking away. Finding out we were father and daughter was a shock for both of us and I don't blame you for how it all turned out, but I need to explain my side of the story. I want you to know how I feel.

You were there for my mother when she needed you the most. You told me how much you cared for her and the evidence I've seen proves just how much she loved you in return, but ultimately it was you who killed her. I'm not sure I can forgive you for that just yet.

Developing your cure for lycanthropy has taken over your entire soul, Sebastian. I can't deny you were trying to help Mum break free from the pack and live a human life, but your frustrations over the flawed serums clouded your judgement and I don't think you realised the damage you were doing.

You began to see me as a second chance, as redemption for her death. By saving me from the fate of the wolves, you would cleanse your guilt. I'm sorry, but it doesn't work like that. I hope you'll recognise why I couldn't let you use me as another lab rat.

I might be a wolf like my mother, or I could be a hunter like you. Either way, I want to discover this on my own. I need space to reconnect with my brother and be a family again.

One day I'd like to return to you so we can try and build a friendship. We've both lost so much. Mum died without telling either of us we were blood relatives, and even your brother was murdered for his part in the horror of my childhood. None of you were there for me, and because of that, I kept you at arm's length.

Trust is something that develops over time, and unfortunately, there have been far too many lies between us. Maybe one day we'll find that bond that every family has. Maybe.

Mia x

I'd reread the words I'd written over and over. They felt forced, almost clinical. It had been Zak's idea to send Sebastian a letter, but the more I stared at it, the more I hated the thought of him reading my innermost feelings.

I didn't hate Sebastian, despite him locking me up and waving a gun at my head. He was my flesh and blood after all and surely if I wanted to be the better person I could offer him some pity.

I rolled my eyes to the sky. Why did any of them deserve anything? My mum had lied about her relationships, died, and left me in the care of a drunk who knew I wasn't his flesh and blood and who punished me relentlessly for it. My beloved brother, Zak, abandoned me to follow his werewolf destiny with the promise of returning to collect me. He didn't. I ended up figuring it all out on my own, as usual. I'd been subjected to abuse for years because of a secret I didn't know.

None of them deserved my pity, or the energy I expended thinking about them. I snatched the letter from the desk and screwed it up, throwing it into the overflowing waste bin in the corner of my room. The blank notepad mocked me as I stormed out, slamming the door behind me.

It had taken me a long time to find any peace in the whirling mess of my brain, but with help from my friends, I was beginning to carve out a life of my own.

The sound of a twig snapping jolted me back to the present, and I gripped the wooden staff I was holding until my knuckles turned white. I sniffed the air just as Cody taught me but all I could smell was the earthy scent of the forest. Then, just as I was about to move forward, I caught a whiff of something else—lavender. Not the soft, subtle kind but a chemical alternative. It was faint but stood out against the aromas of the trees, moss, and leaves. I crouched low and tuned my senses into my surroundings. There were no birds chirping at this time of night, only the nocturnal hoot of an owl and the rummaging of ground feeders. I slowed my pulse and listened. Behind me and to the right I heard the faint sound of breathing. It was a slow and steady rhythm that was almost hypnotic. They'd found me, and I now had two options: stay and fight, or run.

A feral grin spread across my face as I squeezed the staff in my hands and prepared myself to attack. The sound of a soft exhalation filled the space alongside me, and from my hiding spot in the dark undergrowth I raised my eyes to glance at my prey.

In one fluid movement, I lifted from the ground and thrust my staff out so that it swung in the path of the enemy, clipping them full across the chest and flooring them. A yelp followed by a light scream halted my attack.

'Ohmigod, Mia, that hurt!' Elizabeth's bright blue eyes shone in the moonlight as she peered up at me from her position on the floor. Covered in brambles and moss she pushed herself to a sitting position.

'Lavender! Really. There was no other shower gel option for you to choose?'

She giggled, and her entire face lit up.

'I was in a rush, and the lavender one was on special offer.'

'Well, if I *were* a werewolf you'd be dinner by now because your granny-scented soap is stinking up the entire forest. That and the fact you're wearing the brightest pink jumper I've ever seen.'

I extended my hand and helped my best friend to her feet. She grinned at me, zipping up her black jacket to hide the cerise jumper, before launching in for a big hug.

'I've missed you,' she said, squeezing me harder as if to confirm her words.

'I know. I've missed you too.'

'So, you caught me,' she said taking a step back. 'Which makes three to the wannabe werewolf and two to the hunter-in-training.'

Elizabeth dusted herself down as I sniggered at the score. We had spent the last few weeks hunting one another in the forest as part of a secret training pact. In our world, hunters and werewolves didn't mix, but I believed we could flaunt the rules. She was, technically, still a student at Hood Academy, and I was, well, I wasn't sure what I was. There was no way I could return to the academy even if it turned out I did have hunter's blood flowing through my veins. From what Elizabeth had told me, my dear old dad, Sebastian, had vanished without a trace and my nemesis, Felicity, who had made my school life hell, had been parading around school with her evil father, Mr Parker, who was stepping into the role of the headmaster to replace Sebastian.

'Has there been any news from Sebastian?' I'd told myself I wouldn't keep asking Elizabeth for information, but a small part of me just wanted to know that he was safe. He'd appeared broken when we had our standoff on the school lawn right before I left to follow the pack. He'd also resembled a psychotic freak, but under the circumstances, I was willing to forget that. I simply wanted to know that Parker hadn't hurt him.

Elizabeth shook her head. 'Miss Ross has tried everything to get in touch with him, but his phone keeps ringing out. She even tried asking for help from the Governors' Agency, but they refused her request on the grounds of some ongoing investigation they're doing.'

'What's the Governors' Agency?'

'They're the ruling authority over all the hunter academies in the UK. They set the curriculum, hire the staff, and enforce the hunter oath.'

'Ah, you mean the hunters' oath I broke when I ran off with the local werewolf pack.'

'That's the one!'

I laughed, but it felt hollow. In truth, I'd never fully committed to the hunters' oath, merely taking it as part of the façade that I was a normal student. It seemed that the original meaning of the oath had been lost, and the academy had become a corrupt establishment for powerful men to bend the rules and establish their own laws.

'I don't know if I'm supposed to tell you,' Elizabeth interrupted my musings, 'but Miss Ross was sacked today. She was escorted off the premises this morning.'

I wasn't surprised. Miss Ross had helped me escape. Parker wouldn't have thanked her for that, and as he's also Felicity's father, he was always going to be my enemy.

'I'm sure she'll stay in touch.' There was no way Miss Ross would go quietly; it wasn't in her nature. She would find a way to keep in contact with Elizabeth, and I was almost certain she would stay in touch with Zak. She wouldn't just melt into the background, of that I was sure.

'Perhaps she'll head to the Cornwall academy and join forces with Adam.'

Elizabeth's face lit up at the mention of her boyfriend. Following Sebastian's disappearance, it had taken Parker only two days before he transferred Adam to the sister academy in the south, ripping him from Elizabeth's arms. Now, with Miss Ross's dismissal, he'd managed to divide and conquer our little group again.

'I better get back before I'm missed.' Elizabeth hadn't been assigned another roommate after my exit and so sneaking out for our secret training sessions was relatively easy. However, Felicity and her goons were no doubt keeping an eye on Lizzie's movements to see if she could lead them to the pack. Our sessions had to, therefore, involve us hunting one another in the forest, then having a brief catch-up if it was safe, before parting ways.

'I wish you could stay with me at the Mills house,' I said as we strolled in the direction of the academy. 'It's full of boys, and I'm totally outnumbered.'

Elizabeth threw her head back and laughed. 'Oh, and I'm sure the fact that one of those boys is your gorgeous werewolf boyfriend is such a hardship.'

I thumped her playfully on the arm and grinned.

'Having Cody around all the time is the *only* bonus to living on the Mills farm, although I'm not sure Zak is 100 percent happy with Cody and me being a couple.'

'Why? Has he said something?'

'Not in so many words, he just has this look about him when we're together. And, if there's an errand to run he always sends Cody as if he's trying to keep us apart.'

'I'm sure he's just trying to be a responsible big brother, or an overprotective alpha. Either way, it can't be easy to suddenly get his little sister back and find out she's grown into a beautiful woman. You were six the last time he saw you.'

'Yeah, I know. I just wish he'd talk to me about stuff. Since we were reunited, I've been lucky enough to spend all of five minutes alone with him. I miss him more now that he's here than I did when I didn't know where he was!'

Elizabeth giggled and squeezed my hand in her usual supportive manner. I missed having her around all the time too and hated it when we had to go back to our own lives.

The edge of the treeline loomed, and I could make out a couple of lights in the academy. The great expanse of lawn stretched out in front of us as I turned to face my friend.

'Stay safe,' I said, 'and keep away from Felicity.'

'I always do.'

We hugged, and I watched her drop into a low run and sprint across the grass towards the back of the building. She'd have a ladder waiting at the window ready to climb up to our old room, the same ladder Adam used to use when he snuck in for his visits with my friend. That carefree teenage life seemed such a long time ago. I knew that Elizabeth was still in contact with Adam and I kicked myself for not asking about him; after all, he was my friend too.

I turned towards the woods and was about to leave when I spotted two figures running around the side of the academy building toward the old animal cages. An involuntary shudder skittered down my spine as I recalled Felicity locking me up in one of those cages. Instinct told me to return to the pack and report what I'd seen, but I overruled all common sense and decided to follow. Keeping well within the shadows of the trees, I circled the grounds until I reached the dusty trail leading to the cages. I gripped my staff and edged closer, listening to all the sounds that echoed in the night.

From my vantage point in the undergrowth, I could see two students, both friends of Felicity, poking at something inside a cage. No sound came from within: no whimpers, growls, or sobs, and from this angle, I couldn't see what it was. I crept closer.

'I'm glad Mr Parker's using the cages again,' said the first girl. 'This lot don't deserve to be inside the school. Imagine if this thing got out; it could kill us all in our sleep.'

The second student snorted. 'It couldn't hurt a fly. It's weak and useless, but that doesn't matter, 'cause soon it'll be dead.'

The two girls laughed before dropping the prod they'd been using and slinking off in the direction of the back door. I waited. When I believed it was safe enough, I left the sanctuary of the trees and stepped up to the cages. Peering into the inky blackness I thought for a moment that the girls were drunk and had imagined whatever they saw, but then a faint movement caught my eye.

A young girl, no more than ten years old, shuffled to the bars. Her face was covered in dirt and grime, her hair matted to her head. Full, wide eyes gleamed in the moonlight.

'What's your name?' I asked, bending down so I was level with her.

'Arianna,' she whispered, 'but my friends call me Ari. Are you going to rescue me?'

I glanced around the clearing outside the cages, and my eyes fell on the long metal prod the girls had used to taunt Ari. I snatched it up and motioned for the youngster to move away from the bars. Using all my strength, I smashed at the lock until it broke apart and fell to the ground. The door swung open, and Ari emerged sniffing the air.

'Come on!' I reached for her hand and pulled her to the safety of the treeline. We ran hand in hand as deep into the forest as we could before I needed to stop for breath. I collapsed onto a fallen tree trunk and coughed until I thought a lung might pop out. All this training and yet long-distance running was still a weak point for me.

Ari, on the other hand, looked incredibly composed as she perched on the edge of the trunk watching me splutter and choke.

'Do you live around here?' I wheezed.

'No, we come from Yorkshire, but when Daddy needed to visit this area, we all came with him. I got separated from them in town, and then two girls snatched me and threw me in that cage.'

I shook my head. Cody told me when I first arrived how he'd witnessed students from the academy antagonising members of the public but kidnapping a young child from her family was a new low.

'Why did they take you?'

Ari shook her head, her long hair swishing around her shoulders. 'Maybe because I'm a werewolf and they don't like my kind.'

I was stunned. Over the past few months, I'd tried to learn as much as I could about werewolves and nowhere did it say anyone turned before their sixteenth birthday.

'How is that possible? You're so young.'

'Daddy volunteered for my sister and me to have a new treatment. A doctor in a long white coat came to visit our pack leader. He told him about a cure. He said it was safe and that *if* we had the wolf gene, it meant we would never turn.' She kicked at a rock at her feet as she processed the memory. 'It didn't stop us turning, but instead, it speeded up the process. Daddy said we were probably the youngest werewolves in history.' She puffed her chest out and squared her jaw, but that pride didn't reach her eyes.

I licked my dry lips as I processed Ari's words. The treatment she spoke of sounded too similar to be anything but Sebastian's serum, but it was never completed, never finalised, and certainly never administered among the wolf community.

'What did the man in the white coat look like?' I held my breath waiting for Ari to describe Sebastian. I was surprised at the relief I felt at her answer.

'He was short and bald with a funny moustache,' she said. 'And there was a blue picture on the pocket of his coat.'

'What did he do to you?' I wasn't sure I wanted to know, if it was anything like the photographic evidence of Sebastian's lab when it was in action. The horrific image of a man chained to a table was forever stamped on my mind.

'The doctor injected us with something and then kept checking our temperature and stuff. We got ice cream for being so good.'

I huffed at the twinkle in her eye when she remembered the ice cream.

The light in Ari's eyes went out, and she dropped her head, wringing her hands together.

'My sister got really poorly and was sick, even the ice cream didn't help. They took her away to try and help her, but we never saw her again. I turned for the first time on the same day.'

A shiver ran down my spine at her words. Was it a coincidence that this doctor promised the exact thing Sebastian had tried to create? Or had Parker found another doctor to replace my father? I was suddenly filled with dread over Sebastian's whereabouts. His serum had been faulty. What if someone had decided to use it despite the fact that it hadn't been stabilised? Could Parker be behind this?

'Where are your parents now?'

Ari lifted her chin and sniffed the air for a few seconds.

'That way.' She pointed in the direction of the Mills family farm. My home.

'You said your father was visiting the area, who did he come to see?'

'He wants to see the alpha. The nasty doctor is visiting all the packs, and bad things are happening to our friends.'

'You mean other people have died as well as your sister?'

'Yes,' she said nodding her tiny head. 'Hundreds of us.'

TWO

It was well into the early hours of the morning when we got back to the farm and, as usual, Cody was nowhere to be seen. The Mills Family Farm truck was missing from the driveway, and I noticed a delivery note pinned to the kitchen door that confirmed he was transporting the farm's produce to a shop over a hundred miles away. The constantly energetic Byron always accompanied Cody on deliveries so at least the house would be quieter without them.

When I'd emerged from the forest after leaving Hood Academy, I experienced a feeling of contentment upon seeing this farmhouse. It was like something from a picture postcard. Redbrick walls and a grey slate roof with a low white fence wrapping itself around the rose-filled garden. I hadn't exactly given much thought to leaving the sanctuary of a school environment and moving in with werewolves.

That had been three months ago and the joy of being reunited with my brother, and being near my boyfriend, was wearing thin. Boys were loud, messy, and disorganised. The farmhouse always resembled the aftermath of a tsunami. Cody's sisters, who were also part of the werewolf pack, had both moved out to live with their own boyfriends. With Zak's blessing, they had joined other packs and lived in cosy little studio apartments nearer to town. I'd wished them well when they left but secretly harboured an intense jealousy that they were getting away from the smell of wet dog and aftershave.

I kicked the pile of shoes to the side as I steered Ari in through the kitchen door. The large black Aga dominated one side of the kitchen and warmed the stone room to a comfortable temperature. Family photographs in mismatched frames covered the furthest wall, and a picture window looked out over the driveway. In the centre of the room stood an enormous oak table with an assortment of chairs dotted around it. Zak sat at the head of the table with his back to the window and a thin man with a closely shaved beard and greying hair perched on a stool to his right. They had their heads bent together in conversation and didn't see us enter.

'Papa!' Ari released my hand and shot into the embrace of Zak's companion. From the other room I heard the cry of a woman, and then Terry burst through the door with a lady close behind him.

'Arianna, oh my baby girl.'

The small family hugged one another, peppering Ari with kisses as tears of joy and relief slid down their faces and I couldn't stop the tug of a smile as I watched the reunion. It wasn't that long ago that I was hugging Zak that tightly after ten years apart. My gaze drifted to my brother who was studying me in return.

'How did you find her?' Zak asked me, his expression not reflecting the joy of the moment.

Ari broke away from her parents and skipped back to my side.

'Mia rescued me from the bad girls at the academy.'

Zak raised a questioning eyebrow and I waved my hand in a non-committal way trying to play down my part in the daring rescue. Ari, however, wasn't going to let it go.

'She burst out of the trees and smashed the lock on the cage and then we ran away.' The youngster gazed up at me with those wide eyes, and I couldn't help but smile.

'I wouldn't exactly use the word burst, Ari. It was more of a slink.'

I felt my cheeks redden as Ari's parents rushed forward with their offer of praise. Terry chuckled from his position behind me as he watched my awkward acceptance of their hugs and well wishes.

'I think it's best if you all try and get some rest.' Zak's voice boomed with authority. 'You can stay in my room, and we'll talk again when the sun comes up.'

Ari and her parents followed Terry as he guided them through to the stairwell and up to Zak's spacious bedroom. I made to follow in the hope I could escape without a reprimand, but I wasn't fast enough.

'Mia, wait!'

My shoulders slumped as I spun on my heel to look at my brother. He was standing now, his big hands placed side by side on the tabletop. His head hung down as he studied something in front of him. I waited without saying a word, something I'd learned to do over the last few months. Zak had his own ways of dealing with the pack, but he had a unique way of dealing with me, almost like he thought I might break.

'What were you doing at the academy?'

'I wasn't technically *at* the academy, I was training in the woods and didn't realise how close I'd wandered to the school grounds, but if I hadn't then I wouldn't have been able to help Ari.'

Silence. Zak didn't move but continued to stare at the paper in front of him.

'I don't want you going out at night any more, Mia.'

'What! No way! How am I supposed to train properly if I can't get my bearings in the woods at night?' I adopted my what-the-hell stance placing my hands on my hips, a deep frown etched across my forehead. How did this keep happening to me? First Frank had abused me and kept me as a prisoner in my own home, then Sebastian locked me in a hospital cell, and now my brother, who I thought would be different, was trying to control me too.

'If you got caught by the hunters I'd never forgive myself. This is the only way I can keep you safe.'

'No! I'm sorry, Zak, but I'm not going to let you treat me the same way everyone else has in the past. I'm not a little kid like Ari, I'm potentially a werewolf like you, and I want to be ready when the change happens.'

Zak's eyes clouded over, and for the first time, I realised he doubted that I had inherited the werewolf gene. It was like a slap in the face. Was that why he was always trying to keep Cody and me apart? He didn't think I was truly one of them?

Terry returned to the kitchen and slung his arm across my shoulder.

'I can train her,' he said giving me a squeeze. 'She should be able to protect herself, no matter what.' He trailed off, and I examined his face. That same expression, the clouded eyes and uncertainty. I wriggled free and slapped his arm away.

'You don't think I'm going to turn, do you?' I wasn't looking for them to answer the question because it was clearly written across both boys' faces.

'Well, screw you,' I shouted. 'Screw both of you.' I stormed out of the kitchen and down the long corridor to the farmhouse extension where my room was located. It was basic but comfortable, and I had my own bathroom. I threw myself on the bed and willed myself not to cry. I didn't want them to think I was weak in any way because I wasn't. I'd survived so much, and none of them ever gave me the credit I deserved, except for Cody; he knew what I'd been through, and he knew how resilient I could be.

I sent a quick message to Elizabeth to check that she'd gotten back to the academy safely and filled her in on the Neanderthal antics of my pack. I wanted to arrange another training session for the next night, partly to annoy Zak and partly because I missed my best friend so much. Within seconds I received a reply.

```
[Stay away from the academy, Mia.
There's something going on. The place
is crawling with Governors' Agency
agents. I'll message you when I find
out more. E x]
```

I blinked and reread the message. Elizabeth had only told me that night about the Governors' Agency and their involvement in the various academies across the country. Why were they here? Why now? Surely they couldn't have descended so fast after I freed Ari from the cage. No, it had to be something else. Something the alpha needed to know about.

THE LIVING ROOM of the farmhouse was my favourite room. It had an open fire, which was always crackling and alive despite the temperature outside, and a big squishy rug whose pile was so deep you could wiggle your toes in it. There was a huge sofa with faded fabric and worn armrests that was the comfiest seat in the world. Once you snuggled on there you didn't want to move. Dotted around the rest of the room was an assortment of armchairs that the Mills family had collected over the years. The room was warm and homely. It made me feel safe.

Zak was spread out on the sofa with one arm hanging over the edge. He wore shorts and nothing else. His tanned, muscular torso reminded me of how much I'd missed of his life. He'd been sixteen when I'd last seen him, and yet now here he was, a man, and alpha of a werewolf pack.

'Hey, Mia,' he said without even opening his eyes. I didn't think I'd ever get used to the wolves knowing my scent that well.

'Something's going on at Hood Academy,' I said taking a seat in the armchair opposite him. 'Elizabeth sent this message.' I handed him my phone, so he could read it for himself and watched his face scrunch up with concentration and worry. Being alpha must be a huge responsibility, and I wasn't being fair to him.

'I've seen these Governors' Agency agents before. They made life difficult for a pack in Norfolk a few years ago.'

'What happened?'

Zak looked up from the phone, his expression cold. 'They murdered the entire pack.'

My hand flew to my mouth as I gasped. How could they do that? Yes, the pack were werewolves, but they were also human 99 percent of the time. I couldn't speak for other packs across the country, but I knew for certain that Zak's pack never hunted people, or killed in cold blood. They loved nature and living in balance. None of them deserved to be punished for who they were.

'How?' I almost didn't want to know the gory details, but somewhere deep inside me, I had to know.

'As far as we could tell they were poisoned. The local authority covered it up saying it was a leak in the gas line but Terry and Byron saw some of the bodies and they all had puncture wounds around the main artery in their neck. A single needle hole. We think they were all stabbed by a syringe in their sleep.'

My stomach knotted up, and I had to fight the urge to vomit. Those poor people had been murdered in cold blood by a silent weapon.

'Do you think there's a link to the doctor who injected Ari and her sister?'

'Ari's father told me the doctor was a representative from a new pharmaceutical company who were *sympathetic* to the werewolf cause.'

'Sympathetic?'

'The doctor claimed to have a werewolf wife and daughter who had been cured using the product. The alpha bought it and reported back to the pack so they could choose.'

'Choose to let a weirdo experiment on their family?'

'No, choose to cure their children. Prevent them from turning.'

I wondered if Zak ever regretted leaving home and seeking out his werewolf destiny. Our mother had wanted him to see Sebastian before his sixteenth birthday in the hope that he would have completed his miracle cure for lycanthropy before Zak turned, but my brother chose the pack. A bit like I'd done.

'Do you think Sebastian's involved in this?'

'Sebastian is definitely capable of creating a cure, or poison depending on your interpretation, but after hearing what Terry said on the night you escaped, I don't think Sebastian is capable of mass murder. He's crazy, yes, but I don't think he's a cold-blooded killer.'

'You don't have to protect him on my account.'

'I know, but I realise you must be confused about your relationship with him, and I don't want it to come between us.'

I blinked. 'Why would it come between us? You're my brother. Just because we found out we have different dads doesn't make you any less of a brother to me.'

He smiled an exhausted smile. His eyes crinkled slightly, and I felt a tug in my chest. He seemed so young in that moment, and I had to remind myself of the role he played and the responsibility he held for so many lives.

'That's good to hear, Mia.'

The key in the front door broke the spell between us and I heard the low whispers of Byron and Cody returning from their delivery. My mood lightened on hearing Cody's voice, and I jumped from the chair to open the living room door.

In a flash Zak was off the sofa and grabbing my arm, moving my hand away from the door handle. At my puzzled expression he lowered his eyes to the floor.

'I'm sorry, Mia,' he mumbled, 'but I'm going to need Cody to be focused on the pack until we figure out what's going on. I...I don't think you should distract him.'

I yanked my arm from Zak's grasp, unable to hide the hurt and pain I felt at his words. Turning away from him to pull open the door, I stopped myself from calling after Cody and telling him what my stupid brother had said. I stopped myself from screaming to the entire household that apparently I was never allowed to be happy, but I couldn't stop the feral growl as it rose up from somewhere deep in my gut. From the shocked look on Zak's face, it surprised him as much as me.

I stormed off into the darkness of the corridor and back to my room without another sound. If I ever did become a werewolf, the first thing I wanted to do was bite my brother.

I FELT EDGY and out of sorts the next day. Zak's reaction to me being with Cody had not only annoyed me, but it upset me more than I could put into words. How could he think I'd do anything to interfere with pack business? I knew I was sulking, but I didn't care. If it meant all the boys in the house stayed out of my way for the day then I was onto a winner. Perhaps I could tempt Elizabeth to ditch class and meet me in Ravenshood for a hot chocolate at Taylor's Coffee Shop. The idea perked me up, and I burst into the kitchen with a determination to my step.

Any note of positivity was eradicated when I glanced around at the sombre faces sitting at the kitchen table. Zak was at his usual place at the head flanked by Terry and Byron. Cody sat in between Ari's mother and father. There were a few new faces in the mix, men and women I'd never met before, but as my gaze moved to the assembled group, I spotted a familiar face.

'Miss Ross!'

I rushed to embrace my friend, eager to hear her news, but Zak halted my reunion with his booming voice.

'Mia, take a seat, you need to hear this.' He motioned for me to pull up a chair and from the tone of his voice and his demeanour it wasn't going to be in my best interests to ignore his demand.

I squeezed Miss Ross's hand as I took my place beside her, wishing that she could have brought Elizabeth with her too but also feeling elated to see my godmother again. Her eyes were dull and hooded as she stole a look my way and I wondered how hard Mr Parker had been on her before escorting her off Hood Academy grounds.

Zak cut through my muddled thoughts.

'It's come to our attention that the Governors' Agency, or the GA as they like to be known, have taken up residence at Hood Academy while the students are still on summer break. We don't know if this has anything to do with the pharmaceutical company or if it's coincidental, but we all need to be on high alert. As we've seen before, the GA's presence can only mean danger for the local packs.' He paused to make sure he had everyone's attention before carrying on. 'We've received information from a reliable source that a select group of hunters are still on-site at the academy. We know they're working on a top-secret mission but we can't confirm if this is connected with the Governors' Agency.'

'Do you have any more information on the mission?' a broad, muscular man with a shock of red hair asked.

'Not yet, our source was...compromised before they could pass on any further details.'

My mind was a whirling mass of thoughts. I was aware of the giant man talking to my brother and discussing possibilities, but somewhere in my core something didn't feel right. I'd always thought Miss Ross was Zak's reliable source, but she was sitting next to me. So who was their reliable source? What did Zak mean by compromised? I could feel Cody's eyes on me as I wrestled to slot the ideas and musings together in my mind. There was only one other person at the academy who could report to the pack about what was going on and had a vested interest in seeing Mr Parker and Felicity banished—Elizabeth.

I shot out of my seat tipping the chair over as I went.

'Where's Lizzie?'

Miss Ross stood up slowly and put her arm around my shoulders; she moved her hand so she could squeeze my fingers the way Elizabeth always did when she needed to make me feel better. Cody watched my outburst with a pained expression, unable to help, unable to comfort me.

'I'm sorry, Mia,' Zak whispered. 'We'll do anything we can to help her.'

I narrowed my eyes as I tried to process what he was suggesting.

'No, she can't be. I just saw her...' My words sounded muddled.

How had sweet, innocent Elizabeth got herself mixed up with the Governors' Agency?

'Where is she?' My voice didn't sound like it was coming from me. It sounded distant, cold, and detached. Somewhere on the periphery, I could hear Zak talking, but his words weren't penetrating the thick wall of protection I was building around my heart.

'As far as we can see she's been transferred off-site. The agency is holding her on the offence of collaborating with werewolves, which is against the hunters' oath.'

I wriggled free of Miss Ross's embrace and rushed out of the kitchen door and into the garden. The summer sun was rising in the sky, but the warm rays did nothing to thaw the chill that crept along my spine. I bolted for the gate, running into the forest and picking up speed. The wind lifted my hair and the leaves rustled in the trees as I ran, deeper and deeper into the trees. In the distance, Zak called my name, but I kept moving. I didn't want to stop until my lungs burst or my heart gave up. Why had I left Elizabeth behind at that school? Why didn't I insist that she leave the academy and come live with us at the farmhouse?

If anything happened to her, I would raze Hood Academy to the ground.

THREE

Tears streamed down my face as I imagined the horrors Elizabeth must be facing at the hands of Parker and the Governors' Agency. Sebastian and his lab rats were bad enough when they tortured captured werewolves, but these guys were hunters who dedicated their lives to annihilating the packs. Elizabeth had been found guilty of collaboration with the enemy. I could only envision what Parker or Felicity would do to my friend.

I stopped to gather my strength and realised I'd run all the way to the lookout point that Cody and I used to meet at when I ran away from Hood Academy. Ravenshood town and valley spread out below me, but I couldn't see the beauty in the view today, I could only see darkness.

Like some cruel instance of déjà vu, I heard a rustling in the undergrowth. A few short months ago, I'd come face to face with four werewolves in this very spot, not knowing at the time that they were my brother and his pack. My heart thundered in my chest as I waited to see what would emerge from the bushes this time.

Ari broke through the treeline carrying a posy of wildflowers. She grinned when she saw me, and I relaxed my shoulders and uncurled my fists.

'What are you doing out here?'

Ari gawked at the flowers and then back up at me as if I'd asked her the most ridiculous question in the world.

'I wanted to get Mummy a bunch of flowers, but I saw some of those bad girls again, so I decided to go back to the farmhouse.'

My ears pricked up at the mention of the bad girls. Hood Academy students no doubt, but Zak said most of them were on summer break. I had a feeling the select few girls left behind were Felicity's goons.

'Show me.' I turned Ari around and urged her back the way she'd come. We stumbled on the dirt track that the students followed during their training runs; green flags still marked a safe passage through the woods. I huffed as I recalled Felicity moving the flags and throwing me off course on one of our training sessions.

'This way,' Ari said in a hushed voice, pointing towards a crumbling barn. 'They went behind that building.'

I clamped a hand on Ari's shoulder and pushed her gently to the ground. Crouching beside her I put my finger to my lips and urged her to be quiet. She nodded and dropped down lower into the bushes clutching her pretty flowers.

Stay here, I mouthed.

Creeping forward I was able to assess the building. It had once housed hay bales, possibly for horses kept at the academy before it became a school. The wildlife had taken over it now with swallows' nests visible in the roof beams. Ivy grew up one side covering every inch of brick. As I circled the front, I could see where erosion had taken place and the front side had crumbled. It resembled a ruin you'd normally see on castle grounds. The inside was empty apart from an old cartwheel and lots of weeds. There didn't appear to be anything more to the building. I inspected the area to see if there were any other barns where Ari's bad girls could have gone but there were only trees as far as the eye could see. I was about to return to Ari when I smelled something familiar. Lavender. It was faint, but it was there, lingering in the air. My pulse quickened at the thought of Elizabeth being in danger.

A movement caught my eye, and I glanced over to where I left Ari crouching in the bushes. She was waving at me and pointing towards the back of the building. I moved as quickly as I could until I reached her side.

'Look, over there,' she hissed.

I followed the line of her finger and saw a glint of glass in the base of the wall. It looked like a cellar window. Dropping as low as possible, I shuffled ahead until I was alongside the barn. The wall was weather-worn but solid. I inched closer to the glass and lowered myself onto my stomach. It was a tiny window set into the foundations, a small slit of glass covered in dirt, grime, and greenery. I carefully cleared away some of the brambles and using a section of my sleeve rubbed at the dirty glass.

Beneath the inconspicuous barn was a small room set up with trestle tables and boxes. In the centre was a large table littered with drawings and printouts. I could see the backs of two Hood Academy students, both in their training uniform of grey jumpsuits and matching shoes. Another figure stepped out of the shadows, and I jumped away from the window, slapping my hand across my mouth. Sebastian's hair was unkempt and his face unshaven, and he wore a long white lab coat covered in blood. My stomach rolled, and I gulped in great lungfuls of air to calm my nausea. Was that Elizabeth's blood? The thought that my father could harm my best friend was too much to take in.

Voices filled the air, and I frantically scanned the area for Ari to see if she was safe. I couldn't see her anywhere so I prayed that she was nose down in the undergrowth and out of sight. The two academy students sauntered past within inches of where I lay next to the basement window.

'Do you think his serum would have worked?'

'I don't care, the serum was to help the werewolves, so they never had to turn again. I couldn't care less if it helped them or not. We're trained to kick their furry butts and that's all that matters to me.'

'We won't be able to kick anything if this new stuff wipes them out.'

Their laughter carried through the trees as they walked deeper into the forest leaving me reeling at their words. It wasn't bad enough that Sebastian was creating flawed serums that ended up killing innocent people, it now sounded like he was making a weapon to kill *all* werewolves.

Ari appeared above me dragging me out of my stupor.

'I've found the way in.' She motioned for me to follow and I scrambled to my feet dusting off my jeans as I went.

There was a trapdoor hidden under a mound of ivy a few yards away from the old barn. By the look of the well-worn path in the mud around the entrance it was a facility someone used often.

'I saw the bad girls climb out of here.'

'Thanks, Ari. You did really well. Now, do you think you could be the lookout while I go inside?'

Her eyes gleamed with pride as she puffed her chest out and gave a little salute.

'Aye, aye, Captain.'

I smiled at her, pleased that she was by my side no matter how young the little wolf was.

'I'll be back soon.' I hoped that wasn't a lie. I had no idea what I was walking into. The lab beneath the academy had been one long row of single rooms leading off one another, each room holding a fresh horror. Was I about to venture into another evil place filled with test tubes, dusty files, and dried blood?

A ladder balanced against the opening leading down into the darkness. I cursed at not having a torch or weapon with me. When I'd stormed out of the kitchen an hour ago, I hadn't imagined this was how my day would unfold.

Upon reaching the ground, I waited until my eyesight adjusted to the gloom. I was standing in a square space with no way out except the corridor straight ahead. Cut into the wall was a heavy metal door with a small window. I moved forward, tuning into my senses as Cody showed me. The window was made of reinforced glass, which made it difficult to see through or decipher with any real clarity what was inside. However, I saw a man in a white coat moving around the space and assumed this was my deranged father.

The door handle turned with ease, and I pressed my shoulder against the metal and inched it open. Sebastian had his back to me. He was scribbling notes on one of the many pads scattered across the table. The smell of lavender permeated the room, which I scanned for any sign of Elizabeth. To my left was a shelving unit with row upon row of syringes in sterile packaging. Boxes marked with a blue pharmaceutical logo filled the floor space.

So, there was a link between Sebastian and the pharmaceutical company, but was the GA involved too?

The window I'd peered through only moments ago was high in the wall above Sebastian's head casting a dim light over his work. My gaze drifted to the right where two trestle tables were laid with blankets. I'd seen something similar to this in the lab beneath the academy. Sebastian chained the werewolves to the table and injected his serum into their body, gauging the response and recording his findings. Was this where Ari and her sister had been treated? If not, that meant there could be facilities like this one dotted across the country. I couldn't imagine any alpha allowing members of his pack to come here even if there was the hope of a cure for lycanthropy.

I allowed my eyes to travel to the furthest corner of the room. There, on the floor of a small metal cage, was Elizabeth's pink jumper, but my friend was nowhere in sight.

The rage that overcame me was swift. My fingers curled up into tight fists, and all I could hear was the blood pumping around my body. The smell of lavender was overpowering, and somewhere I could hear the slow tick of a wristwatch. Before I could stop myself, a deep growl rumbled from my throat. Sebastian spun around clutching the table behind him. His face registered shock and then fear. What did he have to be scared of?

'Mia! How did you find...? What are you doing...?' His eyes shifted to Elizabeth's jumper and realisation dawned.

A roar in my head drowned out everything else in the room. I was aware that Sebastian was trembling. I could smell the fear rolling off him. Every speck of blood and grime on his white coat stood out, and even the clump of grass stuck to his shoe attracted my attention.

'It's okay, Mia. She's okay; no one hurt her, I made sure of it.'

My hands ached where I was clenching them so tightly, and they felt slick. Beads of sweat dripped from between my fingers and hit the floor.

'Mia, I'm so sorry I couldn't help you.' Sebastian held his hands out in a gesture of surrender. 'But I haven't given up on you, I promise. Please trust me when I say I'm looking out for you.'

A guttural sound escaped me as I swept my gaze between the cage and Sebastian. The sweat glistened on his forehead.

'The GA have her, they've taken her for questioning, something about breaking the oath. I...I told them not to harm her.'

I took a step backward and then another until I was in the gloomy corridor. I reached out for the metal door and readied myself to slam it in Sebastian's face, but instead, I stopped in shock. I caught sight of my hand. Huge claws protruded from my fingers, blood dripping from them. I turned my palm over to see the four small puncture wounds where the claws had dug deep into my hand, although it wasn't a human hand any more, it looked part human and part wolf.

Sebastian took a step forward, and I flinched.

'Mia, I can help you. I've finished my work, and we have a cure.'

I shook my head and took another step backward. The roar in my head was still there, but I could also hear Ari moving about in the forest above. What the hell was going on?

'You don't have to do this alone, Mia. I'm your father, and I will always have your best interests at heart. I can save you from this fate.'

I left the door where it was and spun on my heel running for the ladder. I climbed up the rungs in two leaps and slammed the trapdoor shut behind me.

Ari stood a short distance away watching me with wide eyes.

'What?' My words sounded odd like I had too many teeth in my mouth. I lifted my clawed hand and felt around my lips. A bump caused my top lip to protrude. I ran my fingertip down the lump and met something sharp and solid. A fang.

My eyes filled with tears as I processed what was happening. I was turning. This was it. No more feeling like I didn't belong with Cody and my brother, I was finally going to be a proper member of the pack. I was going to be a werewolf, like my mum.

I grinned, and Ari flinched. Clearly a fang-filled mouth wasn't conducive to a pretty smile. Throwing my head back, I laughed; it felt wonderful to finally belong. I stared up at the lush green canopy of leaves, and the blue sky above. I closed my eyes and soaked up the feeling of the warm sun on my skin. Wait a minute. That wasn't right. Where was the full moon?

'Mia, can you hear me?'

I glanced over at the young wolf and noticed she was still keeping her distance. I nodded.

'We need to get out of here.'

That was an understatement. Not only had I proved to my father that I had inherited my mother's werewolf genes, but I'd also shown him that I could half turn in the middle of the day. He'd have a field day dissecting me in his laboratory.

Ari grabbed my hand and pulled me in the direction of the Mills farm. It was a long walk back home, but we seemed to make great time as we sprinted through the trees.

Looking down at my body I noticed I was still a human: two arms, two legs, a human torso. No hairy limbs or cracking bones. I'd watched Cody turn when Felicity attacked him, and it had been horrific. He broke nearly every bone in his body, changing shape until he became a huge wolf the size of a horse. I was still little old me. My hair brushed my shoulders, and when I lifted my clawed hand, I could feel a human nose and cheekbones. What the hell was wrong with me?

WITH THE FARMHOUSE in sight, I slowed to a walking pace. Ari rushed through the back door, and I heard the commotion in the kitchen as the pack listened to the young wolf's expressive account of the morning. I expected Zak to come barrelling out of the door, but I was delighted when Cody emerged.

He spotted me instantly. I heard the gasp like a cannon blast across the sky. The muscle in his cheek twitched as his gaze dragged from the fangs to my clawed hands. Recovering himself, he sauntered over to where I stood, as if this was an everyday occurrence. His eyes never left mine.

'Hey, Mia.'

He gave me that lopsided grin that melted my heart but all I could do was huff. I didn't have a clue how I'd partly changed into whatever the hell I was so I was clueless as to how I changed back to me; to Mia, the human girl.

A tear slid down my cheek. Cody caught it on his thumb and brushed it away. He pulled me into a tight embrace and allowed me to sob into his chest. His scent was safe and comforting, and I melted into him. I reached up to cling to his shirt and noticed my hands were normal, no claws and no deep wounds. I broke out of Cody's embrace and touched my face. No fangs. I was me again.

'You okay?'

I was shaking so much that my voice wobbled when I spoke.

'Yeah, I think so.'

'Want to tell me what happened?'

'I found Sebastian; he's in a storage facility in the woods. I followed Lizzie's scent but found him instead. I lost it. I felt so angry with him, with the academy, and with myself.'

He pulled me close again and whispered into my hair.

'Why are you so angry with yourself?'

'Because I haven't turned, or hadn't, and I didn't think I ever would. Where does that leave me, or us, or me and Zak?'

'You know what I think?'

I shrugged and snuggled into his arms.

'I think you worry too much.'

I laughed and leaned back to look up at him. His blond hair flopped into his eyes, and I brushed it away with my fingertips. His smile lit up his face, and I felt the ice in my heart begin to melt again. He dipped his head to mine and kissed me gently. All the worry over Sebastian, the academy, my abnormal transformation evaporated as his lips moved over mine.

A small cough behind us broke the magic spell, and we wrenched ourselves apart.

Zak was watching my exchange with Cody with sad eyes. I knew he'd be mad at me for running off and being reckless, and he was probably as confused about my half turn as I was, but part of me didn't have the energy to care. He might be my flesh and blood, but I was still getting to know him. Elizabeth was my family, and I couldn't stand by and do nothing.

'The GA are holding Lizzie for questioning. I'm going to get her back as soon as it's dark.'

I was expecting an argument, or at the very least some resistance from him, but instead, Zak dragged his big hands through his hair and said, 'Okay, but you take Terry and Cody with you.'

He turned to address the assembled pack members. 'If they want a fight, then we're going to give them one.'

He looked every inch the alpha as he took charge and I felt a surge of pride as I watched the assembled group nod their approval.

Cody threaded his fingers into mine, and I relaxed, relishing the warmth of his touch. The heaviness in my chest lifted, and I smiled, feeling calmer and happier than I had in a long while. Finally, I was going to get the opportunity to be a proud member of my brother's pack.

FOUR

ak pulled my collar up around my neck in an affectionate gesture.

'Watch your back, stay sharp, and let Terry take the lead.'

I nodded, stopping myself from pointing out it was Elizabeth and me who rescued Terry from Hood Academy when Felicity and her goons captured him several months earlier. In Zak's warped world anything I'd done before living under his roof didn't count. I was his little sister, and he wasn't going to let me forget it.

'Ready?' Cody poked his head around the doorframe, a black hat encasing his head camouflaging his brassy blond hair.

Smiling up at my brother I spun on my heel and followed Cody out into the night.

Terry was waiting for us beyond the garden gate, and several of the pack had gathered to watch us leave. Having them there disturbed me, and part of me wanted to question their reason for congregating. Their furtive glances to one another told me there was something going on that I wasn't a part of.

Before I could ask the question, Cody had herded me out of the gate and off towards the treeline. As we stepped into the dark forest, any worries I had evaporated.

CREEPING AROUND THE grounds of Hood Academy at night brought back a tsunami of thoughts and emotions. It wasn't that long ago that sneaking out after dark was a highlight because it meant a rendezvous with Cody.

My heart soared as I glanced across at my werewolf boyfriend. I had never imagined it would be possible for me to have anyone to share my thoughts with. My home life had resembled a prison, and my brief stay with Sebastian at school had been turbulent at best. Cody was like a solid anchor keeping me safe. After Zak's brotherly outburst I'd worried that my time with Cody was coming to an end. It was my intention, after this night, that Zak would be able to trust in my abilities and understand that Cody and I being together wouldn't affect his precious pack.

'Do you have any idea where they would keep her?' Terry whispered as we reached the black expanse of lawn that backed onto the property.

I had visions of her chained to the same gurney they'd used for Terry down in the bowels of the academy, but a shadow caught my eye and I breathed a sigh of relief.

'She's there.' I pointed at the patio doors that led to Adam's old room. It was apt that they would lock Elizabeth in that room surrounded by memories of her lost love. It was also the same place Terry and I had escaped from before Sebastian chased after us. A shiver skittered down my spine.

'Well, that's handy.' Terry's wide grin made me giggle as I realised he was remembering the same thing. 'Let's hope your dad hasn't been left in charge of the key to the gun cupboard.'

I rolled my eyes and thumped him on the arm, and his warm laugh rumbled from deep in the back of his throat. Sebastian had shot Terry that night but he recovered quickly thanks to his werewolf healing. I didn't know if I had that ability to heal. I was half a wolf, or a wannabe werewolf as Lizzie liked to call me. If I got shot, I'd probably bleed out and die.

'We'll circle the lawn using the trees for cover. Cody, I want you to keep watch on the perimeter and warn us if anyone approaches.'

Cody nodded and melted into the forest. A warmth spread through my chest at Terry's decision. It would have been much easier to leave me behind in the trees as a lookout, but instead he trusted me to work with him. If only my brother felt the same.

As we approached the back of the academy, I saw Elizabeth through the partially closed curtains. She was sitting on the end of Adam's bed with her head bent forward and her hands bound in her lap. Her slumped posture worried me. Elizabeth had grown over the months we'd known each other. She'd been a sweet and innocent girl who flourished into an accomplished hunter. The girl in that room looked broken and terrified.

I half stood ready to rush towards the patio doors, but Terry was quick to pull me down to my knees.

'Wait! Not yet.' He nodded at the gap in the curtains once more as two men in black trousers and matching jumpers walked in front of the window. The GA. I tuned into my wolf senses and heard the faint rumbling of an authoritative voice.

'It's imperative that you cooperate, miss. This establishment has become a laughing stock and I, for one, will not allow its reputation to remain in ruins. A displaced headmaster, a student running off with the local werewolf pack. Surely you understand why we need to carry out this review.'

Elizabeth nodded, her long blonde hair shielding her face.

'Where did Miss Roberts go? Does Dr Roberts still have contact with her? Why did Mr Parker dismiss Miss Ross? Was she somehow involved? Answer me!'

I could see Elizabeth's shoulders shake as she cried and when she lifted her head my heart almost broke in two. Her eye and cheek were bruised, and she bore a long split across her lip. Eyes puffy from crying, and an ashen face completed the look.

Anger raged through me and it was almost unbearable. I wanted to break down the doors and rip those men apart. As if sensing my rising fury Terry held on to my arm, his warmth seeping through me and calming the roar in my head.

'Be patient, Mia. We're going to get her out of there.'

I believed him. Terry and Elizabeth had bonded when they rescued me from my delusional father, and I knew he cared for her as a true friend does.

'I don't know anything,' Elizabeth was saying. 'I haven't seen Mia since the night she left, or Dr Roberts. I only found out Miss Ross had been sacked when I saw Mr Parker escorting her off the premises. You have to believe me. I don't know anything.' Her voice broke as she sobbed her words.

'Well, we don't believe you. Miss Parker found you snooping in her father's office. Why were you in there? What were you looking for?'

'Felicity is wrong! I wasn't snooping; I was waiting for Mr Parker as I had an appointment with him.'

'Don't lie to me,' the man roared causing Elizabeth to flinch. 'Mr Parker denies that he asked you to his office. He is a respected member of the GA and the new headmaster of this school, and you are nothing. Who do you think we'll believe?'

Elizabeth dropped her head and curled into herself as the man raged on. My mind flashed back to the many times Frank had stood over me like that, his menacing voice the only sound to echo around the small house.

'I've had enough of this idiot,' Terry said with a hard edge to his usually warm voice. 'Stay here.'

I watched as he crept along the building, sticking to the shadows. He skirted past Elizabeth's room and kept going. I wondered what he had planned until I heard the smash of glass from the far end of the school, the rock he had thrown breaking the second story window with ease.

Leaving Elizabeth bound in the chair, the two men left the room as they went to investigate the noise. I heard their heavy breathing mingled with that of others as they all ran through the corridors towards the main staircase.

I rushed forward and kicked at the patio door with all my strength. It smashed open making Elizabeth scream and jump off the bed. The fear on her face evaporated when she saw it was me.

'What have they done to you?' I asked striding to her side and studying the bruises on her face.

'It was Felicity. She tried to get information out of me before handing me over to the GA. Never mind that now, what are *you* doing here?'

'Rescuing you, come on.' I grabbed her elbow, and we fled the room crunching over the broken door and running straight into Terry. Elizabeth screamed again until she spotted Terry's muscular frame. He unravelled her binding and we each grabbed her hands, half running, and half dragging her into the safety of the trees.

Cody was waiting for us as we barrelled through the overhanging boughs and scratched our faces on the tiny branches in our path.

'Four students left the building by the front door and have split up to circle the school,' he told Terry. 'We need to draw them off the girls.'

Terry grunted his agreement and grabbed my shoulder with his big hand.

'Mia, I need you to head back towards the farm as fast as you can. Me and Cody will split up and confuse the hunters so they don't know what direction to go in.'

I gave a short nod of my head and grabbed Elizabeth's clammy hand. She squeezed my fingers, and I smiled at her. It was up to me to get my friend to safety.

We turned and ran, leaving the boys to do what they needed to. We sprinted hand in hand in the direction of the farmhouse, making no sound, until our lungs threatened to burst.

I SLOWED DOWN when I realised Elizabeth was struggling to keep up. I didn't want to ask her what she'd been through. She'd tell me in time.

I closed my eyes and sniffed the air sorting through the scents in my mind: moss, pine, earth, and something else, something that was out of place in this part of the forest. A bittersweet perfume wafted through the trees masking the natural aromas, and the hairs stood up on the back of my neck. I knew that smell; I remembered how it used to make me gag whenever it clawed at my throat in the academy classrooms or the gym changing room. Only one person I knew wore such an overpowering perfume.

My eyes snapped open. Felicity stood in front of us with her staff held out to the side like a broadsword. Her fiery red hair was scraped back into a high ponytail emphasising her sharp cheekbones. She was smirking in that infuriating manner that suggested she'd beaten you already.

'Finally,' she said. 'I've been looking for you all over these woods, Mia. I *really* wanted to thank you for running away.'

I knew she was goading me to get a reaction, but I couldn't help the rush of anger that swept over me.

'I didn't run, Felicity, I was driven away by you and your maniac father.'

She laughed; it was a short, humourless sound.

'The academy is no place for a wolf girl, I told you that.'

A red fog began to descend and settle in my vision, and I took a deep breath to try to control it. The change seemed to be powered by my anger, and I couldn't let Felicity force my shift. I needed to learn to manage my emotions, or the werewolf gene would dominate my entire personality.

'What's the matter, *wolf girl*? You afraid you'll break a claw or ruffle your fur?'

The blood pumped faster around my system, and I tried in vain to slow the rhythm down.

'I owe you a beating,' Felicity continued. 'It wasn't the same using dear old Elizabeth as a punching bag.'

I pushed Elizabeth behind me to safety as I felt the turn snap into place in my mind. The rage overcame every molecule of my body, and the feral growl rushed up and out startling Felicity with the ferocity of the sound.

Any initial shock at my snarling was quickly pushed aside as a calculated grin spread across Felicity's face. This was what she wanted. For so long she'd only been able to prod and poke at my ancestry, but she'd never had proof that I was indeed a wolf girl. Until now.

'There's my girl,' she hissed.

I was beyond controlling anything now. Felicity had always been able to bring out the wolf in me, even before I knew that was a possibility. I'd flipped during a class training session once and beat her until her nose bled and her eyes were swollen. She believed she owed me a beating in return, but instead of feeling disorientated with my transition I felt powerful, strong, and focused. Felicity was the enemy, and I hunted the enemy.

I squared my shoulders and moved my stance so my feet were shoulder width apart, just as Miss Ross had taught me in my training sessions. Felicity moved her staff in front of her and gripped it in both hands, her eyes never leaving mine.

I flicked my right hand out to the side as if shaking something off it and watched Felicity's eyes shift to scrutinise the sharp claws that snapped into place. I stretched my fingers, curling and uncurling them to test the power in my claws.

My top lip ached as I felt the fangs slide into view cracking my jaw as they manoeuvred into place.

It all happened in a matter of seconds, but it felt like the process was drawn out. Felicity was mesmerised by my shift, her eyes blinking rapidly as she inched back a step and part of me wished that I too could see what I had become. The roar of adrenaline in my head threatened to overwhelm my senses, but I managed to retain a thread of my human self and cling to it. I couldn't risk losing myself totally.

Felicity jabbed forward with her staff and struck me in the chest. I stumbled backward with a grunt but quickly recovered.

'You're pathetic, *wolf girl*. You're not even a proper werewolf.' She laughed at me as she moved across my path. 'You can't even get that right.'

I shook off the goading and concentrated on my prey. I couldn't let her distract me into doing something stupid.

We moved around each other, looking for breaks in defence or a weak spot that could be manipulated. Felicity systematically swung her staff at me like a child would antagonise an ant's nest with a long stick. There was no sense of urgency about her movements. She planned to enjoy hurting me, but I wasn't prepared to give her the satisfaction. I was a member of the pack, and this was my chance to prove how powerful we were by sending Parker a message.

I swiped a clawed hand across the air between us and my nails grazed Felicity's cheek. It was so fast that she didn't see it coming and she yelped, jumping backward, with a trickle of blood running down her face.

'You bitch,' she hissed. 'You'll pay for that.'

In a flurry of movement, she advanced on me whirling her staff around like a cheerleader's baton. It hit me hard on the shoulder, thigh, and side of the head, and my ears rang from the impact.

I retaliated with two fast swipes of my claws, slicing left and right until I felt the softness of her flesh. She screamed out in pain, and I grinned at the sound. Any part of me that was human faded away as I was overtaken by the primal instinct to hunt and kill.

Felicity must have felt the change in me too as she backed away clutching a hand across her stomach to stem the flow of blood.

'My father was right,' she heaved. 'You *all* deserve to die!'

With a warrior's cry she launched herself at me swinging her staff from high above to knock me off balance. I skidded to the floor and winced at the sudden impact. She didn't waste any time and was above me in seconds, wielding her staff and bringing it down repeatedly on my crumpled form.

I felt the pain of each blow although I could also feel my body begin the instantaneous action of healing itself. I marvelled at the capability of my partial werewolf form as the beating rained down on me from above.

Felicity began to tire. Her strikes weren't as brutal yet the blood that clouded my vision and poured down the side of my face told another story.

In the distance I heard Terry and Cody approaching, their huge paws pounding on the compacted earth as they tore through the forest.

I needed to end this before they arrived. I wanted to prove to Zak what a valuable member of the pack I could be. Felicity had to understand that the wolves weren't going to give up their lives without a fight.

Bursting from the dirt floor, I leaped to my feet and howled, a deep guttural sound that shook the branches of the trees close by. Felicity baulked. I took advantage of her confusion and launched myself at her, clamping down on her throat with my fangs. I tasted her blood as it gushed from the wound in her. The gurgling sound of her choking broke through the roaring rage, and I let go. She dropped to the ground gasping for breath and clutching her hands to her throat, her eyes wide with terror.

My face screwed up into a snarl as I crouched low over her trembling body. I traced a claw along the side of her face leaving a tiny trail of blood in its wake. Blood frothed at her mouth as she coughed and sobbed. I felt nothing. No remorse, no anger, just a desire to finish her. I spread my hand wide and uncurled my claws lifting my arm above my head in readiness to strike.

'Mia, no!' Elizabeth's cry was cut short as a golden wolf burst through the bushes and skidded to a halt a few feet away. I recognised Cody's scent immediately.

More wolves followed, a mix of colours: light brown, silver, black, and a dark brown, the latter being twice the size of the other wolves. I sniffed the air and my shoulders sagged as Zak's scent filled the small space. He bared his teeth and growled at me. My entire body shook as I tried to resist his cry. He was my brother, and he was trying to stop me from making a fatal mistake. He was also my alpha, and I couldn't act against him.

Lowering my arm, I backed away from Felicity and stood up to my full height. She stared up at me with pure hatred gleaming in her eyes. Blood poured from her neck wound and dribbled out of her mouth. I had no idea if she would, or could, recover from her wounds and the werewolf part of me didn't care. The human part of me, Mia, was slowly returning and my eyes grew wide as I looked down at my handiwork. My claws began to retract leaving a dull ache in my hands and my mouth felt normal again as my fangs disappeared.

'Leave,' I whispered. 'Before I kill you.'

Felicity scrambled to her feet and ran, tearing through the trees on wobbly legs, using her free hand to try to keep herself upright as she manoeuvred through the forest. I watched her until she disappeared from sight and then I kept watching that space for a long time not wanting to look at my brother, Cody, or the other wolves. What would they think of me? What had I become?

FIVE

I stared at my reflection in the mirror, my eyes flitting from the bruises on my cheek to the cut on my lip. Felicity had given it her all when we fought, throwing all her anger, fear, and training into hurting me. I didn't blame her. I couldn't. She was entitled to hate me for the beating I'd inflicted on her all those months ago and now, well, now she had more cause than ever to want me dead.

Is that how Frank had felt when he beat me? Had he lost all control of himself when he kicked and punched me? Was I no better than the man who raised me under a cloud of terror?

The wolves had dispersed quickly following my altercation with Felicity as they sensed the upcoming battle between their alpha and his little sister—the wannabe werewolf. I couldn't deny it any longer. I wasn't a proper wolf, I wasn't a valid or valuable member of the pack. I was a stupid girl who just so happened to have fangs and claws when someone pissed her off. I was a typical teenager.

Zak led me back to the farm in silence. Cody followed a few steps behind. I had an insane and inappropriate urge to giggle as I likened the scene to a prisoner being transported to their doom. I was Anne Boleyn!

No one spoke to me or even looked in my direction as I was escorted to my room. I wanted to express my annoyance that Zak hadn't left Lizzie's rescue up to me, Terry, and Cody but felt the need to follow with the entire pack. He'd had that planned all along, which was why they had all congregated when we left earlier. Zak had prepared himself for me screwing it all up.

The door closed behind me, and I only caught the slightest glimpse of Cody, his shoulders slumped and his eyes sad, before the loud clunk of the wood in the frame. I waited for a few moments and then tried the handle. It opened. I closed the door again, but the heavy weight in my chest lifted ever so slightly knowing they hadn't locked me up as Sebastian had.

That girl in the mirror was an imposter. She wasn't who I wanted to become. I'd survived so much in such a short time, and I knew I was stronger for it. I could feel that inner drive spurring me on to be better than the losers who had hurt me. I wasn't going to make the same mistakes, but here I was, banished to my room because I'd let my emotions get the better of me. I didn't know who to turn to for help. Zak was my brother but he was also the alpha; he had to be extra tough on me for the sake of the pack. Cody meant the world to me, but he was a valuable member of Zak's inner circle. Miss Ross and Elizabeth were like my family, but they didn't have the knowledge to figure this out.

There was only one person who could help me. One person who might know what I was becoming and how to handle it.

I closed my eyes and took a deep breath. Was I ready to deal with the devil? Was I so far gone that the only chance I had at finding the real Mia was in the hands of a maniac? I snapped my eyes open again. I saw a coldness there, a lack of empathy, and something else, something deeper and more frightening. I saw rage buried below the surface. Rage at myself, my mother, Frank, Zak, and Sebastian. If anyone could help me to figure it all out, then it was him. Sebastian could well be my only hope.

THE STARS LIT up the night sky as I sat by the open window. One of the wolves I didn't know delivered my evening meal. Clearly Zak didn't want me talking to my friends, and I couldn't blame him.

I could see the extra cars in the driveway and hear the voices of many visitors drifting up from the kitchen. Packs from all over the country had started to gather, and it was Zak's job to hear their stories and work out a plan of action. I didn't want to cause my brother any more heartache than he was already dealing with but I was also aware that without me in the picture he could concentrate all his efforts on saving the wolves and securing the packs' future.

Yes, he'd be mad, and so would Cody, Elizabeth, and Miss Ross but if I could return to them with answers that might help them rather than hinder them, they couldn't stay mad for long.

I sucked in a breath and slung my backpack over my shoulder, dropping my phone on the bed as I went. If I was going to do this, I couldn't have them contacting me or risk Zak tracing my phone. It was now or never. The warm and musical tones of my family and friends' voices vibrated through the floorboards pulling me in two directions. It would be too easy to slide between the sheets of my bed and wait for everyone else to look after me but I didn't do easy and I didn't do victim. I'd survived more than most girls my age and it was time to stand alone again and fight for what I believed in.

Swinging my legs out on the ledge, I waited until I could train my enhanced hearing onto the sounds from the kitchen.

'Why is the GA here?'

'That doctor has no right to use experimental serums on our children.'

'We don't have all the facts. Elizabeth told us the GA is here to review the academy after recent events. We have no idea if there is any link between them and the pharmaceutical company.'

'Yet our kids are still at risk.'

'It could be a free-for-all. If our kids have that injection they'll either die or they'll turn early. The hunters think they're free to hunt without remorse, killing our children.'

The conversation raged on with voices unknown to me contributing their thoughts. Zak was surprisingly quiet, perhaps taking in all the information and worries before working on a solution. I could hear Terry and Cody adding to the discussion with Terry offering his first-hand account of being held captive at Hood Academy and the many times they'd carried out a rescue.

As quietly as I could, I shimmied down the trellis that ran down the side of the house from my window, dropping lightly to the floor. Crouching for a few moments, I made sure that no one had heard me but I don't think the assembled packs would have heard a chainsaw over the heated discussion they were having.

Through the cosy glow of the kitchen light, I could see Zak at the head of the table, his brow furrowed as he listened to his friends. Cody stood behind him with Terry and Byron on either side. They had each other, and a small part of me was grateful for the fact that they were so close. Brothers united. Miss Ross would look out for Elizabeth, which only left me – the outsider. It was a role I'd played my entire life, and I slipped into it like an old pair of gloves. Sebastian might be a crazy scientist with more flaws than most human beings but he was also my biological father, and I had to hope and pray that this fact was enough to keep me safe, at least until I learned what I needed to about my genes.

I took one last look at my family and friends before melting into the darkness of the forest, their voices growing fainter with every step I took.

THE EMPTY BARN where I'd found Sebastian stood a short distance away. It was cloaked in shadows and looked as derelict as it was supposed to be. Finding my father in a secret room below the ramshackle building was the only clue I had. No doubt he would have moved, or been moved by whoever was in charge, but I hoped there was enough of his scent left for me to follow.

I climbed down the ladder into the blackness below. It didn't fill me with as much dread as when I'd descended the same steps in the hope of helping my friend. That inevitability that I was about to come face to face with my dad had hijacked the moment. At least this time I had a torch.

The room where I'd found Sebastian was now empty, the tables cleared of all paperwork, and the equipment he'd been using gone, the small imprints in the dust the only sign that he'd been here at all. I swivelled the torch towards the far corner, but the boxes with the pharmaceutical logo had also vanished.

A faint scuffling noise filled the air behind me causing the hairs on the back of my neck to stand up. Goose bumps trailed down my arms as I tuned my senses to the surrounding area and the entrance. If Sebastian was still lurking, maybe I would get a chance to talk to him before he launched into an assault or capture.

I clicked the torch off, plunging the room into darkness, and waited for my eyes to adjust. Sniffing the air, I tried to determine what, or who, I could be about to face. I lifted the torch above my head ready to wallop whoever appeared then I caught the faintest whiff of a familiar scent—lavender.

Elizabeth's pale face shone in the muted light cast by the window high up on the wall as she moved into the doorway. Her eyes were as wide as saucers, and yet I had the overwhelming urge to shout 'Boo!'

Instead, I lowered my makeshift weapon and walked to the centre of the room.

'What the hell are you doing here, Lizzie?'

She jumped at the sound of my voice then her eyes adjusted to the dim light, and she could make out my shape.

'I was worried you'd do something stupid,' she said glancing around the room. 'Like return to the scene of the crime.'

I huffed. It had been a reckless thing to do, but deep in my bones, I knew Sebastian wouldn't be here in person. I just needed to inhale his scent, gather my strength, and push forward.

A rustling behind Elizabeth's back drew my attention, and I almost yelped when a tiny figure darted out of the corridor to join us.

I stared from one face to the other.

'When did you think it was a good idea to bring Ari along?'

Elizabeth rolled her eyes and nudged the child with her elbow.

'See, I told you she wouldn't like it.'

Ari giggled.

'I saw you climb out of your window, so I went to get Lizzie. You're lucky I didn't tell Zak!' She put her tiny hands on her hips and tilted her chin looking every inch the defiant young pup she was.

I couldn't help but laugh at her stance. Elizabeth's shoulders relaxed, and she giggled too.

'What's the plan then?'

I raised an eyebrow.

'You don't think I'm going to let you run off on your own, do you? Mia, we've been friends for a while now so you should understand this whole friendship bond by now.'

I smiled. She was right. The two of us had been through so much together, and we made a pretty good team.

'I'm looking for Sebastian,' I said, squaring my shoulders so she knew I wouldn't be swayed from my decision.

It worried me that someone I cared about might get hurt during my mission and I was about to express this when Ari piped up, 'They took that man to Hood Academy.'

'What man?' Elizabeth asked.

'The one in the white coat who was here earlier.' She pointed to a lab jacket hanging on a hook behind the door.

I knelt down, so I was eye level with the youngster. 'Are you sure?'

'Yes, I followed him and another man and saw them go through a back door with a red cross on it.'

'He's going to the lab,' Elizabeth said. 'That door leads to the nurse's station, and we both know where it goes from there.'

A shiver skittered down my spine at the memory of those clinical rooms, and the abysmal experiments that had taken place over God knows how many years.

'He could be visiting Felicity.' I dropped my head as I wondered for the millionth time about her injuries after our fight in the forest. Had she made a full recovery or was she seriously ill and in need of Sebastian's medical assistance?

'That girl would survive a nuclear blast.' Elizabeth squeezed my hand as if reading my mind. 'Whether he's there as a visitor, doctor, or psycho scientist, we at least know where to begin.'

She was right, of course, and it was thanks to Ari's super snooping skills.

'Well done, Ari.' I placed a hand on her shoulder as she beamed with pride. 'Now, I need you to go back to the farm.'

She pulled out of my grasp and crossed her arms over her tiny chest, that defiant glint returning to her eyes.

'I'm not going anywhere. We're a team. You need me.'

I had to admit that so far it was Ari who had found the barn, discovered Elizabeth's captor, and kept a beady eye on my movements. Maybe she would be useful – but from a safe distance. I couldn't risk her life.

'Okay, yes, we need you, but you will do *everything* me and Lizzie tell you, or I'm sending you home.'

Ari grinned and raised a small hand to her forehead. 'Aye, aye, Captain.'

Elizabeth covered her laugh with a hand and moved away to investigate the empty space. I could only gawp at the fierce little werewolf as she clicked her heels together and followed Lizzie. I prayed that keeping Ari close wasn't a mistake.

'Look at this.' Elizabeth handed me a scruffy notepad with a logo printed in the top corner. Evermore Pharmaceuticals. It was the same logo that had covered the boxes, which had recently occupied the small space where we stood.

'I've seen this before,' Ari said. 'This was the picture on the doctor's jacket. The man who injected my sister and me.'

Another link perhaps between the strange pharmaceutical company offering the cure to the packs and Sebastian. Did that mean the GA was in on it too?

Could an agency dedicated to upholding the hunters' oath really step over the line and be responsible for killing entire packs? Entire families? My blood ran cold thinking about it.

I pocketed the notepad and gave the room one last sweep with my torch. 'We're not going to find any answers here.'

Elizabeth smiled, but I could see the glimmer of fear shining in her eyes. We both knew what the next step entailed. We both understood that returning to Hood Academy was necessary, but neither of us needed another run-in with Felicity or the GA.

I squared my shoulders and faced my friends. 'It looks like we're going back to school.'

SIX

I knew my brother was going to be mad at me when he found out I'd gone, but part of me hoped that he knew me well enough to understand my reasons. Since finding my way back to him, I'd battled with those feelings of being an outsider. Not because I hadn't turned, although I knew that was an issue for Zak, but because I wasn't what everyone expected. They had listened to the tales of my violent life with Frank when Terry had spied on me at Zak's request, and then the stories I told them about Hood Academy. They listened, scowled, shook their heads in disgust, and welcomed me into the sanctuary of their home, but I think they were expecting me to be a weak, timid victim. I wasn't a victim. I refused to live my life in fear.

They hadn't been prepared for the survivor in me to be so strong and so I was left on the edges of their lives, circling like the runt of the litter trying to fight its way to the dinner bowl.

Maybe Zak thought he was getting his little sister back, the one who wore pigtails and pleats in her skirt. The little girl who had idolised her big brother before he abandoned her to a life of terror. Instead, he got a teenager with uncontrollable rage and trust issues.

Now wasn't the time to mope about not fitting in. As the daughter of a werewolf *and* a hunter, it was inevitable that I would be odd, but even I couldn't have guessed how peculiar my situation would be.

Elizabeth stopped suddenly in front of me, and I bumped into her, snapping out of my inner musings.

'What is it?' I hissed.

She pointed ahead, and I saw the flickering porch light above the nurse's office door. The windows to the main reception area were dark, and no sound came from the surrounding area.

'Just a short run across the car park and we're in.'

I manoeuvred my way in front of Elizabeth and assessed the area. The main school building loomed up on the right; no lights shone on the dormitory floors. In the distance, across the large expanse of lawn, I saw the patio doors leading to Adam's old room. The door had been blocked off with heavy timber strips following Elizabeth's rescue.

Ari tugged on my sleeve and nodded in the direction of the car park. Felicity and her father pushed their way through the nurse's office door and onto the gravel. As Mr Parker pressed something in his palm, a long black car lit up like a Christmas tree, the lights flashing in time to the loud beeps that bounced off the cold stone of the academy.

Felicity wore a tight bandage around her throat and nursed her arm in a sling. She hobbled as she followed her father to the car. Within minutes the engine roared to life, and they drove off down the winding driveway and out through the gates on to the main road into town.

The three of us let out a collective breath and then giggled.

'At least we know Parker and my archnemesis aren't home now.'

'That's a relief. I don't think I could cope with seeing you...' Elizabeth's words trickled to a stop, and she looked up at me with glassy eyes. 'I'm so sorry, Mia. I didn't want to bring up, you know, *that* fight.'

I understood her trepidation. Losing it completely and nearly killing someone wasn't a high point in my life and I didn't want to discuss it with her any more than she did with me.

'It's fine,' I said. 'Let's get on with finding Sebastian.'

We made sure the area was secure and sprinted across the gravel car park until we stood underneath the porch light. I reached up and unhooked the casing around the bulb, tapping it with my torch until it flickered out. Darkness was our friend.

Elizabeth tried the door; it was unlocked. I mulled this over as we entered the deserted reception area of the nurse's office. If the door was left unlocked, that meant Sebastian was free to leave at any point but chose to stay. Self-doubt bubbled in my gut as I wondered if Sebastian would be willing to help me or if his preference was to lock me up for his experiments.

Visions of my mum rushed forward: her smile, her perfume, her devotion to a man who I wasn't even aware was my father. She'd kept it a secret, even from Sebastian himself, choosing only to tell her best friend, Miss Ross. The experiments Sebastian had done on my mother were done with her blessing. She'd wanted a cure for lycanthropy, not just for herself, but for Zak and me too. She didn't want us to turn. She'd wanted a different kind of life for her children.

That decision cost her everything, but even until the bitter end she still believed Sebastian was doing something good. How then had his work become so twisted that he was injecting young girls like Ari and either killing them or forcing an early turn?

The school hospital wing was exactly as I remembered it. There was a reception area with a small office for the doctor, a storeroom, and four patient rooms. All the areas fed off a large circular space with direct access to the school through the office. To any unsuspecting visitor, it was a mundane hospital wing, but the seventh door, set into a dark alcove, led to another part of the school that only a select few knew existed. The laboratories.

For generations, these secret rooms had been used to experiment on werewolves. Sebastian's reason was to find a cure, but for the scientists who had come before him, the wolves were merely a tool and there to be violated, often killed in the process. Death clung to the walls.

I closed in on the seventh door, turning the handle slowly. Putting my shoulder against the metal, I pushed it open. As we had discovered during our time at Hood Academy, the laboratories were a row of single rooms each leading off one another. Like the rest of the nurse's area, the room we entered was in total darkness, but a sliver of light escaped from under the next door along.

Ari pointed at the floor, and I nodded to confirm I'd seen it. We had no way of knowing who or what lay beyond. It could be Sebastian, or it could be a room full of the Governors' Agency members.

'What do you want to do?' Elizabeth pressed close to ask the question, her fingers tightening around my arm as she spoke.

'There's only one thing we can do,' I said, and took a step towards the door.

Elizabeth sucked in a deep breath and grabbed Ari, wrapping an arm protectively around the child.

THE LIGHT WAS harsh against my eyes as I strode into the room. I didn't have any carefully laid-out plan about what to do next. I decided to adopt Miss Ross's fiery attitude and hope it paid off. As it turned out, the room was empty, and my attempt to look in control was wasted.

'It's okay, guys, you can come in.'

Elizabeth and Ari slid into the room behind me keeping to the edges as they took in the wall-to-ceiling shelving units filled with boxes upon boxes of pharmaceutical products. The logo we'd come across earlier was stamped on the side of every container.

The shelves took up all the wall space with smaller units dotted through the centre of the room. As far as I could tell, all the boxes were sealed and ready for shipping.

'Look at this!' Elizabeth motioned for me to join her.

She'd pulled one of the boxes out and was studying the label printed on the top.

'Its postal address is Cornwall. Miss Ross and Adam worked at the Cornish Academy before coming here.'

I took the small penknife I carried out of my pocket and slid the blade down the centre of the box. The label peeled apart as the box sprang open to reveal its contents.

Short silver tubes were bundled together in elastic bands. I pulled one free and lifted it up to the light. There was a tiny button on one end and when pushed a needle popped out from the opposite side.

Ari gasped and took a step back.

'That's what they gave my sister and me,' she said, a quiver in her voice.

I pushed the button and a green liquid ejected from the needle, spraying all over the floor. So this was Sebastian's serum. These tiny vials could kill, or destroy a child's life with the press of one button. I felt sick.

A loud crash from beyond the next door caused us all to yelp. The blood screamed in my ears as my heart thundered in my chest. Ari flew behind Elizabeth, and I once again doubted my decision to bring her along.

The door handle squealed as I turned it, giving away our position to whoever stood on the other side. It was too late to back out now, so I pushed on the door and let it swing wide.

THE COLOUR DRAINED from my face as I looked around the room. Elizabeth mumbled under her breath as she pushed Ari behind her.

There were five gurneys on either side of the room, ten beds in total, and each one contained a child, some no older than five or six. All wore brightly coloured pyjamas as if this was some upbeat children's ward. I fought against the rising nausea as I moved into the room. Behind the door, a silver tray lay upturned on the floor, its contents spilling out under the nearest bed. A young girl wriggled and squirmed, the terror in her eyes catching me off guard.

I held my hands up as I approached.

'We're not going to hurt you,' I said. 'We're here to help.'

I nodded at Elizabeth, and we both set to work checking each child for needle marks. Ari darted around the room connecting with each child and calming their distress. Seeing someone of their own age seemed to work and all ten captives gathered in the centre of the room looking up at me with an air of expectation.

'What are we going to do with them?'

Elizabeth's question vocalised the thoughts whirling through my head. What the hell were we going to do with them all? Had they been injected? Were they a danger to anyone, or themselves? Damn Sebastian for doing this.

The young girl who had knocked the tray over stepped forward like a pint-sized spokesperson.

'The doctor told us we would be cured if we behaved.' She spoke so quietly I had to lean forward to catch her words. 'He was lying, wasn't he?'

'What makes you say that?'

'They took us away from our families in the middle of the night. You don't do that if you want to cure someone.'

I couldn't argue with her logic, and I wondered if Sebastian had considered this approach.

'Who took you?'

She shrugged her shoulders. 'I don't know who they were; we'd never seen them before. The men wore black jumpers.'

'Men?' Elizabeth stepped forward. 'Not girls in grey jump-suits?'

The girl shook her little blonde head.

Elizabeth turned her back to the group and leaned in to whisper, 'It wasn't Felicity or her goons then. Maybe Parker *is* using the GA to do his dirty work now.'

'We need to dig a bit deeper,' I said. 'There will be files in Sebastian's office. We need to get upstairs.'

We both looked over at the grubby faces of the children, their floaty hospital gowns making them look like a gaggle of ghosts at a Halloween party.

Before either of us could come up with an appropriate answer, Ari stepped forward and cleared her throat. 'Right you lot, it's time for us to leave. My friends need to stay and find the bad doctor, so you need to follow me.'

I was once again astounded at the resilience and strength of someone so young. I knelt down and pulled her into a tight hug.

'Thank you, Ari,' I whispered.

'Aye, aye, Captain.'

Elizabeth giggled and circled Ari into another embrace.

'Be careful, keep to the shadows, and follow the scent straight to the Mills farm. Zak will know what to do.'

The children followed Ari out of the door without question, their backs straight and senses tuned to their surroundings. I had no doubt in my mind that they would get home safely under Ari's supervision.

IT WAS JUST Elizabeth and me now. We knew there were no answers in the rooms we'd been through so the only route to take was forward.

'Let's go,' I said.

It didn't take us long to make it through to the room containing Hood Academy's secret filing cabinets. It was here I discovered the details about my mother's death, and that Sebastian was responsible for the death of Cody's family. It wasn't somewhere I ever thought I'd return to, but here we were digging through mounds of papers and drawers of notes.

I wished we knew what we were looking for. Evidence of Parker's diabolical scheme, Sebastian's involvement, the traitorous actions of the Governors' Agency, anything.

We were both so involved in our search that neither of us heard the door open until it was too late.

'What are you girls doing in here?'

I swung towards the voice, scattering papers across the floor as I went. Sebastian stood in the doorway, his face partly hidden in the shadows. He wore suit trousers and a pale blue shirt rolled up at the sleeves. Once upon a time his sheer presence would have filled the doorframe and radiated into any room filling it with his powerful energy. He didn't seem to be such an imposing figure as I once remembered. What had happened to break him? There was an ache in my chest as I took in the sight of the man standing before us, the man who studied me now with concern in his eyes.

'Mia, you came back.'

SEVEN

Sebastian stepped into the room and closed the door behind him cutting off the only route we had into the main school building, his expression leaving me in no doubt his action had been intentional.

I took a deep breath and squared my shoulders. What I needed to do went against everything I believed in, but this man, my father, was the only one who had the answers.

'I need your help, Sebastian.'

His face crumpled, and he let out a strangled cry. I couldn't prevent the pull I felt to offer him some support, but I also had a strong sensation to hit him and run away.

'I knew you'd come to me in the end,' he sobbed. 'Curing your lycanthropy was your mother's final wish, and I know she would be so happy that you've finally...'

I held my hand up to halt his ramblings.

'I'm not here for a cure, Sebastian, I'm here for answers.'

He recovered swiftly, wiping his eyes on the folds of his shirtsleeves.

'I'm not sure I understand.'

'Your serum is being used across the country to kill children.'

He was shaking his head.

'No, no, that's not true. The serum was designed to *help* save the children from ever suffering the pain of turning. Evermore Pharmaceuticals thinks my work is groundbreaking and they've sent doctors out in the wolf community to share our work.'

'Is that why you had ten kids in there?' I jerked my thumb in the direction of the room we'd recently left. 'So you could *share* your work with them?'

Sebastian glanced between me and the door as he struggled with his conscience. I could see the conflict as it raged behind his eyes.

'You let them go.' It wasn't a question because he knew from my history that I would indeed have let them go. I gave a curt nod of my head.

'You shouldn't have done that, Mia. Mr Parker will be furious, and he will double his efforts to find and kill you.'

'What's Parker got to do with it?' I was fishing for information.

He shuffled his feet as he considered his answer.

'Mr Parker is a silent partner in Evermore Pharmaceuticals. It's his money that's funding our research and production.'

'It wasn't that long ago you called him a blackmailer.'

'I was wrong. Since becoming headmaster Mr Parker has opened up to my way of thinking. He told me he now believes in the work I'm doing for the good of the community.'

'Well, your silent partner is making you create a serum that kills most of the recipients or forces them to turn into werewolves earlier than they should. I've met a ten-year-old werewolf who watched her sister die after your filth was injected into them.'

'No, that's not possible, the serum is designed to prevent the werewolf gene from mutating. It acts as a blocker. I couldn't perfect a serum to reverse the transformation, which is why your mother died, but I'm still working on that. I hope to keep working on that to help you when you want it.'

'I will never want your help in that area, Sebastian. I'm happy the way I am and have no intention...'

'How can you be happy?' Sebastian interrupted me. 'You don't have the power to make a full shift. Your DNA is split between a hunter and a werewolf so you could never be a full-fledged wolf.'

I bristled at his words and sifted through my brain for possible solutions.

'Zak was born of a werewolf and a human, but he's an alpha!' I crossed my arms over my chest and stared defiantly at my father.

'Human DNA can be easily overridden by werewolf DNA, so any wolf who has a human mother or father will always have the wolf gene. You're different, Mia. You're a hybrid, and that's incredibly rare.'

I blinked.

'I'm a what?'

'A hybrid. You are a perfect fifty-fifty split of your mother and me. You're werewolf and hunter in equal parts. It's only after I saw you the other day that I realised. Hybrids are rare as not many hunters and werewolves mix, socially, let alone romantically. I found a few books on the topic if you want to read them.'

I saw Sebastian's gesture for what it was. He was offering me a truce by proposing to give me books that might answer my questions. Yes, his primary game plan was to strip me of my wolf side, but he understood my desire to find out more about who I was.

Elizabeth had remained silent throughout our exchange and only now approached to lay her hand on my arm.

'Mia, if Parker is behind this we need to stop him before he kills anyone else.'

I nodded and turned my attention back to Sebastian, as the look on his face shifted between anxiety and hope.

'If you can help us prove Mr Parker is using you and your serum to kill the packs' children then I'll...I'll take your DNA test so we can find out more.'

Elizabeth grabbed my hand. 'No, Mia. You can't trust him! He might inject you with God knows what and kill you like he did with your mum.'

I knew that I was risking so much by putting my trust and faith in a mad scientist, but he was also my father, my own flesh and blood. Staring into Sebastian's eyes, I saw something there that made me believe in him. Pride. His face shone with the kind of dewy glow that every parent gets when their child surpasses their expectations. It was something I could hold onto during the days

OATH KEEPER

and weeks to come. I was putting my faith in someone who had saved me then tried to destroy me in equal parts.

SEBASTIAN LED US up to the central school building and into the science classroom. Each wooden table had a Bunsen burner and microscope set up ready for the new term.

'Wait here.' Sebastian motioned for us to sit at one of the tables before hurrying out through a side door.

'I don't trust him,' Elizabeth hissed. 'What if he gets the GA?'

'We've got no choice, Lizzie.' I wriggled out of my coat and threw it on the nearest stool. 'He's the only one who can help us stop Parker, because he's here, on the inside.'

'He's not the only one on the inside.' A deep male voice carried across the room causing both of us to jump.

Adam stood in the doorway, a grin plastered across his handsome face. Elizabeth was off the chair and in his arms within seconds. I averted my eyes as they shared a moment. Reunited after so long.

'Good to see you again, Mia,' he said striding over to where I was sitting.

I embraced my friend, clinging to him for longer than was probably acceptable. Having him here filled me with joy, not only for my best friend but also for our cause. Adam had always been a tower of strength during our past adventures.

'What are you doing here? Not that I'm not thrilled to see you.'

Adam chuckled. 'Miss Ross called and told me about Lizzie being taken in for questioning. By the time I'd driven up from Cornwall she was free.' He folded Elizabeth into a warm embrace and kissed the tip of her nose. 'Sebastian told me you were here.'

A lightness filled my chest at Adam's words. It was good to have him back, and good that Sebastian hadn't reacted negatively to him being here.

'Does Zak know we're here?' I dreaded the reply, but Adam laughed and slapped a big brown hand on my shoulder.

'Let's say, I wouldn't want to be you when you get home.'

Shit!

'Right.' Sebastian returned with a large cardboard box. He placed it on the counter and shifted it so the pharmaceutical logo faced the other way. 'I'm going to show you, scientifically, what the serum can do.'

He opened the box and took out one of the silver tubes, unscrewing the cap. He flipped the switch on the monitor linked to his microscope and placed a glass slide on the counter where he emptied some of the liquid out.

'Hmm, that's odd,' he mumbled.

'What is?'

'Well, it shouldn't be green.'

He lifted the slide and carefully slid it under the clips to hold the plate in place, fiddling with the focus controls on the side of the equipment. Leaning over the microscope, he studied the liquid through the eyepiece.

Green swirls filled the monitor screen, and we waited for his scientific explanation. He fiddled with the controls. We waited some more.

'Well? Are you going to give us this science lesson or not?' I asked.

Sebastian stood up and moved away from the microscope, running his hands through his hair in that agitated manner that always worried me.

'This isn't my serum,' he said. 'It's been modified.'

We all watched the screen. It could have been a photograph of the Aurora Borealis for all we knew. The patterns smeared across the image bled from deep green to yellow.

'What do you mean by *modified*?'

He snapped into action, opening the desk drawer and rummaging around until he found a small glass vial. Inching the glass plate out of its restraints he replaced it with a fresh slide and emptied the new, clear liquid out.

The monitor changed the image to show us what looked like a clear puddle with tiny grey blobs floating through the middle of it.

'That,' he stabbed a finger at the screen, 'is what my serum looks like. The serum that prevents a child from turning. I don't know what *this* is.' He waved a hand at the green blob oozing off the rejected slide. It was like toxic waste compared to the clean image on the screen.

Opening up the box, Sebastian tipped out more of the silver tubes and began unscrewing the caps. All the contents were green.

'Can you work out what modifications were made?' Adam asked.

'Not from here. I need my equipment.'

'Let's take it downstairs to the lab then,' I said, already halfway to the door.

'No, my lab isn't here at school, it's at my home.'

'But, I thought you lived here, at the school.'

Clearly it hadn't been on his to-do list to share with his only relative the simple fact that he lived off-site. I felt the strangest feeling of rejection but pushed it aside.

'No, I have a house in the forest, near the edge of town. It's been in my family for generations, but I've never disclosed the whereabouts. Not even the GA or Parker know where it is.'

In that single moment, I realised Sebastian wasn't all bad. For him to own up to the existence of a safe house made me feel warm inside.

'Let's pack up and go then. The faster we get you to your equipment, the faster we can work out what Parker has done and stop him.'

Sebastian scanned the room as if seeing us all for the first time.

'We don't have time. If what you say is true and this modified serum can kill then we need to stop the distribution. It will take me much too long to work out what they've done and rectify it.'

'Okay, so you think stopping the distribution is the best plan, but how do we do that? I wouldn't know where to start.' I realised there was a hint of panic in my voice. We weren't dealing with overdue homework here, this was serious, up to your neck in danger stuff, and as I looked around the room, I noticed everyone was looking at me.

Elizabeth moved first, rushing towards me but deviating at the last second to spin the box at my side. The Evermore Pharmaceuticals logo glared up at us. Of course! We knew who the distributor was; now all we had to do was shut them down.

SEBASTIAN'S OFFICE HAD almost changed beyond all rec-
ognition. His desk was still the same and dominated the centre of
the room, but the books were absent, the paintings stripped from
the walls, and the photo frames containing the happy images of my
mum gone, to be replaced by the smarmy grin of my nemesis, Felicity, and other people I didn't recognise. Parker had commandeered
the headmaster's office after the incident with Sebastian and me on
the back lawn.

I wasn't surprised that Sebastian had been sacked. It was either that or a suspension at the very least. Instead, it appeared that
Mr Parker had taken full control of the academy and relegated Sebastian to the laboratories below the school, a bit like Frankenstein
locked away in his lair.

I shook the thoughts from my mind and walked across to the
mahogany desk, tugging at the desk drawers in search of clues.
The smaller drawers opened without any issue, and an assortment
of pens, pencils, and elastic bands spilled out when I tipped them
onto the floor. The slim-fronted middle drawer, however, remained
locked. I flipped open my penknife and set to work, hacking at the
lock until I heard the crunch and click.

It slid open revealing two folders sitting side by side. The blue
file on the right contained a list of the hunter academies around
the UK and the last known whereabouts of the country's packs. I
stuffed it into my backpack, hoping the information might come in
handy in the future. The folder on the left was thicker and included
pages of formulas, photographs of indigenous tribes, information
on plants and herbs and, most importantly, an address for the Evermore Pharmaceuticals warehouses in Nottingham.

'Jackpot!'

BY THE TIME I returned to the nurse's office my friends and
Sebastian were waiting. Adam had packed bags full of supplies and
was off-loading one of them on Elizabeth who giggled as the weight
nearly tipped her over. Sebastian was wearing a short navy coat and

walking boots with a large holdall strapped across his chest. His brow creased as I walked in clutching the thick folder.

'Thought this might be helpful,' I said handing it over to him. He flipped open the cover and thumbed through the images.

'Interesting. It seems Mr Parker's frequent visits to the native tribes might have something to do with the modification of the serum. It's possible that he used a herb or plant root.'

'The science of how and why is your department, Sebastian, I'm only interested in the address for Evermore.'

'You found it!'

I nodded. 'There's a warehouse in Nottingham. That's the closest one, so I think we should start there. At least it means we can keep the local packs safe while we deal with the rest of the distribution centres.'

I looked at the expectant faces of my friends and smiled.

'Are you sure you're up for this?'

Adam laughed, and it bubbled up from deep in his throat.

'You really think we're going to let you do this without us, Mia? No way, we're in this together. We're family.'

My heart threatened to split wide open at his words. Family. My real family was fractured beyond belief. Mum was dead, my brother had murdered my stepdad, and my biological dad was, well, he was trying. Elizabeth and Adam, on the other hand, believed that family extended beyond your DNA, and they made all the horror and danger we faced worth fighting for.

EIGHT

We drove in silence, Adam taking control of Sebastian's black SUV. Elizabeth sat up front with her boyfriend, not wanting to let him out of her sight after so long apart, and I rode in the back with Sebastian. He had been poring over the contents of the folder for a while, his jaw set in a hard line as he delved further into the information.

'Find anything useful?' I asked.

'Hmm?' He lifted his head slowly as if only just realising he wasn't on his own. 'Oh, yes, it would be quite brilliant if it wasn't so awful. Mr Parker appears to have travelled extensively to search for a specific species of plant. His notes refer to the strychnine tree found in Southeast Asia.'

'Strychnine? As in rat poison?'

'Yes, exactly. I'm impressed you knew that, Mia.'

I huffed. 'I might not have participated a whole lot in science class, but I did listen.'

'Well, the tree contains the poison, and for many years it was used as a common rodenticide, but somehow he has genetically engineered it to blend with my serum. Strychnine causes deadly muscular convulsions, the type of convulsions you would experience during a turn on the full moon.'

'So it's hidden in plain sight because the packs would expect their children to be convulsing?'

'Precisely! What's interesting is that some of the children are able to fight it. Did you say you'd met one who had turned early?'

'Ari, she's ten years old and a fledgling wolf.' I smiled as I thought about her. She was going to make an impressive wolf one day. 'She was taken with her sister up in Yorkshire to receive your so-called cure. Her sister didn't make it.'

'Interesting.' Sebastian's head bobbed up and down as he took in this information and flicked back through the notes.

'Why did Ari survive but her sister didn't?' I asked, hoping I could give Ari and her family some useful information to ease their grief.

'I'm not sure, it's actually more fascinating that your friend survived at all as this stuff should, by rights, kill anyone who takes it!'

'So Parker is distributing a flawed serum under the secret protection of a pharmaceutical company who claim to be sympathetic to the werewolf cause. They're enticing the pack leaders to hand over their children with the hope of a cure.'

'It certainly seems that way.'

'Why would they want to do that? Surely if the alphas cured their kids, the werewolf lines would come to an end.'

Sebastian put down the folder and glanced over at me, his eyes showing a warmth I had never seen before. Or perhaps never noticed.

'Your mother wanted you and Zak to receive a cure so you wouldn't have to go through the pain of turning or having the burning desire to hunt and kill.'

I was briefly reminded of my run-in with Felicity and the fact I'd nearly killed her in my heightened emotional state.

'Not all wolves hunt and kill,' I said, thinking of all the packs I'd met so far.

'Sometimes you don't have a choice, the turn changes you mentally as well as physically, and any harm you inflict is often done without intention.'

Again I thought about Felicity. Had I intended to finish her off? Was I capable of killing her, or of killing anyone? It was true that the wolf side of my personality was ruled by emotions, and I had been struggling to control this, but could it drive me to take a human life?

Sebastian continued. 'As a parent, you would want to do everything in your power to keep your child safe. Just because the alphas are giving their pack the option to prevent a turn doesn't mean they forfeit the lifestyle and community of the pack.'

'I guess so. Although...' I looked away and watched the shadows whip past the car window as I tried to sort out my jumbled thoughts. 'I don't think I belong in a pack, being a hybrid like you said. I feel like I've got one foot in the hunter camp and the other in the pack, but I don't really belong to either.'

Sebastian leaned over and placed his hand over mine.

'Sometimes you create your own pack without even realising it.'

He patted my hand and inclined his head towards Elizabeth and Adam. My pack. I'd been so hung up about being an outsider that I hadn't noticed what I was creating within my circle of friends. We all watched over each other, cared for one another, like a proper pack would. I felt a tug in my chest as I realised, almost for the first time, that I did belong somewhere after all.

Sebastian rummaged around in his bag and pulled out a notebook. It had a creamy golden cover and well-worn pages. He handed it to me with a small smile.

I flicked it open and the word *hybrid* jumped out at me.

'It might help answer a few of your questions,' he said.

I flipped open the first page and began reading, absorbed in the notes scribbled in the book.

The power of the pack runs through their veins, and yet the strength, discipline, and leadership qualities of the hunter are also clearly prominent

It went on to talk about the dual personality of a hybrid, and I was about to laugh at the similarities between me and the notes when Adam broke into my thoughts as he slowed the car down and switched off the headlights.

'We're here!'

We all gazed up at the imposing structure looming out of the darkness. The warehouse was long and thin, its plain grey walls stretching for at least a mile behind to a newly constructed glass entrance, the Evermore logo emblazoned across the top half of the glass with a smoky background to help it stand out.

'Okay, so what do we do now?' Elizabeth's bright blue eyes were wide as she turned in her seat to look back at me.

'We burn it down.' It was the only way I could think of destroying all the serum and prevent the facility from being used. Yes, we could break in and steal the boxes, but that would only put a dent in their sickening plans; I wanted to obliterate them.

THERE WAS A large docking area near the back of the warehouse where two trucks were parked up presumably awaiting their shipments. Adam broke into one and confirmed it was empty, but the other had already been loaded.

'Perhaps we could steal this one,' suggested Sebastian as he climbed into the truck's cab. 'I'm sure I could drive it if necessary.'

'Maybe later, we need to destroy the warehouse first. Did you see any security?'

Adam nodded. 'There are two guards at the front of the building. One of them is asleep at the desk and the other is watching a late-night chat show. If we're careful, we can be in and out before they know it.'

'Okay, let's get on with it.'

We all squeezed under the roller shutter door that Adam and Sebastian had managed to pry open with a crowbar from the truck. From the outside it shouldn't be immediately obvious that anything was amiss if the security guards were to venture out of the comfort and warmth of their office and do a patrol.

The inside space was cavernous, with high ceilings, and long racking units stretching the full length of the storeroom. Thousands of boxes displayed the Evermore logo.

'How do we know which boxes contain the serum?'

It hadn't occurred to me that Evermore probably supplied other products as well as Parker's evil werewolf-killing serum. Did we have time to sort through them all?

'We're going to have to burn it all.' It was the only option. Time wasn't on our side. Parker would sweep across the country like a disease making sure every pack was offered the *cure;* he wouldn't hesitate in his actions, and I had to adopt the same attitude.

We searched around the store until we found five large containers of cleaning fluid with a Warning: Highly Flammable sign on the packaging and began to soak the boxes, leaving a trail in the hope that one box would ignite the next and so on. Once done we all stood by the exit and took in a collective breath. This was it.

Adam lit the match and threw it into the nearest box. It caught light at once and began to crackle and pop as the flames devoured the cardboard.

'We need to leave, now! Once the fire reaches the silver tubes filled with the serum, they'll go up like fireworks, and goodness knows what else this place is storing.'

We scurried under the door and rolled out onto the packing area, taking in a great lungful of air to rid ourselves of the cloying scent of cleaning fluid. The flames reached the first tube as we jumped down onto the tarmac, and the bang caused us all to drop to our knees instinctively. One after the other the boxes exploded, and smoke poured out from under the shutter door.

We pushed backward, breaking into a sprint as the booms got louder, rushing for Sebastian's SUV and the protection it offered.

The entire warehouse was ablaze now, and none of us could turn our faces away as the fire tore through the structure. The speed at which it moved both startled and impressed me.

The glass entrance shattered under the intense heat, spraying shards of the blackened Evermore logo over the car park. The two bewildered security guards stumbled out of the main door sprinting for safety, and as we drove away, the back wall buckled and fell, crushing the two trucks in the loading area under the twisted metal struts.

None of us spoke. Adam sped away and only switched on the headlights when we were at a safe distance. We passed a police car and three fire engines tearing down the main road towards the warehouse oblivious to the fact that they'd been so close to the arsonists responsible for the destruction they were about to find.

'Well, that's one down,' said Adam breaking the tension in the car. 'Where do we go next?'

Sebastian shuffled the files in his lap and opened up the folder containing the academies and locations of the packs.

'Looking at the schedule in Parker's files it says a shipment was delivered to Somerset yesterday, which means they should be rolling out the injections in the next few hours.'

I squinted at the clock on the dashboard, 4 a.m. If we pushed hard, we might make it in time to stop any of the children receiving the serum.

Adam caught my eye in the mirror and winked. 'Somerset then?' he asked.

'Somerset it is,' I confirmed.

MY HEAD BOUNCED off the car window as I was jolted awake. Sebastian snored softly from his seat next to me, and Elizabeth's head hung forward cradled by her seat belt. The sun had risen and as I rubbed my eyes and stretched, I glanced around at the scenery flashing by.

'Welcome to sunny Somerset,' Adam said from the driving seat.

'I'm so sorry, Adam. I never meant to fall asleep and leave all the driving up to you.'

'Do you drive?'

'Well, no, obviously, but Sebastian could have taken over for a while.' I looked across at my father as his mouth hung open and a little snore escaped. 'Or maybe not!'

We both giggled, and I wriggled forward in my seat so I could chat with my friend.

'Do you think we'll find the alpha in time?'

I shook my head. 'I'm not sure. I hope we can, but these Evermore doctors have been so convincing in their argument that no alpha, or parent for that matter, could resist putting their child forward for a lycanthropy cure.'

'Would you take it if you could?'

It was a valid question and one I'd contemplated several times when Sebastian locked me in the hospital wing all those months ago.

'I don't know. It's not like I'm a full werewolf. I don't have to experience the excruciating pain of every bone in my body breaking and resetting. For me, it was easy, apart from my gum aching where the fangs slide out.'

'What's it like? Did anything else change for you?'

'Everything changed. I can hear what people are saying when they're far away, and all the smells are stronger too. It's pretty neat apart from this thirst to rip people's throats out.'

Adam laughed. 'By *people* you mean Felicity.'

'Uh-huh, I only stopped because Zak turned up and did his alpha mojo on me. Don't get me wrong, I'm glad he stopped me, but up until that moment I would have happily sliced her throat open.'

'Good to know, I'll be sure to stay on your good side then.'

I punched him on the arm and laughed.

Elizabeth stirred in her seat and gave a little sigh. 'Is it morning already?'

Adam slipped his hand into hers. 'Only just.'

Sebastian yawned from behind me, and I sat back to take in the sight of my friends and family, fighting by my side to right a terrible wrong done to the werewolf community. It felt good to be doing something worthwhile.

THE PACK LIVED in the woods near the Somerset Hunters Academy, and as we approached the turn for the alpha's house, we saw the school from the road. It was nothing like Hood Academy. Instead of the grandiose setting of Hood's majestic gardens and historical backdrop, this school occupied a modern building with tinted glass windows, and resembled an office block rather than an establishment for werewolf hunters.

'Ugh, it's ugly!' Elizabeth agreed with my first impression.

'The GA have spent large sums renovating this centre following a recent fire,' Sebastian said. 'They wanted it to be the flagship school for the UK.'

I huffed. 'Well it needs burning down again.'

'Oh no! We're not going to burn this place to the ground too, are we?'

I laughed at the squeal in Elizabeth's voice and the unintentional way she still scrubbed at her hands where it appeared the cleaning fluid had irritated her skin.

'No, Lizzie. We'll leave this one standing. We're here to prevent the wolves from getting that serum and nothing else. If we can do what we need to without the hunters even knowing we were here then that's even better.'

Adam pulled off the main road opposite the academy and drove for a mile down a dirt track, which ended at a scenic wooded picnic area. As we all climbed out of the car to stretch our legs, I heard the roar of the sea in the distance.

I turned my face up to catch the early morning sun. There was no real warmth in it yet, but it held the promise of a pleasant day ahead, which was a blessing as I realised I'd left my coat behind at Hood Academy. I tuned my senses in to listen to the surrounding wildlife noises and picked up something different, a commotion that wasn't at home in this environment. It almost sounded like a playground chant, or a bully taunting their victim. Before I could mention anything to my friends, a shrill scream tore through the wind.

I broke into a run, sprinting towards the sound, my senses switching on to full alert. I could hear Lizzie and Adam running after me, crashing through the trees in pursuit. There was a dull ache in my jaw, and I realised my fangs had slid forward, and the pounding in my head increased with every slap of my feet against the dry path.

A second scream ricocheted off the trees, and I adjusted my route, breaking through the treeline and heading deeper into the woods. Nothing could have prepared me for what I found.

Three young children, no more than twelve years old, thrashed around on the ground, their bodies twisting and convulsing as the pain shot through their tiny frames. One black-haired boy and three girls stood over them all dressed in the grey jumpsuits I recognised as the hunters' uniform. Instead of helping the children, they watched the spectacle like it was paid entertainment.

Bursting into the small clearing, I growled at the hunters, startling them into action. By the surprised looks on their faces they'd never seen a hybrid, or at the very least they'd never seen a wolf in the daylight. Their wooden staffs lifted in unison as they circled towards me. From the nervous glances they gave each other, they were unsure how to deal with me. One last look at the children pushed any rational thoughts I had aside and angered me enough to snarl at the foursome. My claws flicked out as I shook my hands and flexed them, clicking the nails together. Beads of sweat covered each of the students' foreheads and the sound of their hearts pounding filled me with surprising joy. I wanted them to fear me, I wanted them to panic and forget their training, and part of me wanted them to run so I could hunt each of them down.

Adam burst through the trees causing one of the hunters to cry out.

'Help us!' she yelled, her eyes imploring my friend to assist them.

Adam ignored her pleas and moved towards the children, kneeling beside them to check their pulse and try to calm the convulsions. Lizzie arrived soon after and skirted around the edge of the clearing to Adam's side. After checking on the children and her boyfriend, she moved to stand next to me.

'Who are you?' It was the boy who spoke, taking a step forward in a bid to assert his authority. I growled, and he jumped back.

Elizabeth ignored him. 'You're students at the academy.' It wasn't a question. 'How many children have been injected with that serum?'

'How do you know about the serum?'

'Because I'm the one who created it.' Sebastian walked into the clearing and stalked over to where the children writhed on the floor in agony. He flipped open a bag and took out a small flask. 'Here, get them to drink this, it might help with the pain.' He handed Adam the container and leaned in closer as my friend whispered something in Sebastian's ear. He nodded and squared his shoulders before moving to my side.

'I'm Dr Roberts from Hood Academy in Nottingham, and the serum you are using on these innocents is defective. I'm here to re-call all vials.'

His voice boomed with authority, and I shifted my stance so I could study him. He looked like he did the night he first walked into my life: dignified, strong, and someone to be respected. Adam had no doubt instructed Sebastian on what to say but he had played his part well. A bubbling of pride lit up my chest.

'We weren't told about any recall. Headmaster Gregory sent us out to do a job, and we've done it.' The boy gestured towards the children. 'Killing werewolves is what the hunters' oath is all about after all.' He slid his predatory gaze upon me, and I felt the corners of my mouth curl into a snarl.

'Bring it on,' I whispered flexing my claws once more.

Elizabeth stepped in front of me sensing my need to lunge forward and tear the kid's face off.

'Our friend is a hybrid, she is part wolf, and part hunter so she understands our oath perfectly well. We don't want to fight you; we just want to stop the killing of innocent children.'

'Well, sweetheart, that's too bad because we came out here for a fight and so that's what you're gonna get.'

For a moment I wondered if we'd found the male version of Felicity before snapping into action and leaping forward to knock the closest girl to the ground. She screamed and dropped her staff, which rolled harmlessly away. Her eyes sparked with fear as I traced a claw down the side of her face.

'Leave this place before I rip you apart piece by piece.' I growled.

She was on her feet and running before her friends could help. Another girl joined her and disappeared into the treeline.

The boy rounded his staff on me and stood his ground. If I wasn't so overcome with rage, I might have been impressed. Lizzie approached the remaining girl, her fists held high as she prepared to fight alongside me.

'Come on then, sweetheart; let's see what a hybrid's made of.'

I heard Sebastian's audible tut as he stepped aside to give me room to manoeuvre. I didn't need the extra space, I only needed enough room to reach across and cut the idiot's cheek. He cried out, and it felt good.

'Nobody calls me sweetheart apart from my boyfriend.' He'd picked the wrong person if it was a fight he was after. Felicity nearly lost her life for calling me wolf girl, so this smarmy kid was in serious trouble. I knew I needed to rein it in this time, as Zak wasn't around to use his alpha connection.

The boy's staff flew through the air and connected with my shoulder. I flinched but shook off the pain, swinging my arm out to smash the wood from his grasp. It hit the floor, breaking into two pieces. The hunter wasn't finished though and pushed forward punching me first in the face and then in the stomach. My cheek stung from the blow, and the ache in my jaw intensified, but I didn't go down. He advanced again, but I swung my leg out high in a roundhouse kick connecting with the side of his head. He dropped like a stone, blood pouring from his ear.

'Enough!' I screamed, the sound echoing off the surrounding trees.

Lizzie held on to the girl's arms as she squirmed and tried to flee, clearly eager to leave the boy to fend for himself.

'I don't think much of your hunter friends,' I said standing over him. 'Two have deserted you and she looks seconds away from ditching your ass. So much for looking after each other and uniting against the common enemy.'

He spat at my feet. '*They* are the common enemy.' He pointed at the children.

'No,' I said. 'They're kids who happen to have been born to werewolf families; they didn't ask for this.'

I realised my voice sounded normal again and a quick check of my hands proved my claws had retracted and the fangs had disappeared. I was Mia again.

'What's your name?'

The boy looked up at me, his green eyes filled with loathing. 'Ethan,' he replied.

I held out my hand to help him up and his brow creased as he contemplated slapping it away or accepting it. 'I'm Mia, and this is Lizzie, Adam, and Sebastian.'

He wrinkled his nose as he took my hand, acting as if I might infect him with some deadly disease. I pulled him to standing where he began dusting off his jumpsuit. I was half expecting him to run, but he didn't.

'I won't say it's a pleasure to meet you,' he mumbled.

'We're not the enemy, Ethan. We're trying to help save these children. Evermore Pharmaceuticals have misled the packs by offering to administer a cure for lycanthropy that doesn't exist. There's a Mr Parker at our academy who's determined to wipe out the werewolf gene for good by killing the innocent.'

'Well, this Mr Parker of yours has probably succeeded,' he said. 'These three were the last of the Somerset packs to receive the serum. We were tasked with escorting them back to their parents after the injections.'

'Instead, you brought them here, and you would have happily watched them die.' Elizabeth was angry, and her eyes flared with unspoken words. She'd released her grip on Ethan's companion, who now took a step back before speaking up.

'We were told that some of the kids might react badly to the injection and if that was the case we should—'

'Kill them!' Elizabeth finished the sentence for her, disgust written all over her face.

'Yes,' the girl mumbled. 'But *he* forced us to do it. Told us he'd get us kicked out if we disobeyed.'

'Who did?'

Ethan crossed his arms over his chest and sneered.

'She's talking about me.'

'What gives you the right to condemn these kids?' I could feel my pulse quickening as I eyed the arrogant boy in front of me.

'Our job is a pretty easy one, sweetheart. We destroy the wolves who threaten our town. Simple as that.'

I bristled at his words. It appeared he'd chosen to disregard my earlier threat about calling me sweetheart. I'd never wanted to slap someone so much in my life.

'No, it's not that simple. These children never asked to be wolves, their parents never asked for it either. They are what they are, and we are what we are.'

Ethan laughed. 'I don't think anyone knows what *you* are.'

I ignored his attempts to goad me and turned my attention to the girl.

'I doubt your headmaster knows the truth about what's going on here,' I said. She was shrivelling up on herself under Ethan's glare. She shook her head.

'I suggest you go back and tell him what's happened. Make sure he knows that the serum is flawed.'

The girl nodded and sprinted off in the direction of the academy.

Sebastian cleared his throat. 'It's obvious that we arrived too late, but hopefully, we can get these youngsters back to their families and help save their lives.'

'Agreed. Ethan will lead us to the packs.'

'What? No, are you crazy? I'm not going to any wolf den and I'm certainly not helping *you*.'

I stood millimetres from his face and growled at him.

'You are going to help me and my friends, and you are going to help save these kids, or we'll let your headmaster know how you twisted his orders for your own sick benefit. I'm fairly sure you'll be expelled and I dread to think what happens to rogue hunters. It's not up for debate.'

His shoulders slumped and I watched his Adam's apple bob up and down in time to his heartbeat.

'Hand over your weapons and phone.'

The muscle in his jaw flinched as he turned out his pockets. Adam confiscated his knives and I pocketed his mobile.

'You'll get them back when you've earned it,' I said.

Turning away from the reckless hunter, I spoke to my friends. 'Once the kids are returned we need to get a message to Zak, so he knows what's going on. The packs need to know the danger they're in and unite before Evermore wipes everyone out.'

NINE

It felt a little bit like going home as we arrived at the tiny house on the beach. Although the building was painted white and looked nothing like the Mills farm, it had a similar vibe to it. A warmth seeped out of every crack in the plaster and the curls of paint at the window frames. A low fence ran around the property bordering a small patch of land with a bench seat facing the sea. I longed to sit and stare at the ocean but the three children we'd rescued needed help.

'The infusion I gave them should help with the convulsions and hopefully counteract the effects of the poison.' Sebastian filled in the anxious parents as they crowded around the children in a spare bedroom. I watched from the doorway and felt a sense of pride as he handled them with care and consideration.

He hadn't even managed that with me on our first meeting, in fact, he'd been so cold and calculating that I half suspected he regretted having a hormonal teenager dumped into his life. I watched as he scooped up the young girl and fluffed the pillow beneath her head, settling her more comfortably. He checked their pulse points, replenished the moist flannels on their foreheads, and cautiously engaged with their werewolf parents on the health of their offspring.

'Can't believe it's the same man from a few months ago, can you?' Adam folded his arms across his chest and leaned against the doorframe. His dark skin still glistened from the exertion of carrying the children through the forest to safety.

'Mmm, he's made a remarkable turnaround.'

Adam raised an eyebrow as he glanced across at me and I rolled away from the doorframe and walked further along the corridor to a small window overlooking the beach.

'You don't sound convinced,' he said catching up to me. I knew there'd been a hint of scepticism in my tone and I also knew Adam would pick up on that as I was fairly certain both he and Elizabeth felt the same.

'I don't know what to think,' I said. 'Sebastian locked me in a hospital room with the intention of experimenting on me! He even shot Terry! Yes, he's helped us, and yes, he seems to be committed to stopping Evermore, but am I supposed to accept that he's a good guy now?'

'What's your gut telling you?'

'My gut?'

'Yeah, you've always been powered by your intuition, Mia. You've got determination and strength, but you're also smart. Both Lizzie and I trust that you'll always do the right thing because, well, that's how you roll.'

I smiled up at my friend. It was nice to receive such a compliment. I'd tried so hard to fit in with the academy students and then with the pack, but that feeling of being an outsider hadn't gone away, so to be complimented on my qualities felt good.

'Honestly, I *want* to believe that he's changed. I want Sebastian to step up and help us defeat Parker and Felicity, Evermore, and the GA. I want him to understand why this is so important to me.'

'And you want him to be the dad you never had.'

Adam's words stopped me short. He was right. Sebastian was my biological father, and I longed to have that father-daughter relationship.

'Yes, I want him to be everything and more. It's not too much to ask, is it?'

We laughed, and Adam threw his muscular arm around my shoulder and squeezed.

'I'm sure he'll manage it, and if not, we can always set the werewolves on him.'

WE WERE STILL giggling as we joined Lizzie in the garden.

'What are you two plotting?' She was sitting on the garden bench with her long legs stretched out in front of her.

'Sebastian's downfall if he doesn't behave himself.' Adam dropped onto the seat next to her and nuzzled her neck.

'Sounds fair to me.' She giggled.

I was about to lay out the terms and conditions of Sebastian's sentence should he mess it all up when a large man wearing biker leathers and a bright red bandana sprinted up the path towards us.

'Where's Liam? Where's the alpha?'

A sheen of sweat covered his face, and from the deep creases on his brow, he wasn't here to deliver good news.

Like a game of Chinese whispers, the Somerset pack members passed the stranger's arrival along the line until the alpha, Liam, a tall man with a quiet temperament, emerged from the front door. The biker wolf rushed to his side pulling him into a private huddle.

I watched amused as the large man flung his arms in all directions, reliving the scene from whatever had him so spooked. I hoped that the academy hadn't retaliated after our intercepting them in the woods earlier and looked around to see if Ethan was still with us. The black-haired hunter sat with his back to the cottage wall also watching the events unfold.

I wandered over and sat next to him ignoring the stiffness in his posture at my arrival.

'I'm not the enemy, Ethan. You do know that, don't you?'

'If you're not a hunter then you're my enemy, sweetheart.'

'So that's it then.' I threw my arms in the air. 'There's no fine line, and no benefit of the doubt? You're either a good guy or a bad guy?'

He chuckled and pulled at a long blade of grass. 'We're not living in some superhero movie, Mia. The hunters and wolves don't mix, it's been that way for hundreds of years. If you followed the hunters' oath then you'd understand that.'

'Is that what's bothering you, that I broke my oath?'

'Doesn't it bother you?' He leaned forward and turned his body so he was facing me, his green eyes sparkling under the bright sunshine. 'You trained alongside hunters, you lived and socialised with them, and you upheld the rules of the oath, but you lied to them. You turned your back on everyone and joined the wolves.'

I was stunned by the passion in his voice. There was no doubt that he was a loyal hunter but I knew it wasn't that black and white. Especially not at Hood Academy.

'There was no malice involved in me leaving, Ethan. My friends understood why I had to follow the pack and they supported me.'

'I could never support any friend who turned their back on the oath.'

Ethan leaned back against the house and resumed watching Liam and the biker's exchange. He obviously didn't have anything else to say to me on the matter.

'How the hell you have any friends at all is a mystery to me,' I mumbled, standing up and dusting off my jeans.

I REJOINED ELIZABETH and Adam. I didn't want them to, but Ethan's words had hit a nerve. I was about to talk to Lizzie about it when I caught sight of Liam and the biker man staring at me. The compassion in their eyes turned my blood to ice, and I slowly slid onto the bench.

'What's up?' Elizabeth nudged me and then followed my line of sight. 'Oh.'

Liam approached, and I fought against the nausea that threatened to take over me. Whatever news the biker had delivered was either about me or for me, of that I was certain.

'Mia, can I have a word?' The gentle lulling of Liam's voice put me at ease as I stood and followed him to the garden gate.

'There's been an incident at Hood Academy,' he said.

Relief washed over me. An incident at the academy wasn't my primary concern, but as an ex-student and Sebastian's daughter I guessed Liam felt obliged to tell me.

'It appears that a rescue attempt was made, but the pack were low in numbers and were overwhelmed by the GA in residence.'

I nodded my head as I processed this information. Why was he telling me this? Who had needed rescuing?

'The alpha and his team swept through the grounds, but when they engaged with the GA, they suffered a great number of casualties. Many of the pack were injured but managed to escape, but a few were captured.'

I listened to the words, and I watched the movement of Liam's lips as he passed on the animated message from the biker wolf, but something failed to connect in my brain. Seemingly understanding my predicament, Liam filled in the blanks for me.

'They have your alpha and his second, Byron, plus two others. We have no more information at the moment.'

'No! They can't. Zak's my brother. They're my friends. Why would they go to the school? I don't understand. Cody! What about Cody?' I could hear the desperation in my voice.

'I'm sorry, Mia, I don't know anything more than what I've told you, but I want you to know that you have the full support of my pack. If you want our help you only have to ask.'

I COULDN'T DIFFERENTIATE between the roar in my head and the roar of the waves as they crashed against the rocks. Both sounds were angry and loud. I'd allowed Adam to take over the conversation with Liam as my distress erupted into full-blown hysteria. Lizzie led me away clinging to my hand like a frightened child, the pair of us trying to comprehend what had happened since our departure.

For the next hour or so I'd screamed, cried, and ranted at Sebastian as if he was responsible for my brother's capture. It hadn't helped when my dear old dad began explaining the probable procedure Parker would use on my brother to Liam's assembled pack members.

I'd stormed out slamming the door so hard I'm sure I heard glass break somewhere.

The sea air didn't have the calming effect I'd hoped for, so I set off at a brisk pace across the sand towards the small lighthouse. Why had Zak advanced on Hood Academy? The only people who needed rescuing when we were there had returned home already. The biker wolf confirmed that Ari had made it back with the other children and they were all accounted for. We'd left nobody behind.

I shivered against the cool breeze that hinted at the end of summer and kicked myself once again for leaving my coat behind. My coat. My scent. A slow-motion film began to play out in my mind. The images were of me climbing down the trellis from my bedroom window and dashing through the woods, arriving at the barn in search of clues as to Sebastian's whereabouts. The inner pictures flashed to our descent into the laboratories to rescue the children and then our subsequent ascent into the school.

Ari had left us in the basement rooms, but anyone following my scent would arrive at the science classroom to find my discarded coat and a missing wolf, driven away in Sebastian's SUV. Shit! Zak had no idea that we were working together, he didn't know Adam was with us, he had no clue that Sebastian had helped us do so much including destroying the Evermore warehouse. To my brother, I was missing, and I knew what that feeling was like. For years I hadn't known where my brother was, but he had always kept tabs on me, until now. I slumped onto the sand burying my head in my arms and let the sobs wrack my body.

I was aware of someone standing behind me and was surprised to find Ethan kicking at the sand a few feet away from me.

'I'm sorry about your brother,' he said.

If I hadn't felt so desolate I might have laughed.

'No you're not.'

He chuckled and crouched down beside me.

'I'll never understand you, Mia, but I'm not totally heartless. Family is important and even though your brother is a freak, I get why you would care about him.'

I stared at him. In his own warped way I think he was trying to be nice, but nice wasn't what I needed right now.

'It's all my fault,' I said. 'Zak took the pack to Hood Academy to rescue *me.*'

If anything happened to him, Byron, or the other wolves, I'd never be able to forgive myself. I realised how foolish I'd been to leave without a word. I should have at least taken my phone with me so I could stay in touch with Cody. He must have been going out of his mind with worry. Cody was the rock I clung to when the rapids swirled around me and yet I'd left without saying a word. Ethan was right. I did turn my back on everyone.

A sob caught in my throat and I jumped up from the sand and swiped at the tears on my face.

'We need to go,' I said with more determination in my voice than I felt. 'I have to return home and fix the mess I've made.'

Ethan joined me as I ran back along the beach. Rushing back towards that small cottage on the seafront I felt a crushing sensation in my chest. What if I was too late?

THE SUV'S ENGINE hummed in the background as we said our goodbyes to Liam and the Somerset pack. I had decided to go on ahead instead of waiting for the pack to assemble. Liam assured us that if we needed their help, his pack would make their way to Nottingham and join us in the fight.

Evermore Pharmaceuticals needed to be stopped before any more children were harmed, or killed, but right now, Parker and the GA were the problem.

Adam and Elizabeth walked up to where I stood shaking hands with Liam and his wife, who nodded their greeting to the pair before moving off to speak with Sebastian.

'Are you sure you're not going to come with us?' After hearing about an Evermore delivery heading to the packs in Cornwall, Adam had decided to travel south and try to get his old school to help. It was at the Cornish Academy that Adam had met Miss Ross and formed a friendship that would see her call on him to help us.

I understood the need to help his old friends, both hunter and wolf, but I felt sad for Lizzie who had to say goodbye to her boyfriend once again.

'I need to see if there's anything I can do. Liam has called ahead and warned the packs to stay clear of the Evermore team, but if none of the alphas bring their children forward, I'm worried the academy will send a team out to force it on them.'

We'd started to hear similar stories trickling in over the past day or two, where the alpha had refused the cure and teams of soldiers had swept through their homes taking the children against their will. The incident with Ethan and the Somerset hunters wasn't an isolated occurrence and the packs needed all the help they could get.

Fights were breaking out all over the country as the packs began to rise up, but without any structure, these small skirmishes wouldn't make any difference. It was becoming clear that Parker had the entire resources of the GA at his disposal while using Evermore as a cover for his despicable plan. That meant he had access to weapons, funds, and hunters.

None of us had yet established if the GA were also involved. They were holding Hood Academy under review but Parker was smart; he could hide in plain sight if necessary, leading the GA into a game they weren't aware they were playing.

'With the new school term around the corner we can't risk the younger students getting caught up in a war,' Adam said. 'They're training to be hunters and will be brainwashed into believing that all the wolves need to die rather than keeping the peace. I need to try and make a difference.'

I understood exactly how Adam felt. The hunters' oath was clear; *to every pack, a cub is born. Unleash the hunter to protect and serve.* Protect and serve, not kill. Over time the true meaning of the academies had been lost somewhere. The role of the hunters was to protect their community from the wolves, not to seek them out and destroy them.

The origins of Hood Academy may have been to assist Queen Victoria in ridding the country of lycanthropy, but the modern teachings had been much more sympathetic in their dealings with the local packs.

Perhaps it was me, but I'd read Dr Neale's book at Sebastian's request and found the message of tolerance to be the stronger theme.

'I wish you didn't have to go,' Elizabeth said, wrapping her arms around Adam's waist and dropping her head on his chest. 'But I understand why you do. Just promise you'll stay safe.'

They kissed, and I averted my eyes, glancing out across the beach and the ocean beyond. I made a vow to return here when all this was over. Being by the sea made my heart soar and filled me with that sense of freedom that I'd longed for all my life.

Yes, when this mess was cleared up I'd be back.

'Time to go,' Sebastian called to us from the SUV, and we ambled over shaking hands with the assembled pack members as we went.

There was a sombre mood hanging in the air, mixed with anger, trepidation, and fear. It clung to me like a physical entity, a burden upon my shoulders.

Elizabeth slid into the back of the car, and I climbed in the front next to Sebastian, giving a final wave to Adam, Liam, and our new friends. Before Sebastian could pull out of the driveway, the back door swung wide and Ethan jumped in.

'What are you doing?' I snapped. I had little patience for the boy as it was, despite his attempts to comfort me on the beach, but the thought of a long road trip with him didn't fill me with joy.

'I'm coming with you,' he said clicking his seat belt into the clip. 'You're not leaving me with a bunch of wolves. I'm a hunter, and I belong with other hunters.' He gave me a sidelong glance as if that last comment wasn't fully meant to include me.

'We might not agree on certain things, Mia, but I can help you.'

I twisted around so I could look into his eyes.

'How can you help us? You don't even agree with what we're trying to do.'

He gave me a wide smile and I almost believed it was genuine.

'I'm a hunter, just like Elizabeth.' He jerked his thumb in Lizzie's direction and she rolled her eyes. 'I can fight and hunt.'

'You hunt werewolves, Ethan. That's who we're going to help. What does your oath-obsessed conscience say about that?'

He shrugged his shoulders and nestled down into the car seat.

260 'If I help you rescue your brother then maybe you can owe me. That hybrid power has to be good for something.'

'Oh, so now it's all about what I can do for you?' I could feel my pulse starting to throb as my anger and irritation grew. The kid was infuriating but I couldn't deny that an extra pair of hands would be welcome.

'Exactly. It's a win-win situation.'

I huffed and sat back in the seat.

'Do you think I could have my phone back now?' he added. 'I want to listen to my music while we're in the car.'

Glaring at him I dug his phone out of my pocket and tossed it at him. At least if he was listening to music he wouldn't spend the entire journey winding me up.

Sebastian caught my attention, and I rolled my eyes in an attempt to convey my unhappiness but acceptance of the situation. Luckily Sebastian got it and moved the car forward.

It didn't matter if Ethan came with us, or that Sebastian was driving us, I was going home to help my family, and that was the only thing that counted.

THE JOURNEY WAS subdued; Elizabeth buried her head in a book and Ethan plugged his earphones in, the muted sounds of some rock band echoing around the car.

'Did you manage to read that notebook about hybrids?' Sebastian broke the silence, pulling me out of my jumbled thoughts.

'Not all of it, I've only read the main references to hybrids, but it does sound similar to my situation.'

'Do you know who wrote it?'

I hadn't given it much thought if I was honest. The word hybrid had stood out for me like a neon marker and stripped away any curiosity.

'It was Dr Neale.'

'You mean Queen Victoria's werewolf hunter?'

'The very same. He was recruited by the crown to defend the country, but he was also a scientist and had a thirst for finding answers.'

'Hmm, bit like you then.'

Sebastian huffed, and I remembered his inability to express emotion faltered on occasion. His little huff was the equivalent to laughing out loud, something I'd adopted as a trait too, I realised.

My forehead crinkled as I drew my eyebrows together.

'What else do you have in common with an ancient hunter apart from both being the head of Hood Academy?'

'Do you remember the conversation we had when you first arrived at the academy? You commented on the cool stuff I'd collected.'

Pushing aside my amazement that Sebastian remembered any of our conversations, I did recall talking to him about the building and its impressive collection of old furniture and books. The place never felt cluttered; instead, it was safe, warm, and cosy. I'd remarked on this right before telling Sebastian I wanted to leave.

'Yes, I remember. You told me you'd inherited most of it.'

'That's right.' Sebastian's shoulders lifted as he mirrored my reaction. We both apparently appreciated the fact our conversations were memorable.

'Well, the academy and its contents were handed down the family line, passing from generation to generation. I'm one hunter in a very long line, and you, Mia, are part of that history.'

'I don't think I'm worthy of inheriting anything as I'm not a fully fledged hunter. In fact, I'm fairly certain that dear old Dr Neale would turn in his grave if he knew you were entertaining a hybrid in his precious academy!'

'That's where you're wrong, Mia. If you'd managed to read the notebook you'd have found some interesting information about our family line.'

'So why don't you tell me,' I urged, starting to lose patience in Sebastian's cryptic ramblings.

'Dr Neale was my great-great-great-granddad.'

My head spun as I processed what he was saying.

'You mean I'm descended from Queen Victoria's hunter?' I laughed. I laughed so loud it made Elizabeth jump and Ethan snarl at having his music interrupted.

'What's so funny about that?' Sebastian's face crumpled at my reaction.

'I'm sorry, but if Gramps knew about me, he'd excommunicate you for fraternising with a werewolf.'

Sebastian did huff at that.

'Everything is not always as it seems, Mia. Dr Neale wrote about the hunters' oath in 1862 when Ravenshood was overrun by wolves. He was a bit like Mr Parker at the time, adamant that the wolves were evil and desperate to destroy the packs. With money from the Crown, he opened Hood Academy in 1866 and began training those students who had come into contact with the wolves.'

'I remember, both you and Lizzie told me that to become a hunter you had to have seen a werewolf. Her sister didn't see what it was that attacked them, so Lizzie was the only one sent to Hood Academy.'

'Yes, there's some truth in that, but it's not altogether correct. I'm fairly sure Elizabeth's sister did see the werewolf, but her young mind wasn't open to the possibility of supernatural creatures being real. We recruit the believers because you can't help what you can't see.'

'Help? You've never wanted to help the wolves! You strapped Terry to a metal trolley and injected him with God knows what.' I could feel the trickle of anger dancing up my spine as I recalled finding my friend trapped in the school laboratories. 'You train the students to hunt and fight. I wasn't at Hood Academy for that long but what I saw during my time there told me you'd do everything in your power to hurt not help the packs.'

Sebastian shook his head, and for a moment I saw true sadness in his expression. I knew he was trying to turn it around and help us fix what was going on but was he really so delusional that he thought he hadn't done anything wrong?

'You're right,' he whispered. 'Dr Neale founded Hood Academy with the intention of destroying the local werewolves, but then he met a girl and fell in love.'

'Oh God, you're not going to get all mushy on me, are you?'

'He fell in love with a werewolf, Mia, like I did when I fell in love with your mother.'

Silence. Even Ethan's music seemed to lower in tone and pace.

'How could he? That would have gone against everything he believed in, and against the Queen's orders.'

'It appears love really can conquer all. The school became a sanctuary and a cover story. He married his sweetheart in secret, and they went on to have a child. A hybrid. The first hybrid.'

I felt like a bomb had gone off in my head; the noise was horrific. My jaw ached, and I realised with horror that my fangs had slid out. I covered them with my hand and prayed that the claws didn't shoot into view too.

'There have been three hybrids in the history of our family line, and you're one of them. The first two wrote about their experiences in that notebook you hold. Perhaps one day you can add your story.'

For the first time in a while, I was stumped for words. I had always had an answer for Sebastian, whether that was genuine or sarcastic, but this went beyond even my comprehension.

Three hybrids. I couldn't help but wonder what they had been like. Had they also felt like outsiders? Had they struggled to separate the parts of themselves that were wolf and hunter?

'Did they stay at Hood Academy?' I asked, relieved to find my teeth were normal again.

'I believe so. The first was Dr Neale's daughter, Emma. She was born in 1868. I don't think the next hybrid appeared until the 1950s when Mary was born.'

'So when you said we were rare you weren't kidding!'

Sebastian huffed again.

'There's certainly been a long time between each hybrid, but perhaps that shows us how the werewolf and hunter communities work.'

'I don't understand what you mean.'

'Our ancestor, Dr Neale, fell in love with a werewolf and got married, and they went on to have Emma, but it was over eighty years before another hunter and wolf would fall in love, marry, and produce a second hybrid offspring.'

'Then you came along and fell in love with my mum making number three, me!'

It had an air of the historical romance about it. Like all these pictures I had in my head were coated in a sepia wash or as if I was watching an old movie play out in my head.

'The hostility between the hunters and the packs has meant the oath taken by the new hunters has evolved over the years. It's this animosity that's gathered speed rather than the protection in the community that the oath was based on.'

'That's why you were trying to create the cure.' It was starting to make sense now. Sebastian's determination and drive to find a cure for lycanthropy wasn't done in malice, it was because he had loved my mother so much and wanted to make a better world for her.

There was a heavy weight in my chest as I thought about all the awful things I'd said to Sebastian over the last few months. I had called him a monster and walked away from him.

'I'm sorry,' I whispered reaching over to lay my hand over his on the steering wheel.

He turned his palm so he could squeeze my hand in return.

'You've got nothing to be sorry about, Mia. I did so many things wrong, and letting your mother down was my biggest failure. That's why I didn't want to make the same mistakes with you.'

I appreciated the sentiment even if he had gone about it in a barbaric manner, but I wondered what he was planning to do next.

'You said Dr Neale used the academy as a cover for his relationship with his werewolf wife. Were you doing the same?'

'In a way,' he said. 'I wanted to keep your mum safe, but we had to hide so much of our relationship from Frank, her pack, and the GA. Eventually, I had Mr Parker's threat hanging over my head, so instead of helping the local pack I ended up being the reason they were captured and tortured.'

I shook off my memory of finding Terry tied to the silver trolley in the basement, and hearing his screams when Felicity and her goons tortured him. Was she doing the same to Zak right now? If she knew he was my brother, I was certain she'd do more than torture him.

'Parker doesn't agree with your view of living in harmony with the packs.'

Sebastian exhaled. 'That's an understatement. Mr Parker's intense hatred of the wolves drives him to destroy the werewolf line. I thought I'd finally got through to him when he approached me about working with Evermore. He wanted to distribute the cure across the country to help the packs. I should have realised what he was really doing.'

'You're not the first person to be tricked, Sebastian. He was using you to create something that contained werewolf DNA so he could add his poison.'

'I should have known though. As head of Hood Academy, I was responsible for every life in that school. Every student was there to train and learn how to protect themselves. I allowed Mr Parker to pull me away from that mission.'

'I know I wasn't there for long, but even I saw how much the students loved it there. They learned so much, they laughed with their friends, and they were safe. You created that, Sebastian, and you shouldn't forget it.'

'Thank you, Mia. I appreciate your words. Unfortunately, it doesn't detract from the fact that I failed and the GA will no doubt strip me of everything I have.'

'Do the GA know what Parker's doing?' It was something I'd wanted to know from the beginning. We all wondered if their sudden appearance was coincidental, but most of us thought not.

Sebastian shook his head. 'I honestly don't know. The GA are reviewing the school after recent events and might grant Mr Parker full headship, but I don't know if they are aware of the links to Evermore, or what Mr Parker has planned for the packs.'

A shudder ran up my spine as I thought about Parker's plans. With help from his evil pharmaceutical company, he had managed to sweep across half of England dishing out his poison. How many had died? How many young children were forced to turn before they were old enough to cope with the pain and hunger? I felt sick thinking about it.

I looked down at the notebook still in my hand. Everything I needed to know about being a hybrid was within these pages. If being half hunter and half wolf could help my brother and the pack then it was time to embrace my unique abilities.

We had a big fight ahead of us, not just with the GA and trying to free our friends, but stopping Parker and Evermore Pharmaceuticals before more wolves died.

I flipped open the book. It was time to find out who I really was.

OATH KEEPER

TEN

T he Mills farm was in chaos when we pulled up in the driveway. I saw Terry through the kitchen window and the weight lifted from my shoulders knowing at least one of my friends was safe.

The first thing I saw when walking in through the old wooden door was the kitchen table covered with blueprints of Hood Academy and maps of the local area interspersed with numerous cups of coffee. How long had everyone been sitting at this table?

'Mia!' Terry was out of his chair and at my side in seconds. His embrace almost took my breath away as he squeezed me tight. 'We were all so worried. Ari arrived with a ton of kids and babbled something about you and Lizzie snooping around the school.'

Elizabeth came in behind me and Terry released his grip on me and circled her in an equally tight embrace.

'We're so sorry,' I said, raising my voice to include everyone gathered in the small kitchen. 'We never meant to worry you. After finding the children and sending Ari back here, we found information about the serum and had to leave to investigate it further. I should have called. I should have let you know we were safe…'

My voice trailed off as I spotted Cody in the doorway. Dark smudges ringed his glazed-over eyes, and he rubbed at his upper arm as if to drive away a chill. I rushed to him, and he scooped me up burying his face in my long hair.

The sound of his sobs ripped a hole in my heart that I didn't think I'd ever recover from.

'I'm so sorry,' I whispered into his ear, trailing kisses along his cheek and blotting the tears that lingered on his face. 'I'll never leave you again.'

He brought his lips to mine and kissed me deeply, oblivious to the watchful eyes of the pack, who began shuffling and moving about in a bid to avoid our intimate exchange.

The sudden silence in the room tore Cody and me apart, and I turned to see what had muted the pack. Sebastian stood in the doorway clutching the files we'd taken from Parker's desk drawer. Terry's shoulders tensed at the sight of the man responsible for his incarceration and torture.

'What the hell are you doing here?' It was Cody who spoke, stunning me with the venom that dripped from his words. I took a step backward and released my grip on him.

'Sebastian's with us. He's been really helpful to our cause, to *your* cause.'

'That man is only out to help himself; he doesn't give a shit about the wolves.'

'No, you're wrong. He helped me and Lizzie burn down the Evermore distribution centre, and he saved the lives of three young wolves in Somerset. He's on our side.'

I looked around at the faces of Zak's pack. Bared teeth, crossed arms, and angry eyes greeted me. They weren't going to accept Sebastian's help without an argument, and part of me understood that. It had taken an epic journey to be able to start to bond with the man myself, and he was my own flesh and blood. I was expecting a miracle if I wanted them to open their home and hearts to him.

I took the files from Sebastian and placed them on the table in front of the pack.

'We have evidence that Parker has modified Sebastian's serum, which is what's causing the children to turn or die. He plans to wipe out the werewolf gene by destroying your kids.'

There was a rumbling of conversation as the files and their contents spilled out across the table.

'If *he* hadn't created the serum in the first place none of this would have happened.'

Sebastian rolled his shoulders and took a step forward, further inside the danger zone.

'I understand your animosity,' he said, his voice clear and strong. 'My intentions have always been for the good of the were-wolf community. I loved a wolf and would have done anything to keep her safe, but my work has been mutilated by a man hell-bent on destroying all of you.'

'It's true,' I said standing at Sebastian's side. 'Parker is behind Evermore Pharmaceuticals, and it's him who's sent the doctors out into our community with the promise of a cure. No one could have known what he was planning. Even Sebastian thought it was the right serum being sent out to the packs.'

'Are you telling me that you've developed a cure for lycanthropy?' Terry stood at the head of the table, in Zak's spot, standing in for his alpha who was captive at Sebastian's old school. How the wolves hadn't ripped my father's throat out already amazed me.

'Yes, that's exactly what I'm telling you. It will only work on the young to avoid them turning, I haven't been able to create a cure for fully fledged wolves, and I think that's a fool's errand that I can't continue.'

Sebastian let the information sink in before going on. 'My serum was tampered with, and I suspect Parker's staff at Evermore had something to do with that. It explains why he kept me working in the school laboratories instead of at the central pharmaceutical facility.'

'What have the GA got to do with it?' One of the visiting pack members asked the question that many of us were desperate to know the answer to.

'I don't believe they've got anything to do with it,' Sebastian answered. 'I don't even think they know Mr Parker is connected to Evermore Pharmaceuticals. The GA are at Hood Academy to review my recent misdemeanours.'

'You mean they're here to find out why you captured and tortured us and tried to kill your own daughter,' Terry added.

Sebastian hung his head, and I felt a mix of anger and loyalty towards my friend.

'Leave him alone,' I said. 'Yes, he messed up, big time, but he's here to help us get Zak, Byron, and the others back. He knows Hood Academy better than any of us. Let him help.'

I HADN'T EXPECTED to be banished from the kitchen with Sebastian in tow. In all fairness, they'd done it so they could discuss our rescue plan in private, but I was fuming at Terry for kicking me out of the inner circle.

Sebastian had taken himself off to sit in his SUV for safety and Elizabeth was checking in on Ari. I'd almost forgotten about our hunter guest until Ethan sauntered over to where I was sitting on the bonnet of a car in the driveway.

'When I came with you I thought you'd be taking me to Hood Academy, not to another wolf den.' He crossed his arms over his chest and settled his dark gaze on me. 'You do know that your hairy friends have been growling at me ever since I arrived.'

'It's a pit stop, we'll be heading to the academy soon enough, although you might not want to join us for that trip.'

'Yeah, I gathered from the raised voices that your pets were planning to attack the school.'

'It's not an attack,' I snapped, annoyed at both his assumptions and disrespect for my pack. 'The GA are holding some of our friends, and the alpha, and we want to get them back.'

He unfolded his arms and leaned against the car watching me with a predatory glance that made me feel uncomfortable. It was the kind of look that made your skin crawl. So far, the infuriating hunter had tagged along with a half-hearted offer of help, but I didn't know if I should trust Ethan yet. He was arrogant but loyal to the hunters' oath and in my eyes that made him unpredictable.

'You think you're going to get past the GA? Jeez, you're stupider than you look.'

I jumped off the car and stood nose to nose with the hunter.

271

'What's your problem with me, Ethan?'

He snarled, actually snarled, and I had to pull on all my reserves not to slap him hard across his smarmy face.

'You say you're half hunter, but you live with wolves. It's like I told you in Somerset, you could never understand the hunters' oath if you don't respect it enough to honour it.'

I was speechless. I'd come to expect a personal attack about my claws or living with a pack, but Ethan still sounded genuinely angry that I'd not upheld the oath.

'I took the oath with every intention of being a hunter, but a lot of stuff happened that was out of my control. Other people weren't happy about me being at the academy, and it made it hard.'

'Oh, my heart bleeds for you. So what, Felicity goes all crazy bitch on you, and you decide to turn to the wolves?'

I took a step back and studied the boy properly for the first time. He was my age with pale skin, which made his dark hair stand out even more. A dusting of pimples on his chin told me he'd recently started shaving and it had irritated his skin. At about five foot ten he was a few inches taller than me, and it annoyed me that I had to look up at him.

'How do you know about Felicity?' Suspicion bubbled in my gut as I waited for his answer.

'Everyone knows about Felicity, she's a legend among the academies.'

I huffed and rolled my eyes. 'A legend! The girl's a freak.'

'Maybe, but she's still badass.'

I laughed out loud, and Ethan flinched at the sudden outburst.

'Did you also hear that I beat her at the last assessment? Thrashed her to take the gold medal and humiliated her in front of her precious daddy.'

There was the briefest spark of appreciation in Ethan's expression before he shrugged and walked away.

'Perhaps Hood Academy has two legends then,' he called over his shoulder.

Was that a compliment? Maybe there was hope for the hunter after all.

TERRY CAME AND found me a little while later with the news that our rescue attempt would happen after dark.

'I suppose if I asked you to stay here you wouldn't listen,' said Terry.

'You suppose right, it's my brother that's in trouble, and I'm going to help save him.'

'Hmm, thought as much. I've asked Lizzie to stay and watch the kids, and your weird friend Ethan has offered to help us too.'

'He's not my friend, but I appreciate that he's trying to help. What about Sebastian?'

Terry ran his fingers through his hair and in that moment he reminded me so much of Zak. Without my brother and Byron around it fell on Terry to hold the pack together. He'd never struck me as the sort to relish leadership. Terry was the funny one, the caring one, the loyal, strong, and daring one. What if it all went horribly wrong and we couldn't get Zak back? Would Terry snap under the pressure?

'I think it's best if Sebastian comes with us. He could be a distraction for the GA if we come into contact with any of them.'

'You mean a sacrifice.'

Terry gave a short nod.

'Do you know where they're holding Zak and the others?'

'We've got our suspicions. The laboratories are the logical choice, but there's also the animal cages at the back of the property. If they have them heavily guarded, it'll be difficult to set them free no matter where they are.'

'We'll get him back, Terry,' I said linking my arm into his. 'We'll get them all back.'

ELEVEN

I felt like I was spending more time at Hood Academy recently than I ever did when I was a student. First, there was the incident with Ari, then finding Sebastian on the school's extensive grounds, rescuing Elizabeth, returning to find the captive children, and now another rescue attempt to save my brother and the pack members.

During the few short months I'd been at Hood Academy I'd run away three times. There was an irony in there somewhere. Running from the academy when I was a student and now returning to the academy when I was supposed to be a pack member. Maybe Ethan was right. Perhaps if I'd been more dedicated to upholding the hunters' oath, I wouldn't feel so displaced.

The pack moved through the forest towards the back of the school, approaching the animal cages first to see if this was where our family and friends were being held. We were all still in human form having decided this was the best way to track and rescue our friends. It meant walking at a slower pace, but I understood how it would be difficult to sneak six huge wolves through the back door. I walked with Sebastian as Terry had given me the task of looking after my father. Ethan had also been placed in my 'keep them out of the pack's way' group. I hoped Terry understood why I had to give Sebastian a chance. He was my biological father as well as being the psycho scientist we'd got to know too well. If there was any hope that I could carve some kind of relationship out of all this mess, then I was willing to try.

Through the inky blackness of the forest, I could see the pack creeping forward, their human shapes melting into the trees with ease. If the GA discovered us, there was a high probability that each of the pack members would turn to protect themselves.

Cody had told me more about the turn after I discovered that werewolves were real. He explained how they always turned on a full moon but other than that they remained human unless attacked. Felicity and her goons beat Cody when he'd come to rescue me. When he turned, I couldn't look away. It was horrific and beautiful at the same time. Snapping bones, shifting limbs, and gut-wrenching screams. No wonder Sebastian had made the cure. Who would want that for their children?

'Wait,' Terry hissed back at us, and we halted our steps.

Through the overhanging branches I could see the twinkling lights of Hood Academy. The GA would be located in one specific area. Sebastian told us that any reviews they had done in the past were carried out from the library, which was on the west side of the building. If we could contain them in one place, it would make it easier for the scouts to search for Zak and Byron.

A runner returned to Terry's side. Would we be heading to the animal cages or had the GA chosen to lock our friends up in the laboratories? Terry waved his hand in the air, and we all moved off as one. The laboratories it was then.

As we reached the treeline, I spotted the bright lights illuminating the dormitory rooms. Why weren't they still in darkness? The students weren't due to start the new term for another week. I tuned into my senses and listened. Through the wind and drizzle, I heard the playful tones of young girls laughing and talking. Panic flooded my entire body, and my hands began shaking. I looked over at Ethan with wide eyes and saw the realisation spread across his face.

'Stop!' He turned towards the pack, attracting Terry's attention with a frantic wave of his arms. 'There are students here.'

Terry appraised the building, casting his eyes up to the second and third floors where silhouettes of students moved across the glass.

'It doesn't change anything.' Terry waved the pack forward.

I watched helplessly as Terry, Cody, and the other pack members crossed the lawns and made their way to the back door, which led to the kitchens. Sebastian had told them it would be the easiest access point, but if the students were back, that meant the kitchen staff would be too.

'Are you going to let them attack students?' Ethan hissed. 'Is this what being a hybrid is all about?'

Panic filled my chest as I struggled with my dual personalities. We had to rescue Zak and the others, but I also had a duty to protect the girls inside.

'Come on you two!' I grabbed Sebastian's hand and dragged him along with me as I sprinted after the wolves with Ethan matching my pace.

I pushed past the assembled pack until I reached Terry's side. He had a crowbar wedged into the kitchen doorframe ready to break in.

'Let me go in first,' I said, unable to mask the desperation in my voice. 'I can keep to the shadows and get an idea of where everyone is. If anyone does see me, they'll think I'm another student. That's got to be better than a werewolf pack bursting into a school full of hunters.'

I could see Terry thinking over his options. He was used to following orders not giving them. Eventually, he nodded his consent, and I breathed a sigh of relief.

'Okay, I need two teams. Ethan, I want you to check out the nurse's office that Lizzie told us about in case they used that entrance. Mia will go this way. I don't want *either* of you to engage with the people inside. We don't need the students seeing you and getting distressed. Find out where Zak is and then get back here as fast as you can.'

Ethan shot off into the night and I felt a strange sense of satisfaction that he was working with us.

Before I could enter the kitchen door Terry grabbed my wrist.

'Mia, I want Cody to go with you as backup.'

I opened my mouth to complain but he held his hand up to stop me.

'It's not because I don't trust you,' he said softly. 'I'd just feel happier if someone had your back. He can stay hidden in the doorway but I want him close to you. Zak would never forgive me if anything happened to you.'

I understood, and instead of getting argumentative with him I smiled and squeezed his arm. 'You need to stay in the treeline,' I said. 'If the students are here that means the staff will be milling about too and I wouldn't want the cook to stumble across you lot in her backyard.'

Terry grinned at me in the way he used to, full of the boyish charm that had been so endearing when we'd first met. I needed to find my brother so everyone could be who they were meant to be, me included.

THE DINING HALL was in darkness; we'd missed the dinner rush, and the staff had fortunately packed up and left. The main entrance hall was on the other side of the dining room through the closed glass door. I could see the light blazing and hear murmured voices. Directly opposite this room was Sebastian's office, or rather Parker's office as he now held the position of headmaster.

'We have to go through that door into the main building,' I told Cody who was tailing me. 'But we need to wait until whoever's out there has left or they'll see us.'

I couldn't remember if this door handle squealed like some of the older ones in the school. I gripped it in my sweaty palm, and I prayed that opening this door wouldn't blow our entire mission.

It twisted easily, and I tugged it open a fraction. The main entrance hall was exactly how I remembered it. Squishy sofas circled the walls, interspersed with chunky mahogany furniture. The lamps were lit, but there were no students lounging there this evening. The voices I'd heard earlier were coming from Parker's room where the office door was ajar. I couldn't help the roll of my gut on recognising Felicity's voice.

'What if the GA let them go, Daddy?'

'They're foolish enough to do something like that. Those damn idiots couldn't organise a bake sale. We've worked too hard for these morons to risk it all.'

'I thought they would have gone by now. Surely they know you're the best person for the headmaster's job instead of that imbecilic wolf lover, Sebastian.'

I bristled at her words and felt Cody's fingers intertwine with my free hand. His warmth gave me the strength I needed.

'Yes, I thought that bringing the students back early might have encouraged them to leave, but no matter,' Parker said. 'Fortunately, my sweet child, the GA are as clueless about my dealings with Evermore Pharmaceuticals as they are about dealing with vermin wolves. They prance around *my* school demanding evidence of Sebastian's ill-advised experiments as if I were the guilty one.'

Felicity's giggle echoed around the rooms. 'You *are* guilty, Daddy.'

Parker's booming laughter mingled with his daughter's as they relished in the downfall of my father.

'My hands are clean, pumpkin. Only Sebastian knows of my involvement with his creation, and a single threat against the life of his wolf lover was enough to convince him to stay quiet.'

'Didn't that cow die anyway?'

'Ah yes, but by whose hand? Sometimes we need to intervene when it's for the good of the hunters' oath.'

Felicity's wild laughter tore through my chest like a bullet. The pain in my heart threatened to rip me apart, and I couldn't stop myself from shaking violently. Cody wrapped his muscular arms around me, sensing my horror. Sebastian believed he had killed my mother, the love of his life. *I* had believed he had killed my mother, as did everyone else, but it was a lie. Parker had interfered with Sebastian's experiments just as he was doing now.

I could barely hear their words as the screaming in my head intensified. Cody clung to me, possibly fearing that I might lose it and murder everyone in my way.

'It's all worked out for the best, my darling daughter. The GA will conclude that Sebastian set up a private venture in conjunction with Evermore to wipe out the wolves. Being a caring parent and governor, I stepped in to look after the interests of the academy and uphold the oath, and if I can time it right, everyone will believe that when his experiment went horribly wrong, he was driven to destroy all the evidence. If they believe Dr Roberts capable of such atrocities as murdering young wolves and silencing their families as they grieve for their cubs then they'll end him, and his filthy bloodline.'

Cody was struggling to keep me in his grasp. My fangs had emerged, and my claws were fully extracted, but I could feel something else, something new happening to my body. The muscles beneath my skin rippled with energy and my blood boiled.

A searing pain shot down my spine as I lurched forward out of Cody's arms. My legs buckled under me and I hit the floor. I braced myself against the hard surface as my claws stretched out before me. The pain screeched through my entire body, and I watched partly in horror and partly in awe as my hands pulsed and twitched. My right leg snapped backward, the bone breaking and moulding into another shape as I wept at the agony. The left leg followed. I'd never known such torture. Even the beatings Frank had subjected me to were nothing compared to this.

I was aware of movement all around me. Cody had alerted the pack. His soft voice lulled me from somewhere that seemed far away. Terry's strong tones carried an authority I'd never heard before, and I tried to remember how to speak. I wanted to communicate with my friends. I needed to scream for them to help me.

I opened my mouth and felt my jaw rip as it widened beyond any reasonable boundary. More fangs slid into place bursting through my gums with terrific force. My shoulders rounded and snapped apart as my spine buckled and twisted.

Sweat poured from me in waves and the nausea frightened me. I strained against the urge to scream as the pain reverberated through my bones. Any cry would attract attention that we didn't need. If it was any consolation, I knew I wasn't alone. The wolves had joined me in the dining hall as a measure of support, but I wasn't sure I relished having an audience.

When would it end? I realised the enormity of what I was going through. I was turning into a werewolf, a fully fledged wolf. No more hybrid fangs and cute claws, this was serious shit. Watching Cody turn all those months ago had been bad enough, I would have done anything to help him as he cried out in pain, but now he was forced to watch me, unable to offer anything but his soft words of comfort.

My hands were no longer hands; instead I could see huge paws covered in silky brown fur. My arms snapped into place allowing me to lift myself off the floor. I could feel the power in my limbs as I rose from the ground. I flung my head back as my spine contorted and manoeuvred into another position. Then it was done. Over. I was a wolf.

I rose higher, my arms and legs settling into position as I looked around the room for the first time. My eyes focused differently. I could see figures all around me, but it was harder to pick out who was who. I sniffed and instantly recognised Cody's scent.

'Don't be afraid, Mia. I'm here with you.'

I wasn't afraid. For the first time in my life, I felt in control. A strength vibrated through me that I had only ever dreamed of. Images of Frank rolled across my mind. Him towering over me with that grotesque snarl before wrapping his fingers around my throat, his heavy boot as it connected with my body. All the times he had hurt me. Suddenly I understood how easy it had been for Zak to rip out his throat. Right here, right now, I knew I could do the same.

My breathing was slow and steady as I waited for whatever came next. The pack remained in their human form and whispered to each other. I could almost taste their energy.

'Parker and his daughter are behind everything,' Cody explained. 'We overheard it all. The GA has nothing to do with the murders; it's all Parker.'

'Then we take out the main threat, rescue our pack, and get the hell out of here before...' Terry's voice trailed off as he glanced over his shoulder at me. His scent was strong and musty, but there was also an edge to it, a rippling of fear that rolled off him in waves. Was he afraid of me, or of what I might do?

Parker's voice interrupted my thoughts as he spoke to his daughter.

'I think the time's come to finish this little project, don't you? I'll keep the GA occupied while you go down to the lab. Here, this is Sebastian's lab coat. Leave it behind for the GA to find but make sure you don't leave any of the filthy wolves alive. I want them *all* dead.'

I heard Felicity leave the headmaster's office and enter the stockroom where the secret entrance to the laboratories was. I'd followed the redhead into that room before, but this time I wasn't going to be trembling in the shadows.

The growl rumbled up from the back of my throat as I edged towards the door.

Cody stood in front of me with his hands held high in the air. 'If you follow her, Mia, you'll kill her, and I don't want that for you.'

I bared my teeth, and his arms lowered.

'Let her save her brother,' Sebastian said stepping out of the darkness so I could see his shape. I sniffed the air and memorised his scent. It was slightly spicy, like a grown-up's aftershave mixed with coffee beans. 'For the good of your pack we have to trust that she can control her actions. I'll find the GA and let them know what's been happening.'

'If the GA see you they'll arrest you on sight,' Terry said.

'I know, and I probably deserve it, but if it gives you the time to rescue your friends and get free of this place, then it's worth the sacrifice.'

I saw Terry extend his hand in offering to Sebastian who took it gratefully. Maybe there was hope for my father yet.

'Okay, let's do this.'

TWELVE

ody hadn't left my side, and for that I was thankful. I needed his support more than ever as I took my first steps as a wolf.

The storeroom was more difficult to navigate since I was the size of a small horse, but I made it through and led the pack down the stone stairs to the basement rooms. Terry and a few others went first, creeping down the steps in silence. I followed with Cody at my back.

The muffled sounds of a struggle travelled along the corridor of rooms, and I urged Terry on. Felicity had barged through every door leaving them ajar in her eagerness to inflict pain and death on the captives. Her poisonous scent coated everything she'd touched.

'You don't have to do this!' Someone cried out in pain.

It was Byron, and the anguish in his tone pierced my heart.

As one we rushed forward bursting into the next room as Felicity held a dagger over Byron's heart. She jumped back from the table, holding the blade at arm's length assessing her assailants. Her widening eyes surveyed the room until that calculated look she was so well known for settled on her face. She took in the human forms of the pack, as if filing their images away for the future when she would hunt them down one by one.

I wasn't going to let that happen, and I relished the shock on her face as I entered the room, my huge paws padding along the floor leaving tiny clouds of dust. Standing to my full height, I growled at her. Even Byron's eyes widened. Cody stood by my side, and I felt the change in Felicity as she put the pieces together.

'Wolf girl,' she hissed. 'You've managed to turn, I see, and here was me thinking you couldn't do anything right.' She brushed her fingers along her throat and the raw scar left behind after our last fight.

'We're here to take our pack,' Cody spoke up, his voice cold and hard.

Felicity waved her dagger in Cody's direction. 'You're the one who nearly killed me in the woods that night, saving your girl.' She moved closer and the pack tensed as one.

'I must admit, Mia, he's cute, for a wolf. I can see why you'd let him slobber all over you.' She winked at Cody and circled back round to where Byron lay strapped to the metal trolley. 'Unfortunately, it's a hunter's responsibility to uphold the oath and rid the world of vermin like you, no matter how cute.'

The pack inched forward circling either side of Felicity who waved the dagger in front of her.

'Stay back!' she screamed, thrusting the blade towards Terry who froze. 'Don't take another step or your friend here dies.'

'You're outnumbered,' said Terry holding his hands out. 'You can't kill all of us.'

Her eyes flashed with anger as she glared from one person to the next registering Terry's words and realising she had already lost.

'I don't have to kill you all,' she spat, that glint in her eye like a warning light to anyone who stepped in her way. 'I only have to kill one of you.'

In one fluid movement she plunged the knife into Byron's gut, blood spurting in all directions as he screamed out in agony. The pack scattered, grabbing for the redhead as she skirted past them and disappeared through the next door along.

'Cut him loose,' Terry shouted. 'Get him out of here.'

Two of the pack rushed to help Byron, who coughed and spluttered from the table. Terry was in pursuit of Felicity before they'd cut the first bond.

I lurched forward almost knocking Cody off his feet as he darted after his friend.

The three of us pushed forward until we hit the last room. This was the same room where Sebastian had kept the children that Elizabeth, Ari, and I had rescued. Instead of kids, the room now held five men. I burst through the door and saw Felicity heading straight for Zak with the blood-stained blade in her hand.

The roar that erupted from my throat silenced the room. Even Felicity stopped and spun around, having the sense not to turn her back on me.

I padded forward never once taking my eyes off my nemesis. Her scent was overwhelming but Sebastian had believed in me. He thought I was capable of controlling my emotions and not killing another human, however evil they might be. I wanted that to be true. Underneath this powerful form, I was just a girl. Granted, I wasn't the same girl I used to be, I'd changed, grown harder, tougher, and more resilient, but I was still just a teenager with hopes and dreams that didn't include taking another life.

Within seconds Terry and Cody had freed our friends, and I had the pack at my back. Zak stood at my shoulder, his dark hair curling up at the nape of his neck. Right now, he didn't look like an alpha, he looked like my big brother.

'You've lost this fight, Felicity. The GA will make sure that because of your actions and cruelty you'll be stripped of your hunters' oath and sent back into the hole you wormed your way out of.'

'Tut, tut, Zak, you should know better than that. My daddy will have the GA eating out of his hand before you even make it to the trees. I'll be able to watch you die at the hands of the agency who'll never know how close we came to wiping your filthy species off this earth.'

'Your threats don't work on me, little girl, you're the most pathetic excuse for a hunter I've ever seen.'

Felicity snarled at my brother, the snide remark at her expense clearly not sitting well with her.

'In fact, once the GA discover what you and your father have been up to, I'm pretty certain you'll be locked away for good.'

'Don't they lock failed hunters up with the murderous wolves?' Terry teased. 'Yeah, I'm sure I heard that somewhere. The kids who don't cut it as a hunter are fed to the prey they tried so hard to destroy.'

'You're all monsters!' Felicity screamed, her eyes sparking with an inner fire. She wasn't going to give up easily.

She swiped at a stack of boxes with the Evermore logo on the side. They crashed to the floor at my feet, and the contents spilled out: hundreds of silver vials like the ones we'd found earlier containing Parker's evil serum. I lifted my paw and pounded at the tubes, smashing the casing and smearing the toxic green liquid across the stone floor.

The door leading back towards the nurse's office burst open, and Ethan lurched through holding his wooden staff. Felicity jumped away from him keeping a safe distance between the new arrival and the gathered pack. Ethan surveyed the room, only lingering on my wolf form for a few seconds.

'You need to leave,' he said. 'The GA are crawling all over the grounds looking for her.' He jerked his thumb at Felicity, and I felt a small tug of satisfaction.

'Who the hell are you?' Zak's voice was menacing as he looked over the hunter.

'It's fine,' Terry said. 'He's a friend of Mia's. Travelled up with her from Somerset yesterday. He's on our side.'

Zak didn't look convinced, but I was in no position to defend Ethan as the only sounds I could make were grunts and growls. I had to hope my brother believed Terry.

'Fine, let's go.' Zak gave a nod of his head. 'We'll leave Miss Parker to her fate.'

One by one the pack exited the room heading for the nurse's office and the safety of the trees beyond. I stalked forward baring my teeth at Felicity as I drew up next to her. She flinched away from me. Cody slapped Ethan on the shoulder in thanks and walked away. I didn't want Ethan getting caught up in this and waited for him to leave so I could protect him from any last-ditch attempt Felicity might make at attacking us.

As I reached the door, I saw the briefest of exchanges between the two hunters. Not a look of fear or revulsion but one of camaraderie. I watched Ethan pull his phone out and tap at the keys. Within seconds Felicity's mobile sang with the notification of a message received. She tapped the screen and smiled across at Ethan, blowing him a kiss. The chill of dread slid down my contorted spine as I worked out far too late that Ethan had fooled us all. He'd tricked me into returning his phone, and now I realised my error. He'd been in contact with my nemesis all along.

In one fluid motion, Felicity threw her dagger at me, and I roared as it struck me in the shoulder. She spun away, rolling across the floor to grasp at the remaining syringes. Ethan swung his staff around to smash into the exposed region of my head. I lurched to the side, momentarily stunned. In my clumsiness, I knocked the door closed, and as I lay on the floor trying to stop the world from spinning away, I noticed I was blocking the exit and preventing Cody and my brother from getting in to help me.

'Time to die, wolf girl,' Felicity spat the words at me as she flung the syringe at Ethan who caught it and brought it down hard on my leg. I felt the sharp sting as the needle broke through my skin and the rush of panic as he pumped the toxic contents into my system.

No! I wasn't ready to die.

My reaction was immediate. I began convulsing in the same way as the children we'd found in the Somerset woods. Sebastian had saved them with his tonics. I needed Sebastian. I needed my dad.

Felicity's shrill laughter snapped me back to the moment. She was draped over Ethan stroking his hair and kissing his cheek. The smarmy grin I'd always wanted to wipe off his face was the only thing I could see. At that moment everything became clear.

If it was my time to die, then I wasn't going alone. Zak had killed for me when he'd killed the bully who terrorised my childhood. So I could kill for him, for Cody, Terry, and Byron, for the pack, and my friends, for Ari and her sister. I would kill for all of them.

I rode the next wave of convulsions then summoned all my wolf healing to protect me from the toxins invading my system.

Neither hunter was expecting my strike as I launched from the floor claws extended. I slashed out at Felicity, knocking her off balance before digging my claws into Ethan's flesh. I felt the warmth of his blood as my nails dragged across his throat. His eyes grew wide in horror as he pitched to his knees clutching at the gash in his neck where his life force was draining away. He stared at me in shock and I realised with some satisfaction that he had underestimated me. Felicity screamed as the door burst open behind me.

'You killed him,' she shrieked.

Her hysteria fed my rage and I growled, readying myself to pounce when another snarl filled the air. It was a sound I'd heard before and one I couldn't ignore. It was the call of my alpha.

Zak stood behind me in his wolf form, his immense size filling the doorframe. He growled at me again, and I dropped my head in submission.

Felicity's screams mingled with my brother's gentle persuasions as I stumbled from the room struggling against the rising convulsions again. The last thing I saw was the redhead cradling Ethan's lifeless body in her arms.

'I will find you, wolf girl,' she ranted, 'and I will kill you.'

The door slammed shut, and she was gone. Zak led me up and out onto the car park where Terry was waiting. They herded me into the forest where I collapsed as the toxic serum burnt through my organs. The spasms rocked my body like a child shaking her rag doll. My bones creaked and groaned as I returned to my human form, and the searing pain in my joints dulled as the damp forest floor soothed me. Cody rushed to my side ripping the syringe from my leg and throwing a blanket around my naked frame.

'We need to get her away from the academy,' he said, a thread of panic in his voice.

'She needs Sebastian,' Terry said.

I wanted to agree with him, tell him that's exactly what I needed but I couldn't form the right words. I was delirious, and anything that came out of my mouth would sound like gibberish. My skin was on fire, and sweat trickled down the side of my face. Cody scooped me up from the floor and cradled me close to his chest. The heat was too much, and I felt like I was being burnt at the stake. I wriggled and moaned, and I knew he thought it was the serum doing its job, but I couldn't tell him that he was killing me with kindness.

A noise up ahead put everyone on high alert, and I felt Cody shudder as he tried to prevent himself from turning. Somehow, I knew he was willing himself to stay human so that he could hold and protect me.

'It's okay, it's Sebastian,' someone called out, the voices travelling back to where we stood. Sebastian was making his way through the trees, heading in our direction.

'Where is she?' His face filled my vision, which swam as I tried to focus. He lifted my eyelid and shone a light on me. I tried to flinch away, but Cody held me steady.

'We need to get her home. Follow me, the academy minibus is behind the school and the keys are always left in it.'

Cody jostled me back and forth as he hurried after Sebastian and bundled me into one of the seats. The engine started, and the vibrations carried through the metal and into my very soul. Everything hurt. The entire journey was torturous as I bounced around in the bus. Cody tried to soothe me as Sebastian drove like a maniac through endless dark lanes.

He finally stopped and I retched, first on the floor of the minibus and then again on the driveway.

'Quickly, get her inside.'

I looked up at the building ahead of us as Cody nestled me against his chest, the blanket tucked around my body. This place was unfamiliar. The stone cottage gleamed as we hurried through the front door. There was a cosy feel to the entrance hall with its flagstone floors, but I didn't get to see much as they rushed me through to a bedroom at the back of the cottage. Cody manoeuvred me into bed making sure I was covered up and kissing my burning forehead.

'What can I do to help?' he asked as Sebastian rolled up his sleeves and set to work unrolling a cloth with an assortment of vials and potions on it.

'Pray for her,' he said. 'The serum was only ever intended for a young child with the wolf gene. The modifications that Evermore made have mutated the strain so that the host gets pure poison. In a wolf child, this will accelerate the turning process as the body tries to heal and protect itself. By rights, all the children should die, but some of them have been able to resist.'

'How can they resist it?'

'I've only managed to look at some of the files so I'd need to do proper tests, but my early findings show that the children who survive have hunter DNA as well as wolf.'

'How is that possible?'

'I believe the barriers between the hunters and the wolves have been changing for some time, but clearly nobody dares talk about it. The horror of what Mr Parker has done might shine a light on a new era, Cody. One that you and Mia are already a part of.'

'What does it mean for Mia? She turned, Sebastian. I mean, fully turned.'

'Hmm, I know, but I'm not sure what will happen now. She was a hybrid with the strength of a hunter and the healing power of a wolf, but now...' He shook his head. 'I never stabilised the serum to cure lycanthropy, I only ended up killing her mother.'

I groaned and tried to speak. He had to know that it wasn't his fault, but I was slipping in and out of consciousness. The ceiling danced above me and joined hands with the walls. They spun together like they were dancing around a maypole. I thrashed my head from side to side trying to stop the whirling, but it didn't help. Cody's blond hair filled my vision as he leaned over me, dragging a damp cloth across my forehead.

I willed him to tell Sebastian that he wasn't the one to kill my mother. I wanted to shout it out loud, so the entire world knew my father wasn't an evil man.

I wanted to, but the world was slipping away. Darkness played at the edges of my mind, creeping forward like a game of hide-and-seek. I felt the sharp scratch of a needle in my arm and hoped that whatever Sebastian was doing would work and bring me back.

The darkness grew, and the voices of my father and boyfriend became fainter. I felt like I was travelling down a long tunnel and there was no way back.

Somewhere in the blackness of this passageway, I could hear my friends. Elizabeth, Terry, and even Miss Ross. They whispered, but I was comforted to know they were there, somewhere.

Before I drifted off into sleep that might very well be eternal, I heard my brother's voice, clear and bright like he was standing right next to me.

'Come back to me, little sis,' he said. 'Come back to me.'

HOOD ACADEMY

THIRTEEN

Through the cottage window I could see the blue sky and noticed the leaves on the treetops were starting to turn. The oranges, reds, and yellows of autumn approached and with them a new school term at Hood Academy.

I'd been lying in this bed for days as Sebastian worked hard to stabilise the poison that pulsed through my body. When I wasn't hallucinating, I was vomiting, and when that was done, I'd start convulsing. It was a cycle that never seemed to end.

Elizabeth hadn't left my bedside unless it was to get me food and water. Her friendship was keeping me anchored to the here and now.

So many times I'd wished that the damn serum would finish me off and let me climb off this wheel of torture, but it wasn't done with me yet.

In between my turbulent fits I'd listened in on the conversations between my friends. The news that the GA had Felicity in custody had lifted my spirits, but the disturbing fact that her father was still missing worried me, and the pack.

Sebastian had been good to his word and handed himself over to the GA. They extended him the courtesy of listening as he explained about Evermore and the serum. He'd exposed his vulnerabilities by telling them about his part in the death of my mother, and the blackmail threat Parker held over him. I was proud of my father, and I made a mental note to tell him that fact when I recovered.

'Morning.'

Elizabeth leaned forward and removed the flannel from my forehead and replaced it with a fresh one, the coolness giving me immediate relief from the burning beneath my skin.

I smiled at my friend. 'What time is it?'

'Ten past two. You've been drifting in and out of sleep for a few hours. Zak went back to the farm with Cody and the others to talk about what to do next.'

I licked my cracked lips and Elizabeth jumped up to grab a glass of water off the bedside table.

'Here, have a sip.'

She lifted me gently into a seated position and held the cup for me. The water tasted so good, and I drained the contents.

'Where's Sebastian?'

'He's back at Hood Academy talking to the GA. They want him to file a report against Parker and Felicity so they can take further action against them. He told me the GA are getting ready to leave as they're satisfied with the review.'

'They're leaving?'

'As far as I can tell. They've sided with Sebastian and there's some talk about reinstating him as headmaster when they go.'

'That's great news,' I said, flinching as a spasm of pain shot through my gut.

'Careful, Mia. You're still very weak.' She fluffed up my pillow and squeezed my hand as she sat beside me on the bed. 'Sebastian's honesty has saved him. They understand the strain he was under thanks to Parker's threat, and they're willing to give him another chance.'

I was happy, truly happy that Sebastian would be staying on at Hood Academy. It was more than a job to him; I understood that now. It was his ancestral home, and, I guess, mine too. I wasn't sure if that would even be a possibility now I was a fully fledged wolf, but I knew Sebastian wouldn't turn his back on me, wolf or not.

'What happens next?' I felt like I'd missed so much since I'd been here. The pack was still rallying around their alpha to eliminate the

Evermore threat, Parker was out there somewhere doing God knows what, and I was stuck in bed drinking foul-smelling potions, and riding each wave of pain as it rushed through my system.

'Zak's liaising with the other alphas around the country to destroy the Evermore dispatch warehouses. Liam arrived the other day with a few of the lads from Somerset. They'd contacted Headmaster Gregory from the local academy and explained the situation. From what I hear the wolves and hunters worked together to take down the warehouse in Somerset, and I also heard that Adam rallied the Cornwall academy to approach the packs and tear down the Evermore branch in the south.'

'Did anyone tell Gregory about Ethan?' I hadn't dared bring up the subject of me killing the hunter until now. I could scarcely believe it myself. When I nearly killed Felicity in the woods, Elizabeth, Zak, and the rest of the pack hadn't been able to look at me let alone speak to me, and yet now I'd crossed that line.

'Zak explained Ethan's part in all this to him but he wasn't shocked. He said that Felicity was a regular visitor at the Somerset academy and the head was worried that our red-headed friend had been leading Ethan astray for some time.'

'That's the understatement of the year.'

Elizabeth giggled. 'He tricked us all, Mia. The bad guy turned good guy ruse had us all fooled.'

I shuffled then winced.

'You did what you had to do to survive, Mia. Anyone would have done the same in your situation.'

I smiled at my friend for her kind words but I knew that Ethan's death would haunt my dreams for a long while.

'Let's just be happy that Gregory is working with Zak on destroying Evermore,' she added. 'That news is something worth celebrating.'

She was right, of course. I was amazed at the news. Hunters and wolves working together was something I never thought I'd hear about, but it stirred something deep inside me. Sebastian had told me during our car journey that things were shifting. There was evidence of hunter-wolf relationships in my notebook. Blimey, even I was a living, breathing piece of that, but something else he'd said swam to the forefront of my mind. I'd been feverish at the time, but his conversation with Cody at my bedside was burnt into my memory. *I believe the barriers between the hunters and the wolves have been changing for some time, but clearly nobody dares talk about it. The horror of what Mr Parker has done might shine a light on a new era, Cody. One that you and Mia are already a part of.* Was it possible that we could create a new alliance between the werewolves and the hunters? Could we honour Dr Neale's legacy and stand by his oath to protect and serve? The thought excited me, and a new surge of power washed over me. For the first time in my life, I knew what I wanted to do, and I wasn't afraid to do it.

MY LEGS WERE still a bit shaky, but I was getting stronger every day. For the past week, Elizabeth had come with me each morning to the garden so we could work on our combat skills. Sebastian had taken a couple of wooden staffs from the academy, so we had weapons to train with.

'You keep dropping your left shoulder.' Miss Ross's voice was like a musical note as she wandered into the garden, and I rushed to hug her.

Elizabeth squealed at the sight of our friend and mentor.

'It's good to see you, girls,' she said lowering herself into the camping chair Sebastian kept handy should I need to rest. 'I'm glad you're getting better, Mia.'

'I still feel like vomiting over my own shoes every day, but Sebastian said that'll stop soon as the poison is nearly out of my system.'

'Glad to hear it!'

'What are you doing here?'

'Your brother told me you were up and about and I thought you might want some help with your training. I know how important it is to you that you stay in control.'

She wasn't wrong. Escaping a violent life changed something inside of me, and when I found that spark in my heart never to play the victim's role ever again, nothing would allow me to slip back into that darkness.

'May I?' She stood and walked across to Elizabeth, taking the staff out of her hand.

'I'll leave you guys to it then.' Elizabeth dashed off inside the cottage, and I made a mental note to yell at her later for abandoning me to the fate of a lethal hunter.

Shit. My lesson in recovery was about to start whether I was ready or not.

I'D FORGOTTEN HOW tough training with Miss Ross could be. I'd only had a few one-on-one sessions with her at Hood Academy before being integrated into main classes, and yet it seemed that now I was a werewolf Miss Ross wasn't going to give me any special treatment.

'How do you know so much about werewolf training?' I asked between gasps. 'I thought you only tutored the hunters.'

Miss Ross's smooth complexion hadn't even broken into a sweat as she'd parried and jabbed relentlessly at me for the past hour. She remained fresh while I looked like I'd been on a triathlon.

'I used to spar with your mother when she was a new wolf. We were only girls back then and didn't really understand the animosity between the packs and the hunters. Call it a naïve innocence.'

'You two were friends when you were teenagers then?' I'd known for a while that Miss Ross and my mum had been close friends, so close in fact that Miss Ross was also my godmother, but I didn't realise they'd been friends from such a young age.

'We were at school together,' she said, jabbing a fist at my head. I dodged and blocked her swing, which got me a satisfied grunt from my tutor. 'We were drawn together by some unknown force. Perhaps it was because we were so different from the other kids. We had an unspoken bond due to our heritage.'

'Did you fight with her?'

Miss Ross chuckled as she spun on her leg and knocked me to the ground with her foot. 'Oh yes! We used to train together like we're doing now. I helped her through her transition to a werewolf, and she helped me hone my skills as a tracker.'

I sat on the floor my chest heaving from the effort of breathing.

'She'd be very proud of you, Mia.'

She extended a hand to help me up, and I took it gratefully.

'Mum never wanted this for me though. She never wanted me to be a wolf.'

'Your mother didn't want either you or Zak to go through the turn. She wanted to protect her children from the pain, suffering, and mental torture of being a wolf. I think, despite the fact you did turn, she would be proud of how you handled yourself, how you coped with the transition, and the young woman you've become.'

'Thank you,' I whispered. It felt good to have someone recognise what I'd achieved. Not so long ago I'd wished that I could turn, longed for it because I thought it was the only way to feel like I belonged, and I'd been bitterly disappointed with my hybrid status. However, the more I read about my ancestors, the more I realised what a great honour it was to be different.

'Can I tell you a secret?'

One of Miss Ross's eyebrows rose as she waited for me to spill my news.

'Well, actually, I need to show you rather than tell you.'

This got her second eyebrow twitching high up on her forehead.

I took a deep breath and extended my arms out a little from my body. As I concentrated, the sharp claws stretched out from my fingers. I lifted my chin and opened my mouth enough to show the smooth curve of my fangs.

Miss Ross's eyes widened as she took in my hybrid frame. She approached and gently lifted my right hand, running her finger along the claw. Turning my hand over, she examined the points of my fingers where the claws replaced my fingernails. Her hands moved up to cup the sides of my face as she stared at my fangs and then right into my eyes. I saw something shimmering in her gaze, something I used to see in my mother's expression: joy, love, and pride.

'It's incredible, Mia, but how is it possible?'

I shook my hands, and the claws retracted along with my fangs. I'd only discovered this ability the other day when Elizabeth had left me alone to fetch a sandwich from the kitchen. Stretching out to grab a glass of water I'd watched my claws shoot out. It had stunned me at first, but also fascinated me. I'd been able to retract and extend them at will for several minutes until Lizzie arrived back. I hadn't told her. I don't know why, but in a way, I was glad that Miss Ross was the first to know.

'I think me hearing that Parker was responsible for my mother's death triggered my turn because I was so angry. I'd never felt rage like it before. I'm not sure, but I think I'm always going to be a hybrid with the ability to turn only if I need to.'

'The full moon is in two days. If you're a true wolf, then you won't be able to resist the turn. It's the law of nature.'

I nodded as I remembered her lesson on full moon activity.

'Are you going to tell Zak?'

I shook my head. Zak had been sensitive to the point of annoying recently. I knew he was worried about me, but I needed him to appreciate how tough I could be. Cody knew how resilient I could be. He had been helping me control my senses as I lay in bed recovering. He understood that my differences were what made me unique.

'No, he'll only worry even more about me. By the time the full moon rises in the sky, I'll be ready to join the pack at the farm. I'll deal with whatever happens when it happens.'

'Probably a wise decision. Your brother still thinks of you as his little sister, and I doubt that'll ever change.'

Our exchange was interrupted as Sebastian strode out of the back door, lifting his hand in a little wave when he spotted his fellow tutor.

'Miss Ross, how good to see you.'

She nodded her head but took a small step backward. Evidently, the breach in their friendship hadn't been healed after my father's craziness, and Sebastian remained at arm's length.

'The GA has left,' he said, either ignoring or not noticing Miss Ross's standoffish manner. 'They packed up this morning and handed the academy back to me.'

He was beaming, and I felt a tug of pride for him. Without Parker's blackmail threat, and with the destruction of Evermore, he was free to run the academy as a headmaster should. Of course, I had wondered what his intentions were in that direction but hadn't been sure how to broach the subject. As it was, I needn't have worried as Miss Ross had it covered.

'Do you intend to train those girls to kill and torture the werewolf community?'

'Absolutely not. There are going to be a lot of changes in the future, Miss Ross, and I hope you'll join me in implementing them.'

'What kind of changes?'

'For one, I've rewritten the hunters' oath.'

I gasped and covered my mouth with my hand. He wasn't kidding when he said big changes. That oath was first recorded in 1862, and now Sebastian was going to rip apart a piece of history.

'Is that wise?' I asked.

'You haven't heard it yet.' He was grinning like an excited schoolboy, and I couldn't help but get swept up in his euphoria.

'Go on then, Sebastian,' Miss Ross said, crossing her arms across her chest. 'Share it with us.'

He cleared his throat, and I stuffed down the urge to giggle.

'To every pack, a cub is born, and every hunter gets their dawn. Nurturing friendships that grow deeper, united together as an Oath Keeper.'

The forest seemed to hold its breath along with Miss Ross and me. It was beautiful. Right there in the heart of the forest, surrounded by the wonder of nature I felt a lightness in my chest. With a few simple changes, Sebastian had forever changed the course of history for the hunters.

'I don't know what to say,' Miss Ross whispered, clearly as much in awe as I was. 'You've done a wonderful thing, Sebastian.'

He huffed and rolled his shoulders back.

'But will the GA accept this?' she added. 'They've stood by the original oath for hundreds of years, what makes you think they'll conform to this?'

He glanced over at me and smiled. 'I shared something else with the GA when I was questioned. Something that I hadn't told them before. They knew I was a hunter, but they'd never traced my bloodline. When I told them I was a direct descendant of Dr Neale they came round to my way of thinking.'

'You're a descendant of the first hunter?' Miss Ross's jaw dropped at his revelation, but then her face changed as she calculated the rest. 'Oh, Mia. That means you were his—'

I held up a hand to stop her. 'Yep, great-great-great whatever! I know, it's cool.'

'Well, if the GA is happy then I'm happy,' she said, offering her hand to Sebastian.

He took it with good grace and beamed at my godmother.

'There's something else. They want me to join the GA as chief consultant. I'll still be based from Hood Academy, but all GA policies will go through me.'

'That's amazing!' I cried, genuinely pleased for him.

'It means I need to find a new headmaster for Hood Academy, or perhaps a headmistress. What do you think?' Sebastian asked Miss Ross.

I'd never seen her so gobsmacked in the short time I'd known her. It was a huge position but an honour to receive. Taking control of the academy and the future of the hunter line was an incredible task, one that I knew, as did my father, Miss Ross was fully capable of handling.

'Yes,' she said softly. 'I'd be delighted to accept.'

I couldn't stop myself from squealing as I leaped at Miss Ross to wrap her in a tight hug. Times were changing, and everything was going to be different from now on.

OATH KEEPER

FOURTEEN

itting at my bedroom window, back at the Mills family farm, I gazed up at the darkening sky. It wouldn't be long until nightfall and the rise of the full moon. Cody had said he'd stay with me for the turn, but I'd brushed him off saying I'd done it once in front of an audience and I quite fancied the next time being a private affair. He understood and went to join the pack for whatever ritual they had on such a night.

The truth was I wasn't sure if I would turn. I suspected that I was back to being a hybrid and only something truly horrific would trigger my inner werewolf.

I'd eventually told Elizabeth my suspicions and hoped she'd help me deal with whatever happened over the next few hours.

'Hey, Mia.' Ari burst through my bedroom door and bounded up to my side followed by Lizzie. 'Aren't you coming down to join the pack?'

I circled the little wolf into a tight hug and pulled her up onto my lap. She had proved herself to be an incredibly capable young girl, leading the other pack kids to safety and keeping them calm. Her parents were bursting with pride and Ari's mother had taken to trailing after her making sure everyone she spoke with knew about her darling daughter. It was cute.

'Not this time, Ari. I wanted to do this privately, you know, until I get the hang of it.'

Ari giggled and pulled on her pigtail. 'I know what you mean. I threw up in front of Ben Clifton when I turned, and he teased me for weeks after.'

'Oh really, is Ben your boyfriend then?'

'Ugh, no way. He's a smelly boy that lives next door.'

Elizabeth laughed out loud at Ari's reaction, and I couldn't help but giggle at her disgusted expression. She was only ten years old and had plenty of time to learn about boys, crushes, and falling in love.

There was a light tap on the door, and Ari's mum stuck her head through the gap.

'Sorry to interrupt but Ari needs to head downstairs, the alpha is addressing the pack in a few minutes.'

Ari leaped from my lap and hurtled out of the room, then thundered down the stairs. I had a sneaking suspicion that the little wolf didn't like young Ben Clifton because she had a crush on my brother.

'Are you okay, Mrs Fletcher?'

The petite lady smiled and walked into the centre of the room. She fiddled with her sleeve as her gaze wandered over the furniture, walls, and my belongings. She couldn't stop fidgeting, and it was making my head spin. I stood up and grasped her hands in my own.

'Are you okay?' I repeated.

'I spoke with Dr Roberts about Ari and Toni, her sister.' Her voice grew quiet as she brought forward the memory of her lost daughter. 'He was interested in testing Ari's blood to see why she had survived that nasty stuff that Evermore was peddling.'

'Did he find anything?'

Her eyes filled with tears and the tiny woman let out a loud sob before collapsing onto the end of my bed. Elizabeth rushed to close the door, and I dropped to my knees in front of her, patting her hands and offering soothing sounds.

'He told me his suspicions as to why some of the children survived, and I was so ashamed.'

I peeked at Lizzie over the top of Mrs Fletcher's head, and she shrugged. No, Sebastian hadn't told me about his suspicions either. I was almost too afraid to ask.

'What suspicions does he have?'

Mrs Fletcher raised her tear-stained face and peered at me, holding my gaze and tensing her jaw.

'Ari is only half wolf. You see, I had an affair and only discovered I was pregnant after we split up. Pete never knew that Ari wasn't his.'

I was amazed that she'd shared such a sensitive secret with us, but the cogs were turning in my mind as I processed what she was saying and compared it with what Sebastian had said.

'Can I ask you a question? Did you have an affair with a hunter?'

More sobbing and shaking and plenty of tears but eventually Mrs Fletcher nodded.

'Yes, he was a hunter, and I was a wolf. My pack would have killed me if they'd discovered our relationship. I couldn't talk to anyone, and I prayed that when she reached sixteen, she would turn like her dad and me.'

It all clicked into place. The serum had killed her sister but only forced Ari to turn. That same serum had caused me to have hallucinations, sickness, and pain but I'd ultimately remained the same.

'Have you seen Ari turn?'

'Yes, we watched it happen over and over.'

'What are you thinking, Mia?' Elizabeth had seen that look on my face before.

'Ari is half wolf and half hunter. She's a hybrid, like me.'

Mrs Fletcher's eyes grew wide. 'Does that mean she can stop the turn?'

'Maybe,' I said. 'If it's okay with you, Ari could stay with me tonight instead of joining the rest of the pack. I'll see if it's possible for us to stay human on a full moon.'

'Oh, Mia, that would be wonderful. Thank you, thank you so much.'

'It does mean that Ari should know the truth about her dad, Mrs Fletcher,' I said gently. Telling your daughter that her dad isn't really her dad would be tough and yet ironically, I couldn't help but notice how the little wolf's life mirrored my own in that respect.

'I know,' she said. 'I'll tell her.'

She rushed out of the room in search of her daughter. I was pretty sure Ari wouldn't thank me for taking her away from Zak's big speech, but if I was right, there was a strong possibility that the two of us could resist the full moon.

'Will you stay with us, Lizzie?'

My friend walked over and sat beside me on the bed taking my hand in hers and squeezing my fingers.

'I'm not going anywhere. No matter what happens I'll stay beside you and Ari until morning.'

THE HOWLS OF the wolves started as soon as the moon reached its apex. I kept the lights off in my bedroom so no one could see us from the woods. Ari and I stood holding hands in the middle of the room, sweat pouring down both of our faces. Lizzie waited by the door, ready to escape if we did turn and Ari's youth and inability to control her actions caused her to attack our friend.

My skin tingled like I was connected to a mild electrical current, but it wasn't uncomfortable. I could feel the same tremors running through Ari's fingers and felt immense respect for the youngster who had paid careful attention to my instructions.

Not once did she moan, question, or argue with me. When Mrs Fletcher dropped her off at my room, Ari's eyes were puffy but she seemed okay with herself. It wasn't my place to get involved in their family discussions, but I'd wanted the little wolf to know she had a friend if she needed one.

'I'm okay, Mia,' she said once her mother had left. 'Daddy is still my daddy.'

I was overwhelmed with love and loyalty for this youngster who was one of the strongest people I'd had the honour to meet.

She happily listened to my story of the hybrid ancestry and the information I'd found in Dr Neale's notebook and this helped her to piece it together with her mother's revelation.

Mrs Fletcher joined her husband, Zak, Cody, and the rest of the pack in the woods, telling them that Ari felt a responsibility to look after her friend Mia. They all thought it was cute that the little wolf was looking after the newbie and they left us to it.

As we both fought the power of the moon, I believed that statement was partly true. We fought it together, hand in hand. The little hybrid wolf and her hybrid mentor. I hoped that this worked and we both stayed human. There was going to be a tough road ahead for the Fletcher family as the truth would inevitably come out now, but if Ari was saved the horrific pain of turning every four weeks, then it was worth it.

Miss Ross entered the room, and I heard her whispered exchange with Elizabeth.

'That's it, they've all turned and are in the woods. The moon's at its peak.'

'What do we do now?'

'We wait and see if they can hold on a little while longer.'

I squeezed Ari's fingers a bit tighter and smiled down into her beautiful, shining face. There was a determination in her eyes, and I could feel her power shuddering through our connection.

My limbs were visibly trembling now but the pain I'd experienced at Hood Academy that night hadn't manifested. Tremors, the sweats, and a thumping headache were all that plagued me at that moment.

Like a wave washing over the pair of us our pulses slowed down, our heart rate settled, and we dropped to sit on the floor together, exhausted.

'We did it,' Ari whispered, her clammy face illuminated in the light of the moon shining through the window.

'We did,' I agreed, circling my arm around the little hybrid. 'I'm so proud of you.'

'Well done, girls.' Miss Ross sat next to us as the moonlight bathed us in its glow. 'You've achieved the impossible tonight, and I think this is going to help many of the children who survived the serum.'

'Surely not *all* of their parents were unfaithful,' Elizabeth said, joining us on the floor.

'No, the DNA has travelled through generations. It might be that many years ago a hunter and wolf married in secret and brought children into the world and their descendants eventually wound up back in segregated communities believing that wolves and hunters shouldn't mix.'

'The hunter gene would remain in their DNA even if they married another hunter and had a baby. There's every possibility that two hunters could have a hybrid baby without ever knowing.'

'A lot of children survived the serum.'

'It's a good thing, Lizzie. With that evidence and Sebastian's new oath we've got a chance of living in harmony.'

We all sat in silence for a few moments taking in the enormity of the situation. History was being made, and we were key players. It felt good.

The companionable quiet was shattered by the sound of gunfire in the woods. We jumped to our feet, and I ran to the window, looking out at the forest bathed in the eerie glow of the moon.

More shots were fired followed by a keening sound that filled me with dread. Howls carried on the breeze, and I tried to distinguish between the sounds. Would I recognise Zak's cry if I wasn't in my wolf form?

'What the hell's happening?' Elizabeth grabbed her wooden staff and headed for the door before I'd even pulled on my shoes.

'I'm not sure, but it doesn't sound good.'

Another shot, another wail. My gut rolled, and I fought the nausea that threatened to overwhelm me.

'Ari, I need you to stay here. Lock the kitchen door behind us and don't come out no matter what you hear.' I grabbed the girl's shoulders and held her tightly. 'We're going to go help the pack, but I need someone here to look after anyone who makes it back home.'

She puffed out her chest and tapped her forehead with her tiny hand. 'Aye, aye, Captain.'

We left her behind, her small face the last thing I saw before she slammed the door and the bolt slid home. She was safe at least. Now we had to find her family and make sure they were safe too.

'We stick together until we work out what we're up against,' Miss Ross said, her authoritarian teacher's voice calm and steady.

As one we melted into the forest unsure of what we might find but ready to take on any danger that faced us.

FIFTEEN

Nothing could have prepared any of us for what we found as we moved deeper into the forest. Elizabeth fell over the first body, and I found the second. No longer in their wolf form, the two pack members lay sprawled across the floor, their naked bodies smeared with blood and grime.

Lizzie threw up behind a holly bush, but by some miracle I kept control of the bile rising up my throat.

'Are they dead?' Elizabeth's voice was barely audible.

'Yes.' Miss Ross felt for the pulse in their neck. 'There's nothing we can do for them. We can return later to recover their bodies, but for now we need to press on.'

More shots echoed through the trees, further ahead of us nearer to the academy.

'Have the GA changed their mind and come back to finish off the pack?' It was the only logical explanation I could come up with.

'The GA doesn't use guns. A hunter uses natural weapons to defend themselves, like the wooden staff. This is something else.'

By the gleam in Miss Ross's eye, I believed she had her own thoughts on who, or what, we were about to find but I wasn't sure I wanted to know in advance.

A series of snarls and cries to our immediate left had us running in that direction. We burst through the trees to find a small brown wolf pinned down by two students, one holding a gun in shaky hands and the other a small crossbow. Shock reverberated through me at the sight.

Hood Academy students, kitted out in their grey school jumpsuits, were attacking the wolves in the forest at gunpoint. My mind tried to make sense of it, but before I could fathom an answer, Miss Ross had struck the nearest girl with the butt of her staff and was rounding on the other.

'Who sent you here tonight?' she snapped, circling the girl.

'The headmaster,' she said, her voice shaking almost as much as her hand. 'He said we were under attack, rounded us all up, and gave us a weapon. I've never killed anyone…anything before.'

The brown wolf hadn't run away, and I realised it had a bullet wound in its back leg.

With Miss Ross dealing with the student it gave me time to tend to the wolf. I dragged my scarf from my neck and wrapped it around the leg. Before my eyes, the wolf disappeared, and Mrs Fletcher lay before me. I'd never seen the wolves return to their human form before and I had been in no fit state to remember my own return. It was like the fur melted away exposing broken bones which shifted back into position as one.

Ari's mum moaned as she collapsed to the forest floor.

'Oh my God.' The student dropped to her knees, throwing the gun away to the side in disgust. Elizabeth scooped it up and slid it into her waistband.

'The headmaster you're talking about, is he called Sebastian?' Miss Ross continued her interrogation.

'No, the head is Mr Parker. He's been head for a few months now.'

I sat back on my heels and stared at Miss Ross, a message passing between us. The girls didn't know Parker was no longer head.

Parker had armed the students and sent them into the woods even though most of them weren't fully trained. He'd used young girls as a weapon and didn't care if they were slaughtered in the process. We'd found dead wolves, but I was under no misconception that somewhere in these woods we'd find dead students too, young girls who faced the wrong wolves and never lived long enough to see the yellow of their eyes.

'Go, find Zak and the others,' said Miss Ross. 'I'll take this girl with me, and we'll help Mrs Fletcher. It's probably nearer to the academy than the farm so I'll get her to the hospital wing. If you find any more wounded send them there.'

I nodded and left Mrs Fletcher moaning on the ground. Elizabeth joined me as we sprinted off into the night.

We found other pack members wandering the woods, dazed at the sudden attack. Fortunately, my scent was familiar to all of them, and I was able to guide them in the direction of home or the school and Miss Ross.

'I wish we could find Zak and Cody,' I said pushing the branches out of my way.

'I know. There haven't been any shots for a while. Do you think the wolves have killed all the students?'

'God, I hope not. Parker's used them to try and start a war, and it's up to us to make sure that he doesn't manage it.'

'How the hell are we supposed to stop him, Mia? The man's dangerous. He's prepared to sacrifice teenagers.'

I couldn't answer her. I had no idea how to stop someone like Parker. I'd spent so long fighting his daughter that the prospect of coming face-to-face with her dad never dawned on me. I knew that he probably wasn't in these woods though; he wouldn't want to get his hands dirty. I shivered as I remembered his conversation with Felicity about framing Sebastian for everything. Parker had turned getting away with murder into an art form.

The trees ahead rustled and we both braced ourselves ready to fight. Together we gasped as Terry staggered into view, his naked body covered in blood. Elizabeth shrugged off her coat and wrapped it around his waist, nestling herself in the crook of his arm to help support him. He'd been shot before, but it was a clean wound and healed quickly thanks to his werewolf healing abilities. This was an altogether different situation.

From this angle I could see two bullet wounds, both in his leg; he had a crossbow bolt sticking out from his shoulder and another in his abdomen. He coughed, and a cloud of blood spurted across the floor.

Pitching to his knees, he crumpled to the ground taking Elizabeth with him.

'Where's Zak?' Panic laced my voice as I watched my friend bleed all over the earth. 'Where's my brother?'

'We got separated,' he wheezed. 'Near the school.'

He was spent, that small piece of information enough to wear him out beyond exhaustion. Blood poured down his chest from the injured shoulder and mingled with the fresh blood seeping from the hole in his gut.

'I don't know what to do,' I said to no one in particular.

'Look for Zak. I'll try and get Terry to the school. Miss Ross will patch him up. He's tough, Mia, don't worry.'

I nodded at my friend and taking one last look at Terry I shot off into the trees.

The forest was silent, not even the nocturnal animals dared to move. The moon had begun its descent but still lit up the area like the floodlights on a football field.

I was close to the school now and crept silently to the edge of the treeline to see if I could spot Parker or the wolves. Soft cries filled the air, and I felt a tug on my heartstrings as I saw the huddles of young girls clinging to one another. They hadn't asked to be put in this position. They'd arrived at school ready to start their training in the safe environment of the academy building. At no point were they expecting to be sent out into the woods during a full moon armed with guns and told to kill on sight.

Should I speak to them? Could I convince them that Parker wasn't the headmaster anymore and they didn't have to follow his orders? I doubted they would believe me after everything that had happened. It was common knowledge that Mia Roberts had followed the pack and rejected the oath. If only they knew about the changes Sebastian would make.

My skin crawled as Parker emerged from the back of the school building, Felicity at his side. How the hell did he get her away from the GA? That didn't matter now. I had the two of them together in one place, and all I needed to do was find a way to stop them.

I watched Parker move around the girls appraising them with predatory eyes as I contemplated various ridiculous acts of bravery. He flicked at something on his jacket, dusting the sleeve and rubbing his blackened hands on a handkerchief from his pocket. I didn't want to think about the stains on his hands or the blackish smudge that now coated the cloth. No doubt he'd tortured some unfortunate soul. His stance reeked of authority as if he'd already won when I knew he'd lost everything. Perhaps this was his plan all along; return to the scene of the crime and kill everyone in a blaze of glory.

Blimey, I needed to stop watching Cody's action films.

I surveyed the students. They clung together wearing matching jumpsuits and school regulation pumps, but that was all. A large crate of guns lay open on the lawn a few feet away from them but they eyed it nervously. I couldn't see a weapon of any kind on their person apart from the wooden staff Felicity was twirling. Even Parker appeared unarmed.

He really believed he was safe. Safe from attack, safe from discovery. This was my chance. Taking a deep breath, I stood up, strolled out of the treeline, and headed across the lawn towards the assembled group.

Felicity was the first to spot me and screamed with fury. She sprinted to meet me, but her father grabbed at her arm stopping her in her tracks.

'No need, pumpkin, she'll be dead soon enough.'

I came to a stop a few feet away and held my arms out to the side readying myself to release my claws. I didn't want to freak the students out, so if I could keep them hidden for as long as possible it would be for the best. It was tough to ignore the itch just beneath my skin as I watched Parker and his red-headed daughter snarl at me.

'You're a tiresome creature, Miss Roberts,' Parker barked across the lawn. 'You've managed to unravel my carefully crafted plans and bring about the destruction of my entire business empire. If I didn't have to kill you, I'd be of a mind to offer you a job. You've got a certain way with manipulation that I admire.'

'I'm flattered. First I beat your daughter at the assessments, then I impress you with my handiwork. Perhaps I'm the daughter you wish you'd had.'

Parker was way ahead of me and kept a tight grip on Felicity's arm. Goading her was a cheap trick, but it felt great. Divide and conquer them was my only plan.

'Perhaps you should have left her to the GA where she couldn't show you up.'

Felicity's face matched her hair colour as she tugged at her father's grip, but Mr Parker held firm.

'The GA are a bunch of fools, my dear, and can't see the corruption in their ranks. Did you know there are a dozen GA agents loyal to me? No, I don't suppose you would.'

That explained the kidnappings. The children from the lab had spoken about men in black taking them from their homes. Parker clearly hadn't heard about Sebastian's reinstatement or his new role at the GA. I smiled to myself as I thought about Parker's men getting their comeuppance.

'Do you find something funny, Miss Roberts?'

'You've broken Felicity out of the GA using their own men. Don't you think someone will notice and come looking for you both?'

'Oh, I think the GA will have enough to deal with clearing up all the dead vermin from the woods.'

I flinched. He wanted the wolves dead. All of them. I had to stop him.

'You don't belong here anymore,' I said, loud enough for the gathered students to hear me. 'The GA dismissed you, arrested *her*, and reinstated Sebastian as head of the academy. What you're forcing these girls to do is against the oath.'

Murmured whispers rippled through the assembled students.

'That's right,' I shouted. 'You've all broken the hunters' oath and could be punished. If I were you, I'd make your way back to your dormitories and wait for Dr Roberts.'

'Stay where you are!' Parker snapped. His words echoed through the night air and startled the group who began crying again.

I needed to get the girls to safety before engaging with Felicity and her father. I had no idea if Parker could fight. I'd never seen him in action even though he was a hunter. I'd seen him intimidate, bully, and embarrass, but I'd never seen him swing a staff.

The low howl of a wolf in the distance followed by the response of others answered my prayers. Zak's call. I did recognise it after all. I breathed a sigh of relief on hearing the sound. He was calling the pack, and that could only mean he was rounding them up for an attack. As he wasn't too close, I could only assume he'd found more students in the woods.

The sound briefly distracted Parker and his daughter, and without giving it too much thought, I burst into a run and barrelled straight into Felicity knocking her to the ground. Parker snatched at me grazing my arm with his fingertips but missing out on a firm grip. I kept running until I reached the girls, who shuffled backward in fright and surprise.

'Run, all of you!' I shouted. 'Get to the hospital wing and find Miss Ross. She'll tell you what to do. Go!'

They didn't need much persuasion as they sprinted off across the lawn towards the school building. The howls in the woods grew louder. Zak was heading this way.

'You stupid bitch.' Felicity jumped at me, punching me square in the face. I staggered backward almost losing my footing. I could feel the blood dripping down my face, but within seconds I felt my claws snap into place and my fangs appear.

I swiped at my nemesis catching the top of her arm. She yelped and jumped clear. The sound of approaching wolves filled my head, the soft boom of their paws on the compacted earth, their breath a faint whisper on the wind.

I only needed to stall these two long enough for the alpha to arrive.

Felicity thrust her staff forward but I blocked it with ease. I was getting better and faster at anticipating her moves.

'I'm going to kill you for what you did to Ethan,' she hissed.

'He'd still be alive today if you hadn't involved him.' I knew it was a low blow to turn Ethan's death on her and from the flash of anger in her eyes I'd hit a nerve.

She snarled, and I almost laughed. If she wanted to know what a real snarl was like I was only too happy to show her.

I filled my lungs and roared, releasing my full hybrid power. The startled expression on Felicity's face was worth it. I reached back ready to strike another blow when Parker assaulted me from the side. He wielded a long cane like something out of a Sherlock Holmes movie with a heavy brass ball on the end. My teeth shuddered as it connected with my head. Stars danced across my vision as I tried to keep Felicity in my view. They were tag teaming me now, circling me like vultures around a fresh kill.

The cane landed on my shoulder blade, and I heard the loud crack as it fractured. Pain seared through me as I howled. Felicity flicked her staff up, catching my chin and sending me sprawling onto the ground. Parker stood over me his cane poised, ready to bring it down onto my skull. I tried to lift myself up but the pain shot through my arm and I slid back to the floor. Parker's eyes clouded over as he lifted his cane.

'Time to die, Miss Roberts.'

I waited for the blow, but it never came; a blur of fur and fangs filled my vision as a huge brown wolf hooked its teeth into Parker and dragged him away, his screams filling the empty space he'd left behind.

Felicity became hysterical, whirling her staff in all directions trying to cause damage but not hitting anything in the process. The gurgled sounds of her father's demise distracted her. She screamed her fury and threw the staff at a golden wolf who guarded me where I lay, but the wood fell harmlessly under the claws of the pack. Wolves swarmed the grounds, and I caught the scent of everyone I knew and loved.

Surrounded, Felicity still refused to give in. She lashed out at anything that came too close to her as she crept closer to her father's body. Parker's lifeless eyes stared into the star-filled sky, blood soaked the front of his shirt, and his torn throat glistened under the moonlight. I tried to push down the need to vomit. Sobbing and shaking, Felicity knelt over her father and the wolves seemed to hold their position as if giving her that split second to grieve.

That split second was all she needed to unhook the gun from Parker's belt, the gun I hadn't spotted before, and wave it at the wolves. She settled the barrel on Zak, and I saw her finger twitch as she squeezed.

The gunshot made me scream, the sound too loud for me to deal with. I struggled to my knees, my eyes darting all over for Zak, but he remained where he had been, as strong and powerful as ever. My brain couldn't work it out until I spotted Sebastian, his arm outstretched with a smoking gun in his hand.

Felicity was on the floor, blood pouring from a wound to her shoulder. She screamed and swore, and for a brief moment, I was relieved to hear it. He hadn't killed her, but Sebastian had stopped her from killing my brother.

HOOD ACADEMY

SIXTEEN

Miss Ross was in full control when we arrived at the hospital wing of Hood Academy. Students and pack members sat together, helping each other. My heart swelled with pride at the sight.

Cody helped me through the main door where the young girl we'd met in the woods greeted me. Her face was tear-stained and her eyes ringed with bruises from crying, but she looked like she'd pulled herself together.

'I'm Jenny,' she said stretching out her hand and helping me into a nearby seat. 'I wanted to thank you for not killing me earlier.'

I huffed and instantly recognised the family trait.

'Mia,' I said with a wave of my hand. 'I never had any intention of killing you. I only wanted to stop Parker from starting a war between the hunters and the wolves.'

'I know, Miss Ross filled me in on everything on the way back here. She's a wonderful tutor. I hope she stays.'

'Oh, don't you worry about that. Miss Ross will be around for a long time.'

'Do you need anything? Bandages, pain relief, water?'

'No, thanks, I've got it covered.' I knew that my bones were already healing and knitting back together as I could feel it like a burning sensation beneath my skin. 'How's Terry? Did Elizabeth make it here okay?'

Jenny shook her head. 'I haven't seen anyone called Terry, and if Elizabeth is the blonde girl you were with in the woods, then she hasn't been here either.'

Panic bubbled up in my chest. Terry was in a bad way and needed help. Yes, he would heal eventually but not if there were bullets lodged in his body or crossbow bolts still wedged in his side.

Cody scanned the assembled group but finally he glanced at me and shook his head.

'We've got to find them,' I said to him.

'I know. We'll head back out into the woods, and hopefully we can pick up their scent.'

Jenny left us at the door as we hurried out into the car park. Zak was still in his wolf form refusing to return to being human in case he needed to protect his pack from further attack, which was fortunate for us.

His immense head swivelled in our direction as we tore across the gravel car park. The other pack members who stood with him melted away to give us privacy.

'Terry was hurt, badly, and hasn't made it to the hospital wing. I think him and Lizzie are still out there somewhere.'

Zak bobbed his head to let me know he understood and then lifted his head to howl into the sky. From within the trees, I heard the returning cries of the wolves still patrolling the area. My brother approached and nudged my elbow with his large snout, pushing me towards the forest. He wanted me to run with him, brother and sister.

I stared up at the full moon still visible in the sky. I'd passed my own test to see if a hybrid could control its shift, but now I was about to see if a hybrid could turn when the need arose.

Cody's warm fingers intertwined with mine and I gazed up into his sparkling blue eyes.

'Together,' he whispered.

I leaned in and kissed him.

'Together,' I agreed.

Taking a deep breath I concentrated on my body, feeling for the bones and muscles, picturing the tendons and ligaments that joined it all together, and then the heat washed over me like an explosion. The pain was instant as my bones began to break and my skin rippled.

I was aware that some Hood Academy students were standing outside the nurse's office door watching as Cody and I turned, but I didn't mind. I was proud of who I was, and I wanted everyone to know it.

WE RAN THROUGH the woods as one pack, sniffing out injured wolves and startling any stray students. Zak ordered some to stay behind and help guide everyone home. As we ripped up the earth with our paws, we found pockets of hunters and wolves huddled together.

Ari's father stood as we entered the clearing where he and another pack member sat with a young girl from the academy. The two men were draped in blankets but were unharmed.

'I heard your cry, but I didn't want to scare the young lass by returning to my wolf form,' he told us. I could understand his words perfectly even though it was his scent I recognised rather than his physical looks. 'I saw young Elizabeth with Terry. They were heading back to the Mills Farm. He didn't look good, but the lass was looking after him well.'

A deep rumble erupted from the back of Zak's throat causing the student to flinch and shy away from the wolves surrounding her.

'I will,' Mr Fletcher said in response to Zak's request. 'We'll take her back to the academy straight away.'

It was a relief to hear that Lizzie and Terry were making their way to the farm. I knew Terry was injured, and they were both probably shattered from the exertion of manoeuvring through the woods, but if they made it to the farm I knew someone would be there to tend to Terry's wounds.

I hoped Ari was okay too. The young wolf had been left alone and in charge of the farmhouse. I knew she could handle it, but

I hoped hearing the cries from the woods hadn't worried her too much. Strong or not, she was still only a little girl.

We left Mr Fletcher and adjusted our route to take us back home. I was eager to see Elizabeth and check she was okay.

Running through the woods, I marvelled at the sensation of my powerful frame. Long ago I'd run through these same woods as a tearful teenager hiding from my problems. I'd come such a long way, and now I was free. That freedom felt incredible as the wind tore through my fur and my paws pounded the fallen leaves. The moon illuminated everything that was beautiful about the forest. The colours that changed with the shadows, the textures of the moss and bark, and the crunch of the leaves as the seasons turned. I'd never felt more alive.

Zak and Cody growled at the same time, and it took me a few seconds to sense the problem. The stars in the sky disappeared behind a haze, and the scents of the forest changed, becoming harsh and toxic. Something was burning.

My eyes caught sight of the flames above the treetops in the distance, and my stomach knotted. There was only one thing that would burn so fiercely out here, and that was the Mills farmhouse.

Panic clenched my insides as I understood the connection. Parker had been dusting ash off his coat and wiping soot from his hands when I saw him on the lawn. He had found the house, discovered where the wolves lived, and destroyed it. We had brought Ethan here and in our naivety we'd trusted that he'd keep the location a secret. His deceit ran deeper than we had realised and suddenly I wasn't so upset that I'd ripped his throat out.

The wolves darted in all directions unable to comprehend what was happening. I broke through the trees into the back garden of the house and came to an abrupt stop. Flames engulfed the entire building, licking up the sides of the walls, and blistering the paint on the wooden window frames. Smoke poured out of the kitchen door, which stood wide open. A sob caught in my throat and came out as a growl. The flames fanned out, leaving nothing untouched.

A strangled cry bubbled up from my throat, and I realised I was back in my human form. I hadn't even felt the shift or registered any pain. Looking around me I saw only wolves, all of them staring at the house, the flames dancing in the reflection of their eyes. I snatched a pair of joggers and T-shirt off the washing line and hurried to dress.

There was no way I could get close to the house; the flames were too fierce. Crumpling to the ground, I broke down. Ari, Elizabeth, and Terry were in there. Had they realised what was happening? Were they trapped? Or did the smoke kill them before the flames? Even after his death, Parker was still able to inflict pain and misery.

I tilted my head back and screamed into the night.

A soft shout caught my attention as if someone had heard my screams and was answering from the heavens. I opened my eyes and looked around. The wolves moved off as one towards the back of the house, and I scrambled to my bare feet and followed.

The white picket fence was blistering from the heat of the fire as we trailed around the edge of the property. Zak led the way, his deep brown fur glistening in the firelight. There was movement up ahead, and as the thick smoke parted briefly, I saw a blonde head of hair shining like a beacon.

'Lizzie!' I shouted as I launched into a sprint, barging past the wolves who stood between my friend and me.

She barrelled her way towards me, and we flew into each other's arms. Her hair smelt of smoke and her face was covered in soot and grime, but she was very much alive.

'This way, come quickly.' She herded me to the side and urged the wolves to follow. We headed for the garage adjacent to the farm, still untouched by the flames that decimated the farmhouse.

'Mia! You're here.' Ari shot out of the doorway, and I dropped to my knees to hug the little wolf. Relief flooded through me, and I sobbed once more.

One by one the wolves' masks dissolved until everyone was in their human form. Blankets and random pieces of clothing were distributed from the laundry that backed onto the garage block. Elizabeth tugged me through the door and there, lying on the flatbed of the Mills family truck, was Terry, languishing among the sacks of potatoes, his wolfish grin shining out from his sooty face.

'I don't know about being a wolf, you should be a bloody cat with all those lives you have.' I leaned across the side of the truck to kiss Terry's cheek.

He laughed out loud, and the sound melted something in my chest. I had thought they were gone, all of them, and for the briefest of moments, I was utterly broken.

Cody snaked his arm around my waist and slapped his brother on the shoulder, which made him wince, and all of us laugh. Zak stood on the other side of the truck and smiled at his friend, the relief clear on his face as much as on my own. Ari swung herself up onto the truck and nestled in next to Terry, a beaming smile on her beautiful young face.

I glanced around me as if seeing my friends and family for the first time. We were all hot and sweaty, covered in twigs, soot, and blood, and wearing mismatched clothing, but we were together. This was my pack, and I would follow them to the ends of the earth.

SEVENTEEN

The car pulled through the tall, wrought-iron gates and into the winding driveway of Hood Academy. It seemed a lifetime ago that Sebastian first brought me here as a new student.

The massive wooden doors of the school stood open as we pulled up outside and I saw the throng of people congregating in the entrance hall. Miss Ross stood on the top step greeting everyone as they arrived and I had to smile at her choice of wardrobe.

'I thought headmistresses had to wear stuffy suits and billowing cloaks,' I teased as I joined her.

'Then you're at the wrong school.' She winked, her bright blue tracksuit perfectly complementing her dark skin and reflecting in the twinkle of her eye.

I left her shaking hands with another group of students and wandered inside to see what other changes the new headmistress had made. At first glance everything looked the same. The comfortable sofas, the wood panelling, and the chandeliers were still there, but there was a new sign on the glazed office door. Miss Ross was in charge of Hood Academy now, and the wording on the plaque told everyone that fact. To the right of the head's office had been the small store cupboard, which housed the secret entrance to the basement laboratories. The cupboard was gone now, and with a bit of remodelling the space had been developed into a respectable entrance to the science labs.

It had been Sebastian's idea to continue working on natural remedies that could help both wolf and hunter. He'd abandoned his cure for lycanthropy and had instead begun to work on salves for dressing wounds, tonics for fever, and a serum to reduce the pain of turning at the full moon. The GA had agreed to fund the venture and were hoping it would create a pioneering science-based diploma for future students.

The excited chatter of the girls who came and went down the stairs to the labs told me the corridor of rooms, which had housed such barbaric activities below, had also received a remodel.

'Mia!' I spun around to see Elizabeth and Adam making their way through the masses of students.

'The place looks great, doesn't it?' I said as we hugged and exchanged cheery hellos. Adam had arrived back at the Mills farm as the fire brigade were damping it down. The sheer terror on his face evaporated when he spotted Lizzie safe and well.

We'd all suffered scary moments over the past few months, some more terrifying than others, but we'd come through it and were much stronger for it.

'When's Zak getting here?' Elizabeth asked, her voice betraying the excitement I also felt at my brother being invited to the grand opening of a new Hood Academy.

'They should be here soon. Cody dropped me off and went to park the car.'

I never thought I'd be talking about the local werewolf pack's arrival at a hunters' academy, but a new head, and a new oath were only a few of the changes being made this year.

Miss Ross and Sebastian had approached the GA with their proposal to work with the local wolf community to build a better understanding of each other's roles in society. It was groundbreaking stuff, and we were all eager to be a part of it.

I spotted Sebastian through the crowd and waved him over to where we'd found a small space to stand at the side of the room.

'Welcome back to Hood Academy,' Sebastian said beaming at us in turn. 'Let's hope this academic year is a bit quieter than the last.' He winked at me, and I couldn't help but laugh. It certainly had been a whirlwind year with many transformations.

I pulled him to one side so that we could talk privately. So much had happened recently and I hadn't had a chance to tell him that Parker was guilty of my mother's death. Sebastian had held himself accountable for too long.

'I owe you an apology,' I said, suddenly feeling nervous. 'I blamed you for Mum's death and now I know that wasn't the truth. It was Parker.'

Sebastian leaned forward and took my hands in his. 'I know it was. I read his notes in the file you took from his office.'

'Why didn't you say anything? You let me carry on thinking you were responsible.'

He smiled at me and his eyes lit up. 'You were dealing with enough without having to think about me and your mother, Mia. After Ethan injected you I spent hours at your side trying everything to save you. Cody told me what the two of you had overheard and I realised that was the trigger that forced your full shift to werewolf. I couldn't spare you the anguish and pain of turning, but I most definitely wanted to save you from further despair.'

'So you would have allowed me to think the worst of you to keep me safe?'

'Always,' he said softly.

It was at that moment I realised how far we'd come as father and daughter. He had lost the love of his life, and very nearly lost his only daughter, but instead he'd shown a strength of character that made me proud to call him family.

It wasn't only me he was helping either. With the destruction of the Mills farm, Sebastian had offered his cottage to Zak and the pack. He had moved into rooms on the third floor of the academy so he could stay close to his work.

We had all found our way in the end. Elizabeth and I were due to return to our old dorm room. Lizzie wanted to continue with her studies but Miss Ross had other plans for me. With my personal knowledge of being a hybrid, and the realisation that it wasn't as rare as we first thought, I'd been offered a position as a tutor. I was in the process of developing a new course about the history of the hybrid and the talents we possess to share with the students.

A hush fell over the room as Miss Ross called for attention.

'I'd like to ask all the students to make their way through to the library, so please take your places as quickly as you can, and we'll begin.'

We followed the crowd and spilled out into the library. The shelves had been pushed to the sides of the room, and hundreds of folding chairs filled every inch of the thick burgundy carpet except for a walkway through the centre.

We took our place on the front line where Miss Ross had put reserved signs on a row of seats. My skin tingled, and my stomach fluttered when I thought about the future. Not only the future of Hood Academy and its students, but my own outlook. I was a hybrid: half hunter and half wolf. I could do things that neither hunters nor wolves could do. My skills were unique, and I took a tremendous amount of pride in being different.

Miss Ross and Sebastian stood on a raised platform at the front of the room and addressed the group.

'Welcome to Hood Academy, everyone. It's a joy to see so many of you here.' Miss Ross's voice was clear and strong, and I glanced around at the shiny faces of the new students as they hung on her every word. They'd heard the stories of the war between hunters and wolves, and the sickening way the old headmaster, Parker, had used the students as weapons.

They'd also listened to the stories of hunters and wolves working together, of students lost in the woods and being rescued by the packs, the tales of wolves standing over students to keep them warm until help arrived, and the aid given to wolves by the girls who helped Miss Ross in the hospital that night.

Good overcame evil. Darkness turned to light. Miss Ross knew how to capture the imagination of these girls and mould them into honest, caring, and tolerant human beings.

'It's my pleasure to introduce a special guest to you all today. Someone who is a large part of this community and who has been a tireless friend to both Sebastian and me, and a champion for this school. May I present Zak Roberts, alpha of the Ravenshood pack.'

I felt the air leave the room as the students turned in their seats and sucked in a collective breath, watching the alpha pad down the red carpet. Zak had chosen to attend in his wolf form so that he could show the girls what they were up against if they decided to follow the old ways.

He was as big as a horse, his powerful limbs visible beneath his glossy fur. He looked magnificent, and I savoured the lightness in my chest as I watched my brother mount the platform and stand beside Sebastian.

The students remained silent as Miss Ross cleared her throat, none of them taking their eyes off Zak.

'I'd also like to introduce a few other members of Zak's pack. Gentlemen, if you could join us here for a moment.' She motioned for Cody, Terry, and Byron, who bashfully inched out of their seats and strode to the front.

Terry grinned at the young girls in the front row, and I watched the red flush touch their cheeks in turn at his attention. Elizabeth giggled at my side too, and I rolled my eyes at her. Only Terry could manage to get half the school crushing on him.

'These young men helped to secure the future of Hood Academy and the hunters' oath. They fought side by side with some of our most determined hunters to banish evil and bring us into the light. Can we give them a round of applause?'

The library erupted into claps and cheers as my friends waved and grinned at the audience. Elizabeth and I joined the chorus of cheers and laughed as they each took a bow in turn.

Once the noise had died down Miss Ross winked at me from the stage.

'Finally, I'd like to present to you one of our newest tutors, an ex-student, and a unique young woman. Mia, will you join me?'

Elizabeth squeezed my fingers as I stood and I felt her strength mesh with my own as I faced the sea of expectant faces. They seemed so young, and yet they were only a year or two younger than me. I'd turned seventeen during the weeks we spent destroying the Evermore warehouses and saving our friends. I'd registered the day but didn't tell anyone. At the time it wasn't important, but now I knew it had marked a new beginning for me.

'Thanks, Miss Ross.' I smiled across at my godmother, and she nodded. She knew I was ready to face the future and embrace who I was and I was grateful for her continued guidance. 'I'm here to share something very special with you all. Something that will cement the future of this academy and give us all something to fight for. Standing together makes us stronger, and we can learn so much from one another. Zak is—' I swept my hand out towards the alpha, who held his head high as he watched me speak. 'Zak is not only a fierce and loyal alpha, but he is also my brother.'

There was a rippling of whispers from the students.

'Cody isn't just another member of Zak's pack, he's my boyfriend. Miss Ross is my godmother as well as my headmistress, and Dr Roberts, well, Sebastian is my father, and I am proud of each and every one of them. We have been through so much together, but we're still here standing shoulder to shoulder, and that's a beautiful thing.'

There were tears in Elizabeth's eyes as I glanced over at my friend. Adam smiled up at me with a fire in his eyes that told me he was as much a member of my pack as everyone else. Cody, Terry, and Byron beamed at me from their seats, and near the back of the room, I caught the twirl of a pigtail as Ari bounced up and down in her seat.

History had been made today, and we were all a part of it. I felt the warmth of Zak's fur as he moved to stand beside me and the touch of a cool hand slip into mine as Sebastian stood on my other side.

'I'm so proud of you, Mia.'

I smiled up at the man who had saved me, even if I hadn't known it at the time. I smiled at the man who had loved my mother unconditionally, and I smiled at the man he would become. 'Thanks, Dad,' I whispered.

I turned back to the assembled group and cleared my throat. 'I'd like to share the hunters' oath with you.'

As one, the students stood up and placed their hands on their chest. They waited eagerly for me to recite the words and invite them into the community. I'd never felt so proud in my life. Finally, I knew where I belonged, and I knew who I was, and as I glanced over at my friends, family, and pack, I knew I was home.

'To every pack, a cub is born, and every hunter gets their dawn. Nurturing friendships that grow deeper, united together as an Oath Keeper.'

OATH KEEPER

ACKNOWLEDGMENTS

Thank you first and foremost to my parents for their unwavering support of everything I produce. Mum, you are the best saleswoman in the world. Thank you.

Thank you to my daughter's friend, Elizabeth, for the loan of your beautiful name—I hope our Elizabeth did you proud.

A huge thank you to the team at BHC Press for working on my book and turning it into a living entity. I'm pretty sure I shall continue to squeal with delight at every cover you produce for many years to come.

Thanks to my wonderful editor, Sooz, for believing in my story, guiding me when I had my dark moments, and patiently waiting for me to emerge from the treeline.

ABOUT THE AUTHOR

Shelley Wilson's love of fantasy began at the tender age of eight when she followed Enid Blyton up a *Magical Faraway Tree*.

Inspired by Blyton's make believe world, Shelley began to create her stories, weaving tales around faeries, witches and dragons.

Writing has always been Shelley's first love, but she has also enjoyed a variety of job roles along the way; from waitressing to sales and marketing and even working as a turkey plucker.

Shelley lives in the West Midlands, UK with her three teenage children, two fish and a dragon called Roger. She is at her happiest with a slice of pizza in one hand, a latte in the other and *Game of Thrones* on the TV. She would love to live in the Shire but fears her five foot ten inch height may cause problems. She is an obsessive list writer, huge social media addict and a full-time day dreamer.

www.shelleywilsonauthor.co.uk

www.bhcpress.com

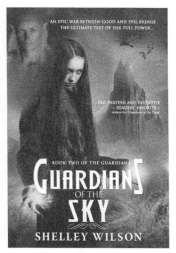

CPSIA information can be obtained
at www.ICGtesting.com
Printed in the USA
LVHW111703260919
632367LV00005B/63/P

9 781643 970097